Shall Not be Forgiven
and other stories

Charles Nightingale

DEDICATION

For Dominique

CONTENTS

ACKNOWLEDGMENTS

I am very grateful to Erica Wildwood who helped me edit the stories, and who ran an excellent creative writing class on which I met other keen writers including my friend Christine Page, who has been a constant source of literary discussion, Andy Derbyshire, and Katy Matthews. Also to other friends who have commented usefully on the tales, including Martin and Margaret Redstall, Alwyn Lewis and Diane Rich. Last, but by no means least, to my dear wife Dominique who has stood by my side through thick and thin.

1 The Ride of the Valkyrie

I hear the precision locks respond to my firm but gentle press on the remote control. The on-board computer deduces my mood from the way I handle the remote,

Brunhilde selects a Schubert string quintet – *The Trout*. How's that for *Vorsprung durch Technik*! I slide onto the immaculate Morocco leather seat, start the engine and draw out into the road. I feel, as usual, at one with the vehicle, whose silent power is under my foot, controlled by my own keen reactions and supreme powers of judgement. I manoeuvre the big silver beast discreetly but efficiently through the town traffic. I have to follow an old green Nissan estate which wavers uncertainly along, but I have no need to overtake - as a mature responsible citizen driving an acknowledged masterpiece of engineering, my stake in society precludes the taking of stupid risks. Nevertheless I can feel that Brunhilde hardly likes to have her way blocked by this down-at-heel vehicle. As we come off the roundabout onto the dual carriageway I gently press the accelerator. The whole lovingly engineered gestalt of harmoniously inter-working engine components breathes a gentle note of urgent response to my desire. Together we sweep magnificently past the rusty obstruction whose aged driver is still fumbling with his controls. My hand moves with decisive articulation through the sweetly meshing gears. Brunhilde surges ahead onto the appetising vista of open road. Now I am up to my cruising speed of eighty-five. My vehicle is nevertheless safer than an ordinary car at seventy. I can stop on a sixpence, or slip through any gap like a salmon on his way upstream. The engine is just audible as a deep whispering menace, a fire smouldering in its depth, ready to flare up to boost me to a hundred and forty if it is needed. There is my trump card. *I* can burn my way out of trouble if I have to, like a Tomahawk missile bursting from the ocean into the freedom of the skies. The music centre has deduced my new mood from my driving-style and is playing *The Entrance of the Gladiators.*

I blast past an Astra which had underestimated my speed, momentarily holding me up. I give the driver a glance of reprimand. He looks straight ahead to avoid having to face out the consequence of his own bumbling obstinacy. The joy and peace of being a liberty-loving but law-abiding leader of men in a smoothly functioning society suddenly comes foaming and bubbling into my soul and the music switches to *"Ode to joy..."*

In my mirror I perceive a Mondeo approaching very rapidly. His reckless neglect of speed limit and safety is a disgrace. His face is exactly what I expected: that of an irresponsible lout. He is dressed in a clean white shirt and tie. A cigarette hangs from his mouth. He will have a fat beer belly and run some barely-legal business. He will have bullied and bamboozled his way to the surface of the cesspit in which he has been spawned. Still his car harasses me. I'll give him a taste of Brunhilde's power. Here goes, foot down, I've had enough of him. I feel the sudden thrust as she leaps forward, smoothly and silently accelerating. He's still there though, hanging grimly on. Now both of us are careering down the carriageway in the third lane, pushing towards a hundred. I don't see it as breaking the law if one is in a car like mine. Obviously the speed limits are set with an average car - like a Mondeo - in mind. In Brunhilde I have a marvel of engineering excellence to cope with these speeds safely. But he doesn't. I'd better let him pass - if he's that irresponsible. There he goes - selfish pig, no concern whatever for others. The music steadies but strengthens me: the march from *Tannhauser*. I'll just pull out again to gun down this guy grovelling along in his Skoda...uhh? Who's hooting at me? Blast! A Porsche - I didn't see him! He's had to brake and let me out. *I* look as if I've made a *cock-up* now! It's better to make it seem as if I meant it! I'll just stick two fingers out of the window, in a mechanical sort of way, as if I routinely cut people up – a jack-the-lad type! I'll let him go - I've kept face at least. Look at him! He's going to leer in as he passes. I'll mouth the words 'Up yours mate!' if he does. I'm almost up to his speed now! Here's a little convoy of container-lorries. Keep out of my way you sluggish mechanical brontosaurs! The music's onto the *Ride of the Valkyrie*. Past we go! China Shipping – glass beads for the hoi-polloi. Another Chinese box ahead of him! Yang-Ming; well you're the yin matey - I'm the yang and here I go. I'm doing nearly a hundred and ten! Banzai! ... Oh my God he's pulling...

*

"Mummy, there's a policeman at the door."

2 Leaving Home

I'm leaving! I've lived here a very long time. I couldn't say exactly how long - it seems like a thousand years. I can't remember what it was like before I came here. Perhaps no one can remember what it was like before they were at home - and after all, this must be my home, whichever way one wants to look at it. I can even regard it with some premature nostalgia, now that it's soon to be in the past. I've come to see that, claustrophobic though the place is, it's all I've ever known. But now I've got to go!

Everything I know now becomes irrelevant, except when I come back here which I suppose I will from time to time - although I haven't been given the precise arrangements yet. Worse than that, I'm not even sure what I'm going to do out there - what I can do. In principle, of course, I can do just about anything; you all know the traditional wisdom. And it's the same for everyone in my situation - we are expected to be able to cope. But I'm not at all confident - and probably Mustafa is right in saying it's all in the confidence. (Yes! It's not all solitary here - one gets to meet others in the same boat.) He makes quite a lot of sense actually, if I can *only* drum up an air of confidence!

I ought to absolutely hate it here really. That's as it should be. You never meet anyone in my position who doesn't, it seems. But it's all a part of people's expectations of course. Dealing with other people's expectations is possibly the very worst aspect of my case! People look, and think how cramped I must be - and imagine how gloriously free I will feel, and they put two and two together and get five. But it isn't nearly as cramped as it looks, and although in a way I do hate it, I wouldn't leave if I didn't have to. It's not, I hope, that I'm afraid of freedom, or of the big outside world. I'm just afraid I might be incompetent. I'll let down the whole of my kind, the whole team, so to speak; the first flop since time immemorial. Imagine the son of a great dynastic ruler who goes and loses his first battle against infidels, or barbarians or other group of despised enemies! He would keep seeing his ancestor's faces before him, wouldn't he? He would probably prefer impaling himself on his own sword, or requesting a faithful comrade to sweep off his head with one blow of his scimitar, to facing the wrath of his father. Not that I can remember my father. Obviously I must have had one, but that's the extent of my knowledge on the point.

After the ages I've been in here everything about the outside world, including my own origins become very fuzzy and blurred. Even so I have wondered ceaselessly about that world, and have had the time to study it. As I said before it's seemed like a thousand years. And I have been able to read things that others might not have had the patience for. Gibbon's *Decline and Fall* for example. In fact, believe it or not, we are encouraged to read the works of great masters, although I didn't like that particular one. The ideology isn't up my street. I've read many modern works too, and could hold interesting conversations on any number of topics. I have theories on everything, and would love to try my steel on the great minds of this age! The trouble is, I'm very unlikely to meet any great minds - the chances are negligible. And in any case, of course, no-one - savant or otherwise - is likely to hold conversations with me. That's not what people want with my kind. It's not that I don't want to fulfil their expectations, even if, as is well known, they are selfish and often mercenary or prurient. The problem is I'm not at all sure I can make a success of my new role. I've applied myself to the task of acquiring all the necessary skills, and have seemingly passed the various tests. But no amount of study of the traditional methods can put my mind at rest. I know I'll panic the minute I set foot outside.

There's so much I don't know. What sort of people will I meet out there, for example? I hardly know what people look like nowadays, only from out-of-date books, or sometimes, flickering images through the dirty green glass. No one could have led a more sheltered existence than I. And what will *he*, (or *she* for all I know), be like? That's going to be crucial. We all end up working for someone, I suppose, and if one thinks about it, one sees that that person controls one's destiny to a large degree. I admit it will be that much worse for me though, however I try to water it down. I'll end up having to just abrogate my own will utterly, and live for *him* as it were.

Behind the excitement of the moment I've been very depressed by all this. I've been moping around and generally giving people the pip. It was all right with Mustafa to cheer me up, and make me realise that I was about to begin living for the first time, but now he's gone. Mind you I gather this happens to quite a few people, and can be expected. It's like the doubts the most devout believers are said to experience - it evidently strengthens their faith. But faith in the Most High is one thing - faith in oneself quite another!

Even so, in the light of all this anxious anticipation I'm at least getting my act together as much as I can. I'm OK on the basics and I could deliver on a whole range of requests. It isn't as spooky as it sounds, once you understand the reasoning behind it. One can't complain that we are not given very sound training here, for the world outside. You can rely on it. But training is only half the story. First impact is of course terribly important, more so than any number of party tricks and jiggery-pokery. I know Mustafa - who has impact - will have made a great success of going out. For all his cynicism he's just the sort of person who will carry all before him. He's probably an omnipotent aide to some dictator by now, resplendent in a specially designed uniform. But what do I have? I still have my youth, but first impressions go beyond mere youth. They are everything. Absolutely everything. In a way one *should* be overdressed in that situation, not *under*dressed. But overdressed in the right way. I know what people wear at the moment, more from verbal description than pictures, although I have seen a few pages from various recent magazines. They wear suits, casuals, trainers, anoraks, and of course, jeans! I haven't actually seen jeans, but I know what they are like, and could have at least had the option of wearing a pair. One would, of course, have had a pair in an unusual colour which would have given me the necessary distinction, but in every other way they would have been conformed to the norm.

One should *not* be obliged to enter a new life dressed in an outrageous costume that will immediately mark one out as an eccentric at best, and as a complete idiot at worst. It's quite ridiculous, and they are hopelessly out of touch with the real world, with any concept of human dignity, and more importantly, with the feelings of people like myself, and in my position. I'm not saying that flamboyance is absolutely out. But why not something which modern people will relate to? There are *flamboyant* sports clothes, and sportswear is evidently very popular now. I could have been issued with a brightly coloured tracksuit, for example, in a silky material. The effect would be similar, but without the ridiculous associations. After-shave I wouldn't have minded, it's still considered a little vulgar, but perhaps in my case it would have seemed fitting. The headgear is a lot more difficult, it's generally so unpopular nowadays in any form apart from a baseball cap (And even I can see that a baseball cap just wouldn't meet the case, whichever way round I might have worn it). I recently saw a picture of a grand prix driver in goggles and a helmet, and something like that might have done - but of course none of this makes an iota of difference. I'm afraid you are probably dismissing me as a vain person by now, obsessed with shallow trivialities like clothes. But ask yourself how you would feel if, say, you found yourself at an interview for an important job dressed like the principle boy (or even a lesser character!) at a pantomime? People don't expect anachronisms - for example if Mephistopheles appears in a play or film nowadays he's always very sharply dressed - often in an impeccable evening suit. That would be fine with me - or, and this would be a last resort, even one of those stage escaped convict suits with arrows stencilled on them, which would at least be appropriate in some way.

Now let me tell you what they have just actually put on me. A pair of orange trousers the like of which haven't been seen since the Sultan Ibrahim tipped his entire harem into the Golden Horn in 1646, for reasons that have comprehensively escaped me. And, as if that wasn't enough, a golden chain round my neck, which will make any red-blooded woman burst out laughing at the first glance. I gather such a thing will be seen as the humiliating badge of a macho poseur, if my current reading is to be relied upon. The headgear I can't bring myself to mention. Apparently at one time it helped terrify the infidel. The prospect of wearing such a thing in public now terrifies *me*, so we can confirm that the wheel of history turns at least through a hundred and eighty degrees, if not a full circle. Finally, and this is the worst of all, my bare torso has just been rubbed with oil which exudes a disgusting sweet fragrance, which will raise all sorts of unjustified questions about me in the world I'm to enter. As they rubbed it on I implored them - 'In Rome do as Rome does' I begged - but it was useless. You can't undo thousands of years of prejudice with a few sentences of reason. Talking of rubbing, I can hear a scraping sound now! By Allah, my time has really come!

The seal has been broken! I'm trembling like a leaf; all my worst fears are descending upon me. I'm going to fail I know it! Suddenly I am exposed to the brightest light I've ever encountered. The top has come off, and just as I was told I'm being sucked out! A strange traumatic feeling, like being born, I suppose. I am enveloped in green smoke... I get confused, I had forgotten about this, and begin to fear that they are burning me after all! But no, of course they aren't... in fact it's horribly cold wherever this is, half dressed as I am. As the smoke clears I see that I am standing in a muddy, untidy place strewn with bottles and other rubbish. I look up to see my first people of the outside world! They are two boys, the one a pallid roumi of the barbaric north. They wear the very tracksuits of silk that I had desired for myself, emblazoned with the words 'The Reds' - some team which they evidently favour - like the old Blues of Constantinople in times even before my own. They cower together in their fear of my sudden appearance, their eyes wide in their angelic but impertinent faces. Emboldened by the success of my hated costume, and the fearsome impression I have created, I feel my nerve to be coming back - and I seem to grow in height. I address the boy who holds the bottle and stopper in his shaking hands, in my most booming voice: 'I am the genie of the bottle! What is your wish, O Master?'

3 In the Square

I sit on a seat in the square, and one thought cycles through my mind, again and again and again. 'Why, in heavens name, have they done this? Was it something I said? Something I've done? Or what...?' It is a pleasant day – and a pleasant place. Where could be more agreeable than this large southern town, with its Bougainvilleas, its Washingtonias, its famous statuary, its beautiful architecture, its galleries, concert halls and theatres and last but not least its plethora of cafes and restaurants? It is nearly lunchtime – yet there has been no sign of any of them. We were to meet here for breakfast to plan our day. I was keen to visit art galleries – but would have been delighted to participate in any activity that was proposed. I have a birthday card for Anna – which I bought in the little bookstall on the station. There must have been a meeting at which they unanimously decided that I was to be dropped, and this sudden boycott adopted in the interests of making a clean break.

I feel no animosity toward them – I liked them all, each and every one. I felt a certain rapport had emerged between me and the others. I had struck a careful balance: I had paid attention to interests and preferences of the group where it was possible to do so without insincerity, offering opinions which resonated with those I heard expressed. At the same time I would venture some ideas which were more challenging in areas where I thought they would not characterise me as a philistine, yet would give me an air of one who thinks independently. I had developed an interest in one or two of the female members of the group, but tried to prevent it from giving offence by steering clear of unctuous flattery or repulsive attempts at familiarity. Rather I maintained what I thought of as a quizzical and good-humoured masculine airiness, accompanied by opening doors and lightly touching an elbow when it seemed to me that protectiveness was required, as at a road crossing for example.

With all of them I was able to engage in subjects of mutual interest on which they had touched. With one I would discuss developments in the art world, and whilst listening with apparent interest to his appreciation of the contemporary scene, I offered on my side a knowledgeable insight into the psychology of habituation which I felt lay at the heart of the popularity of the works he praised. I did this with some delicacy so as not to give any idea that I felt myself his superior in any way in this field. In addition I treated him to a small poster reproduction of a famous work by Jasper Johns, an artist he had mentioned. Another was an enthusiast of mathematical puzzles, and I showed myself to be on his wavelength when he outlined a neat problem in probability. It was relatively trivial to work out the answer in my head, but I deliberately made a show of scribbling on a piece of paper to give an impression of serious effort before vouchsafing my answer after some time. This maintained his respect for me without threatening his own self-esteem, and I felt I had clinched the relationship by presenting him with a small book of such puzzles by a Russian author.

I also tried to make myself generally useful by giving brief histories of the iconic places we visited, as well as drawing their attention to lesser known buildings and landmarks whose significance I happened to know; and I discreetly settled many restaurant bills before anyone realised what I was doing.

Yet somehow I must have given offence and I rack my brains for an explanation for their having deserted me so abruptly, after they had seemingly agreed on the time and venue for this morning's gathering. It was a serious decision for them, since my fluent grasp of the local language would be severely missed, as – at their original request – I had taken on the duty of dealing with situations in which a good grasp of the language was needed. They would now be thrown back on the halting phrases of Vera, who would soon be in the Sargasso Sea if called upon to deal with any complexities such as 'My friend asked for Gilthead Sea Bream but has been given Sea Bass which she doesn't like.'

It is even possible that the argument which broke out with Vera a few days ago might have caused her to influence the group in arriving at their decision. During a discussion over after-dinner drinks I had needed to correct a slight misunderstanding she appeared to have on a point of economics, but perhaps my explanation had been a little too glib and academic, for at its end she raised her voice and invited the others to confirm that I was, to use her own angry words, 'a pompous prick'. They declined to concur with her somewhat hurtful description of me, whilst showing by their demeanour and gestures that they understood the frustration which had prompted her outburst. They kindly smoothed the situation over and reassured me that she was overstating her case. Since then she had been a little aloof from me, her only words being a gracious apology for having thrown the beach ball directly at the back of my head when I was eating an ice-cream. I felt that she had probably aimed it at me, but had estimated that from the range from which she launched it, there was little possibility of achieving the strong accurate strike which she did, with the attendant disintegration of the confection, and inconvenience to me.

I have to admit, as I watch groups of people pass me, chatting enthusiastically, pouncing upon vacant tables outside cafes, and looking ready for a pleasant day of exactly the sort I had been anticipating, I feel a little despairing. I had had idiotic hopes of this holiday. But in my heart of hearts I had known they were on the point of ejecting me – I knew the signs so well. The situation is a repetition of many I have experienced. To some it seems to come naturally to be popular and always surrounded by friends. Not so for others, however hard they may strive to win acceptance. As usual I find myself rejected by a group, for no reason that I can comprehend. Perhaps this time it was my insistence on answering Vera's points, which she made so passionately, with cool detachment, that may have been responsible. Yet spirited and prickly woman that she is, she had not struck me as one to slyly undermine someone behind their back.

Someone joins me on the seat.

'There's only me today, I'm afraid. Do you want to take a walk, to those Saracen ruins you told us about?'

Looking round in surprise I see Vera, smiling tentatively.

'Perhaps we might have lunch on the way' I reply

We walk off and she takes my hand.

4 The Next Territory

I needed a holiday - badly. When a man's marriage breaks up, he loses his job and his home all in the space of six months he *needs* a holiday. To quote Dunsany I wanted to go somewhere beyond the fields we know. 'I'd like to go to the end of the world really', I told the serious young lady in the travel agency. 'But I'm more or less broke.'

'I'm sure we can sort something out.' she said - 'just bear with me a moment please.' Something about her – maybe the strange faded black of her suit – made her seem out of place. Her jet eyes reminded me of my ex-wife.

I only had myself to blame for my present solitude. I'd always had an idea a man needed to go beyond a one-woman relationship – to go farther afield. The second time she had been stubborn. 'You promised; this is the end of the road, you can't come back!' I saw that she would not relent and I left.

'There! This should suit you sir.'

I came out of my reverie to find the young travel agent showing me a brochure. A town I'd never heard of in a country which had, until lately, been off limits politically. A country with pleasantly grotesque myths surrounding its mountain ranges. 'For the man who wants to go that one step beyond' it announced. The weather looked good, the countryside looked superb and the town very appetising.

'I'll go!' I announced, when she told me the very reasonable cost.

'It is the best thing for you' She said, her dark eyes friendly, but unsmiling 'if you deal with it the right way.' I wondered what she meant.

She almost echoed the board's words when I had lost my job. Each advance I had made, each new office, each new company car, and each new privilege - each had given me a glow of happiness. Yet within a few months it had always seemed a humiliating sideline - until I made it to the board where I had to make difficult decisions, and was judged on their results. As a result I got fired. I had made the final step beyond the end of the old road and fallen into the abyss: once again I couldn't go back.

The holiday began by exceeding my most extreme hopes. I made friends - local friends, not just tourists. I met a woman who, whilst maintaining some distance, seemed anxious to form a lasting relationship. The town was a fairy tale. Everything was very cheap, the wine was excellent, the food new and exotic. The country around was very picturesque, and I returned to an old pastime of mine, painting in water-colour. My skill returned, and I occupied each day with my hobby and each night socialising with my new friends. All around, I could see a never-ending supply of subjects, getting better and better toward the green distant hills in the east.

For a while I was happy, but then one or two small clouds came on to my horizon. First were the *Inspectors.* These were a group of people, jet-eyed men and women, who one saw in ones and twos around the town dressed in light casual clothes of a sort of washed out black. For some reason I feared them. I took them to be some sort of internal spies left over from the old days.

The other problem was my attempt to paint the beautiful high country and villages I could see to the east. Every effort I made to get within reasonable painting distance failed. The roads marked on the map were not there - and since the map had been produced before the second world war this was not a surprise. The invaders had punished severely those who did not acknowledge their sphere of influence and whole valleys had been bombed into oblivion. The marks of those cruel days were now covered with aromatic pastel-coloured herbs and stunted parasol-like conifers; the roads and paths of former times were quite lost. Always I got almost to the point I wanted, but never exactly, and the resulting works, whilst saleable, never achieved the qualities of which I dreamed. Always at the range I attained, the whole eastern landscape had a heavenly, almost unreal look - yet too far for my brush to capture.

My friend seemed concerned when I became obsessed with visiting this range. '*They* do not like it' she said, waving at two of the *Inspectors*. But I became more and more determined to visit these mysterious hills. I began to find ways to get closer to them. I took a compass and when the hills sank behind local features as I approached I was still able to move along minor roads and villages in the correct direction. By taking great care, noting my route carefully, and resuming each day at the place I had reached previously, I made slow but steady progress. The closer I got the more perfect the hills in the distance looked. But things still worked against me. Always something thing happened in villages which stood in my path. An aggressive group of youths, a barbed wire fence or a checkpoint in the street where some morose *Inspector* would shake his head over my papers invariably forced me to retire. In the end I grasped that I would never get through one of the villages that seemed so frequently to block my path. The problem then was that the only bridges over a raging mountain torrent which certainly had to be crossed were in these unfriendly places.

I was on the point of giving up when, one day, through my binoculars, I discovered a place where a rock-fall had split the river into manageable streams. And after much difficulty, late in the afternoon, I found it. Suddenly as I started to make my way across the rocks a very large black dog appeared out of the blue on the opposite bank. It looked at me with smouldering eyes, yet made no menacing gesture, so I scrambled across and found myself beside the creature in the lowering gloom. It let out a strange growl, and seemed almost to place itself in my path to prevent my advance. But I am at home with dogs, and I patted it as confidently as I could and it let me pass. It was too dark to see much, but I felt an exhilaration to have discovered what I felt was the final answer to my quest. I could just see the path ahead, and it went straight as a die to the hills I sought. I knew it was too late to go further, and I decided to retrace my steps. It seemed much more difficult to go back than it had been to go on: each of the rocks which I had easily mounted on the way across the stream seemed to be at particularly awkward angles for the return. Indeed at one point only the near presence of the great dog enabled me to scramble onto the central rock, by using his strong shoulder as a handhold. He showed great pleasure at my painful return, and I left him wagging his tail as I hurried back along the route I had so tortuously unravelled over the weeks.

I told my friends of my success, but they did not share my pleasure

'Why must a man go to the end of the earth to find a subject to paint when there is so much beauty nearby?' one asked.

My woman friend echoed his sentiments. 'The dog had more sense than you have' she said.

The next day I took my water-colour materials and left at dawn. I passed no-one as I headed for the crossing, except one *Inspector* who seemed to spy on me from a high point. The sun was warm, the sounds and smells of the country were perfect - and ever ahead were those inviting hills of paradise. I would return with a painting to silence their carping once and for all.

There was no dog at the river and I easily crossed into the beyond. Each step I took made the woods, houses and hills look more like a masterpiece of Dutch landscape painting. Only an artist of omnipotent ability could truly produce such an image. I saw no one ahead, although way off to the side I seemed to see tiny figures who peered steadily at me - *Inspectors*, I was sure. The walk became easier and easier, and the effect of hills seemed to have been an illusion. As I looked back it almost seemed as if I was coming downhill - the whole town seemed above me. I knew enough of the effects of perspective to know that such optical illusions were common in hilly territory, and I pressed on until I seemed to be on the threshold of the promised landscape.

But then something happened which brought a great uneasiness over me. I had reached a cottage only to find that it was a sort of decoy - like a wooden aeroplane painted to look like a real one, to waste the guns and bombs of enemy attacks on an airfield. And as I puzzled over the phenomenon I noted that other features of an artificial nature were observable. Brilliantly though it was all fabricated, I suddenly realised that the whole area which I faced was like a huge stage backdrop. Flowers, trees shrubs, cottages, barns, rocky outcrops, all seemed to be brilliantly fabricated from a wondrous substance that could be formed into any shape or colour, however complex. I had strayed into some giant project where no doubt serious security measures were in force. I thought to move away to safer places, and walked along at the same level, but constantly found myself facing only the false and now menacing landscape of the project. Worse, whatever I did I seemed always to be further into the backdrop. Behind me what had seemed at first downhill, then flat, then slightly uphill now towered away so that the town seemed perched high on a green plateau above me. And it looked like at least a day's effort to attain the town once more. But with rising unease I admitted defeat, and began to retrace my path; suddenly I had realised that there was nothing in these hills that I wanted!

I scrambled back up the slope which had been so easy to descend, but the material of which it was made now displayed a new quality - it was almost impossible to move upwards - it slid and crumbled to a fine dust which had no adhesion whatsoever. After an hour I had gained no more than a few feet. I fought off an attack of panic when I imagined my dried bones in this lifeless desert, victim of a ridiculous accident. I threw away my painting equipment, to lighten my load, but made scarcely any more progress. Finally, at my wits end, I made the hard but only possible decision, to go on down the slope, hoping to reach a more normal terrain further ahead. At first I felt sure that the false landscape - which I now knew to be of immense proportion - was the result of some insane totalitarian land-forming project. But as I went on I found my blood chilling as I looked back. The terrain behind me now towered up, higher with each furlong I went. First the town appeared perched precariously amid the haze of an alpine mountain chain. Then as it faded in the thickening mist, it was as high as the Himalayas. Finally it topped a cyclopean range such as is not known on this earth - and I cowered beneath it as it overhung me, an insane landscape over my head, casting a shadow that added gloom to the horrific power of the optical illusion. And worse, the slope was increasing ahead, and soon I was staggering, trying to control my pace, until at last I fell, and went bumping, grazing and slithering on down, crying out in fear.

But just when I felt that I was doomed I was finally brought to rest by a jarring blow against something hard. I had been caught by a metal bar right on the edge of a precipice which I could sense from the total absence of any visible terrain beyond what was a perfectly straight line going off in both directions either side of me - an abrupt end to the false landscape. I could not yet see into the drop as I was not in a good position to do so. The slope I had come down was dangerously steep in its final twenty feet. I had been lucky to be caught by the metal bar; else I must have plunged over the edge in my fall. I had no means of going back, but even so I took some time before pushing up on my shoulders from the prone position and peering over the edge of the gargantuan structure where I fond myself. I was already afraid, as one might be, clinging precariously to a niche in a strange landscape, but as I peered over the parapet I went dizzy with panic. I was looking down a straight drop of what I guessed to be a couple of thousand feet into an ocean of still, black, oily water, which stretched out in all directions from the towering wall at whose top I was perched. The whole atmosphere below me was dank and chill and the view partially obscured by a dreary grey mist. The bar on which I rested was in fact the securing of an iron ladder which went vertically down the slimy black wall toward the horrific ocean of turgid water which lurked in the murky gloom below. Perspective and mist obliterated my view of the descending ladder after the first thousand feet or so. I could see other such ladders at intervals along the wall, which went as straight as a die to horizons on each side of me. How long I remained clinging to the bar I cannot remember - I cried out for help - despairing wails which went unanswered. Finally, after an age, I set off in the only possible direction - descending.

Down the iron ladder I went - hanging in space hundreds of feet up, fighting off panic and vertigo. I went slowly and deliberately, but never looked below. At first the ladder seemed very sound, and I was able to control my fear by holding tight and stepping cautiously from one rung to the next. But further down, the ladder began to feel rusty and after about half an hour it became corroded and weakened and its rungs bent and gave under my weight. A few were even missing. But I kept going, with pounding heart and twisted innards, never looking below, until I seemed to have been on the ladder for hours. Then one section suddenly shuddered and creaked - and for a moment I thought I was about to plunge to my death. I screamed as I felt the section above me break loose, and fall away, leaving no possibility of return. For a moment I was clinging on to struts which were palpably bending under my feet, until the ladder hung precariously out from the wall from the fixing of one side. I dared not look down for fear that vertigo would claim me. I only lowered a leg until I was ready to gain the next hopefully more secure section. But my foot searched and found only a shifting, disintegrating tangle of rotten iron. The slightest weight and it began to give. Waves of terrible panic surged through me. I could feel even the piece to which I clung creaking and slowly moving. I looked up - always up. I knew if I looked down now I was lost. I feared the dizzying drop, but I feared the black oily water even more. I remembered my wife and children, my old life and job, then my new friends. I decided to let go, rather than await the collapse of the disintegrating ladder which still supported me.

'Get in'. A voice sounded from nearby - I looked down and saw one of the *Inspectors* in a boat on the black waters. I had finally reached the bottom!

'Where the devil is this place?' I said as I scrambled to get into the boat, still trembling from my horrific experience.

He smiled - the first time I saw an *Inspector* smile. 'Why it's the end of the world, as you might have guessed.'

'There's nowhere like this!' I stuttered out - before falling silent.

'It *is* nowhere' he said.

*

I live simple life now. And I'm not looking for the next territory. I had a second chance, and I took it.

5 The Road to Nowhere

Saturday Morning

What could be more agreeable than a weekend break when you stand on the verge of the fulfilment of your life's dreams? The world will perhaps be at one's feet by the following weekend; after a long private struggle, one is to experience a public apotheosis. Of course one must not count one's chickens. But to have been selected for a one-man exhibition at the White Gallery, my exhibition catalogue filled with eulogistic interpretations written by respected critics and to know that pre-sales have already exceeded one's most grandiose secret dreams! To know also that numerous influential well-wishers are ready to carry my torch into the omnipotent photosphere of the world of art. These are surely the warm breezes that herald the approach of the white heat of fame! Only one fading cloud remained in the sky. Celia: just before her exhibition in a tuppeny-ha'penny gallery somewhere south of the river had bombed, I went to see her up in our old bed-sit in Lewisham where she still lived, with news of my imminent arrival on the London scene. Her mock-offer to write my biography and especially the last words I ever heard her speak - still rankled.

I was now sitting on the promenade taking the sea air in the very town where my journey began, debating whether to go and look in the self-important little provincial gallery in which the locals took such a comic pride, with its three Monzos, which had been donated by the artist who had spent some time in the town, in the 1860s. I had been taken to the gallery when I was very young – seven or eight – but I couldn't remember a thing about them. They were probably portraits of pompous local dignitaries – ones that even he, a now little known but heavily derided example of the evils of the era, hadn't valued.

I recalled my primary school where my drawings had attracted the interest of my first teacher. Trolleybuses, ships, aeroplanes and dinosaurs and been my favourite subjects, the first seen all around me, the last – and best - seen in pictures and models in the museum, where once the local celebrity, Eoanthropus, had been its centre piece: until he had been unmasked as the Piltdown Hoax. How easily distinguished experts can fooled!

In the next class I found I didn't attract much interest. There was a boy who was rather disruptive in normal lessons who used to toss paint around, but the teacher got him to hurl it on a large sheet of wallpaper, and he was praised very highly, getting into the local paper once or twice. My work had got better, and although the art teacher didn't praise it like the earlier teacher, he would make suggestions and didn't seem opposed to it. I got into a secondary school which specialised in art and design. I had moved away from my original subjects and painted portraits and landscapes. But once again found myself in the shadow of pupils who worked on a large scale, and some were doing installations. There was a girl in the class who I realised was actually better than me at drawing, a thing I had never experienced before. Only about half the class could draw at all, and most of the ones who were praised never drew, so one didn't know whether they could or not. On our first day in year 11 the teacher told the girl that she was 'too controlling' and she looked totally crushed. I put some bolder less fussy strokes on mine before this teacher got round to me, and I escaped that reprimand. Celia – for it

33

was she – who had previously received fulsome praise, went home very tearful. We later became quite friendly, and took to going sketching together. She used to like painting the Abbey, visible over a bank of flowers, but I knew from the art teacher, Mr Priest, that these pictures were in danger from his ire. 'She's got a rather chocolate-boxy style, you know;' he had said to me once when we were taking in the entries for the school exhibition. I had rather liked them, but soon saw what he meant.

I admired him greatly – he was a thin nervous-looking man with a straggly beard, who had had pictures in avant-garde exhibitions. I had become an aspiring impressionist, using vivid colours to good effect. If there was anything grey in a scene I would gaze at it until I either saw, or imagined I saw, a faint tinge of some hue, whereupon I would mix a bright saturated version of it and boldly dab it in. Mr Priest nodded at my stuff, but would say, kindly things like: 'This is OK at the moment, but I think you could become a fine artist if you wanted, and your style is a little old-fashioned by the standards of today.' I was rather shocked at his use of the word fashion. Art was supposed to be eternal and universal according to some books I had read.

But I scored a signal success in sculpture. I had a technical streak in me, and the whole gestalt of clay, armatures, casting and glazing caught my interest. After a few successes – 'just getting the feel of the materials,' Mr Priest had said of my bold reliefs – I essayed a full length nude. I used an armature and chicken wire, and had just got a vague human form with a rather small head by winding on some plaster impregnated strips of cloth and slapping extra plaster on, when Mr Priest came beaming up to me. 'Don't do any more. It looks like a Giacometti – look.' He opened a book, and I saw some statues of thin almost skeletal figures by this famous artist, which I hadn't known of at the time. I saw that mine did indeed bear a resemblance. There was a moment when I thought of my plan, with its beautiful female form, like a Greek statue in a garden; then I looked again at the book with its glossy high-quality photos. 'Don't go for some pedestrian Greek pin-up,' he had said. As quick as a flash I had replied: 'Oh I wasn't going to. I was going to stop here.' I could see now how much better his idea was, and what ambitious youngster could have resisted the white lie? 'Great!' Mr Priest said. 'You'll be in the White Gallery yet.' Celia, who was nearby, said nothing, although she had seen my painstaking sketches, front and side views. There was a very faint flush on her cheeks, I noticed. She went on carving her leaping cat. Mr Priest looked at it, but said nothing.

They still asked for portfolios at the art school where I applied after my family had relocated to South East London. I proudly showed my portfolio to Mrs Lacksey and anxiously watched her look through it. She looked solemn, and went rather quickly over what I thought was my best impressionist style work. She stopped at the photograph of my Giacometti figure and a slight interest appeared in her eyes. There was also one painting that I had thrown in at the last minute on Mr Priest's recommendation – thank goodness – a very free fiesta of paint, with most of the figurative content expunged beyond recognition. She gave this an even more positive signal. 'Yes – this and your 3D piece – they interest me. Most of your others are just attempts to show off your technique and your drawing. You will find that those will be an encumbrance to you here, just evidence of an incipient elitism. Innovation is our watchword. I will be pleased to accept you on the basis of your more honest work.'

I heard later that Celia had got in at the local art school where I had lived before – a place which I soon learned was beneath contempt at Shortham. God knows where I would be now, if I had ended up there. In the years I spent at Shortham I learned a great deal. I was occasionally downhearted, as when several of us – including Mrs Lacksey – visited the Klinthkoe exhibition in a new gallery in London. I was stunned into silence when I saw huge canvases covered in gigantic blobs, streaks of garish colour with solidified piles of paint all in soft seductive lighting, sparsely spaced around the white walls. 'Stunning, aren't they?' Mrs Lacksey said. One or two students echoed her words, but for a time I said nothing. 'You are all coming to the stage where you will begin to understand the significance of the subconscious, and the impact of raw emotion in painting. One knows what the public will say, and the reactionaries in the press, but you only have to let the works in, embrace them and they will reward you with a surge of empathetic feeling. Just note the contrast with the callous and relentless hypocrisy of the Victorian painters as they concocted their false emotions and their routinely boring images. You are lucky to have come on the scene when you have. The rigid mould is broken, and the sky's the limit. If there are any of you that can't appreciate these exquisite masterpieces then you might reconsider your choice of career.'

I could relate to the pictures after a while, and I picked one in particular that from a distance could have been birds in flight. The colours were good and I thought I could attempt something like it. I began to produce paintings in a Klinthkoe style and found myself going through materials like there was no tomorrow. Mrs Lacksey was very encouraging. 'You obviously got a lot out of the Klinthkoe exhibition – but you are developing an individual voice, with a sort of spiky roundness which works so well,' she said. At the final year exhibition I was thrilled to see my paintings dominating the space. I could see Miss Liggins looking resentfully at them crowding out her students' careful routine paintings of local scenes, urban landscapes and some foolish attempts at genre painting with social comment. Her day was gone; her reactionary attitudes had at last been exposed for what they were.

At the private view my mother and father looked dutifully at my work, although it was manifest that they couldn't understand it. Mrs Lacksey joined us. 'You must be very proud of Jonathan,' she said. 'He has achieved an amazing wholeness of being for one so young.' I heard a snort and the words 'Good God!' coming loudly and indignantly from behind me and to my left. I turned and saw that Miss Liggins was staring at Mrs Lacksey, her eyes blazing with anger, her wild grey hair haloing her face like a lion's mane. I saw that, for a moment, Mrs Lacksey blanched, but Miss Liggins turned on her heel and strode off ostentatiously. When she was out of earshot Mrs Lacksey shrugged. 'Don't worry about that, she's a poor old thing really. I feel sorry for her students having to produce that frightful kitsch,' she said, indicating some modest paintings in a rather Camden Group style. 'Some of them were quite talented when they came, but that's all been squashed out of them by now.'

Both Celia and I applied to get into the Royal School in central London, but Celia was rejected. She ended up at a rather minor establishment, but undaunted went on with her admittedly kitschy style, hoping to find some job in commercial art whilst aiming at an exhibition. My interviewer was very enthusiastic. 'Some of the candidates haven't understood that figurative art was rendered redundant by the invention of the camera,' he said. I smiled pityingly. 'What do you think of the Turner short list?' he went on to ask. 'I think it's marvellous,' I had answered. 'Yes, but some of these youngsters haven't yet realised that if they can't relate to every work on it, they might as well become estate agents, that's our problem.' I had nodded and smiled again. I was accepted. I was soon attracting attention at the Royal. I began to move away from the Klinthkoe School and develop ideas of my own. I used collage with stuck-on atrocity headlines about a war that was going on at the time and then washed coffee over the canvas at the end; later I moved on to using plywood on which I painted smoky looking backgrounds and nailed on old metal boiler plate labels. I got one of those exhibited with the London Brotherhood group. 'A wry comment on our past industrial sins with a burnish of brass bravura,' I read with excitement in the evening paper, written by a well known critic. Noticed for the first time!

There was a flat period when I left the Royal, and Celia and I got a summer job in the Botanic gardens. I recalled the long summer days, when she and I had spent our time hosing the beds inside and outside the hothouses, and then chased and hosed each other to cool off. But that carefree time was long gone. I remembered the cruel reviews of her exhibition. 'A farrago of saccharine sentimentality' …. 'a nauseating tour of Never-Never land and Toytown, with Tinkerbell at the helm. Don't clap your hands readers, let her light go out'…'Techniquey kitsch – well painted but not worth painting.' And last, but maybe not least, the single word 'Help!' I hadn't seen the exhibition, partly because of her remark, and partly because being seen at that private view wouldn't have been good for me in view of my rising status.

Saturday Afternoon: 2 PM

Out of the sunshine, the gallery smelt a little musty, but it was cooler and I was glad to be out of the heat. It had one large space and one door to a smaller room through which I could see more contemporary-looking exhibits. The main room was exactly as I expected. Ranging from pedestrian and techniquey landscapes and figures, to some saccharine genre scenes, it made me realise how far we had come. There was no doubt that they could paint – indeed I doubted if I could have ever achieved the effects they could produce. Even Monzo with his Greek pin-ups, his false emotion, and what one could only describe as his relentless hypocrisy, had a mastery of the medium he used; it was only a pity he had wasted it on his promotion of his controlling elitist ideas. One could hardly have found a better collection of the conventional daubs that the Victorian art foundry cast from its rigid mould, than the one in this gallery. One yearned for a bonfire. One last look at the routinely boring works sent me out for a cooling tonic-water in the garden of a nearby pub, where I ruminated on the past that hopefully lay behind us, and the future that hopefully lay before me.

Saturday Afternoon: 4 PM

I walked into the contemporary room of the gallery and felt better immediately in the white-walled and sunlit space. I was pleased to see a small installation by a former fellow student at the Royal, who had begun to have some modest success before my own rise. I had recalled her building hair curlers into the form of a giant hammer during our last year. It had some political message which she had explained to me, but I couldn't recall what it was. I reminded myself that soon people would be looking at *my* work in the grandeur of the White Gallery, and I felt a surge of joy as I stood amongst the white plinths with their innovative toppings. Then out of the corner of my eye I saw three conventional paintings on the wall – looking quite out of place amongst the cutting edge collection. I turned and one caught my eye, and unexpectedly I felt a sudden pleasure in looking at a portrait. I immediately walked over and had the shock of seeing Celia herself sitting in the bright window of our old Lewisham flat. I saw planes of light and shade, and a halo round her head where the direct sunlight was scattered by her dark, dark hair. On her face she had captured the placid joy she felt when she painted. Beside it were two other of her works – the run-down garden of the house in which we had lived, and her latest version of that old Abbey. I knew what was likely to be printed on the card below. I read: 'These paintings by the late young artist Celia Trueman were purchased for the gallery shortly after she took her own life.' It gave the date of death as the week after her exhibition had finished.

I left the gallery in haste. Recalling her last remark to me helped to expel sentimental thoughts which have no place in the mind of a rising artist with a hard-edged reputation. 'I'll call your biography *An Artistic Journey from Hoser to Poser*,' she had said with angry tears in her eyes, before slamming the door on me.

6 The Lost Bomber

Strangest thing I ever heard was when I was flying back from Canada, with Nobby Clarke. We had been on a sudden servicing emergency, and were in uniform. The old fellow saw the uniforms and introduced himself. 'Raynes is my name, Chief Tech Raynes. I was in the mob for thirty years. Course we didn't get flown around in Jumbos in those days! It was the middle of the cold war, you know.'

We humoured him, and talked of the mob and the way it had changed. But he had something he wanted to say. He never once looked out of the window at the grey waters of the North Atlantic. We finally got him going, in the belief that until we did we couldn't watch the film.

'It was the height of the cold war, you see', said Raynes. 'We were constantly on alert, and a man could only take so much. But Barson, I thought he'd really cracked up. He was the Master Technician, and he was a meticulous little weasel, not like old Wildes, his predecessor as I recall. We were awaiting AOC's inspection. It was a stupid affair - a big nob - the group commander, who in our case was an Air Commodore, came around once a year to see if everything at Saddington was OK. Of course the camp lot would go into panic mode, and everything had to be cleaned, or painted, or whatever. It'd all be done three days before he got there, and then the silliness would start. 'Maybe we should paint white lines round the windows!' some fool would say. Or 'why not have all the lorries in the MT pool in an exact line with the biggest ones at the end?'... And so on, and so on: fart-arsing around, bulling up the whole place. That's where tales of spraying the grass green come from - AOC's inspections; or GOC's in the army. And they went even pottier than us - the pongos always go over the top you see...we at least had our planes to fly. They had nothing to do but bash around the square and blanco their bloody belts. But aircraft could be a problem too! And as often happens, when all the pratting about's been done, the evening before the big day, a problem arose. Barson ran into the sergeants' hut, at 'A' Flight dispersal. 'Hey Jimmy!' he shouted. He was as white as a sheet, and I asked him what was up.

'You'll never believe this, Jim, but I seem to have lost a bleeding kite.' he said.

'Come off it, Les - you can't lose kites: folk'd notice.'

'Well I've just checked my inventory - I went through all the brooms, the tools, the towing arms, the land-rovers, the garries and the rest of the paraphernalia, and I found the kites are on my inventory! It seems crazy, having a Master Technician with millions of pounds worth of Vulcans in his charge. But they are! And one's not here, and furthermore I don't think I've ever seen it since I came last year!'

'Well you should never sign for an inventory until you've checked it, Les,' I said, to wind him up, 'First rule of life in the mob! It might not have *been* here when you came! Someone might have just forgotten to strike it off when it went, and old Wildes probably never got the inventory list out of the drawer'

'Well that's the point. I didn't realise the *bombers* were *on* the inventory – I just told you.'

Poor chap, he was in a blind panic. He couldn't see things straight.

'What's the number?'

'ZA908!' he said.

'Oh - 908 - that's around alright. I saw it yesterday, I think. It's been on a major - that's why you haven't seen it!'

He looked relieved. But do you see the point? How the hell could anyone lose a festering four-engined jet bomber? Or even think he had? It was the cold war, you see. It did funny things to us. We knew there were atom bombs being carried around up there, for real. We were jumpy. But Barson was still worried. It was a bloody nuisance, because I was due to go drinking at the Horse and Jockey, that night, with my old flight crew, Jim Lewis, Aubrey Clay, and Vince Washington - they were all officers, but we used Christian names when we went out. Obviously with me being only an NCO we didn't fraternise regularly, but once a year we met: a sort of reunion. So I was keen to get away. But a mate's a mate, and I wanted to help him.

'Well where've you looked then? This airfields a big place you know. There are lots of old unused dispersals around - someone might've parked it on one of them - you can't even see the south pans from here!'

His face relaxed.

'Yes - I'm being a prat - it must be around, mustn't it?

'Tell you what, Les', I told him 'I'll just get in the garry and have a look over in the old ILS hangar - you could check the south pans. Let's get it off your mind.

You'd look a bit of a Charley if the AOC wanted to go and see if 908 was all nice and clean, and you had to admit you'd somehow mislaid it; mislaid a bleeding Vulcan - bloody rotate!' 'Thanks Raynsey, you're a pal!' he said.

I got in the one-ton and drove off round the peri-track, the engine pinking all over the place. I knew ZA908 was around. I'd been palmed off with the job of looking after the paperwork by then. I had Barson's inventory documents. I also had the pre-flight inspection records, including the one for 908 in my filing cabinet. I'd glanced at it that very day and seen that it had been all properly signed off before its last flight. All those erks couldn't have signed off their pre-flights if the kite wasn't around, now could they? Oh no! You can't check the airframe of a ghost bomber, nor the engines, nor the radar. You can't put the test gear on the Alt5 if the plane has already disappeared in the ocean, now can you?

Anyway, I parked the garry outside No 7 hangar - it wasn't used regularly at the time, but I had a set of keys, and soon got in. There it was, 908 - I could have recognised it a mile off. Typical of these Halton trained crew chiefs: panicking at the first whiff of a blot on their copybooks. Not that it would have been Barson's first blot. I heard that when he was an erk one of the kites he'd inspected went up with an Alt5 test set still attached to the gear! You wouldn't know, but that feeds in a constant signal - 200ft. The kite could've piled in if the crew had trusted it, but they had more bloody sense. He was a lucky bastard, dead lucky, that's all.' Raynes seemed to become quite agitated and flushed.

'I took a look at her. She shouldn't have been put in No 7 - it leaked, and she was wet. The whole scene was dank, with greenish vapour lit up by the hangar lights, which I'd put on. The condensation dripped off her, and she'd gathered algae on her fuselage. What a way to look after an aircraft! It wasn't like that when I was in charge of her. You could have believed there was seaweed growing on her, in that strange misty illumination. If the AOC got to see this, then poor old Les would wish I had never found it! I switched the lights off and left. I caught Les going out of the flight hut. 'Found her!' I said.

'Where was she?' he asked – bloody relieved he looked.

'In No 7 hangar' I said. 'And if I were you I'd get a few of your lads over there to tart her up. She looks to me like she's been at the bottom of the sea for a year or two! Iron Jack won't like it.'

'No 7 Hangar? That's more or less derelict, isn't it? Who put her it there?'

'Who knows? I said. 'I'm off - got a date with my old crew at the Horse & Jockey.'

'Strictly you should ask me, Jimmy...I need every man...'

'Strictly, bollocks: I was in this lot when Pontius was still only in flying training and I've had more kites on my inventory than you've had hot dinners!'

'Not any more' Les said with a cold look in his eye, and I looked at him hard. He shrugged, and said, 'OK go on'

'I was going to' I replied.

They were already at the Horse and Jockey. What a bunch they were! They were got up in fancy dress, all three; something new, every year. This year it was green skulls! I ask you. And they had got themselves up to look as if they were all wet and covered in seaweed, all three of 'em. I laughed fit to bust! Jim and Vince let Flight Lieutenant Clay do the talking. They just sat looking at me through these black sockets. Clay was no snob. He put on a mysterious hissing voice. 'Help us Raynes!' he said. 'It's cold down here! We're cold and it's all your fault. Get us out of here Raynes!'

I laughed again. 'Come on you blokes, what are you going to have?' I noticed people edging away from our table. Drunken airmen aren't so popular in peace time. Some were looking at me pretty strangely.

When I got back Les was still in a panic. 'There's no aircraft in No 7 hangar' he said. But I just went to the mess and to bed. Any Crew Chief who loses a kite...I ask you! Of course the AOC never asked to see it. So there you are!'

The plane landed and we went through customs. Nobby and I were taken to Lindham, and there we got on a train, which wended its tortuous cross-country route to the station where we were now posted.

'You think that old git was ever in the mob?' I asked, once we were ensconced in the refreshments coach with pints in our hands.

'Well he had all the jargon', Nobby answered. 'And funnily enough his name's vaguely familiar. Funny sense of humour his goulish friends had.'

'Yeah; I thought it was just fighter pilots who pulled those sorts of silly bloody capers.'

But just before we reached our destination Nobby suddenly spoke.

'Hey, it's all come back to me where I heard of Raynes. It was from a Senior Technician Instructor I came across when I was doing my tech training. He had been one of the bods on Raynes' crew at the time, and he told us the whole tale as a warning to be meticulous in our servicing. Yeah, Raynes was the guy responsible for that Vulcan that went into the drink off Cape Finisterre in the fog. He had a new erk who left the Alt5 test gear on his kite - the pilot must have thought he was at two hundred feet, and he went straight into the drink, and sank without trace. Raynes had over-signed the pre-flight confirmation, but he didn't check whether the job had been properly done. Apparently the plane went in on the very night the aircrew were to take him out for his annual treat. He recalled Raynes standing around for hours hoping 908 would turn up, even after it had been off the radar for far longer than its fuel would have lasted. The erk confessed, Raynes got on a technical charge and he ended up stripped of his stripes, and apparently spent the rest of his career shuffling round hangars with a broom and filing the paperwork at the end of each shift.'

We looked at each other.

'Bloody hell' I said.

7 A Holiday in Bloggsville

It's funny the way things happen to change ones life. How much my self-esteem has gone up – all indirectly as a consequence of a holiday!

I had never felt like taking a trip to Bloggsville, having heard nothing especially interesting or unusual about either Bloggsville, or the surrounding Bloggs country. But my wife had a good friend there - called Annggs - which is apparently a Bloggs name - the equivalent of Ann. Annggs often asked my wife whether we would like to go and visit her and her husband at their villa on the outskirts of Bloggsville. Finally we agreed, and took the long train journey to Bloggsville, where we were met at the station by Alanggs, her husband, who I knew slightly, as he still worked in the capital, which in Bloggs is called Krunggspoop, in an office near mine. He was an eager ambitious sort of chap, I had heard, and he was known as Alan by his colleagues.

'What do you think of it!' he said shaking hands vigorously, then spitting over his shoulder, which, as I had heard, was a Bloggs greeting for a friendly stranger. In the case of my wife, who he knew better, he used the familiar form of greeting to a woman, which seemed a bit over the top to me, smoochy as it was. Surprisingly - for Sylvia is very hot on sexism - she accepted this with a smile, presumably because it was a genuine tradition. 'Takes your breath away, doesn't it?' Alanggs said.

I nodded, smiling, without any idea whether he meant the hilly country we had been crossing, or the first view of Bloggsville, which we had now sampled. I could see that the buildings were different from those in the capital where I lived, but only like many others I had seen in similar latitudes. I guessed he probably meant the hills, which were pretty enough, although they wouldn't really take anyone's breath away. He ushered us straight to a cafe where Annggs sat. She smiled at us - almost sympathetically I thought.

'That's the Bloggs flag, there, on the garage - you'll see that a lot here' Alanggs said, indicating a grubby piece of cloth flying over a run-down looking garage. 'We rarely fly the national flag here you see - in fact it can be a bit risky. There's nothing personal, of course, but the Bloggsoes - that's what people from the Bloggs country are called - hate Oafenpoopers - that's what you people are called here - and it's not specially complementary either!' he lowered his voice and nudged me with a conspiratorial air: 'But what about the architecture then? Annggs tells me you are keen on architecture. You'll be amazed at our villa - I had it built in authentic Bloggs style, designed by a Bloggs architect - it was a ruin of a sheep-shearing shed that my grandfather left us. I'm Bloggs through and through, back as far as you can go, although my fathers family were originally from Krunggspoop (That's what we call the capital, you see!), but here it's only the mother that counts. Briggs, you know, the boxer, he's Bloggs, because his grandmother on his mother's side, she was Bloggs - lived in Bloggsville in fact. That's where he gets his toughness - Bloggsoes are as tough as hell - a Bloggsoe would smash your face in as soon as look at you, you know. We have a saying, 'Beware an angry Bloggsoe'!'

Just then a waiter arrived. Alanggs insisted that I tried a traditional Bloggs beer, and I agreed, being an open minded sort of person. At other tables people seemed to be drinking perfectly normal beer, and I was surprised when the Bloggs beer appeared. It was called Breggs, and was a livid yellow in colour, slightly cloudy, and served warm with a living beetle dropped in from a little jar at the moment of presentation.

'That's really the tradition, and you can't get the Bregger - that's the beetle - in many places now.' said Alanggs. 'Well – here's to a great holiday.' We lifted our glasses - Sylvia was drinking a glass of white wine that looked chilled and tempting. The Breggs was quite unpleasant, and it seemed a strange tradition, if such it was. But Alanggs smacked his lips with gusto, and spoke enthusiastically about the beverage. 'This is marvellous - I count the days until I get my first glass of Breggs!' he said, crunching the Bregger with relish. 'You can't get it in Krunggspoop at all! Oh there are places where it's sold in bottles, but real Breggs is always kept outside in a Grutbluggs - that's a big tin bath, and the surface should be covered with rotting bay leaves. The bottled stuff is just, well frankly it's worse than Pooperdreggs - that's what we call ordinary beer here.'

Alanggs wanted to get home to see how the Bloggsville soccer team were getting on in an international tournament.

'If it wasn't for us Bloggsoes you wouldn't have a team left in Europe,' he said. 'The national team is usually more than half Bloggsoes anyway, you know.'

I pointed out that at the moment only our goalkeeper was a Bloggsoe. 'Ah yes, but then the selectors will never pick a Bloggsoe if they can avoid it - they hate us, they are all Oafenpoopers you know! Same as in the war, the government always send in the Bloggsoe

Dragoons first, partly because they are the best troops, and partly to get as many Bloggsoes killed as possible, they hate us Bloggsoes, as I said.'

At home a few minutes served to show that the Bloggsoe team were on the receiving end of a good beating, and Alanggs turned off the TV.

'In fact I'm not that interested in soccer these days - the real game down here is Bloggsoe League Football. Bloggsoe League is the toughest game in the world. The average Bloggsoe League player is twenty-three stone, and stands six feet five in his Bloggsoe League socks. I saw a lot of Bloggsoe League players in an Oafenpooper pub once - boy did they scare everyone - you know, one of those prissy little places. Lots of middle-class Oafenpoopers in their weekend jerseys and cravats, and then these huge touring Bloggsoe League players came in, you know, having a laugh, and knocking over a few tables, and accidentally breaking chairs, I mean they were just so big! No one dared say a dickey bird, of course, and a few local yobboes got roughed up a bit I gather. '

No trouble had been spared to keep us entertained. That evening - having admired his house, which was quite sufficiently in the Bloggs-style for my taste, and in every other way a highly desirable residence - we went to sample some of the delights of Bloggs food. I felt uneasy on being told that we were going to a 'Real Bloggs restaurant...not some touristy dump serving Oafenpooper food passed off as real Bloggs.' Initially, on being told that the national dish was actually third-fried chickens' heads served cold in dripping I furiously tried to think of an excuse to drop out. But the other dishes weren't too bad, and it turns out that sea anemones in a tasty fish sauce are pretty decent fare. The wine of the region was just like any other wine, although a little expensive, and after a few glasses, I began to feel a bit better. I instinctively recoiled from a beige substance which was put before me with a flourish at the end of the meal, and which exuded an unexpected, but rather disturbingly familiar, aroma. Alanggs immediately piped up 'This is Gutbuckitta, a traditional cheese which recalls the siege of Bloggsville by the Oafenpooper army in sixteen-thirty-seven. The inhabitants survived the famine by drinking their own urine and eating...' Ann hastily cut him short: 'We don't need to know the details darling...lets look at the drinks menu again...' she said.   Nevertheless Alanggs attacked his Gutbuckitta with a robust if slightly mechanical looking enthusiasm   After a little glass of a traditional spirit which was not unlike many another such local liqueur - a cross between paint-stripper and a cough medicine - we were only too eager to see some Flaboggia, the famous dance of the region. Silvia likes dance, and I had noted that Flaboggia dancers, as seen on TV at their carnival, seemed to wear only a bare minimum - or less than a bare minimum in some cases. We passed several promising looking shows, but Alanggs was not easily satisfied. 'Oh no: they're just tourist shows - *that's* not *real* Flaboggia. I know where we'll see *absolutely authentic* Flaboggia.

After a while, in a more dimly lit part of the town, we entered a run down looking cafe, which was almost empty, apart from an oldish man with a strange stringed instrument, an embarrassed-looking youth with a small drum, and two very mature, stick-like women in black trousers. 'This is it, Silvia, this is a real Flaboggia bar... you're going to see real Flaboggia. No-one under sixty has a clue about it now, but if we give 'em twenty apiece they'll do it!'

He ordered us normal beers after discovering that they didn't do Breggs. Then after he spoke in halting Bloggs to the large barman and handed over a hundred smackers, the two musicians shuffled onto the floor and set up a most horrendous cacophony, aided by the barman himself who blew some loud disgusting raspberries from a giant Kazoo which he suddenly produced from beneath the bar. After a suitable period in which we were able to concentrate fully on the musical aspects of Flaboggia the two unlikely dancers creaked out onto the floor, and performed a dance consisting of very slight jerky movements, some of which appeared to be only the natural effects of the stiffness which comes with age, and the instability which comes from inebriation.

'This is it, you people...this is Flaboggia, absolutely uncommercialised, it's been going on since the Dark Ages, and they used to do it here before the Romans came. Of course it's all been ruined - and quite deliberately - by Oafenpoopers; they hate any expression of Bloggs nationhood!' We watched the strange spectacle for about fifteen minutes before the dancers left the floor and resumed their seats, with a disconsolate air.

Next day Alanggs wanted us to go to a Moggida, at which cats were chased up poles by specially trained dogs after which their heads were bitten off by the Moggeritos, who leaped to the poles from the backs of Arab stallions. The Moggeritos were athletic young men who wore stylised feathered costumes representing various birds that figured in Bloggsoe mythology. They had huge followings and their photographs appeared everywhere. If the Moggerito failed in his attempt to bite off the head, the job was finished by an assistant called a Chopperito who used a special pair of giant secateurs; one could buy prettily decorated versions of these in tourist shops. As he did it he would utter a strange hysterical yodelling sound, which was apparently the phrase 'The land of Bloggs is safe once more!' I told Alanggs that I didn't really want to go, but he was adamant. 'It's not about killing cats at all!' he said. 'It's the colour - the ceremony - the costumes, the dust and heat - the drama of good and evil! You haven't seen a Moggida, so you don't know. You've no right to dismiss what you haven't seen!'

'Well look, the cats get killed don't they? And I happen to like cats'

'You...you don't know how we *love* cats. The Bloggsoe loves a cat more than any other animal. It's our national symbol for goodness sake. Read Pinkington! He was a *real* man, not one of your *sissies* from Krunggspoop. And he said it was the most exciting spectacle he ever saw. We get fed up with you Oafenpoopers coming down and sanctimoniously condemning us over issues you know *nothing about*! If you think it's cruel what about the *slaughter of Bloggsoe children* that used to be perpetrated by Oafenpoopers every year in the thirteenth century? They were beaten to death, then fed to the kings hounds when meat was in short supply. Yes! That's real cruelty! Whereas the cats! They enjoy it. They live only for the Moggida! You come along, and you'll be won over, I promise! It's traditional for a Gaggelweggsoma - that's a woman who is at her first Moggida - to be given the Bruggom - that's the first cats head to be bitten off. A Bloggsa - that's a Bloggs woman - treasures her Bruggom all her life. Sylvia will get a Bruggom with luck'

'Look Alanggs - I just don't feel like going to a Moggida, that's all. I'm sure it's all as you say!' I said.

'Well that's OK then! Only we're a proud people, we Bloggsoes, we don't like to be lectured by Oafenpoopers about cruelty. We're the kindest people on earth. We have a terrific sense of community, you see. We aren't like Oafenpoopers; if, say a Bloggsoe falls on hard times, then all his neighbours will just help him out, there's no thought of selfishness. The chappie that used to own the little vegetable shop next to me - he went bust when they halved his regional trader grant. That's how we got our garage, actually, he had to sell his shop in a hurry, and we helped him out, got it very cheap too. Mind you he was very bitter about it all - I gather he joined Bugga - the terrorist group.'

The rest of the holiday was in a similar vein, and after a while Silvia and I took to sneaking off, buying national papers and sitting in touristy cafes reading about the world outside. By a co-incidence we met the chap who had sold his shop to Alanggs. He had seen us with him, and was surprisingly friendly. He hadn't joined Bugga at all, but using a compensatory grant from the government, plus what was a apparently a ridiculously high price he'd got from Alanggs for his lock-up shop, he now owned a franchised electronic consumer goods store, and was doing well. Property prices were now rock-bottom, and he'd bought himself a big Bloggsville style house. 'I hope you enjoy the rest of your holiday!' he said. 'I could show you some of the real Bloggsville, you know, you won't see anything with that Oafenpooper Alanggs!'

We gently declined, and a few days later returned home, glad to get away from so much tradition.

But things weren't so wonderful in the capital. As I sat trying to read my newspaper in my local cafe a yob left his noisy friends and accosted me in a threatening manner, having noticed my Bloggsville sweatshirt.

'What do you want in here, Boggoe?' he enquired, using a derogatory name for a Bloggsoe. 'We don't want any stinking Boggoes around here!'

'Look, I'm not from Bloggsville' I said. 'It's just that I recently went on holiday to the Bloggs region.'

'Oh you did, did you, well if you don't bog off out of here I'm going to *smash your face in*!' His friends were all grinning away.

I decided that it might be as well to leave, and he made no move to stop me, only saying 'now we can have some fresh air' as I went out the door. I'd like to see him say *that* to a Bloggsoe League player! But I was getting fed up with life in the capital...this was only one of several such incidents, and the traffic was getting infernal. I missed an important opportunity for promotion, and I yearned for some respite. I remembered Bloggsville with some warmth, and recalled the Bloggsoes words about low property prices.

A year later and I was holidaying in my new villa in Bloggsville, and a finer place doesn't exist. I knew that my great-great grandmother on my fathers side had come from Bloggs country, which meant that he was Bloggsoe, by Alanggs theory, and therefore, so was I, in some sense. We therefore bought a house in Bloggsville, for a good rock bottom price, and we go there every spare moment. I've learned a bit of Bloggs, more than Alanggs, and Sylviggs - that's Sylvia's name in Bloggs - has learned a whole load of Bloggs recipes. And she's taking Flaboggia lessons, and intends to just wear a Flaboggia thong at the fiesta when the weather warms up a bit. And I have to admit Alanggs was right about Moggida. It's a fantastic spectacle. I've done several watercolours of Moggidas, and sold them all - such colour and drama! The moment when the cats heads are tossed up by a good team of Moggeritos! And yet I love cats - it's the Bloggsoe in my blood! Tears even came to my eyes when I saw a cats head that reminded me of Tinker, who had sadly disappeared a week earlier, tossed up at a little ad hoc local Moggida. Of course the cats are bred specially, and have to be trained for months, but even so it provokes strong emotions. But it toughens one up! Last week, back in Krunggspoop, I went to a restaurant with Sylviggs, and recognised the man eating at a nearby table with his girlfriend. I immediately did what any Bloggsoe would do, and went across and smashed his plate of chiperons into his stupid Oafenpooper face. It was none other than the Oafenpooper who had insulted me a year earlier. At least I think it was, and we Bloggsoes are a proud people. I'm sure it was him. Beware an angry Bloggsoe!

Well, we're off to the Moggida now, after we've picked up some Gutbuckitta and a case of Breggs at the local shop.

8 The Electric Bullshitter

My fortunes were at a low ebb as I sat disconsolately in the corner of the carriage on a miserable November night. My wife had left me for Tom Grabber, who was miles higher than I in the company, and she had taken the kids. I had just heard that my promotion prospects were zero, and as the compartment emptied at the more fashionable suburbs I was left on my own watching the rain streaming down the grimy window of the train I daily used. Splashes came in through the disintegrating seals on the windows. I got one or two drops in my mouth, which seemed to taste sweet. I recalled a legend from the land of my ancestors, and sure enough a train passing in the opposite direction gave a piercing whistle like the wail of the banshee. I looked through the window, as the train loitered past a signal and seemed to make out an old woman sitting on one of the mileposts. I sat back again into the lighted compartment, shaking my head. We Celts are an imaginative people.

I picked up an abandoned magazine that I had not previously noticed and idly flicked through it. It was an *Exchange and Mart* type of thing, with lists of all sorts of second-hand and dubious things one could buy. One could learn to be a concert pianist in ten easy lessons, for example. Or buy a suite of software worth ten thousand pounds for a mere fiver. One advertisement caught my eye. 'Kiss goodbye to those 'can't advance blues'. Own your very own bullshitter! For details call us....'

Smiling wryly I put the number into the contact list of my mobile, and prepared to alight at my dingy station. My house was very near the railway, although it was some walk, due to the awkward configuration of the streets. I glanced at the unkempt state of the front garden with its faded chrysanthemums, and got in out of the rain. I fried myself a steak, microwaved some chips and took a four pack of Murphy's from the fridge. I ate the meal and drank steadily through four pack. Then I tried the number, although not really expecting to get an answer on a Friday night. But almost immediately a friendly female voice took my details, and by some miracle I received a colour brochure the next morning. It showed a whole range of men in business suits, together with one or two women. Each had a name. The first to catch my eye was a model called Mike Guttersnipe. It was the cheapest. The blurb offered was as follows.

Entry-level model for use in the most basic situations: the Guttersnipe can cut through layers of your opponent's bullshit using a streetwise cut-and-thrust delivery often succeeding in complete character assassinations of diligent and experienced colleagues. It has a careful diction in which one can detect traces of an original cockney accent almost eradicated by elocution lessons. It comes in three choices of neat business suit, Ex-Barrow-boy Green, Common-as-Muck Brown and Getting-On Grey. Can be upgraded right the way through to a Slimebag, just slot in your new head and you have your next bullshitter. The Guttersnipe comes complete with a degree in Business Studies from the University of Lewisham.

As a further recommendation for a Guttersnipe a cutting from trade press was quoted in which 'A Guttersnipe entered a modest-sized but thriving manufacturing company as a junior clerk, rose to the board within five years, gutted the finances, got away with a hundred and twenty million, and left the firm bankrupt. No crime was involved, only a steady stream of dynamic bullshit.'

At the top of the range was the Crispin Bluffer. He spoke in impeccable Oxford drawl and his suit alone retailed at three thousand pounds, but was in the package at only eighteen hundred. His virtues were boundless apparently, and we learned that one Bluffer was a serving MP, two were directors of nationally known companies, and there were dozens coming up behind them. There was a race on with a rival manufacturer to be the first to get a bullshitter installed as Chief Executive of one of the big four banks, or into the cabinet. The rival model, though newer, and with a better record, was said to be 'badly engineered and over hyped. One had apparently recently exploded in its office, covering the walls with disgusting and evil smelling organic slime. The police failed to solve the case, and the electric bullshitter was listed as a missing person.

I looked carefully through the brochure before choosing a 'Charles Buckpasser'. I opted for a dark blue suit, Cambridge Degree (it could have been Oxford) and an RAF tie. It had an upper middle-class accent with a priggish tone. Of course when I made the order I had no idea what would happen - it didn't really matter, the cost wasn't more than a top-of-the-range new PC, and I had found my motivation aroused out of its numbed stupor by the strange opportunity. I eagerly filled out the form which included the text: 'Please rush me my Buckpasser within three days. If I am not completely delighted with my bullshitter I may return it and receive a full refund immediately.'

A few days later a huge parcel was delivered and I unwrapped it in a fever of excitement. As I did so I could hear the head already bullshitting in the bag in which it was enclosed. 'I think maybe we could put Keith's idea on a back-burner', came through in a muffled tone, followed by 'The company should be provided with a raft of innovative capabilities, which I feel I am uniquely positioned to instantiate given a suitable team ' Once I had him out of the parcel I turned off the bullshit stream which had been triggered by the sound of a Porsche door closing outside the house. I examined the electric bullshitter and was deeply impressed. It had numerous controls under the left breast of the jacket, and one could adjust the number of lies or buzzwords per minute, the range of topics, or the degree of fawning, all with superb analog knobs. The suit alone looked worth the investment, and it came with a shrink-wrapped pile of documentation plus a beautiful oilskin bag containing the qualifications and CV of the bullshitter.

I assembled it in twenty minutes, and tried it out. Although according to the manual the analog knobs 'put *you* in command', I preferred to use the programmed mode which had, apparently, been developed in-house by the world's finest team of computational bullshit experts. It went smoothly into action when I tested it on a telecommunications theme.

'I'd like to develop a platform for a wide range of new products and services in which a customer-facing data-centric mode of pro-active object-oriented new modules is key to the enabling technologies we shall require.' it began, smoothly. 'I'd like to take a few moments to show my vision of a global virtual network in which each capacity-provider is tributary to ourselves as a managing shell, with fiscal opportunities falling out with no costly provision of new facilities beyond our current mandates.' It had set up an overhead projector, and now a sequence of obscure diagrams appeared with numerous references to 'revenue amplification', 'competitor disadvantage' and 'ultimate sector domination'.

Next day I got it an interview at the company, and it passed with flying colours. I didn't see it very often at first as it was always out of its office, generating a whirlwind of apparent activity. It was able to achieve great success by seeming to its bosses to be setting up exciting new ventures and activities, which promised to bring glory to them. It always seemed to know just that bit little more about new winds blowing through the company earlier than anyone else. If it suddenly started talking about 'hothousing' you could bet your last cent everyone would soon start taking about hothousing. If 'concern for our people', was the current theme, and it suddenly started saying things like 'lunch is for wimps', you could safely fire your staff, freeze promotion and incorporate pay cuts for people who couldn't really leave - for a while. It always managed to get promotion before the plethora of useless projects and procedures it had initiated collapsed in disarray, and within the year his replacement's head would roll as he became the scapegoat for the bullshitter's blunders.   It spent most of its time divided between its boss and its boss's boss. It rarely appeared to its own staff - hardly seeming to recognise their existence. I worked directly for it for a brief while as it rose up through the layers. Every morning ones in tray was full of its opened mail, with little scribbled notes attached, signed by it in shorthand, - 'Can you dl pls? - Rbt' or 'Can you sort ths pse? - Rbt' (I had christened it Robert). Of course I soon scotched that by reading its manual which dealt with such cases - it was an excellent product.

"**Cases where the bullshitter becomes part of the owners own supervisory chain:** *All directives, orders and other imperatives from the bullshitter can be* *either ignored by using the command OWNER MUTE, or switched off altogether with the OWNER DISABLE command."*

I used the disable, because all my work then went onto Jackson's desk, and I could even send queries about my own work to the bullshitter and it farmed it all out to Jackson, who whinged, but it, of course, ignored that with phrases like, 'People have got to just put the company first old chap - if you cant handle the heat....' I also picked up its salary every month, and soon decided I could move and leave my job. After that life was simple - I lived like a king on the fruits of the bullshit, my only work consisting of following the maintenance procedures. New versions of the bullshit software were issued, and I downloaded them. I seemed to have at last achieved the sort of success that I had always craved - even though it was rather second hand.

The problems started gradually. First, having eliminated most of the old company stalwarts, the bullshitter began to find that it was increasingly in competition with other bullshitters. These could not be so easily disposed of, especially as my bullshitter was an older model, with certain fundamental limitations. But more seriously, as the miasma of bullshit around the place grew in leaps and bounds, it became clear that even the technical side was being infiltrated and taken over by bullshitters. Both managerial and technical decisions were being taken by a fewer and fewer number of real people who had somehow been able to hang on. Each was now surrounded by a crowd of smoothly verbose electric bullshitters who picked his or her brain unceasingly, whilst desperately manoeuvring not to lose access to the dwindling resource of meaningful thought. Inevitably cases arose where bullshitters mutually mistook one another for people, and ridiculous changes were initiated into which no real thought had gone. Technical bucks were passed furiously down the chain of command until lowly technical people found themselves taking decisions which affected the whole thrust of the company. The bullshitters in desperation turned to consultants, and contracted technical staff, but it soon became apparent that the consultants themselves were mostly well known bullshitter models, incapable of making any useful contribution.

In the end the firm went bust, and a legion of modern bullshitters were left with no jobs. Of course they were dispersed to the rest of industry, the civil service, charitable organisations and so on. Management consultancies in particular seemed particularly vulnerable to the ex-high-flying bullshitters. My life fell apart once again, and I had to take a job of much lower status than I had had before, with a Chinese-owned manufacturer who had set up recently, having moved a factory here from the now higher paid labour market of Taiwan. Bullshitter after bullshitter applied to join the company, but they seemed to have a sort of sixth sense with regard to electric bullshitters - and none had any success.

I was coming home one night on a similar evening to the one when I had found the original ad for my electric bullshitter. I heard the same wail, tasted the same sweet rain, and saw the same figure loitering beside the track. I picked up a magazine, in a sort of dream, and again flicked through some ads. 'Buy your own electric pimp.' caught my eye. Further on 'Buy an electric dope-pusher. Send for details, stating that you are at least twelve years old'. But the one I settled on was 'Electric Artists. Gallery success guaranteed within six months.' One could choose between a Freudian Anal Retentionist, a Performance & Installation Poser, a Conceptual Con Artist and an Innovative Gasbag. I chose a Gasbag. One had to sign an agreement which stated 'I understand that my Gasbag will not have technical art skills of any kind. At present our 2D models come with paint-squirting, paper-sticking and scribbling capability. 3D models specialise in ready-mades.' But along with this disclaimer I noted that the Gasbag came with a sophisticated range of text and speech modules covering a wide range of topics from scientific analysis of colour relationship via radical political polemic right through to Freudian analysis, cognitive psychology and primal scream therapy. The software, the ad boasted, had been 'engineered by the same teams who programmed our triumphant range of Electric Bullshitters, who now hold high office in every corner of our land.'

As soon as I got home I filled out the application form.

9 Instantaneous Transformation

'There's no such thing as a discontinuity in nature: an instantaneous transformation is a useful mathematical idealisation, and that's all'

'What about a square wave sir? With a Schmidt trigger you can...'

Lance knew about things like that – he had an oscilloscope his father had got from work.

'Have a careful look at a square wave on your oscilloscope Lance...you'll soon see.'

I didn't care whether instant change was possible or not. Mr Bartram thought I was going to the university to do maths. He was so proud of us. I hadn't had the heart to tell him I wasn't...I had filled in the form and he had added his reference and sent it off.

*

I had walked briskly but sensitively from the bus stop to the school, portfolio in hand, new corduroys flapping around ankles, a young art student on his way to his first session. The very room I was in smelt of the essence of art physically and psychically. There were posters on the wall: Matisse, Picasso, Mondrian as well as many I could not identify. Easels were dotted about the room; I was almost faint from joy. Senior students with beards came in, picked things up and then left. I heard one say to another 'Did you know Malcolm has gone straight up to the painting group?' A dark girl a little older than I came in; she picked up a canvas displaying a stylised plant, very Braque-like. She had long brown hair, dark blue make-up all round her eyes, and wore a black jersey and long black skirt. She gave me a faint but slightly seductive smile as she passed – I was thrilled. Real art students, I thought. And *I am* one. The future was becoming more appetising with each passing moment. I looked with a little feeling of superiority at the other new students standing nervously around clutching their boxes of paints.

Miss Liggins entered. She was very young, rather tall and somewhat frail looking, with bone white skin and shaggy black hair. A young woman driven by her art I thought. A recent returnee from the left bank; my dreams were starting to intersect the old dull, realities.

I made direct thrusting brushstrokes. Vivid streaks of saturated hues, no grovelling homage to nature would emasculate my canvases. I knew that painting now was about colour, emotion and significant form. Alfred Munnings, Frederic Leighton and their ilk were dead ducks. Miss Liggins walked slowly round, saying encouraging things to her new crop. To one: 'Don't worry about shading and modelling, just concentrate on getting the feel of oil paint' And to another: 'You have obviously used oils before'. Sometimes there was a nervous tremor in her voice.

She stood behind me for a minute or so – stunned, I hoped, by my virile and avant-garde rendition of the still life she had set up. Perhaps, like Malcolm, I would be going precociously up into some more advanced group. Then she spoke, noticeably gently. 'I don't know if this is perhaps an under-painting?' She looked very kindly but steadily into my eyes, the white hand she held up just perceptibly trembling. I mumbled something and nodded. My work had been instantaneously transformed into an under-painting by her question. I heard nothing of her next words. A knot formed in my stomach, and I felt the colour draining out of my face. As she walked soundlessly away I began the over-painting.

At the end of the day's session Miss Liggins, looking very self-conscious, gave her general feeling about the productions of her new class. 'The first and foremost quality I like to see in my students is honesty' she said. Then she stopped, and made a determined attempt to look at us, rather than at the back of the room. 'I don't mean, of course, to suggest that any of you are dishonest. But one or two of you are painting in a somewhat affected way. There lies the first step in the direction of artistic dishonesty. To those few, who will hopefully recognise their tendency, I say that I sincerely trust that you will arrive tomorrow with the idea of making a fresh start'

My cheeks burned. Her long serious face etched itself into my memory. There was something admirable, beautiful even, in this awkward forthright creature, but I never wanted her to see me again. Kind eyes are so savage.

I instantly realised that no mathematician worth his salt would wish to rub shoulders daily with such a collection of hairy young poseurs, misfits and bohemian strumpets as had assaulted my vision that day. And especially would not wish to operate under the direction of an escapee from the tomb of Ligeia! I was headed for the university the very next day; I couldn't understand why I hadn't done it in the first place. I walked to the bus stop with a gait that projected logical thought in every nuance of its choreography.

How wrong Mr Bartram was – there *is* such a thing in nature as an instantaneous discontinuity – oh yes! There is nothing ideal about it though.

10 Almost Perfect

It all happened again – twenty years after the first disaster. Melissa fell head over heels in love! Losing her job had had something to do with it – she had had to snap out of her routine, and the part time teaching jobs had forced her to be a bit more social. The contrast with her old desk-bound job made teaching almost like being on the stage, a performance every night.

His name – or his nickname - was Kaz. That intrigued her from the start. And he reminded her of Peter. He rather kept himself to himself, but not in a stand-offish way. He was refreshingly different from the loud and shaven-headed Derek – who could be intimidating. His hair was that of an artist, covering his neck – no military short–back-and-sides. He would occasionally join in the conversations at his table – where Doris and Shirley reigned, although there wasn't much for him to contribute and Melissa was rarely close enough to know exactly what was said. She had gathered that Doris' daughter was getting married in two months. And the whole class surely knew that Shirley's son was just finishing a PhD, and her other son his BSc. She saw Kaz occasionally say something with a smile, but never caught what he said in his soft voice.

Her liking for him grew up too slyly for her to be aware of it at first. He treated her with great respect when she offered advice, usually restricting his responses to smiling and making sincere-seeming nods of his head. He was a caring sort, offering the infirm Susan a regular lift home and getting on well with Chris Starling, the old moustachioed chap, who sat on the next table, making his plaques. Kaz dressed very well, in an understated manner. He had undeniable physical presence, yet he was not burly and didn't swagger about as some good-looking men do. And his voice wasn't always booming around the room as Derek's did and even Chris's sometimes. Sadly she was sure that Kaz had no very great liking for her. This was due to an incident that occurred in an early week of the term.

She made a point of stressing the more innovative, without disparaging the craft aspects of the field. She wanted to move students on, creatively, from their often rather conservative ideas: vases, bowls and, in Kaz's case, tigers, zebras or leopards. She encouraged them to go to exhibitions of modern ceramics and 3D work, and occasionally took in brochures from exhibitions of modern sculpture. One evening she had asked Kaz what he thought of a piece illustrated in one. She had hoped some students might like it in spite of its provocative nature. It featured shapes formed from spaghetti which had been cooked, formed, dried and then mounted on a blue plinth. He looked politely at it, but then gave her one of his enigmatic grins and turned rather pointedly back to his giraffe. He then made some remark which she didn't hear very well, but, felt it was probably cutting and dismissive, even though it was spoken in a soft and gentle voice. She let her anger come to the surface immediately. 'Where have you been hibernating for the last thirty years?' she said, flushing. Infuriatingly he just went on slyly smirking, and they had been rather cool with one another for a couple of weeks.

It was in the period leading up to Christmas that another incident occurred, which made her face her real feelings. During the year the college asked her to provide one work to be exhibited in the foyer in the art department's permanent display. Only four students responded to her request for work. All but one produced run-of-the-mill traditional items. There was a hand built Bonsai pot from the capable Doris, a stylish teapot from Shirley, an ambitious but run-of-the-mill thrown vase with an ugly outline from Derek, but encouragingly, a delicate and very simple paper sculpture with a modern air about it from a young art teacher, which she chose. Although Doris and Shirley laughed it off they were both obviously disappointed. But Derek – who was a habitual and sometimes aggressive complainer – was not pleased. He had put a lot of effort into learning to throw, and with a lot of braying about the technical aspects of potter's wheels and firing temperatures he had finally produced a pot of which he was very proud.

'Frankly I'm not at all happy with your choice, Melissa' he said. 'I think you're just trying to curry favour with that lot in the art school; feathering your own nest. You are not really interested in our work'

He walked sulkily away and put his vase on the table; Melissa noticed him crush a paper coffee cup in his hand. She was furious with his insulting and false accusation, and immediately responded.

'If you want to be exhibited you had better listen more and pontificate less!' she said, heatedly, knowing that she shouldn't have risen to his provocation. But she wasn't prepared for what happened next. Derek took two steps back toward her and hurled the screwed up paper cup with all his force, hitting her on the forehead. For all her verbal feistiness she was easily intimidated physically and felt suddenly afraid as he seemed to continue toward her. Suddenly Kaz was up on his feet and standing protectively in front of her. Not a word was said, and for a moment nobody blinked. Then after a few seconds Derek went back to his workplace and began to pack up, obviously meaning to walk out in a huff. Passing her on his way back to his workplace, Kaz rested a gentle hand on her shoulder for a moment. She felt it as an electric shock. As he returned to his seat Chris gave him an unostentatious 'thumbs up'. Doris and Shirley led the class in crowding around and warmly supporting and comforting her once Derek had gone, and she felt a slight recession in the oppressive solitariness of her life.

For the whole of the week before the next class Kaz was in her thoughts. She knew she was being stupid, but what use was it to know that, when she couldn't control her thoughts and emotions? She had only gradually come to notice him over the weeks that had passed since he had first walked in on the night of her first session with the class. Of course his tigers and giraffes were simple stuff and had no contemporary feel about them – but they were exquisitely made, and real craft skills always inspired her respect. And she had slowly begun realise that his work was not the result of thirty years blinkered attachment to a dated idea of creativity as she had implied, but an admirable empathy with the beasts he sculpted. And she had discovered that he admired all sorts of art whatever he had said to her about the pasta forms. He praised the sculpture which she had selected. She saw him talking to its creator, and made out him saying something to her involving the words 'ethereal', and 'beauty' above the general noise of the class. Later the student told her she was changing the name of the sculpture to *The Unbearable Lightness of Being*. 'Kaz suggested that' she had said smugly Now Melissa wondered why he had chosen to make these flattering comments to *her*, of all people. And why did he want to let *her* know that he was also well-read, in addition to his other virtues? She tried to think of the few things Kaz had said to her during their acquaintance. There weren't many.

From then on she had difficulty in acting naturally. She knew, in her professional capacity she should neither extend, nor attenuate, her tutorial sessions with him. She got their discussion over right at the start on the next evening. He listened to everything she said, nodding and smiling. Even so she found she was avoiding his eye in the most cowardly fashion, for one in her forties. She looked up and glanced furtively at him as she worked on the ritualistic paperwork generated by the college apparatchiks. She was sure that he liked her, especially since their eyes still met many times

In the break, when some had gone for coffee, she sat romantically day-dreaming at her table. She longed for his arms around her; she imagined candlelit dinners in continental bistros where they gazed into each other's eyes. She knew what her staunchly feminist friends would have said if they had known what degenerate and idiotic thoughts were in her head.

She probably could have contained herself if it wasn't for her history, and the slight resemblance he bore to a figure from her past. Peter, the fatal Peter, whose features still floated before her eyes when she thought about him; the very features which she could sometimes discern in Kaz's face. Twenty years before, Peter had shattered her world, and perhaps blighted her whole life when he had told her he was gay. And that was that. He was young and somehow he had let her build a dream of longed for happiness and security before he had told her after his trip to Scotland where he had met Hamish. Now she was beginning to fear the same fate for her dreams of Kaz. He was a perfect gentleman; perhaps too perfect. He had his own rather delicate bone china mug from which he drank his coffee. He projected such quiet self-sufficiency in this female-weighted class. He seemed not to act in the macho way of Derek, or even the aging Chris who still gave off some faltering signals of interest in the women of the class. Not so Kaz. There was worse. The week after the fracas with Derek, Kaz had been absent, and Doris had said that he was suffering from a bad cold. Melissa had asked - out of simple curiosity - if he was married. The two of them had looked at each other with infuriating complicity and grinned. Shirley answered. 'No he is not married' and they both sniggered. They had, of course, known him a lot longer than she had. Even so, she felt in her heart that he wasn't gay. And that, was mainly because of the way he sometimes looked at her. There was a longing in his eyes, she was sure of it. But she couldn't go through months of agonising doubt that would arise from her experience with Peter. There was only one thing for it. She would have to take the initiative. Perhaps as one of her students he felt that it was for her to initiate things out of respect for her status. It was *her* call, his eyes seemed to say. And her friends would all approve of her taking things into her own hands – not waiting for the lordly male to snap his fingers.

By good fortune that evening he had to transport his large giraffe, which had only just come out of the kiln, back to his car. He still had his toolbox to carry and she brightly offered to carry it for him. He graciously accepted. 'That would be very welcome. This piece needs both hands, elongated beyond nature, as happily it is.' He looked at her with a charming acknowledgement that the sculpture had greatly benefited from her recommendations. As they stood by the boot of his car, alone together for the first time in their lives, she popped the question as quickly as she could in the abbreviated period allotted to her.

'Kaz, would you be at all interested in going out to dinner one evening?' she asked, keeping her voice as steady as humanly possible. 'Why yes, that would be very pleasant!' he replied. Melissa floated a few inches off the ground. They made the assignation immediately, over the noise of cars starting and sweeping past in the damp evening air, and he gave her a gay wave as he drove away in his. She was so excited that she could hardly eat for the few days to the Friday of the dinner. Now those two could wipe the leers off their faces. All insolent conjectures would soon perish in the dust.

They met at a Greek Restaurant that was a favourite of Melissa's, but which she seldom had reason to patronise. On her way she saw other couples, and felt so good that she too had someone to be with that evening, someone who had once stood by her when she felt threatened, someone who surely respected her, and her art; someone who might soon be something big in her life. But still the nagging thought. Some gay men particularly enjoyed the company of women, she believed. Peter certainly did. Suppose this was such a case. Suppose he welcomed the idea of having a platonic friendship with the elegant tutor of his sculpture class? She flattered herself that whatever her shortcomings may or may not have been in the conventional beauty stakes, she dressed stylishly even when teaching, and her hair had often been complimented, as had her cultured and well-modulated voice. She was deeply attached to creativity, and had a high local reputation as a sculptor of which he surely knew. Perhaps it was these modest attributes of mind and manner which attracted him, and not the female body hidden under the tasteful ensemble. She couldn't bear the thought of the desolate months she had gone through after Peter's abrupt announcement. Things must be settled tonight before it was too late.

He was already in the little lounge bar of the restaurant, and looked up smiling with evident interest in her as she came in. She wore all black, with a single jewel around her neck, the only one she possessed, a sapphire from her mother which had been her pride and joy. No plaster powdered denim or patches of clay tonight.

'You look fabulous!' he said, with as much animation as he had ever displayed. She smiled noting that apart from their newer appearance his clothes were much like those she already knew. They chose from their menus, and followed the waiter side by side down the aisle in the middle of the room. As they did so Kaz lightly ran his hand down her back, stopping its trajectory only just before it would have encountered the rise of her hips. This sensual but restrained stroke set her heart singing. Of course as a gentleman he wouldn't go further in public, but she thought perhaps he would have liked to.

They sat down and she felt that at last all was well. She intended nevertheless to confirm the truth, because she knew that she could well end up wondering again. Had he curtailed the gesture so abruptly because he had an instinctive repulsion from some aspects of womanhood? Yes, she had to be bold!

After a few formalities about the pleasantly muted sound of a bouzouki and the quality of the wine, he gave her an opening.

'I must say that the decor and so on in a restaurant is very important for me. However good the food, I can't enjoy a meal in a brightly lit, plasticy sort of place. And the same goes for so many things – down to the glasses, even. Look how nice this one is. It's so simple – so perfect.'

He held up a glass that was very well proportioned. It was indeed *almost* perfect, but a scintillion too curvaceous for Melissa's taste.

'I knew you were fastidious about that sort of thing' she eagerly replied. 'That mug you bring with your thermos – it's so elegant. That made me think you could be gay!'

He was silent for an instant. But then he smiled. 'Well I don't know why *that* made you think it! But you were quite right, I am gay!'

She felt as if I had been hit in the stomach with a pile-driver. In spite of all the reassuring things that had happened, her dreams lay bleeding to death in the sand once more. After that the meal fell horribly flat. No matter how much she tried to be civil, and converse with Kaz as a platonic friend, she couldn't raise her spirits. And although *he* had seemed quite chirpy when he had revealed his orientation, he now seemed to have picked up on her gloom. She could hardly wade through her Moussaka, and he picked at his Kleftiko with little enthusiasm. She drank more Retsina and felt as if she was going to stupidly burst into tears. Still, there was one final thing she wanted to know, and this was the last chance she would get to find it out. After they had dealt with the bill she asked him.

'So, what *is* your real name? It surely can't be Kaz.'

He looked desolately up from his Tia Maria.

'My real name; no it isn't really Kaz. It's Katharine.'

'That's ridiculous.' Melissa blurted out. 'You can't be called...' Then she shut her mouth with a noisy intake of breath. A supernova had exploded in her head and time stood still whilst its planet-forming remnants fell into place, for both of them. They sat staring at each other, mouths open, noticing nothing around them, for many minutes. Then Kaz looked across the table and shrugged. She stood up and started moving slowly toward the door. Melissa caught up with her and together they walked out of the restaurant.

11 The Blind Spot

I had been on a misty and rather eerie stretch of dual-carriageway for some time and I had seen no other cars. I probably wasn't concentrating properly but was brought to attention by a car which momentarily appeared in my wing mirror as it passed. I waited for it to reappear but it didn't. It seemed it was just sitting in the blind spot, neither dropping back, nor moving on. Finally I slowed right down so it would overtake, but it still didn't. I glanced over my shoulder in irritation but saw only open road. I shrugged, knowing that such things often happen, especially when one has been driving for a long time. I drove on, moving back into traffic, once more enjoying my first long drive in the new Jag. It was mid-evening and there was little traffic about and I soon found myself on an empty road again. Suddenly I again sensed a car's lights on the periphery of the view in my wing mirror. I turned to look in my blind spot, but again nothing was there when I checked. Could it be that some idiot was deliberately hovering just out of my vision, probably jealous of my brand new vehicle? On the last part of my trip home, along a B road the sensation weakened, but still persisted. All in all I was glad to get home and drink a glass of sherry with my wife, who shrugged off my weird tale. 'You are tired and stressed', she said. 'You do too many long trips.'

For a week or so things were normal: I forgot the unpleasant drive. Then, once again in early evening, driving back from Wales it all happened again. It came on very suddenly just after I crossed the Severn Bridge. There were cars around, and I thought nothing of it when a car went to overtake; but ominously it didn't reappear in front of me. The fear surged up, especially as the road gradually emptied. It was raining heavily and I kept seeing the dim glare of yellowish lights at the edge of the mirror. I turned my head expecting to see nothing, but this time, for an instant, I saw it, solid and real through the spray and rain, something low with lights too dim, driver not discernable, but clearly following me. When I glanced again over my shoulder I couldn't see it for the rain and spray. Somewhere nearby I heard dogs barking. On the last lonely sixteen miles of empty B road I drove on and turned my head no more. I focused on the digital displays – turning up the illumination. I was safe inside the car I thought. But suddenly the elusive vehicle appeared in my wing mirror, fleetingly tangible. I made out that it was probably a sports car - open topped in spite of the damp weather, with something flapping. For some reason I couldn't make out a drivers head but I could see that he was wearing a mackintosh – a Burberry I thought, chillingly although it was only a vague lurking shape. But the idea that it was a sports car began to haunt me. It was too horrible to contemplate.

My wife saw that I was badly scared. When I told her what I had seen she still shook her head. 'Take a holiday Gavin. You are working too hard. See John Bowman' - he was our doctor. I had three straight scotches and went to bed. But as I lay there, I began to think: I was getting obsessed. I recalled the glimpse I had had of the rainy blur of an old fashioned sports car matching my speed in my side mirror, its driver wearing a Burberry. I remembered something else I had seen: the thing which had been flapping on the driver's side had suddenly lifted and blown away in the wind. Could it have been a tie? And how on earth could his tie blow away? I knew damned well how it could blow away.

I had been driving home on a short leave after a long cold war exercise. I was with a comrade in my old sit-up-and-beg Ford Anglia and resentfully watching much better cars being unloaded from the free ferry over the river. A middle aged woman with three wolfhounds on the lead was walking on the pavement. I felt waves of jealous rage when a young man about my age, wearing a Burberry, drew alongside us in a pale blue Jaguar – the latest model. He was smoking a pipe rather pretentiously. There were two slow moving lanes of traffic, we on the inside lane, he on the outside. He gave us a wave with his pipe as if he felt some rapport with us. I assumed he just wanted to impress us with his wonderful car. In my whole life, I thought, I would never be able to have a car like that. But him! His Daddy had bought it for him. That was certain. He would be at Oxford. Me? I didn't have a single A-level. Even the way he drove his car infuriated me. He'd wait for a reasonable gap to open up before him, and then he'd gun his car urgently forward so that we could all see the power of its acceleration and the efficiency of its brakes. I started laughing loudly, ostentatiously, directing it at him through my open window. I hoped he would realise I found him ridiculous, a principal boy at a pantomime, a sissy, a rich idle drone, a daddy's boy, a poseur, a boy racer. Anything! He noticed my loud fake laughter, turning his head round uneasily to look at us several times. The last time he looked he was seemingly about to say something. He did it whilst in the act of accelerating his car, but that little turn meant that he didn't see the menacing back end of a left-turning flat-back lorry swing out across his lane. He saw it too late; the power of his car was his undoing. It shot under the metal corner and decapitated him in the fraction of a second. The pipe hit the side of the bus in front with a loud rap, followed by something else which made a bang like a cannonball. The car careered on; his tie suddenly flipped up, and blew away in the wind amid a fountain spray of blood, the headless body still clutching the wheel. The car careened into a bus on the other side of the road. I saw the woman with the dogs faint, and the freed dogs yelp and eagerly begin to lap at the blood running in the gutter. I didn't enjoy that leave at all.

*

As the days passed after that first time in the new Jag I was always aware of the blind-spot phantom. Several times I nearly crashed as my attention focused on the barely-seen sports car with its decapitated driver. I was beginning to shake as I got into my car when it was dark. Soon I would not be able to hold down my job.

I took my wife's advice and went to see John. He gave me some tranquillisers. He offered me a week off but I just couldn't take the time. I went to see specialists in the paranormal. Some would sit with me in the car whilst I drove along a dual carriageway at night, but the ghostly car never appeared at such times. They seemed genuine enough, but the last one suggested I visit someone she knew. When I found out that the 'someone' was a psychiatrist I was furious. Here was a ghost buster who didn't believe in my ghost. But it was that or my job.

I ended up in the consulting room of Dr. Okon, a man with the dark complexion, resonant consonants and tonal vowels of Africa, but a distinctly Oxford air about him. His consulting room was not the antiseptic cube I expected though – there were lots of very striking masks, shields and assegais hanging on the beige walls amid a thousand books.

'I gather you have a problem for me?' he said in an open friendly manner.

'Well you are the doctor - you tell me,' I said in a rather sulky defiant tone 'but I'm not potty, so you won't find anything' I wanted to show that I didn't consider our roles such that I had to play the inferior.

'Indeed I am a doctor. So come on: what is your problem? Why have you come?'

'I wouldn't have come, but my wife and some ghost-catcher persuaded me against my better judgement.'

'Well here you are, so tell me about things. I'm sure your time is as valuable as mine.'

I reluctantly told him the story, and the memory that I connected it to. He listened politely, raising his eyes at appropriate points, and looking gratified.

'This is interesting: very interesting. We have a haunted car!' His eyes glinted in anticipation.

'You don't believe in ghosts, obviously.'

'Oh I do, my friend I do. You are plainly seeing a ghost.'

'You think I'm mad - you are humouring me! *I* know what I see!'

'I am not humouring you. I believe you see a spirit of the dead!'

'You think it's just in my head.'

'Everything you see is just in your head. Something in the real world stimulates you, but you make the pictures in your brain. Real things, ghosts, fantasies, illusions or dreams, they are all in your head.'

'Don't give me that soft soap. *You* think you wouldn't *see* it if *you* were in the car, don't you?'

'That's what ghosts are like isn't it? Who saw Banquo's ghost? Only Macbeth I think.'

'You know what I mean. You don't believe the dead man is actually there.'

'I know what you think. But I am well placed to know that there are ghosts – I know the spirit world very well. You are not mad as you fear. You are hunted by a ghost my friend.'

Now that he believed me, I had no confidence in him at all. The ghost hunters thought I was crazy, the psychiatrist thought my car was haunted. So he's a witch doctor, I thought. 'Oh, right,' I said.

He read my mind. 'And no, I am *not* a witch doctor. I am a psychiatrist'

'So what pills do you recommend?'

'No pills. We must deal with him. When did he first appear?'

'Oh a month ago - something like that. I remember it was after I got my new car; at first I thought it was some artifact of the mirror - an optical illusion. But it isn't.'

'How interesting, that you should say that!'

'What?'

'A new car!'

'I don't see what bearing that has.'

'What sort of car is it?'

'Oh it's a Jag. I hardly even enjoy it now. When I first got it I was over the moon. I never thought *I'd* own one!'

'What sort of car was the one involved in the fatal accident?'

'Oh it was a Jag as well: a pale blue one, with open top.'

He nodded his head slowly – and looked rather grave.

'You have to find out what it wants. If you don't, it will kill you. It's as simple as that.'

'How can I speak to someone with no head? Ghosts can't speak anyway. They are insubstantial. And how could it kill me?'

'They can do many things my friend; and they are *particularly* good at *killing* people'

'African ghosts maybe, but here that's all just mumbo-jumbo. This isn't Africa.'

'But I am African. And believe me it isn't mumbo-jumbo. You must find out what it wants.'

'Well how?'

He leaned forward. He fixed my eyes in a hypnotic stare.

'The world is not as you think, my friend. You have led too sheltered a life. You make too much distinction between the external world and the internal world. I can't help you except to tell you that you must find out what this ghost wants. It doesn't make any difference if it's in your mind, in the spirit world, or in the physical world; it will kill you, my friend, if you can't discover what it wants.'

I told my wife what he had said. He had left a very powerful psychic footprint in my mind for all his unscientific talk. 'Who would know what it wants to tell me?' I asked her, who seemed incredulous that her formerly oppressively rational husband was asking about a ghost. But something from my subconscious had been stirring. I remembered: he had been trying to speak. He still wanted me to know what he had been going to say before he had been cut off for ever.

'No-one knows what someone else wants to say' she said, shrugging, almost sullenly; but then with inspiration that often came to her she added: 'Except maybe a mother...' I remembered how good she had been at divining babies' desires.

I said nothing. But I knew what I would do. *My* mother was dead – but perhaps *his* was not. She need only be seventy-five or eighty. I phoned my old friend Marley, a private investigator who took only two weeks to come back with a name and address. He didn't ask why I wanted it.

Spring was in the air as I drove down into the heart of Kent, to the little village whose name Marley had sent me. There, in a row of workman's cottages, was her house. I rang the bell with nervous anticipation. The door was opened by a slender woman, with white hair and striking dark eyes in her sad still beautiful face. I told her that I had come to ask her about her son. At the mention of him she closed her eyes tight for a few long seconds. Then she let out her breath and faced me.

'He was my beloved son; for whom I lived. There was only he and I. He was twenty-one. He was desperate to have a car – he had got his license. But he had no money you see. He had just finished National Service. He was going to go to Woolwich Polytechnic to do chemistry. He was looking forward to it; he already had the college tie. His great friend lent him that car for the afternoon – and he drove it off, dreaming what it would be like to own it. He was posing – but at twenty-one why should he not? Poor boy, we had little enough. But he wasn't used to such a powerful car. The police said he had been distracted.'

'It wasn't his car then?' I said.

She shook her head.

'I have to tell you – I saw that accident – he was about to speak to me when it happened – I was in a car beside him.'

Her eyes widened. 'Tell me then'

I told her the whole story, not hiding anything apart from the gruesome details; my own contribution to his distraction was included. And I ended by saying 'And after all these years I have become obsessed with discovering what he was going to say.' I didn't tell her about the car in the blind spot. She sat silent for some time, a hand over her eyes, shaking her head. Then she spoke.

'Your jealousy killed my darling boy' she said, in measured tones over some great emotion; I could see tears brimming in her eyes. I said nothing.

'I think I would like you to leave now' she said.

Her eyes were insupportable. My trip was wasted. As dusk was falling I was uneasy. But as I walked down her little path amongst the chalky flower beds I heard her call out.

'He wanted to say that it wasn't his car. He would have known why you were pretending to laugh at him. He was very sensitive. He would have wanted to put the record straight'

I left her there, with her thirty empty years and the bitter sweet memories.

On my way back dusk fell, and a chill went down my spine as I saw the lights again in my peripheral vision. Panicky feelings spread through my body. But when a suitable gap in the oncoming traffic appeared, a car pulled out and overtook. An old pale blue Jaguar, with the driver turning and smiling, waving his hand, his tie flying out in the breeze – it disappeared over the crest of a hill, and I never saw it again. He had got what he wanted.

12 The Welsh Dragon

I don't often go to Wales - but I was there, in the mountains - the heart of Welsh Wales. I don't like the Welsh. I am afraid of them. A deep tribal recollection of the time when my ancestors drove them from their ancient land, out of the green plains and woods of England into the impenetrable maze of valleys and mountains, where they licked their wounds and nurtured their hatred of the fair-headed people who stole their birthright. Small dark people skilled in magic...druids, sorcerers - like Morwenna who told us she was a witch, trained in the arts by her grandmother, and who had the dagger supposedly forged from the broken Excalibur... I ask you! Harold took this as a joke, asking her if she performed her spells sky clad. But, as I could see, she took it very seriously. Perhaps she had a race memory of grovelling around in caves, running down the mountains to take helpless fair-haired captives - women, and children, and sacrifice them at black rites conducted in dank caves lit by smoky fires. Of course one hardly thinks consciously of these dark origins when mixing with them nowadays - but make no mistake, these feelings are bubbling away underneath on both sides in dealings between the two peoples.

Harold denies all this - he trades on his reputation as a hearty companion, ready for any joke - about the Welsh or anything else, or any crazy escapade that might suggest itself to him. Gold in the Welsh hills! It was my idea, but I would never have actually taken any practical steps myself. I wouldn't have gone along with him either. But Morwenna immediately determined to go with him and begged me to join them. She seems to fancy us both, but says that he is too headstrong for her. Once on a holiday in France he swam away from us right across a lake. We had no idea where he had gone. He reappeared only hours later, on a bicycle he had hired - he had had no thought for our fears. We imagined he had drowned and were in the local *gendarmerie*, when we saw him cycling along, no care in the world. We looked very stupid, after finally convincing a sceptical Gallic policeman of the urgency of the situation in our rotten French.

Here in this part of Wales we had Morwenna to intercede between us and the suspicious natives. She spoke Welsh in her husky contralto - sending shivers down my spine. She conceded all my theories as to the root of the problem with the Welsh; but not he. 'It's all the sort of garbage people dream up when trying to sound erudite' he said. 'The Welsh are no different from the English - it's just a sort of ongoing conversation piece.' I knew he was wrong. Just one careful look at their stupid flag is enough to see what deranged thoughts they entertain - en masse, so to speak, as an operative group: a red dragon - on a green and white background. All aimed at the Saxon invader. 'This'll scare 'em' some ancient Welsh designer must have suggested. Their whole mind still focuses on these bland invaders after nearly two-thousand years. There's no big world out there for your nationalistic Welshman - only Wales, and next door the enemy, who they must ultimately destroy. Anyone who sees further than this must leave - and go out into the blazing sunlight of the whole wide world. Why don't they look for their gold themselves? Why, I say? Because they think all the gold of the world is next door, in the blessed land they had to abandon to the mindless unfeeling men who now ignorantly occupy it.

Harold dismisses all this as my imagination. 'It's just a flag, John', he says. 'They have to have one just like we do. We have that red cross, don't we, but who cares about it?' I remind him that it is the cross of St George who slew a dragon. It's all there, the same story: conquest and simmering hatred. 'Nonsense, John', he says. 'It's a myth. There are no dragons, John, and never were. Nothing that size could get up in the air. Simple as that.' Morwenna pointed out that dragons seemed to exist in the mythology of east and west. I pointed out that a Jumbo jet was bigger than fifty dragons and it could fly. But he had lost interest. 'Myths', he said 'Myths'. And that was that.

I was discussing him with Morwenna. We were uneasy. The drizzle had turned to heavy rain. We rested in the big tent where he and she slept. They weren't doing anything, they said. It was an equal relationship - like *Jules et Jim*, only completely platonic, Morwenna said, whoever *they* might have been. 'It's up there, I can tell,' he had said indicating the jagged outcrop of granite that we could see a few miles or so up the miserable rock slopes of lichen and couch grass. Wales was more or less what I expected: dank, dark and depopulated. A place for ineffective dysfunctional Englishmen in wet weather clothing to hike around with the huge strides that they substituted for the sexual activity they could never experience. 'Ah, but it's marvellous country' they say. 'Next year I'm doing the Grampians...look at that!' That would be a picture of some barren granite landscape, where no-one in his right mind would want to venture.

Harold wasn't like that though. He had had half the women in Humanities as far as I could see. But he had the gold bug. Off he had gone with his precious drawing which Morwenna had persuaded some old Welsh fraud to do of the strange shaped rock formation which marked the entrance to the high valley where the gold was known to have been mined in Roman times. 'It's a rich vein he says. His grandfather went in search of it, but never came back. You can't get within fifteen miles of it in a car - even a four-wheel drive. The last five is a trackless waste. He had an army surplus Land Rover - but it was never found.' she said. We had had to ply the man with beer all evening, and play shove-halfpenny with him whilst his cronies openly laughed at us.

'You'll never get there and back today' I told him. Why not wait till tomorrow?'

'I can bivouac if I need to. I may go down the other side; he said it was possible to come back this way. If there's a signal I'll text you - otherwise follow me - if it's the pukka thing I'll still be up there. But most likely you'll see me about dinner time - have the chili con carne on the hob'

We had eaten the chili - very good it was - and drunk the *vin rouge ordinaire*. Now we just waited. The question as to where I would sleep had not been raised. We saw glowing flashes of lighting, and heard distant rumbles, but if there was a storm it was very distant from us. When I tentatively suggested it wasn't worth putting up another tent Morwenna was most insistent. 'Usual arrangements I think!' she said. 'The rain has stopped, might as well do it!'

It wasn't difficult. I had my hurricane lantern and as I usually do I read a little in my sleeping bag. I was jerked out of my detective story by a loud cry rising from baritone to a strange counter tenor, then ceasing abruptly. 'Did you hear that' came Morwenna's voice, a little questioning. I confirmed that I had. 'What do you think it was?' she went on. 'Oh some ridiculous Welsh bird or sheep or something' I said. Then I lay down to sleep. Why had I come on this foolish expedition? Looking for fool's gold? Foolish hopes of some sort of adventure with Morwenna? I could be at some pleasant barbecue now, chatting to some of those girls from the art college - filling our glasses amid the pleasant aroma of roasting spare ribs. It seemed to me that I could almost smell them. Perhaps later I might have shared a plate of them with some liberal-minded and half-inebriated city girl, instead of being cast into the outer darkness by this Celtic faerie who was no more likely to engage in sex than she was to put on a display of Indian Rope Dancing. Yet her beautiful face and the semi-tangible aroma of roasting ribs remained in my mind as I drifted into the healthy oblivion that comes to hikers in the hills. An hour later I awoke to find Morwenna shaking my shoulder. I looked at her and saw that she was highly agitated.

'I am frightened. There's a funny smell in the air. And have a feeling that something awful has happened.'

I could smell the smell. It was almost indescribable. A pungent mixture of foul excrement, struck matches, dank ponds, and something of rotten squids I once found in my refrigerator after a fortnights holiday; and finally something else, unique unreferential.

'Come to my tent!' she said. It was no seductive invitation, although all she had on was the lumberjack shirt she wore in the day.

I followed her; outside the rain was beginning again, and the smell seemed to be dissipating. We instinctively looked toward the dark mass of rock where we had last seen Harold. There was a flash of lightning and Morwenna screamed, and gripped my arm. I thought saw it too: something large and slimy, something saurian, standing, still as death. Then another flash and I saw it for what it was - a rock, vaguely animalian in shape, head wet and pointed with a cavity for an eye. For Morwenna though, the reptile still existed, and she was frozen with fear. I pulled her into the tent and we lay, she clinging to me, I still shaken, but in good heart. We were a prey to the fears of a night on bare mountain, I thought, with the diabolic figure at its summit, sending his demons to the valleys below. 'Calm down, Morwenna - it's all your imagination. There are no dragons nowadays even if there once were which I doubt.'

She seemed to relax, and sat, white faced on her sleeping bag. 'He's the sober logical Englishman - he won't see any dragons' I said.

'Not in Surbiton he won't!' she croaked - her eyes blazing with anger - 'He won't see anything except his bank balance and his BMW. He has no soul! Ice people, coming down from their frozen wastes, all the warmth and blood frozen out of them. The children of the Snow Queen, ice that never melts; no you won't see any dragons in the kingdom of ice you have made - and there's no Aslan coming to set the green shoots growing. You spread it across the earth, taking everything giving nothing. Whoever heard of an English nationalist? No one, because he doesn't want what he's got, he wants what you've got, and he takes it. Money always money! The English disease! You've come here for gold.' She said, seemingly forgetting that she had started the whole blasted gold seeking expedition.

She was in full rant now. 'But here the world is different! You saw what was there! I saw your face. But you blocked it out - like you blocked out the dreams of half the people of the earth! But you can't block this out. It saw us. You know it did! There's nothing here to dissipate its force. No BMW's, no Macdonald's, no Marks & Spencers, no Tesco's, no air-conditioned offices full of arse-licking yuppies. You better believe it John, else you're doomed.'

I thought I *had* seen a Tesco's on the road to the hills, I thought she was illogical - wasn't it Welsh soldiers who had shot up all those Zulu's at Rorke's Drift? But I said nothing - emotions were in the ascendant in her fey head.

'Perhaps you're right Morwenna. But Harold is one of us ice-people, I hope he's not going to suffer for all the Saxon's of history.'

She said nothing but I saw tears come to her eyes.

'He has already suffered some horrible thing - and I wasn't there for him. I could have saved him,' she sobbed.

She reached for her mobile, and punched in a number. I doubted she would get anywhere the signal was poor, and Harold's phone was on answering. She gave a half-hiss, half-whimper, and punched in another number. This time someone answered, and seemingly was not put out by the late call. Morwenna spoke in Welsh, and sounded eager and focused. She began to repeat a phrase that sounded like another language. She kept asking then repeating - then she finally hung up, and got into the sleeping bag.

Eventually she slept. I watched her beautiful features in repose. I regretted having made the mocking quotation. Perhaps if ... I thought; perhaps if. As she slept I heard a series of wet squalls against the tent, sudden hissing sounds like the rotation of the wet sails of a windmill. I felt those sorts of silly fears one can suddenly work up in dark lonely situations. I kept awake by some male instinct when the female rests in a perilous situation - however imaginary it was. But the weather began to calm, and eventually I slept.

In the morning summer had returned. Even Morwenna was reassured.

'He probably bivouacked under rocks' she said. We'll find him if we set out early. Back in her trousers she seemed her devil-may-care self again. We looked for the 'dragon' rock but didn't decide which one it was. In the dry, with no watery reflections, the rocks looked quite different.

We climbed in the warming landscape, the sun creating steamy mists rising around us. Other visitors had been here rather recently it seemed; we passed a campsite where there was a recent fireplace, a blackened area of sward with sharp curved and blackened spikes thrusting up amid the cinders, where it had burned out, or been extinguished by one the frequent cloudbursts that the region experienced.

'Your tame Welsh savant has told plenty of people his phoney story, it seems. It's a wonder there's no Macdonald's up here. I could use a few barbecued spare ribs'

'Oh shut up John.'

Her face reddened with a sort of panicky anger. I had no idea what I had said to change her light mood for this sudden storm.

'You are the most insensitive prick I have ever met!'

We plodded on, higher and higher, passing no more campsites. We took an early lunch, having contented ourselves with hot coffee before setting out. We mixed the last of the vin ordinaire with the water from a mountain stream - ice-cold and refreshing; then onward and upward. I noticed a gravelly patch with a clear impression of a hiking boot and pointed it out to Morwenna.

'It is the exact pattern of Harold's boots' she said. 'But it's pointing the wrong way. Whoever made that was coming down.'

'It could've been him, returning.'

'Well if it was, we would have seen him.'

We saw several more of the prints, and I noticed that the toe impressions were much greater than the heels - which were sometimes barely visible. I said nothing to Morwenna. But from diverse sources I knew that whoever it was must have been running. They looked recent.

The gravelly patches petered out and the prints with them, and we were beginning to feel again reassured by the blue sky and sunshine when we skirted a huge boulder to be confronted with what at first seemed an amorphous lump of twisted metal, blackened and rusting, with no clear division between it and the soil in which it was partially buried. We examined it uneasily; I soon recognised some features - those of a Land Rover - which had survived by their original durability. I pointed it out to Morwenna, who had already suspected it.

'You wouldn't get that up here nowadays - with all those bridges that have since gone. I wonder whose it was?' I mused.

'I don't. I think it was his grandfather's - the man we were introduced to - Harold's man.'

'It's possible. It looks old enough. I wish Harold were here. He would have liked this. He could have explained its condition, maybe.'

'It's just old isn't it? It crashed.'

I was all the while searching for any human remains - but there were none that I could see. Bone wouldn't have lasted long exposed like this in the burnt conditions it must have been in from the beginning. The unmistakable signs of heat were there to be seen, twisted and deformed steel, lumps of fused metal even teardrop shapes of melted glass. One could only hope the occupants either escaped in good time, or had been killed instantly. We turned to go on. Above the talon shaped rock where the cave was supposed to be loomed large now - maybe another hour's walk. But there were more clouds appearing, dark and threatening. If the weather held we could be there safely enough, but we might get caught on our return. I was uneasy about the land rover. It was a corroboration of the evidence in favour of the Welshman whom I had dismissed as a self-serving charlatan, taking drinks from gullible tourists.

'Maybe we should call it a day' I said. The weather's going to turn nasty. And I think we need to alert the authorities to Harold's disappearance.'

'We can't do that. He may be up there - with a broken ankle. You go back - as soon as your mobile gets a signal you can alert them - they will be able to use the GPS to locate you - send a helicopter.'

The darkening sky induced darkness into our thoughts. There was more at stake than a half pretended search for gold. We should have met Harold by now, if he intended to return today.

'Maybe you go down, I'll go on.'

'I don't really want to split up. It's dangerous. We have our bivouac, we have food - we are OK as long as neither of us gets injured. And then it's essential to be together.'

We walked on along an increasingly gloomy trail between edifices of rock, scrambling awkwardly over uneven rocky contours. The sky was darkening more quickly than I had thought possible. We should have turned back, but we didn't. We had to cross a patch of muddy earth - and once again we saw the prints - coming down. The mud must have been hard after the drought that had been ended the evening before, and not yielded to his weight as he climbed. The prints were not those of a man running. He had been returning - joyfully, I thought. Now the sky began to blacken, as it sometimes does, beyond what we expect. Afternoon turned to dusk, and dusk began to turn to night. We were in the shadow of the great ugly rock - not a peak, invisible from anywhere further than our camp, but now a great talon clawing the sky. A false night fell - and with it total darkness, and rain. We dared not continue - we could walk over the edge of a ravine - there were many rock parapets that we had seen before. We cowered in a rocky corner, looking uneasily at the rock which we could still see against what glimmer of light remained in the sky.

Morwenna clutched my shoulder in a convulsive grip.

'It's here!' she said.

'Don't panic. It's a storm and it will pass. We saw a great flickering of lightning above, through the now gushing torrent of rain. Again and again it came illuminating the wet walls of the miserable gully where we hid. There was no danger, because the thunder was negligible - asynchronous aspirating salvoes of deep resonance inseparable from the hiss of the intolerable rain. Morwenna was moaning, and suddenly pointed during a short spurt of lighting, unleashing an unearthly scream. I looked, fear induced in me in spite of myself. I saw nothing more than the horrible rock illuminated by an orange glow of reflected light from shrubs somehow ignited by the strike. The rain soon doused them. She had broken away, and I could no longer see her. I was terrified - running down the mountain she had no chance - she would be over a precipice before she got half a mile. Suddenly there was a searing, blinding light, and a simultaneous roar of thunder. Then I did see something - something real, something winged, something demonic...amid the flames of hell - moving inexorably toward me – something from deep in the memory of humankind...and around it a disturbance of the ether, a huge reciprocating vortex dispersing the smoke that constantly swirled and reformed. I was engulfed in the steam and smoke, and sank to my haunches as my knees gave way. I raised my head at a human cry. Between me and the infernal entity was the dark form of a naked woman, who stood, straight backed, rigid, one arm raised bent at the elbow, holding a knife horizontally above her head. The other arm pointed straight into the blurred mass of flame and smoke; around her head; her black unkempt hair blew out in a radial halo, flapping like a flag in a gale. And in a loud voice came those words she had recited over the phone, those ancient words from her deep past, clear and commanding, echoing along around the rocks. For a moment the white hot focus of the threatening disturbance brightened, raised, like a serpent preparing to strike, then it dimmed, and all around the smoke and flame swirled less strongly. The figure staggered back, and I ran forward, before she fell back into my arms. She looked into my eyes:

'Get away - it will come back...'

Then she went limp. I threw down my harness and lifted her, fireman style. There was enough glowing light to see my way over the perilous path, and with my great strength I could keep going as long as I could see. But as we extended our distance from the scene so the clouds began to disperse, and by the time we passed the land rover the sun was beginning to beam through the receding black clouds. The rain had stopped. Ten minutes later I heard Morwenna sigh. I laid her on a gentle sward of grass, and stole a look at her bony but moving nudity. No glamour girl she - but an earthy sorceress, flat-chested and meager-limbed. She sat up and adopted a pose which restored her modesty. I took off my anorak and long jersey - which she hastily pulled on, covering her to mid-thigh. We said nothing - there was nothing to say. I was as near exhausted as I could be and yet still walk. She was drained, her face white, her hair and eyebrows singed, her face smoky.

We walked, side by side, in that peace of mind that comes from total understanding. The sun filled the hills, and eventually we came to the beginning of that gentle slope where grassy softness came under our feet. We passed the last patch of gravel where Harold's fleeing footsteps were discernable.

She shook her head.

'It was stormy wasn't it at about the time he would have got here?'

'Yes it was' I said.

We passed near the place where the campers had left their fireplace. I walked over to where it was, the pointed blackened embers still curving out. It was no campsite. I thought of the barbecued spare ribs, and of Harold – and I shuddered. I took my tobacco pouch, and emptied the tobacco, before gathering some black ash. As I did, I saw something glinting in the sun. I foraged and found a misshapen lump of golden metal: something that had been melted and reformed. I went back to Morwenna who stood sufficiently far away to miss the characteristic shape of the pointed embers of the fire.

'Looks like somebody found something here.' I said. I handed it to her. She looked at it - for a long time; then she handed it back. I made a pose as if to cast it into the rocks beneath, but she shook her head. I offered it to her again but she shook her head again.

'Keep it. He will reappear. Then we can give it to him – it's what he came after.

Morwenna and I have never spoken of that day again - I don't think we ever will. I think of it, when I talk to our eldest boy - who reminds me of it - or of Harold at least. The nugget has been recast into a Celtic cross that he keeps in his den.

I can't honestly say that Harold will never turn up - it would be just like him if he did. I'd enjoy telling him our tale. Ball lightning I think it must have been - not much understood by science even now.

13 The Pilots

His son Thomas's remark sent Don into a reverie. He recalled that time when things weren't going too well for him. Tiger Moths were one thing; Lancasters were a different kettle of fish. The other trainees seemed to get on fine…some had even arrived after him sporting recently acquired wings above their left hand pocket, and were now on ops. One had already been killed with his crew. There was something about the aircraft that seemed to overawe him: maybe its size – maybe something else. But surely the Jerries deserved everything they were getting - they'd asked for it hadn't they?

But his problems with the aircraft were such that he spent his days doing circuits and bumps; sometimes he was too near the end of the runway and had to throttle up and take off again in a hurry. Other times he landed too hard, and the gigantic plane made an undignified bounce or two as it came in.

'It's a damn bad show Manley', the CO said to him. 'If I had my own way you'd be out on your blunt end old chap – no hard feelings. But it seems it's easier to make planes – even these bloody things - than make pilots. So if you smash one up you better make sure you … well I won't say it, but for God's sake pull your finger out.'

Don was desperate. 'You'd think I'd be only too keen to get chucked out', he thought, 'given the number of the chaps that are failing to come back,' Some planes just exploded in mid air, when they were hit by the enemy night-fighters defending their wives and children. Some crews got out. Even then there was a good chance that some jerry farm-hand would do you with a pitchfork, before anyone who knew about the Geneva Convention appeared. He couldn't blame them. Yet when he saw everyone walking out to the planes in the dusk he couldn't wait to be one of them; just as he couldn't wait to sit in the mess with the returned pilots laughing and joking with relief after an op. That feeling far outstripped his survival instinct.

Dolly and he had been meeting in London for six months. Whenever they could both get a furlough they would meet there. She was a WAAF who worked as some sort of courier; of course they never talked about the war. He wore his uniform, complete with pilot's wings of which he was very proud. She wore pretty print dresses, and talked about helping her mother cook the Sunday lunch. She envied a friend who had got a pair of nylons from a Yank, although she'd got pregnant by him, as she found out two days after he was killed over Schweinfurt. They joked about it. It was all they could do. 'She must've worn those wartime utility knickers' Dolly said, with a mischievous grin. 'Why?' Don asked. 'You know: one Yank and they are down!' she said and they laughed. She told him the other girls were very tough characters, and this sort of joke was usual. He didn't tell her the jokes that were usual on the station. She was his refuge. She looked up at him when they met, when they embraced. He felt her eyes giving him thanks for the strength needed in those troubled times. She wasn't suited to service life, he was sure. He longed to come home to her when they were married after the war, with the scent of baking pervading the house. When he heard aircrew talking about the 'little woman' he yearned for his own. What the little women thought when, babe-in-arms, they heard their husbands

105

growling out over the North Sea at night never occurred to him.

'You're out old boy' the CO told him. 'You're off to train as navigator next week. You don't have the right temperament for flying a Lanc. You'll be in Coastal Command – out of the firing line. I had to call in a few favours to keep you in as aircrew so don't look a gift-horse in the mouth, there's a good chap!' He had made the worst landing of his flying career the week after she had told him her joke: so hard that the undercarriage of the bomber had collapsed under him, and he had been lucky to escape with his life. The two starboard propellers were sheared off and the outer engine was a write-off.

One evening while he was waiting for his posting Don went and watched three new Lancasters coming in. One was to replace the one he had 'bent', as the saying went. The other two were for the ones lost during the last week. He watched the menacing shapes coming down so slowly, terrible birds of prey, nemesis for the women and children of the evil empire, who were to be burnt.   One perfect touch-down, two good ones; three monstrous dealers of anonymous death rumbling around the perimeter, parking in the dispersal pans in front of No 6 Hangar. He would never have to deal with those thoughts of his victims now. Yet still he felt a terrible pang of loss. He watched the planes disgorge their crews and one or two visitors, and saw them immediately surrounded by ground crew, who would put them into a service-ready condition. Some force impelled him to walk toward the first of the Lancasters, the one that had landed so daintily, a dragonfly alighting on a water lily pad. He momentarily hated the pilot who had ferried it in, showing off his skill to the whole airfield, aware that many experienced eyes would be critically appraising his consummate skill. He still had the humiliating task of telling Dolly that he had failed. A group of people were walking toward him. He suddenly froze and a shock went through his body. He saw a figure he knew - that figure he knew so well. She must have come in on one of the aircraft- she looked at her most attractive, hatless in RAF slacks and blue shirt, hair blowing wildly in the gale of the propellers. He knew her job involved visits to operational camps, but she was the last person he wanted to see at that moment. He thought to slope off, but she had spotted him, and ran over, leaving the group she was with, amongst which there seemed to be two of the pilots of the incoming planes. They discreetly embraced, but before they could begin to speak, a flight sergeant came dashing up and shouted loudly, over the angry racket of the grounded bombers, to the group which included the two men walking along in bomber jackets. 'Where's the pilot of WS-K? I've got a message for him from the CO.' For some reason one of the two pilots pointed to Don and he was about to correct him when Dolly spoke.

'That was me!' she said, chirpily.

'Don't try to get funny with me young woman, or *you'll* end up in front of the CO. You're not in the girl guides now. There's a bloody war on, in case you hadn't noticed,' the flight sergeant barked.

'She *is* the bloody pilot, flight-sergeant, and she's an officer too, so you'd better belt up' one of the two pilots said. 'There's a lot of 'em ferrying planes from the factories, so we might have a chance to get on ops. And good on 'em I say.'

The flight sergeant looked as if he might have a different opinion about the matter, but he handed the message to Dolly, and turning to Don gave a slovenly salute. 'Excuse me sir, are you Pilot Officer Manley?'

Woken from his shocked, daze Don nodded. 'Yes I am'

'An Anson's picking you up at half ten tonight, sir, to take you to Gosport. Better get packed, sir. No holidays over the Ruhr for you; you must be glad to hear that sir.' There was a slight sneer in the flight-sergeants voice.

Dolly looked at Don in surprise.

'That's enough, Flight-Sergeant,' Don said angrily

Dolly had read her message. She was to take the plane straight to a maintenance unit – it was to have a special modification for a new radar gear.

They said little as they walked into the shadow of the ponderous aircraft through the squall and clamour of its impatience to depart once more.

'Don't you have a navigator?' he asked.

'I've got a map' she replied.

Her dark tresses blew around as she climbed back into the aircraft. Once she was in the cockpit high above him he could just see her head with her intercom in place, looking at the marshal. The volume of sound from the four engines increased as she gently pushed the throttles forward making the controlled roar that Don knew so well; it became an insistent jeer at his failure. She looked down at him with a wan smile as she coaxed the huge bomber steadily off down the perimeter; he stood watching until it was at the end of the runway, ready to take off. It slowly accelerated and the roar turned into a great thunder as Dolly pushed the four throttles forward as far as they would go, and the satanic spirit of the sky took eagerly to its airy domain, where the white fluffy clouds welcomed it. Don watched it as it headed into the golden band across the horizon until he could see it no more.

*

Don remembered the long patrols in a Sunderland looking for U-boats and never seeing any, dropping depth charges on peaks of foam which might have been periscopes but weren't. Nothing to be ashamed of, he thought. Dolly was in the kitchen and the delicious smell of a Sunday roast came wafting through to the lounge. Dinah and Thomas were arguing – she was holding the model aeroplane and Thomas wanted it. 'It's mine, he said, and as Dolly came into the room he added: pilots are men anyway! Dolly said nothing – neither did Don. But he smiled. They rarely talked about the war. They had found peace.

14 The Ugly Sister

You've all read it – Cinderella. You knew you were going to get a dispassionate and objective account of the affair when you heard of the *wicked* stepmother and the *ugly* sisters, didn't you? The *ugly* sisters. Ugly ugly ugly. Am I ugly? I suppose I'm not so attractive. Jane isn't much to look at either – my dear sister Jane. Were we beastly to Ella? (Yes that was her real name. She made up Cinderella herself, to make Dad feel guilty). Yes sometimes we were beastly. That's what sisters do, and I have a reputation for caustic wit. Jane never said much – she is so loving and kind – but she got lumped in with me. If we tried to be inclusive Ella complained to Dad that we were mocking her, by pretending to be nice, and he believed every word. Ella made everyone feel guilty – that was the name of her game. She *did* work hard; she *did* get covered with cinders, all done in this sanctimonious pseudo-dutiful way, with constant sidelong glances at everyone. Big kitten eyes for Dad, secret smirks for us, and eyes of poisonous hatred for Mother. Did Mum forbid her from going to the ball? Well she said it *once*. We all tried to buy smiles from 'Cinderella'. But they didn't come cheap, so Mother bought her a beautiful and expensive dress for the ball. Of course Ella had been too busy grovelling around with a dustpan and brush to go with Mum to try it on and now said it was ghastly. So poor Mother was goaded into naively saying what Ella wanted her to say – 'Well then you can't go to the ball, can you dear'. There was a silence like the moment when a doodle-bug engine cut out. She had won! Of course she knew damn well she would go to the ball. But there was now a psychic mountain of buttering-up to climb before she could possibly comply with Mum's terrified imploring. So who had to dress up as a fairy godmother do you think? Mum, of course. Who had to order the silk made-to-measure ballet shoes? No of course they weren't glass; glass shoes would *really* be good for dancing wouldn't they? Who had to buy a bespoke dress from Dior, and bang went my year's riding sessions? Who had to order a carriage to come and then fool around with a wand and a pumpkin? I know what I would have done with the wand and the pumpkin! Jane and I got to the ball alone, and sat, as we always sat, together, feeling dreadful, but looking as if we didn't care if neither the Prince nor anyone else gave us a second glance. But as always, he did. We each had one heavenly dance. Obviously he wasn't really a prince, but he was a man to die for – or cut off one's toes and heels for. He was handsome, intelligent and articulate. But he was also kind and considerate, and could make one feel very special, even when one was not, as in my case. Darcy himself couldn't have eclipsed him. But he had one weakness. He stupidly couldn't see through that slender ultramarine-eyed brunette. (No she wasn't a blonde as those fools at Disney in the United Blondes of America made her). She became his instant goddess. When she came into the room, she took even *my* breath away, and tears flooded into *my* eyes. It's a good ploy to go round looking like a scarecrow and then suddenly appear looking the whole business. And that *did* do the business. I won't go into the rest, all the phoney running off down the road at midnight waggling her delightful little bottom at him; the idiotic returning of the slipper, the humiliation of trying it on – under the fear of her frown which might freeze the house for the rest of the day.

What now? You want me to say I never married, and that Jane topped herself, don't you, as in real creative writing? No, I have my husband and beloved daughter Dinah. Jane is a very successful diplomat. We meet Ella quite often, and are still in awe of her. And she still hates us, but not as much. It's true I haven't much of a social life. I am still ugly, I suppose; and as Dinah says when she is not invited to parties: 'They go by what you look like, Mummy'. But I have long since forgiven Cinderella; I know now that Jane and I had had two things more precious than anything she ever knew. We had our mother. And we had each other.

15 The Estavian

It was beautiful summer evening in Highgate, and a pleasant exercise in cultural exchange was taking place in a large dining room into which warm summer breezes blew through a magnificent open window. Outside one storey below was a flower bed, laid to French marigolds.

Simon and Ursula Cohan, their daughter Jemima and Davin the Estavian were enjoying the excellent dinner prepared by Ursula and Jemima. Jemima in particular had seen to it that there were plenty of traditional English features.

'He'll be interested in seeing how we normally eat; it's no good doing a Bolognese, that's Italian.' So they had done a steak and kidney pie. It wasn't what they normally did - they liked continental cookery. But Ursula liked cooking, and took the afternoon off from her tutoring to sort things out.

Davin was as good looking as Jemima had hoped, but wore a rather conventional old-fashioned suit. Jemima and Ursula were soon put at ease by his studious and attractively accented English. Simon asked him rather dull questions about the economy of Estavia, its current relationship with Russia and whether it had a football tradition. Davin answered very politely and informatively, but looked from time to time at Jemima with a smile, which seemed to say that sometimes the older generation were a little too earnest, a smile which Jemima returned warmly. Soon Ursula was talking about dance in Estavia, of which they had heard a little after enquiring from friends at the cultural association. He nodded as she talked of Kovapiskoi which was said to have originated in a Russian dance called the Komarinsky, a rough vulgar affair of pre-revolutionary peasants.

'Yes, we dance sometimes the Kovapiskoi' he said. 'But we prefer also the Rock and Roll.'

He ate as he spoke, getting somewhat behind as he was obliged to answer questions from all sides. He drank a little, but not in excess, and mellowed a little but not too much. Ursula asked if wine was grown in Estavia. 'Of course not, it's much too far north', Simon said, which created a moment of tension, since it appeared as a put-down to Ursula. But Davin took centre stage, lifting a finger high, and adopting an informative tone. 'It has been done.' he smiled, his eyes twinkling. 'It has been done. There have been bottles of Estavian wine!' Ursula looked at Simon with a slight air of triumph, but no malice - for she was a kind and loving person. 'But of course you are right in general, that it is not such a climate for that'. He was silent for a few moments, but then, half rising from his seat he said to Simon 'If I may be permitted?' He rose and walking to the window took advantage of it to urinate directly into the outside world. The sound of the hose-like stream striking the richly scented French marigolds below with the momentum gained by height, temporarily filled the silence. The act was performed discreetly, but incontrovertibly. Having completed the whole operation Davin asked if there was a wash basin he could use.

When he returned to the table he continued the conversation where it had left off, and told them that the Teutonic Knights had been able to produce wine from grapes grown in the sheltered courtyards of their castles which had sunny walls. At the end of the evening he left amidst the good wishes, fond hand-shakes and kisses of the family. It was generally agreed that he was a cultured man, and that his unusual act came from habits of being bought up in an admirable country in which nevertheless, plumbing was in a primitive state, through no fault of its own. He was in fact a man of exceptional qualities, although Jemima deviated from her original plan by excusing herself when he telephoned to invite her to go out to dinner with him on the grounds of a heavy program of study.

As it happened the Cohan family didn't invite any more Estavians - there were few enough around - and plenty of Russians, Poles and Ukrainians to sample. There was one, a female, but although nothing to that effect was said, there was a feeling of unease about the prospect of entertaining her, that somehow couldn't be put into words.

It was two years later at university that Jemima met Simin - who was studying aeronautical engineering at the same university. He was at the flat of a colleague of Giles, her roommate Helen's boyfriend, where they had gone after a folk concert. She sat beside him on the futon, as a dozen or so students debated the problems of the world, most of which, it transpired, could be surprisingly easily solved if it were not for the economic system under which the rich countries currently operated. Simin was a young man with considerable personal attractions in both looks and a pleasantly soft though manly voice that contrasted with some coarser and more strident utterances that dominated the conversation. He spoke with a noticeable accent yet with great articulacy, and Helen and Jemima were both rather taken with him. He seemed definitely to prefer Jemima - which was a nice change, although Helen, as she sometimes did, made considerable efforts to distract him, using clear body language to indicate that Giles was not to be seen as a defining factor in her life and using even clearer body language to suggest how she could perform if suitably approached by an acceptable male. Yet Simin only turned to her when it was necessary to avoid rudeness - gentlemanly man that he was. To Jemima's delight he asked if she wished to go with him to a play that was showing at the university theatre the following day. She had seldom felt the thrill that now throbbed through her - a delight in Simin's youthful maturity; he seemed light years ahead of the oafish young English boys who competed with each other in loudness and vulgarity.

The next day they met, and sitting in the garden bar of the university theatre on a fine late August evening and answering Simin's manifestly sincere questions about herself Jemima felt that the world was as right as it could be. She felt like a tulip gently opening under the rays of the rising sun.

'What about you, Simin? We are talking too much about me - and my life has not been an interesting one. I have been wondering about what country *you* come from. I'm sure you are not French, German, Italian or Spanish - not even Russian I somehow feel.'

'Ah you are right. Not even Russian! I come from a rather humble country, although I am proud to do so - I am Estavian - a nationality you may not even have heard of!'

A cold shock went through Jemima's sensitive soul - the confusing horrors of that evening when she had last met an Estavian recurred to her mind. She was a genteel person, unable to really cope with the idea of bodily functions unless they were hidden away.

'I have heard of it.' she said in a very different voice.

Simin looked at her - she could tell he sensed her unease.

'The play is about to start; just one moment.' The sunny French doors were wide open, and he walked seemingly in their direction. It was too much for Jemima and she scuttled furtively away.

He didn't ever ask why she had done so - although they often met, because he married Helen eventually, and made a great success as a writer. Jemima remained single, and although she did not consider this to be a failure, she would not have considered finding a loyal loving partner with whom to walk in the trackless wilderness of life a failure, either.

Years later she accompanied Helen and Simin on a trip to France, to buy cheap wine with them. As they sat on a terrace in a cafe near Boulogne Helen suddenly recalled a message she hadn't given to Simin.

'That chap Davin phoned again last week - forgot to tell you.'

'Oh yes? Did you invite him?' Simin replied.

'No, I wasn't sure what you would want, and anyway the next few weeks we're away, seeing the girls at their colleges, and then the wedding.' Her eldest son was getting married.

'I assume Davin is a common name in Estavia. I knew an Estavian called that, once.' said Jemima tensely.

'It's actually a very rare name,' Simin answered. 'It's surely the same fellow. He is a very fine man, except that he has a terrible habit – almost a personality disorder - that causes him to suddenly do ill-mannered and even unpleasant things when in social situations. In particular I have known him to use a window instead of going to the bathroom even in company. He knows the problem, but there's nothing he seems to be able to do about it – it could be related to Tourette syndrome. Do you think it could be the same Davin, Jemima?'

But Jemima didn't answer. She was looking out to sea, her hands clenched, and her eyes staring.

16 The Inundation

He had clearly been unbalanced. A Dutchman by his accent – it's striking the way that regional accents like his have almost turned into foreign languages over the centuries. He was speaking as correctly as he could, but now and again he slipped into his broad dialect when he became animated. He had a way of looking at one with his head angled down, so that in order to make eye contact he had almost to glower from under his eyebrows. He had joined me at a table – I had had no problem with that, the café was very crowded – it was rather small for a big station like Ipswich Junction. He had a rather desolate look, as if his life was at the last point of desperation, and I gladly responded to his overtures. After all life is good, and one must make an effort to engage the unfortunate few, who, even in a world as seemingly perfect as that in which we are fortunate enough to live, find themselves out of step, due to some inner turmoil, or external blow.

'You are going far?' he asked me.

'About fifty miles or so,' I answered.

'You go to Norwich, perhaps, Lowestoft, Cambridge – or toward London?'

'No. I'm going east!'

'Ah – east' he answered, looking at me as if a little puzzled. 'Well that's the same as me – I'm going back to Holland; getting the Harwich boat. It's a lot more than fifty miles. But it was worth the trip. I've a landed a job at last'

He said it as if landing a job was a major achievement. I assumed he had some specialised qualification where jobs were not so easy to find. Some sort of research or university post.

'I guess you're well qualified – sometimes it can be tricky finding the right post.'

'I am indeed qualified – a PhD in Engineering - but I long since gave up hope of finding a job in engineering. All I've managed to get is a temporary job pulling up sugar beet.'

I saw it in a flash. His strange remark about getting the Harwich boat had alerted me. Of course no respectable manufacturer or university would take him on if he gave the delusional state of his mind away by some remark like that, even though industry was crying out for engineers with any credentials whatever. But a farmer wouldn't mind if he rambled a bit. A sugar beet is a sugar beet, and no great mental stability was needed to pull one out of the ground.

I thought of my own sons: one had just received his first royalty payment on his debut novel, which was selling better than I expected in my wildest dreams; and the other was in America leading the design team on a new animation project. Qualified people were in great demand, and the elder boy had supported his wife and new baby by freelancing in the lucrative world of copy-writing in the advertising business, whilst he penned his first novel. I thought of him, his strong face, broad shoulders and confident gaze, and I gloried in the thought that as my life moved pleasantly toward its final years, he was already carrying the torch for me with his steady advance in our excellent well-organised world.

'Well I am sure you will soon find work in engineering' I said reassuringly. 'Have you thought of getting a job in academia?'

For a moment he looked almost angry. 'I have thought of everything, *everything*: where have you been? There is nothing out there! Unemployment is rife – twenty percent if you believe the lies coming out of the press, forty if you don't. Why don't you mock me with a suggestion of considering becoming the President of the United States – or the Emperor of China?'

I nodded. I thought it best to humour him. Yet I recalled reading only that morning that the shortage of manpower in every sector was beginning to result in the economy overheating. Job advertisements produced few applicants.

'If you had sons and daughters of working age rejected by the world we have created, wilting before your own eyes, like beautiful lilies in a drought, you wouldn't be talking like that,' he went on, his voice rising in pitch and volume. But he abruptly stopped his harangue seeing a sudden change of expression on my face.

Just for a moment I had had an instantaneous but frighteningly vivid flash of my son: white-faced and gaunt, alone and without hope, typing out a futile job application on his computer.

'I'm sorry', he said, it's not your fault. I know I sound crazy – but that's the way it takes one.'

'I understand' I said, back in the real world from which this sad outcast had torn me with his dystopian rant. 'But I am confident you will soon have a job commensurate   with   your   qualifications;   with unemployment down to just a few thousand, here and in Europe, you will soon see.'

A train rumbled into the junction, and he got up. He looked at me – almost sympathetically.

'Don't worry about me' he said, smiling broadly 'I have what I came for. I have a job!' then he smiled even more broadly. 'You enjoy your trip down to the coast – although surely it is not fifty miles, not unless the Pleistocene inundation has retreated since I arrived.' And cutting short his strange illogical rambling he departed, his coffee unfinished.

I am on the way back to my beloved home, where my wife will be waiting to greet me warmly, after my day's absence. The ramshackle nature of the single coach train is a surprise feature in view of the affluence of our nation, and I must say I notice it more than I usually do. I try to recall my last trip, but it eludes me, and I settle to look at the landscape as the formerly azure sky is gradually replaced by a grey overcast. I cannot help but recall the strange mad Dutchman who had somehow held my attention in a way that such people sometimes do when encountered on ones journeys. What had driven the poor fellow out of his mind: the tragic loss of a loved one; some horrible injustice that had led to the collapse of a promising career; or just some ever present cross he had had to bear which had finally ground him down? Who knows? But as the train slows to an intermediate stop at some station I have never heard of, life surges back into me. I amuse myself by translating its name back into its roots: Felixstowe. The first bit's Latin, the second is Anglo-Saxon: Happy Meeting Place. How about that?

A voice bellows into the carriage 'all out – this is the end of the line.'

I jump up – I've been on the wrong train.

I accost the guard. 'I want to go to Sunhaven – I got the wrong train. How do I get there please?'

'Never heard of it mate!'

'It's about forty miles to the east of here!

'Is it by Jove? Well you better get your wet suit on mate, that'd be under the sea.'

'Can you tell me where I can get travel information somewhere nearby?'

'There is a Tourist Information Centre. Go down the high street, right down Bent Hill – and turn right at the bottom, carry on until you come to it; they'll know. Or hop back on – we'll be off in a moment.' I have a strange urge to go back where I have just come from, but I quickly dismiss it, and stride briskly out of the station and on down the road through the grey drizzle. I pass the shops one sees in every town, although there is no Woolworth's which you normally see in a high street. Then round a bend: a sudden mind-bending shock. An icy shudder goes down my spine: what I see cannot *be*. Grey morose-looking waves out to a distant horizon, and a gigantic ship wallowing in them. I run down the steep hill and out onto the wet shingle; the sea, the sea! And there's no sea between Ipswich and Holland; just the Rhine on whose banks my happy home is situated. I stop a passer-by, who looks alarmed at my urgent grasp.

'What sea is that? Tell me its name, please.'

He looks at me with his now steady honest grey eyes.

'That's the North Sea, sir. Stranger in these parts are you?'

'How long has it been there, can you tell me, please?'

'As I understand, it's been there about half-a-million years, sir.' I stagger off and slump down on one of the damp seats on the promenade. My home is under the cold unforgiving North Sea, its rolling billows so certain of themselves, beside which no other certainty can survive. My life, my boys, my wife, my hope, all perished in the nightmare inundation. I hear a voice call my name. I turn and see my wife. But she is bowed under the weight of something unspeakable. Her old smiling face is gone; gone forever.

'It's alright. Where were you? You're safe now dear. Come home and I'll make a nice dinner – we can watch the last night of the proms together.'

'But Sunhaven…what has happened to Sunhaven?'

'Sunhaven is fine. We'll go there tomorrow, perhaps.'

I walk with her along the familiar road: the long, long road.

17 The Enemies

'Keep me safe for this night'

'And keep Daddy safe for this night'

'Keep Daddy safe for this night'

'Now get into bed...'

'I want to play with the aeroplane that Daddy gave me.'

'You can get up and play with it in the morning. Be a good little boy.'

'Will you sing me the song?'

'Yes darling, sleep well, happy dreams.

Go to sleep, go to sleep, go to sleep now my darling ....'

*

'We've all been recommended for gongs...'

Daddy didn't care about that.

'I'm not really interested in gongs. I only want to get back to my wife and son...it's different when you've got a child you know.'

*

'*Behüte mich diese Nacht*, and bring *Vati* back safe.'

'That's good. Now get into bed...'

'Can I hold the aeroplane?'

'No darling. You must sleep... *Sicher bis zum Morgen.*'

"*Mumie*"

'*Ja Liebling?*'

'Might they bomb us tonight?'

'No darling. They won't come here'

Mumie looked at her child; she was worried about a rash he had developed. The doctor said it was nothing, but how could one be sure? She lovingly applied the special cream to his delicate body. Surely he would be alright now?

She went to the window. She peeped out from the blackout - there was a clear sky and a moon over the ancient city. One day things would be right again. Daddy would come home each night, and talk about the school.

'*Mumie*'

'What is it little boy?'

'Supposing they do come here'

'*Vati* will stop them'

'In his fighter?'

'*Ja Liebling*, now sleep.' She suddenly shivered. She remained in the bedroom, looking at the sleeping child, so bonny, so trustful. Was there some almost inaudible humming in the air

*

'But!'

'I know, *Kapitän*, they should not. They know it has no reason. That it is undefended. But what do they care?'

Vati started the engines. The comrade adjusted his radar screens.

'We will never intercept them - it's too late!'

'We can get some as they go back: one less for tomorrow!'

'Too late! *Oh, mein Gott*! They are going to kill my wife and son...I pray God I shall never hear that news...'

'I too, *Kapitän*.' The comrade was soft-spoken, and he was the best kind of *Kamaraden*.

*

She looked out at the stars, and wondered as she did every time. She knew the odds. She remembered Daddy, holding the child, his face radiating his love. What happiness there would be, a tiny mote of paradise, when it was over. She had heard them go out over the North Sea, the sound had not woken the sleeping child, his eyes closed, his breathing so smooth. She would hear the sound of the return, then wait, wait, until the sound of the old car. Then blessed peace would return.

*

'My God, they've started a blaze there.' said Daddy.

'It's like daylight'

'No flak!'

'It's undefended'

'The night fighters will be coming'

'Not before we're out of it'

'What have we got?'

'Incendiary - no need for explosives; it's a medieval town the whole place will go up like matchwood in that heat - I can feel it from here!'

'Well here we go - starting bomb run now.'

*

She had heard it, a faint hum, like the murmuring of myriads of bees. She had felt fear - not for herself, not for *Vati*, but for the *Kind* who still slept. He dreamed on, as the noise got louder. She shook with fear, prayed: 'Oh *Gott* who looks after us, preserve him. Why are they doing this?' She heard the sounds far away across the city, rumblings, and saw light flickering on the moonlit horizon. The sounds increased, the flickering lights became orange, and got brighter. Nearby explosions sounded. Then all around there was flame, the sounds of burning - screams. She began to feel hot. She saw the child stir. She began to cry, but stifled the sound as the child woke.

'*Mumie!*'

'It's alright darling.' She took him in her arms, and he became calm. There was nothing else she could do.

'Why is it so hot Mummy?'

'It's just the sun, darling!'

The house opposite caught fire and blazed up. The flames flashed across the gap, engulfing their house and neither mother nor child spoke again. There was just the sound of screaming for a few moments, then nothing but the noise of *Krieg und Schlacht*.

*

Daddy was on the homeward journey. The merciless swarm had done their work - not to reason why, just to do or die. Daddy thought of his son, the roses in the garden, the wife who loved him, waiting to hear. Soon he would have them in his arms.

*

The comrade looked into his radar screen. 'There's one not far ahead... his trace is strong...two o'clock!'

Vati looked out into the dark night miles from the blazing town. His hands were cold with the fear. He had sent them there for safety. He had failed them. He saw it now, the flames of its four exhausts first, then the dark evil shape.

*

Daddy heard the gunners beginning to shout, their voices high-pitched, not like heroes of films about war. 'He's coming in at eight 'o clock'...'he's in your field...why don't you bloody fire'...'how can I when the bloody bomber's weaving around like a ...I can't see a fucking thing! He's in your field...' 'I can't see him....he's gone!'...'he's here for fuck's sake, let's get the hell out of here', '...he's ...' the voices were panicky, almost screams. Daddy could see nothing. He had nothing to occupy him...he thought of home...so far now.

*

Vati pressed the firing button and delivered the power of his cannons into the front of the black shape, and its starboard engines. It stopped its weaving and bobbing, and peeled away in an increasingly steep dive, the cockpit half shot away, fire streaming from it and the outer starboard engine.

*

Daddy felt the icy wind from the ripped open front, and got out of his seat checking his parachute. But the steepness of the dive and the huge g-force flattened him against the bulkhead, and his navigators table. He heard the increasing whine, as the doomed aircraft made its final plunge and he despaired. Someone was shouting - screaming. For Daddy the world suddenly stopped.

*

She heard the first return, and then one by one, two by two they came over and returned to the airfield. She listened to the sounds - she felt she knew the sound of Daddy's plane, but she didn't hear it. It was only a silly fancy though, and meant nothing. Most of them always came back.

*

'*He* won't be going home for breakfast.'

The comrade's voice was soft, but hard. 'But the others got away, I'm afraid.'

There was no triumph in his voice. Nor did *Vati* feel any. He could pack up now, and he had work to do.

'Let's get back. I'm driving over there as soon as we debrief. I am afraid for them!'

*

130

Still she waited. It was longer than usual. Still not as long as it had been a couple of times though.

*

Something nasty had come out of the wood-shed and was sneaking around the airfield where *Vati* was anxiously circling as he waited to land. Invisible and swift it was. Inside were two enthusiasts, looking for sitting ducks.

*

Vati lowered the undercarriage - ordinarily this was the prelude to a moment of relaxing: writing:

He always started the writing with the same phrases:

To my beloved wife,

I thought of you and the child as I returned safe tonight...

The hunter swooped and annihilated the tail-plane, sending the aircraft crashing off the runway, over five hundred meters of grass, ripping off propellers, half a wing, and ending up hitting a concrete pillbox at high speed.

*

'Damn good show: another one of the bastards off to hell!'

'Yeeeas! Bloody good hunting! Well let's get back and have a late beer in the mess'

*

Her stomach was pulsating jelly. It was half an hour more than ever before. Waves of panic spread through her. She went to the child's bedroom and sat by his bed, watching his even breathing. She would have given everything she had, entered any horrific life, to see Daddy pick up the child at that moment.

*

Vati was dead - a corner of the pillbox had struck his head, which no longer really existed as such. It was just as well.

The comrade went through the broken glass and slid over the lush grass, until he finally stopped, a mass of bruises and cuts, in a haystack a further hundred meters on. He stood up, and began to walk back towards the wreck.

*

The morning light was filtering through the windows when she heard the sound of the gate. She went with heavy heart to answer the discreet ring. It was Joey, the Canadian, who had been with Daddy in flying school. He met her eye for a moment, and then looked away. 'They went down, I saw it' he said 'I didn't see anyone get out.'

'Oh. I guessed something had happened.'

'Can I do anything? I wanted to tell you, before they...'

'Yes - no'

And so now there was only Mummy, and all that had gone before was nothing but a few photographs, which told of a different world, where there had been Daddy - a very different world it seemed as the boy grew older.

*

The comrade didn't fly again. There was no new plane, no new pilot, and no fuel. He made the pilgrimage to the burnt city, and looked at the destruction wrought, and the carbonised husks which a few days previously had been moving around, giving life to the town. He could find no recognisable trace of the house, or even the street. 'It is actually very pointless, in fact' he said out loud, the sentiment applying to everything in his life, and as much beyond as he could comprehend.

He had a vision then, an important vision.

*

She watched the victory celebrations, the bunting, the flags, the street stalls, and singing round bonfires. Daddy's name would live for evermore, it seemed. The child asked less about Daddy now, but still played with the model bomber.

*

The comrade thought he had realised his dream a few years later. He found a small park, where there were some neat flower beds, cropped lawns and a pond on which a half-dozen ducks of various varieties swam. Bees hummed harmoniously, and the sun warmed his icy limbs. For a while he used the same green park bench to spend his days, reading and watching mothers with children feeding the ducks. He had to put up with some inconveniences though. A well-meaning man, seeing his scars, told him that war could easily be stamped out. It was caused by a particular group of people behaving very selfishly, who should be brought to book. But he persisted in his dream until one day he saw an argument between a boy and a girl as to who could stand in a favourable spot

133

for feeding the ducks. Beautiful children, both, but very cross with each other: the girl called 'Daddy', and a man appeared, and told the boy to be off. Immediately the boy called his Daddy, and another man approached, asking what right Daddy had to send his boy away. They began to argue, and push came to shove. The comrade left his beloved seat and never returned. *His* dream was unrealisable.

*

'You know I miss the Mob.' The enthusiast had appeared in his demob suit, getting out of his sports car and entering the pub garden. He shook hands with his former radar operator.

'What you doing - now that peace has broken out?' asked his former comrade when they were ensconced over two beers.

'Oh I've got into teaching in a prep school. Don't need a degree or anything. War rather put the kibosh on my studies you see. But you know what I've taken up, at last?'

'Go on!'

'I only went once, and I was hooked! It's bloody marvellous - just the job!'

'Well go on, tell me!'

'Duck shooting!'

'Duck shooting?'

'Yes, Duck shooting: shooting bloody ducks!'

'Right'

'It's been a sort of dream of mine, and now I am realising it. Do you fancy coming along?'

His former comrade didn't speak for a moment. Then he said somewhat sheepishly: 'You know I think I've had enough of all that shooting' He grinned. 'I don't really have any quarrel with ducks I suppose.'

His enthusiasm had waned.

18 The Blackheart Man

Tik'ya the Blackheart man Children

I say don't go near him

Tik'ya the Blackheart Man children

For even lions fear him - Bunny Wailer

I sit here in fear now – fear of my fellow men, and worse. I fear my son. Why? How has it happened? When did it happen? How did he become one of them?

Long before I went there I think! Before I was here, I was there, in that place where I had gone in desperation; that strange city, in a far land; I who once never strayed beyond my comfortable suburb, except for a pleasant safe holiday in southern Europe. In that hot shadowy city I searched amongst the alleyways, questioned the fierce-eyed men, entered even the dark churches, and skulked amongst the columns that supported the incense-clouded vaults. All around there was an effluvium of fear. Forces long forgotten in our northern lands still haunted the close packed mud-walled buildings. I had been afraid. But I had stayed to seek what I desired most in the world.

It had happened long before, in a that cool green land where I dwelt in happiness and ignorance. When did he turn? When did the world turn? Many years ago after some problems I fathered a son. He was the first of several healthy children, and I rejoiced in the pleasures of family life, earnestly working, with my wife, for the welfare and advancement of these children. But the first one, who we had named Godwen, for his flaxen hair, always aroused a fascination and deep emotion in me. He was my firstborn, and had come when I had lost all hope of having a son - or a daughter for that matter.

As he grew I spent many hours with him, delighting in his company, and seeing him develop like a young beech tree, tall and straight. His faults of quick temper and a tendency to domineer over his siblings seemed to decline as our relationship grew in trust and mutual respect. I tried to imbue him with my own code of morals, stamping on racist tendencies or contempt for minorities, firing him with a dislike of political oppression, giving him an understanding of sexual equality and generally passing on my liberal philosophy of life. And I taught him honesty, loyalty and compassion. For a time he became almost a model of friendly but disciplined behaviour. His interests still contained the essence of his old nature: conflict in the form of games of battle, both mental and physical: chess, martial arts and computer war-games. He also liked myths and legends of old wars, and especially outré creatures, gods and devils. He had no time for conventional religion, but held to the moral principles I had taught him, especially the habit of truth, with dogged zeal.

Then there came a time when problems began to develop at his primary school; they arose out of his proud and sometimes bellicose nature. At his school the boys had to relinquish the area where they had formerly played football – it was felt that the girls were being denied a fair share of the playing area, and that they should be able to engage in their more sedentary pursuits wherever they wished, without the sudden incursions of the ball, or boys running into them in pursuit of it. Godwen seemed to take an angry dislike to this development, although as far as I knew he was not especially keen on the game. He got it into his head that one particular teacher had promoted the idea, and that she was 'down on boys'. My wife and I pointed out to him that fair was fair, and that the girls were entitled to sit where they wanted. The fact that this same teacher had also been the one to confiscate his Jedi light-sword didn't help. We had always forbidden him toy guns as playthings, but the light sword we allowed as he was so attached to it. Nevertheless we supported her decision. Looking back I think we were wrong.

As it happened from around this period I became unable to give the amount of time to him that I had up until then. Both my wife and I were becoming increasingly successful, and our careers began to burgeon. Work often encroached on evening and weekends. The happy little trips we made out into the country, or to visit local zoos and gardens became fewer and fewer. I caught him looking at me in a disappointed sort of manner as our old relationship seemed to fade. I told myself that he needed to be less dependent on me for his social life.

Looking back I see how precious those times were, and how worthless the bigger cars, expensive ski holidays and sense of satisfaction that came from our success at work were, compared to the earlier simple but joyous engagement with our children. Indeed I have to confess that my wife and I engaged in a sort of foolish rivalry as to who might be in more demand for working late or at weekends, or who might be sent on more foreign trips to the USA, Europe or Japan. On the plus side we always made sure that the youngsters were in good hands, and that they reaped the material benefits of our gain in affluence. Indeed I gradually equipped Godwen with a computer gaming and multimedia system which was the envy of all his friends, and of most of their fathers. He took to it like a duck to water, and sometimes it made me uneasy to see him change that old innocent real world for the new virtual lands which he eagerly explored, and began to inhabit. Sometimes we had to veto particular games he had acquired – some with Second World War connections in which we felt that the Nazis were not clearly shown to be totally evil, others when there was too much machismo on show.

When Godwen was twelve he gradually began to develop some unpleasant characteristics that seemed to arise from malice of which had I thought him incapable. He got interested in graphic art, and began to show me the results of his work. At first I was most impressed. He seemed to have significant talent, especially in terms of figure composition. But his work went increasingly in directions I didn't like. There were pictures of muggings and street crime; hurtful pictures of people with physical imperfections, or even racial stereotypes whose message one couldn't quite put ones finger on. Some had people with prominent hooked noses weighing piles of gold and there were street muggings in which black people were shown as aggressors.

I severely reprimanded him over these. He rejected my criticisms. 'It isn't against black people, dad. It's about street crime. We've talked about it at school. Ephraim and I are friends aren't we?' Ephraim was an African boy who, like Godwen, was very athletic. He was in Godwen's class, and they went together to Karate, and were seemingly very close. 'Well I don't like it. You are stereotyping and wasting your talent. How do you think Ephraim would like that?'

'Well he doesn't mind. We play at muggers and victims. He plays the mugger, and I play the victim, and also Mr Babylon'

'Who's Mr Babylon?'

'He's a policeman dad!'

Annoyingly, it wasn't easy to deconstruct his arguments. One was used to mixing with adults who never ventured into the dangerous areas on which his graphics encroached. Parroting a phrase that was commonplace in our house, he would say 'I'm breaking boundaries, Dad! You said it was good to break boundaries'.

'The whole thing is vile, Godwen, absolutely vile!' I replied without taking the trouble to answer his points. He replied civilly enough, but I felt very uneasy.

'Sorry Dad. I'll make them both white. But will you still play Age of Empires with me tonight? You said you would.' I curtly told him that I had to take a visiting Chinese client out to an opera that evening – I hadn't really got the time. 'Ask me again tomorrow – or maybe at the weekend.' I said. On the other hand I greatly approved of his pictures of men with no particular ethnic stereotype in pinstriped suits receiving wads of notes from similarly dressed figures.

Nothing changed though. His next works showed Islamic looking terrorists beheading Western-looking victims. I carefully explained that this was too narrow a view and he seemed to take it on board. I told my friend David, who was a psychiatrist, about the problem, and he came and looked at some of the work, when Godwen was out at Karate. He looked through scores of the pictures, pausing on one that had the Jewish stereotypes – it might have been from Der Sturmer itself. I wondered how David who was Jewish, would react – but I saw no knee jerk reaction of horror. He was an impressive man who took a strange unclassifiable view of the world. He nodded and passed on. In the end he just shrugged and looked at me.

'It's most likely just a phase. Goodness knows where he's getting these ideas from. Do you find that you spend a lot of time with him trying to sort out this problem?'

'Of course – it horrifies me.'

'If it didn't he probably wouldn't do them,' he said with a reassuring smile. 'Just keep talking to him and gently push him back onto the path of truth. He's only twelve.'

Later Godwen came back and David talked with him, and of course Godwen was very civil and pleasant, and talked very articulately for his years, as he always did. Then he showed us his new brown belt. We weren't too keen on this activity, and as it happened I had forgotten I had promised to come home early specially to go to watch the grading – but he didn't complain. He was pleased as punch with his new belt, and cracked it the air like a whip before disappearing to engage in one of his mindless computer war-games.

'Unusual lad, Godwen; a lot of potential there,' David said, lighting a pipe, which he smoked in the face of almost universal opposition. I couldn't understand why he was not more incensed by my son's graphic art. 'The thing is boys nowadays tend to be seen as the bad guys– which doesn't help.' David went on.

Finally, a week or so after he had seemed fully repentant, he showed me another of his latest sexist pictures - showing harpy females clawing cowering men. I lost patience with him completely, and struck him for the first time in his life, knocking him down. I ignored his insolent appeals. 'What did I do wrong dad?' he said as he went upstairs. 'I'm breaking boundaries aren't I?' He reappeared and I wordlessly watched him walk sulkily off down the garden, finally shouting after him. 'Yes, clear off...go to the devil'

I'm sure it wasn't just this incident that had changed him; he had already rejected all the important moral values that I had tried to teach him. He still had some good qualities. He was a dutiful son – as when he actually redrew his mugging picture as I had asked him. He didn't steal as far as I knew. He was scrupulous about telling the truth. He never seemed to be motivated by greed, jealousy or covetousness. I never saw him display cruelty to animals, or his sisters. But on all the more important issues that meant everything to me –as he well knew – he had gone horribly wrong.

I assumed he would soon return with his tail between his legs, but he didn't. When he failed to come home we contacted everyone who might have seen him. He wasn't at any of his friend's houses, but when I spoke to Alice Okon – Ephraim's mother - she sounded worried. I couldn't get from her what her fears were; it only made us even more worried. But search as we might, we couldn't find him. You can imagine the progression from slight unease, through mounting fear to blind panic, when night came and went without the blessed moment of his return. The police were involved, the press got hold of it, and he became a national celebrity for a while, as vain appeals over national media failed to locate him. Finally his case was put on a back burner and he became just another missing person.

But I never gave up. I tried private detectives, internet appeals with huge rewards offered, and finally even spiritualists and clairvoyants. No sign of him ever emerged. Most people thought he was dead, victim of a child-killer, or had fallen into some disused pit, in his disconsolate wanderings. But one thing always kept my hopes alive. Although he had gone off in what he was wearing, with no evident preparations for a serious attempt to run away, he had taken the one thing he had always valued. It was a strange object, a stick with the seemingly perfect head of a lion on it. He had seen it in a collection of antiquaries that my grandfather had passed on to me, accumulated from his days as a missionary in Africa. He had immediately evinced a great desire to have it for his own, and I had given it to him. He had never tired of this artefact, and indeed it was an object of supreme envy in his peer group. Ephraim insisted they showed his mother. Alice told Godwen to burn it. 'It is from the spirit world, Godwen. Get rid of it' she said, but Godwen didn't. I knew that Godwen would never have taken it unless he meant to leave.

I gradually found myself at odds even with my wife, when I seemed unable to accept that I would not see Godwen again. 'Do you have to keep bloody reminding me?' she would sob. His sisters, who had adored him before the shadow fell on him, never mentioned him. I spent large sums we could hardly afford on advertisements in the national press, with Godwen's dear face there for anyone to recognise who might have seen him. I neglected our other children, believing that I could make it all up to them when Godwen should return. I became like a stranger in my home.

I became unbalanced...believed he had been abducted...that the horrible drawings and outbursts were signs that some evil influence had already begun its work. I listened to Godwen's favourite record night and day...'He lives in the gullies of the city...t'kya the Blackheart man! O! T'kya the Blackheart Man' On the cover was a powerful painting of a frightening looking figure in a lion's mane head-dress, with wild and

143

intimidating eyes who held in his hand the replica of the artefact that Godwen had valued so highly.

Alice told me Ephraim pined for Godwen, stopped eating, kept going off, then returning; finally he didn't return. I took to visiting Alice. She seemed lifeless and distant. Her old zest for life was gone with her beloved Ephraim. And on several occasions she mumbled, barely audibly 'I know who has got them' or 'He has got them!' Finally I asked her who He was, and she turned away, mumbling 'It's the Blackheart Man'.

After that I stopped searching for Godwen, and decided to search for the Blackheart Man as a last hope. The cities of the west have their dark corners, where horrors are perpetrated day and night...especially night. Behind the tall noble facades of stone, off the illuminated boulevards, far from the leafy avenues and the bountiful stores, unknown and dangerous to the law-abiding citizens, lurk the terrifying emissaries of chaos. In their drug-infested, whore-haunted quarters, they wait and watch as the bright light of civilisation slowly begins to recede, and the Dark Age begins once more in the twilight ebbing of hope. Here I learned to live in a nightmare world of stabbings, rapes, trained killer dogs, and the terrifying dictatorship of the gang tyrant. Always I felt myself nearer to the Demon himself, the black-hearted lord of it all. Yet I never found him, nor any sign of the fate of Godwen. Mad I was, lost to all the calming currents of rational thought, a wild-eyed, bearded fanatic, striking down the servants of darkness when they crossed me, until I was avoided even by the dope-crazed burrowers of the world beneath.

Finally on a break from my wanderings I talked with David. He told me of that ancient city in the birthplace of humanity where I would finally go in desperation. 'I don't say this Blackheart Man of which you speak is real. But if he is, that would be a good place to start looking. There are people there who will know where he might be. .If you do go, and you do find him, I'm not sure any good will come of it, for you, him, or anyone; there is something growing somewhere that I fear, and it may be there.

Not long afterwards I found myself in that strange Christian city, where the Christian God is not the liberal touchy-feely figure he has become in the land where I was born. A hot city of mud buildings built one upon the other, with alleys and ramps, stairways and tunnels running through it. Its inhabitants are dark black-bearded men in loose turbans, dressed in kaftans, boubous and burnouses. There are fiery-eyed black-haired women clad all in blacks and purples. And there, in a dark complex of interconnected buildings I found one who nodded when I told him of my quest.

In a tavern lit by guttering oil-lamps I drank dark wine with him. He led the way to the lion-guarded labyrinthine citadel for which I had so unceasingly searched, but shook his head at me as I made to pass within. He spoke little English, but his face said what his tongue could not: 'No good can come of this. Go back to your own land, fool!' Inside the cyclopean structure I wandered until I was lost, despairing of my hopes. Then an icy hand gripped my innards as I saw lions gather around me. As I felt my end approach I yearned, at last, for the cool air and gentle breeze of my green and pleasant land. But as the beasts moved silently toward me they stopped, and lifted their heads, listening. Then they slunk away, heads bowed, and a dark and monstrous figure dressed in leopard's skins, wearing bones and skulls at his waist, and a great lion's mane on his head stepped from the shadows, only two blazing eyes visible in his shadow-darkened face. In his hand he held a larger version of Godwen's lion stick.

He gripped me, and led me into his unholy domain. We passed through halls upon halls where boys learned the science of war, the skill of the hunter, the art of combat...the reflex of the killer, the ways to deliver sudden death...and the urge to enslave. One after another all the nations of the earth were represented there. At last we came to a long room where there were boys I knew. Boys from the land from whence I had come with their cropped heads, earrings and thirteen-year-old spindly legs, their game-boys and their warcraft cards, their eyes glazed over with the images of death and violence that they had absorbed. Their insolent faces turned to reverent respect when He came into their hall. He turned to me, and in a voice which resonated with the aeons-old stones of the citadel, said: 'All these have been given unto me. And they shall inherit the earth.' I looked for Godwen, and saw him, right at the back, and Ephraim beside him. But when I called out to him he laughed, spat and turned away. And I was cast out of the citadel that had been raised in the dawn of civilisation, and returned home to a darkening world. Was it there, under the tutelage of the Blackheart Man that he had turned?

I didn't see Godwen again for many years, until the world had changed into the evil empire that it now is. One day, as I sat reading, two of them came in. They looked at the book I was holding. After a brief consultation one tore it in half with one flex of his powerful arms. They turned over my bookcase, and poured paraffin on my books. Fluttering down came a crumpled sheet. One of them looked at the picture, and I saw that it was one of those harbingers of Godwen's doom.   He looked at me and I recognised him, and Ephraim, also: 'Dad!' I heard him say, and the years rolled back. They looked at each other – then Godwen smiled, and he was himself again. He lit the pyre of my last connection to the old world, saying 'Put some steel in your bones, old man, don't waste your time with this enfeebling pap. Today belongs to us!' He adjusted his black beret and he was gone, to the festivities to come. I put out the blaze as best I could. My books were finished. David came later, making sure he wasn't followed, and whilst helping clear the mess told me they could never eradicate all the books older people were hiding on memory sticks. But I like real books. They should be out in the open, on the shelves. He looked glum. 'Ah well - I suppose I'm still safe – It seems they think my lot got the full treatment last time.'

I nodded. 'I wish I'd spent more time with him'

He shook his head sadly. 'We all should have. It takes a community to bring up a child. But we had forgotten that. We were almost afraid of them.'

Now we are very afraid.

19 Charleville Circus

I live in a small rather dull seaside town. Some years ago   a curious thing happened to me. It is only because I have thought about it since that I have come to realise that it was curious at all.

I was making an irregular living as a consultant at the time, and went through periods of adequate finance, to much more affluent days. I was in the doldrums, when I received a fax which promised some rich pickings. As luck (and some lack of efficiency on my part) would have it, my printer was out of paper and I had no refill. I walked briskly into town, feeling pleased with myself, to obtain the necessary supplies. I wanted to reply quickly, so that I might preclude the possibility of the potential client going elsewhere. It was a lovely early autumn afternoon and I could hardly keep the spring out of my heels.

My pleasure was only clouded by the generally boring aspect of my town. I had few friends there, and usually went to a larger town nearby to take part in such small social life as I had. Yet I felt that this little town must have a more congenial part. I often saw people who appeared much like myself, yet who seemed to be happy and satisfied by the ambience of the place. They seemed to know one another, nodding and smiling as they met in the excellent second-hand bookshop the town boasted, or walking round the periodic art exhibitions. I had joined one or two clubs and societies, in the hope of meeting these apparently interesting   people, but never encountered them, even in associations for promoting literature and fine art. I am somewhat of a wit and raconteur, at least in my own eyes, and thus sorely missed a platform for exercising these talents.

I had always felt sure that in the absence of some quarter where local artists and writers met, there must be some inner circle to which I might hope to be admitted, if I could only find it. I felt that, having no wife or girlfriend, I was at a disadvantage, since women seem better able to pick up the faint echoes of undiscovered social life than men.

On this day, as I was coming back along my quiet street I suddenly remembered that I had been meaning to sort out an oddity of layout of some of the Victorian villas further down my street. There was a largish gap between two houses, and there seemed to be a large house set back behind the one of those which faced the street at the side of the gap. It seemed a ridiculous arrangement where suddenly instead of the usual string of single houses edging the street someone had had the silly idea of building two deep. Now I could check once and for all if this were so, and come later to photograph the anomaly - interested as I was in humble urban architecture. As I came to the place, in the gathering dusk I noticed a lamp post at the rear end of the strangely placed house, and all of a sudden a realisation came upon me like a flash. The gap was not a gap, but the entrance to an alley - a proper little street that I now saw clearly. The streetlight I had noticed seemed to throw its light down the continuation of the alley into the houses which I had previously assumed were the backs of those in the next street to mine. The dog-leg, which the alley followed, gave an exact appearance of a dead end, in normal sunlight, and similarly in full night - only under the present conditions of lamp-lit dusk did it reveal itself.

I was probably more amazed, and perhaps excited than most people would have been. Firstly I am very observant and could barely believe that after ten years residence I could have missed the little road. Secondly, I am keenly interested in the geography of my neighbourhood. Gossip about local people rarely interests me, but the humble geometry, history and architecture of leafy Victorian streets fascinates me. As soon as I saw the street it solved a problem of which I had been vaguely aware. The triangular section of the town that was delimited by the three streets I knew was much broader at the base than could be explained without the existence of some area of land within it - a very large garden, perhaps, used as a smallholding: an allotment for the use of those whose houses backed onto it.

Now I saw it all, there was a street - possibly streets - a whole enclave of my town which I did not know, and one on my own doorstep. I immediately decided that I would explore it at the first opportunity, but that for now I would merely glance beyond the place I knew - like Alice seeing for the first time the strangeness of the parts of the mirror-world which she could not usually see. I turned the little corner and stopped, frozen momentarily by what I saw. A group of people sitting around a cafe table complete with parasol, talking and laughing in refined tones, a flask of wine in front of them. Further down the lamp-lit street I saw a discreetly lit restaurant sign, with people eating outside in the warmth of an autumn evening, and further down, a division in the street which disappeared to left and right, but with guitar music emerging from what looked like a cafe window, on one side, and a group of men and women talking animatedly together. The scene had a wonderful continental atmosphere, and it solved the problem of where the town smart set went every evening. It was here

- not fifty yards from my front door! And the music I sometimes heard wafting into my house from this direction would annoy me no longer. It was not the mindless *continuo* of some local resident's sound system, but the outward sign of the inner grace of the little oasis of cultural life that I hoped soon to be a part of.

My first instinct was to plunge straight in, seating myself at a table of the nearby cafe, but I prudently kept to my original plan. If I couldn't get a consultation from the recent fax then I would have little money to spend in my newly found demi-paradise. I went home, replied to the fax. I received a reply before I went to bed, and soon found myself engaged in a big and lucrative contract, which kept me very busy. Almost everyday I told myself that that very evening I would go for a night-cap in the Circus. I knew the name of the street now for I had consulted my street map where the little streets were clearly marked. They were missable to the untutored eye, because they were drawn in broken lines in accordance with the maps way of representing pedestrian only paths. In addition, it occurred on a meeting of four folds of my old map which was now very worn. I had been pleased to see concrete evidence of the existence of *Charleville Circus*. Strange mixture of romantic and rationalist that I am, I had kept seeing the words '...but he was never able to find it again!' floating in my vision, silly though it was to believe in such clichéd literary magic. Now I found that each night some new complexity kept me at my desk or my computer until even the most continental of cafes would have long been closed.

The final stages of the project involved trips to the continent, in which I had to sit through a number of long boring meetings with chain-smoking representatives of various continental organisations, interspersed with elaborate lunches and dinners. I was sustained through this period in the knowledge of *Charleville Circus*, where I would soon have the time and money to become part of the intellectual community of my home town. I barely listened to the wife of one representative as she spoke animatedly about the history of the town where we sat, even to the time of the Visigoths. Not that she was boring, or other than charming, but because my thoughts were far away, in that little, magical oasis where at last I should have a toe-hold on a satisfying social life!

Once home I chose a early Saturday afternoon to explore *Charleville Circus*. The weather was bright but there was some of the chill of a late September day in the air. I went with pounding heart, and soon walked through the gap to the new world. My first reaction was of shock. The cafe where I had seen the group was not a cafe at all, but a patio with a set of tables and chairs. Behind it, in the next garden another set of green garden furniture had helped to create the illusion. I know enough of the power of the human vision system to flesh out unseen details, to realise how easily illusions can be created. I saw that a woman was tidying some of the plant arrangements, a perfectly normal householder - with no thought of a cafe in her mind. I hurried on, remembering that I had seen, with absolute certainty, the restaurant, called *The Big Top,* after the Circus. I walked the necessary few paces to find, indeed, a restaurant, but with little sign of life - and an aura of being closed. As I glanced to left and right I saw no sign of further hostelries of any kind. My disappointment was overwhelming. As I looked at its facade a voice called, irritatingly. 'Its closed you know'. I turned to see the woman who had been in the house I had mistaken for a cafe. I shrugged. I felt unreasonably annoyed with her. 'I thought as bloody much' I replied, ungraciously.

'I know what you thought!' she said, with a kind smile. 'I saw you, in August, when you looked down the alley. You thought this was a little Greenwich Village! All tucked away! It isn't though -- but it could be! My husband did the gaslight and the *Kronenbourg* sign.'

I felt a fool. 'Oh really?' I said. 'Why doesn't he go and live over there, if you both like the atmosphere so much?' I could have asked myself the same question. She tossed her long gypsy locks, and looked to the side before smiling again.

'Ah well - he did! Unfortunately he didn't take me!'

'Oh, I see! I'm sorry!'

'Oh it was a few years ago now - I'm over it. I'm on the shelf, but it's not a bad place to be!'

'I wouldn't know!' I said, feeling that she had probably spied on me going past on my own. I don't like people who try to somehow pull one down to their level. I was polite, but far from warm. Nevertheless she was a friendly and sympathetic person. She smiled and beckoned.

'Look, I've got a few drinks in, including some Pelforth, why not have one here on the terrace - it can be the Cafe Charleville for an hour!' If I hadn't been so unreasonably irritated I might have accepted her offer.

'Ah no, thanks, I'm going out tonight, you see.' I was: to watch a video with a former colleague and his wife - a reprise of the last world rowing championships - they were rowing enthusiasts.

'Oh, OK. Well, sorry to have been the bringer of bad tidings, I can see how disappointed you are!'

'I wasn't *that* disappointed!' I said, as she bade me a smiling farewell. I was though, as she had correctly guessed. The next days I was heavily depressed and wondered at the dull bare wet earth of my life. That I could have been such a fool as to dream that impossible dream, and that I should have found my mistake in such a humiliatingly public way!

Luckily the consultancy was doing well and I soon lost myself in a round of work, much like the earlier collaborative contract. I spent some time abroad, and began to approach my dream of saving enough to invest in a quiet life. No more boring meetings and evening conversations with important clients or their wives! But I still blushed at the thought of my foolishness, and brooded over the resulting emptiness of my life. I am a polite and kind person at heart, and felt shame at the gruff responses I had given to the pleasant mannered woman I had met in the Circus. She had seen almost into my heart so easily, and had been so ready to play along with the Charleville village idea. Once - in Atlanta a kind expression reminded me of her so strongly that it brought me to very clear memories of the original. I could no longer remember my irritation, only her exquisite kindness, laughing, almost provocative eyes, and her slightly faded, but undeniable beauty. The more I thought, the more I realised what a chance it was to have so suitable a potential woman friend living at such close quarters. She evidently liked me enough to remember me, to speculate as to my feelings, and to make a gracious invitation. I felt a cur. I realised I liked her great deal. As my sojourn in Atlanta neared its end I became increasingly impatient, and thought endlessly of the moment when I should encounter her again. I rehearsed several opening gambits designed to undo the evil of the past, and open a door to the future.

On the plane back I dreamed of the beautiful neighbour constantly. After sleeping off my jet lag, at seven o'clock on a fine summer evening, almost exactly a year after my first discovery of Charleville Circus, I went in search of the object of my new found love with reasonable confidence - if she were not in tonight I should call the next day. I had an excellent present in the form of a set of bottles of fine Colognes and perfumes which might please her.

When I stepped into the alley I was, if anything, more shocked than on the previous occasion. Against all logic and common sense, her house was now, definitely, and unmistakably, a continental style cafe. My heart leapt, and I entered in excitement, seating myself at a spare table, and preparing to greet her once she should see me. I was disappointed to see that she was not behind the bar, but I ordered a beer. I noted that the restaurant I had seen had reopened under the name *The Inner Circle,* and had adopted the London Underground as its theme. Both it and the cafe were doing very brisk business indeed. A group of street performers were amusing the customers in the warm evening sun. I breathed deeply. The Circus had arrived! I drank slowly, and noted that a middle aged couple seemed to be behaving in a patronly fashion in the cafe where I sat. I looked around uneasily. At the tables I saw many of the people I had so longed to meet in the town before my discovery of the Circus. I touched the arm of one who sat close to me. 'Excuse me, but could you tell me who actually owns this excellent establishment?'

The man turned, and smiled, leaving the conversation about the comparison of virtual reality to the emergence of the novel, and spoke.

'Yes, it's Jan & Peter there!' He pointed to the couple.

'Oh', I said, a little shocked. 'How long have they been here?'

'Oh, they opened about six months ago. It's a great improvement to the old town, isn't it? Mind you they don't expect to open in winter - they think it's a summer thing mainly. But the pub people say they'll be open all year, and the restaurant too. My wife Laura, that's her in the yellow pullover, she did the decorations in there, its all very John Betjeman of course but she hasn't got much work on at the moment anyway ...'

I listened impatiently to his gushing. When he paused momentarily I quickly put in: 'Any idea what happened to the woman who lived here before - you know, last year?'

'I don't know, but Laura will' he said. He turned and asked his wife, who called out. 'Oh she sold last Christmas and went off to Canada, she got a good job. She didn't like it here!'

My world went black. I could hear the vague twittering of these Muscadet Matisses and Heineken Hemingways, but the words made no sense, they were like gulls crying. Finally I felt a tap on my shoulder, and looked up to see that the man was attracting me to his wife's calling 'Why don't you pull up a bollard?'

I made some graceless reply, I don't know what, and staggered away, hearing the man say, in a slightly aggrieved voice 'Suit yourself old man!'

I could think of nothing but the lost woman, one whom I could have responded to, warmly and perhaps formed at last a happy relationship. I was sure of it; and now she had gone to Canada, where no doubt she had been wooed and won by some drawling giant of a man, with far superior credentials to mine. I licked my wounds, and it was some time before visiting the Circus again. News of my rudeness on the earlier occasion seemed to have spread, and no invitations were proffered, and my attempts at friendliness pointedly rebuffed..

I didn't visit it again for a couple of years. When I did, the results were possibly the most disastrous of my three visits. I had not forgotten my *femme fatale* but I had pushed her to the back of my mind. I had made progress at work, and more, I was just married! I had met a continental woman at one of the interminable lunches, and we had developed a friendship. She seemed very favourably disposed toward me, and soon we were very close. She was a divorcee, and had a young son, with whom I did not form a good relationship. The fault was, as I now admit, on my side rather than his. But she made my life very pleasant during a long stay on a consultancy. We married quietly and she returned with me to live in my house. I was reasonably pleased with her, and she was as devoted as ever. She did find town life very dull, and alien though. She couldn't get used to the early closing of shops, the male aura of the pubs, and the lack of companions of her own nature.

But one day she came home from the shop where she worked (for amusement rather than necessity) in an excited state. She had heard of a place that sounded very continental - from someone who had once been to Charleville Circus. We must visit it! She was now expecting my child, I couldn't see the point of revisiting the place, but she was so eager that I foolishly gave in. She insisted that we take Edouard, and so together we went. As I had feared, the cafe was now closed. I knew such ventures often started well then fizzled out, and the Charleville was no exception. But my wife was ready to be pleased with the *Inner Circle,* and so might I, but for the sight of my *femme fatale* gazing thoughtfully at me from her old house, as I passed arm in arm with my wife. From that moment I found my marriage a frustration and a prison. I ceased to preserve the civilities of life, and returned my wife's true devotion with barely concealed irritation. Yet she bore it whilst it did not extend to her son, a fine big boy of eight. But soon she found that what should have been fatherly feelings for the boy were in in fact almost non-existent. And the boys' evident wish for my approbation, and the appellation 'Eddy' only hardened my heart. Edouard he was, and Edouard he remained. Finally, when he complained of some bullying I dismissed his problems. When she remonstrated I merely expressed the hope that the expected baby would not prove to be such a wimp. This heartless behaviour, of which I am deeply ashamed, was against countless fruitless attempts to behave in a decent manner.

The day after this outrage, my wife left with Edouard, and I have never seen either since.

The remainder may be easily told. I formed a relationship with the woman I had dreamed of, whose Canadian venture had been planned as a year's absence. She had not sold the house, but let it to the couple, whose business had wound down to a bare living. They had started a new and apparently successful venture in the capital, and she had re-occupied the house she owned. After a brief spell of pleasure I soon discovered that I had my wife constantly in my thoughts and found little pleasure in my new relationship. I soon decided to contact my wife. I located them and wrote a letter to her, and another addressed to 'Eddie'. But I received only a curt and hurtful reply, the news that she had a new partner and a request that I should refrain from further contact other than with respect to her desire for a divorce.

My new partner ended our relationship abruptly when she came across the sequence of emails that had passed between my and my wife.

As I write now, two years later I live as I did before I found the Circus, my business having suffered during the disruptions of the break-up of my marriage. I have no more foreign trips, but still receive a sufficiency of contracts. I have few friends in the town or elsewhere. I last visited the Circus a year ago. The restaurant was open, but completely empty. Its boards were faded, and one didn't expect them to be painted. Outside the restaurant now a pub I saw a scuffle with two hefty local youths settling some primitive dispute. One a had a bleeding lip, the other torn trousers. As I hurried past I saw a man vomiting into the garden of the next door house. Nevertheless, a year can make a big difference in the Circus and I am planning another visit soon. Most of the setbacks I have suffered, which have been very hard on me and which I think you will agree are undeserved, stem from that place, so it owes me something. Third time lucky perhaps!

20 Everybody Knows

Everybody knows that the moon isn't made of green cheese, don't they? They know what it *is* made of – bits of it have been brought back to the earth by those who made the great step for mankind all those years ago. The bits were just rock – silicates, aluminium and iron. More or less what they expected.

But it wasn't like that when I went there, all those years ago, when my steel soul was prompting me, imploring me, and crushing me with its need to spawn a child. He couldn't do it but he knew I could. 'Don't put Cornelius beside anyone who has children' they used to say before we visited. 'He gets very depressed.' I averted my eyes when I passed all those mothers waiting for the emergence of the pixies from the kindergarten I passed every day.

At night, in a high room, whilst my wife slept peacefully, I threw the window open and saw the moon and sensed its silent beckoning. I raised my arms, and prayed to it, as we are forbidden. I floated out and upward, into the indigo yonder, over the sentient city on the tide of love she bore me. Like an albatross I flew beside an ascending Boeing feeling the warmth of its engines until it could rise no more, and I left it, the last homely house, and rose into the kingdom of the air and the spirits. I saw the great ball which I was leaving, as it slowly turned its face. The sky changed from indigo to black, and I was alone, as I had never been.

But I looked toward our guardian goddess, who pitied me and sent her cold white rays to turn the firmament from night to dusk, the grey light of the North Sea which recalled the despairing urgency of my quest to my mind, and drew me on. I saw a cloud in the void between the heavenly sisters, a cloud that moved so purposefully in the opposite direction, from the goddess to the mother. Like Galileo, when he saw that the Milky Way was made of stars, I saw that the cloud was made of human beings. A shoal of babies, their eyes still closed, swimming in the ether, slowly but inexorably, their tiny limbs thrusting them on, sending warm waves over me. I looked with a sudden hope. Was my child on its way? There were so many that I could not hope to see it if it was. But one of the shepherdesses looked at me with pitying eyes and shook her head as she glided past. 'Go on, go on' she said. I passed the living cloud and saw that a few of the tiny space travellers were tiring, and at the back were those who had stopped swimming, their life-force spent, and they faded away as I left the cloud behind.

I fell gently to the surface and was enveloped immediately in *Mare Imbrium*, the Sea of Showers, where I set out for the shore, my head warmed by the gentle and eternal rain that replenished the ever evaporating waters. I found my feet and waded out onto sands washed by the flooding tides raised by the moon's gigantic sister; I came to a prairie of dank reeds and struggled through their cold unwelcoming spikes hour after hour, then came to the shore of *Lacus Doloris,* the Lake of Sorrows wherein I saw a figure that I had long forgotten standing on the water with flowers in her hair. I had seen her once before beside my bed when the blitz was at its height and my parents had clung together awaiting the end of everything in the orange flickering light of the burning docks. She looked at me, raised her arm and pointed steadily the direction I must take around the lake and across the grassy plain, up the mossy damp ring walls of the craters great and small that scatter that ancient land. On through their marshy depressions I went, and sometimes through bogs that would have sucked me down had the earth's gravity acted upon me, I half-ran half-glided mile after mile until I saw glistening *Mare Fecunditatis*, the Sea of Fertility, twinkling ahead in the sunlight of the lunar dawn. I launched myself into the warm amniotic brine and gloried in the achievement of my quest.

But when I returned thr Sea of Fertility had done its work – a child was coming to us across the boundless void. He grew strong and another came. Together we made their home on mother earth, and a time of love and hope stretched out. But the first was made of lunar stuff and it touched his very soul. As he grew up he found the earthly world of men and women could not match his stratospheric dreams and he withdrew and walked alone.

I look now again at the moon from the high window on a night when the goddess beams as brightly as she had in my youth. I shall go once more with him, and seek *Mare Tranquilitatis,* the Sea of Tranquillity, and if he will not come, then by myself, to find *Mare Nubium*, the Sea of Clouds, where I shall see nothing more as everybody knows.

21 The Entertaining Mr Jones

I looked around the luxurious yet severe conference room. It was impossible not to feel it filled by the presence of Jones. He seemed bigger, solider and more upright than all the others. We each had a document in front of us, illuminated by the cold filtered light which came in through skylights, making an impressive reflection on the huge oak table. On examination the documents proved to be reviews of a weeks viewing on our various film channels. I read mine trying to look keen and able, but finding it rather boring, something I had read too many times.

Your Entertainment Tonight: The pick of the weeks films

The Children *(Thriller)* Three children befriend a delightful old vagabond, but he turns out to be a serial killer.

The Gynaecologist (*Erotic comedy*) A doctor finds his life complicated by a bevy of beautiful naked women. But he turns out to be a serial killer.

The College girls *(Drama)* A number of attractive young women are brutally horrifically disgustingly mutilated, murdered and raped one after the other at an exclusive girls' college.

The Sabine Women *(Historical Drama)* A group of attractive young Sabine women are brutally horrifically disgustingly mutilated, murdered and raped one after the other at an exclusive Roman camp.

Child Abuse! *(Family drama)* An attractive woman tries to stop her husband abusing their ten year old daughter, but he brutally murders her, and the child his next target!

Rotten Cop. (*Police drama*) A cop brutally murders his wife's lover, and then goes on the run pursued by his ex partner, who he has to kill using a flensing knife given him by his Norwegian grandfather. He then embarks on an orgy of killing starting with his wife and children, and finishing with his superior officer after which he escapes to start a new life in the purifying atmosphere of a Tibetan monastery, where he once again goes on the rampage.

After Jones had finished reading the film summaries he paused, and looked up at us.

'So what do you think?' he said. No-one spoke. They all wanted to know his own reaction before committing themselves. He looked aggressively around, and picked on the newest member of the entertainment steering group, Henry Jenkins, who'd just put his kid into public school.

'What do you think Hank?'

Jones' stentorian American voice had softened fractionally. Henry looked half pleased at the distinction, but desperately anxious to avoid the saying wrong thing. He looked panickily around, but we all kept straight faces. This was a competitive company, and he had to take his chance. Only Sharon Trace, Jones' secretary made a microscopic movement of her head. For some reason she didn't want Henry to put a foot off the fairway. It was a shake...a negative.

'Well sir! I'm not sure I'm wholly convinced that this sort of programme is precisely commensurate with the company mission.'

'That's right, its garbage' Jones said, with a black look.

'…precisely my thoughts!' New voices chimed in.

'I've been thinking just that, these last months!'

'I was just thinking that those review writers should be kicked out on their asses!' This was Charles Holdsworth - a successful and experienced toady, and currently my boss. But he went white, and could have bitten out his tongue after Jones next words. His first boob for two years!

'They are OK; nothing wrong with them!'

Holdsworth sat in blue funk during the silence that followed. Fifteen seconds to suffer knowing that he had made the blunder! He of all people! And we were all enjoying it.

Then Jones looked at him for a split second. 'It's not them ... you see that don't you, Chuck?'

'It's the films!' Holdsworth blurted out, exposed, the moment of life or death.

'Right, Chuck! We are showing garbage! Isn't that what we are doing?'

'Yes sir! We seem to be doing that sir!'

'They *are* a little violent' Sally Horn said - she wasn't as tough as she liked to appear. Jones went on as if she hadn't spoken. But his lips seemed to somehow show irritation with her remark, in the way they articulated his words.

'We are buying garbage! That's what we are doing. There's a reason for that. What's the reason for that, Chuck?'

'There's only crap out there!' said Lydia - she had to say that, she signed the purchase orders for the films we were showing.

'RIGHT' Jones banged his fist on the desk. 'RIGHT: there's only crap out there!'

He looked around, with a lizard-like smile. 'We want more than just serial killers. Of course we want serial killers. But you don't advertise a brothel by saying there's whores inside! Of course there are! You don't get people to go to church by saying we got preachers inside. We've got serial killers but they are used to that. They want violence beyond their fondest dreams'

Everyone relaxed. The casualties cursed themselves; the others rejoiced that the battle was over. Jones had pointed the finger away from us. The next time I saw Sally Horn she was pushing a pram, her dream of power and glory at an end. I think she was sacked three days later, in front of her staff, for going a few pounds over budget.

Jones then got the real meeting going, having let us all feel the heat of the red hot poker in our backsides. He showed us the charts that proved that for the last year we were the biggest customer of all the film companies. They were going to learn who the boss was. And they were going to make good films. Or else. We were all sent off with a mission to invent suitable film scenarios. We were going to do the creative part; the film makers were just going to implement our ideas - adding a few arty touches to bamboozle the censors.

The showdown was at a presentation that the film producers were summoned to. They were told to bring their new film plans, with synopses, highlight descriptions, and some scene mock-ups. They had already been told to 'soup up' their plans. 'More blood and snot, less piss and wind' was Jones's prescription.

Jones watched the first company – *Raptor Films* do its thing. They were very nervous. Their films were a series of thrillers dealing with trendy themes. There was some child abuse with the father getting lynched in an exotic fashion; date rape getting out of hand with some murders; a series of killings in a moral tale about a rain forest being exploited. The director tried to sound enthusiastic about the violence. He looked young, and even a little creative. 'The lynching is gonna be a pretty robust scene Mr Jones, the guy's really gonna get his comeuppance.' Jones cut him as he started saying: 'In the date rape we're getting into a more serial kinda thing with the guy...'

'How many killings in the child abuse thing...'

'Well, just the one actual killing, but ahhh...he beats his wife up too, y'know, pretty strong stuff with ...er a coupla harrowing scenes with the kids...'

'Only one killing...harrowing scenes with the kids? What *is* this? This is even softer than the stuff you palmed off on us last year. Harrowing scenes with the kids? They get harrowing scenes with the kids at home! They want to see the kids bust open.' he stopped, and winked at us. 'Bust right open' he said.

The director looked horrified, and a little nettled. His producer seemed aware that he might now say the wrong thing, and tried to come in with 'This is of course a framework, it can be worked up from here, we can have the abuse going a little further...some physical abuse, death even', but now the young director began to speak.

'Well sir, we thought that these scenarios are going to give your company a positive image vis-à-vis the current moral climate, they all present a final harmony, whilst perhaps shocking the viewer out of the couch-potato acceptance of the viciousness of modern western society....' Even he could see that Jones was looking thunderous...we all flinched. He tried to back pedal.

'We thought that the moral overtones would help us steer films which you would find ah... suitably realistic and robust past an increasingly hostile censor. Ah violence against children…'

Jones silenced him.

'I got lawyers and they tell me we can bust kids apart. Isn't that so, Simon? That's what we want.'

Simon Strachan our legal beagle nodded vigorously.

Jones turned to the producer.

'You got all these guys sitting on their asses cooking up stuff like that, whilst my customers are being deprived of entertainment they want. We can't use these films OK? See if you can do better next year.'

Raptor Films were ignominiously ushered out, with their tails between their legs. Stiletto films took the stand.

After that Jones began to weave a magical tapestry of delights to come.

'We should do a sort of feminist thing, a cult, where they go round castrating all these guys, captains of industry, engineers, preachers, family men etc. The women will like that, and the guys will get dragged along. And we can do another, to balance the books, where a cult of guys goes round popping off feminists, those weird ones with the shaved heads and earrings. 'Aim right between the earrings, that could be their battle cry! Y'never know, it might catch on!' he added with a wink at me and Strachan, our legal beagle.

'These are exciting concepts!' said Strachan, even though he was always putting his wife's feminist views forward. His daughter was in my daughter's class. She'd been taken out of the local high school after she got her nose broken. Who said boys are the only ones who fight?

'Well I'm looking for *more* exciting concepts! Something historical - real brutality just faithfully recreated...'

I spoke 'What about the massacre of the McDonalds? That included everything - battles, women and children - lots of costume with creative possibilities'

I waited. This was it. I hadn't made a suggestion for too long. But if this worked - I was safe for six months - with things going well. He sat stock still, with everyone watching my life in the balance. Then very slowly he began to nod. Finally it was a very positive gesture.

'I like that, Ed!' he said. 'I like that!'

I smiled. 'I think it could be a nuke sir!'

'Yeah...who were they, the McDonalds? They were Scotchmen weren't they? What are Scotchmen really? We'd need the historical stuff perfect. They do bagpipes, don't they, and wear skirts, is that it? Do the English do the massacre?'

I said nothing, but Jenkins spoke up, hoping to sink my idea.

'No sir it was other Scots...Scotchmen'

Jones glared at him momentarily. Jenkins flinched. 'Right; what about the IRA - is this part of that same thing?'

Nobody spoke.

'Whadya think Chuck? Can we use the IRA?

Holdsworth stammered out: 'Ahhh...the IRA was not operative contemporaneously with the time-slot occupied by the proposed cinematographic project, sir'

Jones looked at him for some moments.

Then he turned to me. 'So we can't use the IRA...and we can't have the English massacring these McDonalds ... right Ed?'

'I'll get onto the English angle sir... I think the government in London may have been behind it.'

'That's the stuff, Ed. I like that Ed!'

'And we can use Claymores, sir, they were enormous swords sir, twisty ones I think!'

'Yeah? Could you have two Scotchmen being chopped in half by a Claymore, at the same time...that'd be good wouldn't it Ed?'

'It would sir, it would. I think that may be stylistically novel.'

'And we could cut to the top halves, shooting up, almost in formation, Ed. Playing the bagpipes...by a sort of reflex, couldn't we Ed?'

'I think so sir. The logistics sound achievable...do you have that capability?' I looked at the people from Stiletto Films. John, who seemed to be the main man, turned to one of his lackeys.

'Yes we could do that, couldn't we Mike? He looked at their technical man.

'Ah yes that's not a problem' he replied.

'Or we could cut to the bottom halves... the guys legs still running a few paces, still in the skirts. Whadya think Chuck?'

'They're both stimulating visualisations sir, but maybe the top halves are better. With maybe three guys instead of two. The bottom halves would need very good directing to steer away from Guignol, sir. I think your instinct was right first time, with the top halves'

'OK...and with blood squirting out of the bagpipes, Chuck. You'd want blood squirting out of the bagpipes wouldn't you Chuck'

'Yes you would sir.'

'OK so we've got the gist of this thing, you guys can take it from there on the same line can you!' He looked at the Stiletto people again.

'Yes we can run with that' the senior man said. The artistic director started to say 'Yes, but John, what about the Lovecraft idea...'

'Let's take that off-line shall we Keith. Mr Jones ideas are so vital; we need to take them on board with no distraction.' Keith scowled sulkily.

'I'm looking for some credit on this one...my name can go in as art director...or would it be author?' Jones said.

'Creative consultant and co-author?' Holdsworth ventured.

'And we want to get some awards for this...we need awards'

John nodded. 'Awards' he said, and wrote something on his note book.

'And no ass and tit in this, it's got to have a sort of reverent feel about it. That's how it is with ethnic stuff you see.'

'No ass and tit' John intoned, adding another note.

'Scotchmen are an ethnic thing, aren't they Ed?' Jones said.

'Yes they are sir.'

'That's what I thought.'

'Now, Ed. I want *you* to work up a scenario for me.'

'The massacre of the McDonalds sir?'

'No. This is my special project Ed. I want one of these school massacres. I thought we could set it in a private school - not a public school...lots of rich kids getting hacked around...people like that. Girls I think...your daughter goes to a public school doesn't she...and that's like a private school isn't it?'

'That's right sir.' I said hollowly.

'You could probably do an authentic scenario. Right, Ed?'

'I could sir'

'This could be a big break for you, Ed. We'll soon want to start our own subsidiary film company, you know, Ed. And I'll need someone to head it.'

'That's a stimulating idea sir' I said.

'I want girls who look like real kids; the audience gets to know 'em. They are getting on with their sports, lessons, friendships - they are nice kids, with parents and so on...the guy...a real maniac...gets into the place. I want the fear on their pampered little faces...'

Holdsworth had been looking at me. He thought he saw a chink in my armour. He chimed in:

'This is just right sir! Ordinary girls hacked to pieces...blood all over the dormitory, the showers and the classrooms...the gym. He could have a chainsaw, and a lot of other stuff. We could focus on kids at home talking about their hopes...an obese kid, say...nicknamed The Whale ... 'I'm going to be in the swimming team dad!' Then the same face just before he gets her with a harpoon...she could be somehow pinned to the wall in the pool...this is going to give audiences a whole new dimension of pleasure!' Kathleen was going through a slightly overweight phase and Holdsworth knew it.

'That's good Chuck! I like that! You got that Ed! I want that in the film Ed!'

'I'll get it in sir!' I said.

'This one's going to be a classic - like a ball*ay*...and specially a lotta decapitation. That's to be the um...*eeday fixay* of the thing do you see? We can use the 'Blue Danube' as the heads fly.'

'Um...that's a great sound/image concept sir! But they used *Blue Danube* in 2001.' That was Holdsworth.

'OK...yeah...well we can maybe...yeah, the Mexican Hat thing....da-da-da-da da-da da-da-da...da da-da-da da-da-da da-da! Lots of blood like fountains going into slow motion...very serene in some way...I'm getting a real spiritual thing here, aren't I, Ed?'

'Yes sir, that's what you are doing.'

I was glad to get out into the sun. Surely I wasn't weakening. My big chance and I was getting squeamish. I felt better when I got into the BMW. It made me feel calmer and stronger. Maybe I did need to get out. I might be able to get in somewhere on the technical side again. Maybe things weren't right for me on the creative side right now. I purred into the leafy lanes of the green belt, and up our chalky drive. Tim was playing on his bike, and waved to me. I was pleased he wasn't inside playing on his computer on such a nice day. But his words dulled the pleasure.

'Dad! Will you set up *Nazi Nightmare* for me...Brian reckons it's better than *Nazi Dawn*...you can actually *be* the SS in Slaughter'.

'Not now, Tim, I'm just going to relax and have a drink.'

Sharon bought me a much needed beer. I didn't say anything to her about my plan, but I was already half committed.

Kathleen could go to the local High School. I had heard nothing bad about it. I could get dad to coach her - he'd enjoy that. She'd make a good scientist - I could be proud of her. The school had high standards of security, and were said to be well on top of bullying. She knew some other thirteen-year-olds who went there.

Tim didn't particularly like his prep school - he wouldn't mind. We could move to a smaller house. I needn't replace the car for ten years. I'd write to Judson at Standard Software. He could get me something - middle management - low pay - but it would be OK.

Kathleen suddenly spoke - having come up through the formal box hedges unnoticed by me in my reverie.

'What's up dad?' She still wore her mulberry coloured school dress. I wondered if I should break the news to her.

'Come here...sit with me Kathleen' I said, and she joined me on the rustic seat overlooking the downs. 'Dad...I can cheer you up! I'm to be in the school chess team! Mrs Romanova was amazed! I'll be on board two! And I'm the youngest! What about that dad!'

'That's excellent darling.'

'And, Dad...and!'

'Well!'

'I've been invited to go for the weekend at Cleo's...she's the most popular girl in our year...I'm to take Ned...they'll pick us up with their horse-box and Cleo and I will ride all over their estate. I really am part of Upside now dad!'

I said nothing. I patted her head. 'That's super dear...marvellous' There was no escape.

I went and found Tim. 'Let's go and set up *Nazi Nightmare*. Only don't be the Nazis...be the American Secret Resistance...I don't want you to be the Nazis son.'

'OK Dad...but will you be the Nazis...it's a two player game!'

'No son. You play on your own.'

'Oh Da-ad...just for a bit...you promised...will you be the Nazis? It's not like the real second war was...in this most people are Nazis...'

'Oh well...if most people are Nazis I guess I'll be the Nazis...just till dinner mind you.'

22 Out of Babylon

As he grew colder and hungrier he grew increasingly angry. This was no way to treat somebody! He'd always hated being kept waiting. He checked the time, and yet again the sight of his bare wrist gave him a jolt. He never realised just how much he'd taken having a watch for granted, how often he looked at it. He had no idea how long he had been here: more than an hour, surely. Two hours? Without daylight there was no way of checking.

His stomach rumbled again. He could really do with a drink as well – a double whisky or, failing that, a cup of tea. 'A nice cup of tea, that'll make you feel better, dear'; he could almost hear his mother's voice. Dear Mum. Poor old Mum, if she could see him now. He quickly suppressed the self-pity that was threatening to creep up on him.

At long last the door opened and in the oblong of light he saw the silhouette of a tall figure. It stood, perhaps looking at him, or waiting for him. He had intended to loudly complain about his having been left to his own devices when he had expected to be treated with the deference due to his status. But his anger, instead of boiling up to bursting point, as he had hoped, was partially displaced by wariness and he said nothing, but waited hoping that the figure would soon reveal itself as some subservient type who would respectfully facilitate his encounter with some elevated official. But it just maintained a potent stillness in the lighted doorway. It neither spoke, nor moved, and acquired a greater air of importance by these omissions. Momentarily the circumstances of his finding himself in the ill-lit windowless chamber had slipped his mind. The figure, although it could not yet be described as menacing, was affecting his psyche in such a manner that he had lost his train of thought. The absence of his watch seemed to have disrupted the flow of time itself and with it the continuity of his stream of consciousness. He knew that he was here on some significant mission, but, purely because of the disturbing aura of this silent motionless figure, he could not recall the nature of the mission. All he could feel at that moment was hunger, thirst, and a profound unease but finally he mustered the courage to speak. All he could think of to say was: 'Is there any possibility of a cup of tea?'

Almost immediately the figure moved back from the door, leaving it open. He found the energy to follow it into the daylight. He expected some sort of urban scene, fashionable-looking people walking along with busy purpose. He found he was clutching a book, and suddenly remembered what he had been doing; he was to be interviewed about his second book titled: *Bend over Darling*. One critic had said, appetisingly '...his leading character makes the Yorkshire Ripper look like the hero of a Mills & Boon'. That had mollified his fears that he could never top the success of his first blockbuster, *Fuck my Old Boots*. In that he had enchanted the public and the literary establishment alike, with a scurrilous farrago of sexual violence beyond their wildest hopes.

Outside was no place that he recognised. A plain of greyish grass stretched out toward the horizon on all sides, like Dorothy's Kansas. But just outside the building was a table on which there was a tea tray with elegant cups like those his mother had loved. Sitting at the table the figure beckoned to him. It indicated the side of the little redbrick building from which he had emerged. Around the side came a woman, with a teapot, whom he recognised after a short moment of shock. The blood drained from his face, and his mouth went limp.

'Have a nice cup of tea, that'll make you feel better, darling!'

She poured him a cup. She was not as he had known her in the last days, blind and suffering from bed-sores. She was the beautiful lady of his boyhood, the lady whose compassion engulfed the universe, and whose love and care for him was unique and eternal.

'There's nothing to worry about darling, it's just a one in a million chance for us to see you. That what we've been told.' She gestured toward the figure. He looked but he couldn't really see it properly.

'What is the book you're holding darling? You always liked books didn't you?'

Before he had thought, he blurted out as his writers pride dictated:

'Oh this is the latest of my published works. I write books now. My last one is already a best-seller.'

'Oh, that's wonderful! I always *knew* you would be successful!'

Her face was as her face had been at his graduation, like a picture of innocent girlhood receiving a precious gift. 'Can I see it, then. It's so exciting!'

A sudden knowledge of what was at stake paralysed him. He found himself discreetly keeping the title from his mother's sight.

'Oh not just yet Mum, its better to just talk after so long. How are *you*, Mum, you look so well!'

'I am very well darling; of course we can leave the book till your father comes, if you'd prefer'

'Yes, Mum'

He didn't mind if his father saw it. He wanted him to see it. It would do him good; the sanctimonious old poseur.

'Oh here he comes; he will be so thrilled that you have done so well.'

He turned, trembling as if he was eleven years old, and saw his father. His stern, lined face was suffused with joy at the sight of his beloved son. It was as if he had never seen his father before. How kind and honest he looked.

'Show Dad the best-seller you've written darling.'

No way could he bear to extinguish the love and pride in his father's face for all eternity.

He turned to the only one he could, and it got up and walked toward the door from which they had emerged. He followed it into the blackness.

*

'You're as right as rain now old chap.'

The dark doctor looked at him.

'Count my fingers.'

He had no conscious memory of anything after setting out that morning in confident spirit. He counted the eight fingers that the doctor held up.

'Eight'

'Yep! Right as rain now: but you were dead there for a while – heart stopped. But we got your heart going and your breathing just when it looked hopeless. Look where you're going when you next cross the road – don't be so eager.

'I'll try harder'

'Looks like it's you, on the back of the books you were carrying. Doing well with those aren't you?'

'Have you read them?'

The doctor grinned under his bushy moustache.

'Nope – just the blurbs; one man's meat and all that...'

As he lay recuperating he knew things had to change. He didn't know why – just somewhere, presumably, where his conscience had led him. For some reason he kept thinking about Mum...and more unusually his father. He must acquire fame with more ennobling work. But that wasn't going to be so easy.

23 A Bad Journey

I was already late, having been stuck behind a tractor for ten miles or so, and I knew that there would be an attempt to exploit my absence if I arrived after they started. There were recent studies that appeared to support their scepticism, and I needed to get in with the line I had worked out, before they started their brazen opportunism.

The guy must have heard my car in the distance long before I started hooting, which I did when I was still a hundred meters away from him. I didn't realise he wasn't going to move until too late. I took some steps to miss him, but the road was too narrow to avoid him by swerving. It was his own fault, and his stubborn stupidity proved his undoing. There was a thud and he got flipped over the hedge. It's typical the way these things happen at the worst possible times, but as I assessed the situation I came to the conclusion that no real damage was done; I obviously didn't have time to stop and in consequence I soon found I was making up the time that I had lost due to the tractor.

I parked in a dark and deserted street near he chember, and noticed that there was a dent in the plastic bumper, but I easily pushed that back out with the jack handle and it popped back into place. I then wiped some extraneous material that had been smeared across the bonnet in a trajectory from roughly where the dent was, to the place where it disappeared; it was too late to worry about it now and I only had to carefully wash my hands once I arrived and the world was more or less as it has always been.

I scotched their little game with some statistics which they were incapable of understanding, and pointed out that their stance was a blatantly self-serving act which would have severe consequences for us all, a fact that would not be forgotten when the chickens came home to roost.

On the way back I listened to a beautiful concert coming directly from the Albert Hall. It was very late when I got home, but my wife had waited up for me to commend me for my speech which she had heard on the ten o'clock news. We took a glass of port each and looked out over the marsh. In bed I did momentarily recall the unpleasant event of my journey, but couldn't help recalling that the chap looked very like someone I had seen at a Britain First rally earlier in the summer anyway.

24 The Alien Alien

Have you read all that stuff about alien visitors, Roswell and so on? Well I can tell you that those of us who know, have been mixing with aliens for some time. It isn't worth going into in any great detail, but you should know that they have been here for years - since just after the Second World War, in fact. You only find out about them if they want you to. I have to deal with them. It's been a bit cloak and dagger. They appear where they say they'll appear, they buy what they want - I won't go into what they want, they wouldn't like it. They seem very like us, no tentacles, no green skin, nothing obvious – just a little bit foreign, in a clever sort of way. And their fingernails are more substantial than ours, and slightly pointed – hardly noticeable if you don't look very carefully. They tell me that their studies show that the humanoid form is the only one that works for intelligent beings on planets like theirs and ours: inevitable convergent evolution it seems. They even have monkeys where they come from as well, carnivorous ones though, they said. Before he came I had thought of it as if I had just been dealing with the Chinese – or even the Americans. But I'll tell you something: they are alien alright, alien to the core as I now know.

I was asked to have a chap stay with me for a couple of weeks. When he arrived he told me would he use the name Sharpe, which he said was the English word for his real name. He seemed all very civilised and sensible - well able to take care of himself. He appeared to know what he was doing. He was very interested in everything – us and the world we have made, like a businessman on some sort of secondment, behaving like a tourist. He seemed to know a lot about us, but gradually I came to suspect that there were fundamental misunderstandings. I must say that from the first he reminded me of a cat more than a monkey, carnivorous or otherwise. Not in any obvious way, just his personal mannerisms. He usually sat very still, his eyes looking almost out of focus, but as soon as he wanted to do anything, however trivial, he would spring to life very suddenly in a smooth and almost silent manner. But that wasn't enough to make him seem any more alien than many people with other personality traits in I knew. I was also stunned by his physical skills: I taught him to play squash, at which I am a competent player, and he thrashed me of the court in the first game, after only a very few mistakes in the first exchanges.

The first thing that really got me thinking was innocent enough. As we were driving home from the site, on a rainy evening, we passed a motorcyclist on a low-powered bike. He looked elderly and poor. Sharpe suddenly tensed up and looked at him with an excited and concentrated gaze. As can happen occasionally and partly because Sharpe's subtle movement had distracted me I went a little closer to the rider than I had intended. After I quickly steered the car away from the moped Sharpe turned to me with a strange expression. One I couldn't read.

'I expected him to get off the road when he heard us coming. You could have got him, no-one would've seen; you would probably have killed him stone dead!'

I was puzzled by the way he expressed himself in suggesting that I hadn't taken adequate care.

'Oh I was reasonably clear of him, he was quite safe.'

He nodded slowly, but to my eyes uncomprehendingly. I didn't really think he knew what I meant. I drove on, and we spent the evening as usual. Mostly he worked all the time. I found myself thinking about the incident, and wondering whether in fact he had been expressing surprise that I hadn't deliberately knocked the poor chap off his moped. I dismissed that idea – realising that perhaps his body language and style of speech would naturally be different from mine. And I *had* gone rather close to the rider. Around the same time another misunderstanding occurred when, as he occasionally did, he was watching the TV. He called to me and I saw that he was watching a hospital sequence in which they were attempting to resuscitate an old man. He was in his more animated mood and asked if they were trying to kill the man: 'Of course not!' I replied. He nodded again, looking a little puzzled.

A few days later, he saw me watching one of those programs where real life emergencies are sorted out. A disabled man had been on a climb, raising money for a charity. He had slipped and broken his ankle. Sharpe saw a helicopter winching the man to safety from the rock he'd been trying to climb. He seemed fascinated, and when I explained it to him he started to laugh. He seemed to find the situation utterly hilarious, especially the last scene. When he saw the brawny air-sea rescue man lift the injured climber to safety, he went into near paroxysms of laughter. He put aside his work and watched the remainder of the program. He found most of it amusing but nothing quite matched his response to that first item. He asked if I could transfer the program from my hard disk to a USB, telling me that he wanted to take one with him when he went back when he went. I supposed, he would take a laptop, or they would devise some way of using it when he got home – their technology was streets ahead of ours so I copied it for him. After this he always made a point of watching that particular series and getting it put on to USB. He would chortle away through all sorts of terrifying ordeals – but it was always the final rescue that sent him off into hysterics,

These incidents were disturbing enough to me. But it was something more tangible that finally caused me to feel a real fear and suspicion of *them*. On the last but one day of his visit we had a pub meal which he had asked about. As we strolled back we encountered by a harmless person, whom I often encountered and who was mildly deranged. He passed us - as he usually did – loudly braying: 'In the na-me of the law!' My companion became excited - not uneasy in any way - but alert and ready.

'That chaps abnormal isn't he? Calling out like that'

'Yes - he's harmless enough though.'

'Does he often pass this way?'

'Yes – he's as regular as clockwork – just about this time every night.'

Sharpe nodded. The next evening, which was the final one of his stay, he asked to go out to the same pub again, which was unusual for him. He didn't often want to repeat things – trying as he was to take in as much as he could whilst his visit lasted. Before we left, to my uneasy surprise, he put on a pair of menacing-looking hob-nailed boots, which he had bought that day, giving me a sort of knowing grin as he did so. In the pub, we enjoyed a drink, and a snack, and Sharpe rose to leave at more or less the same time as the night before. He dawdled along the road, as if he was waiting for something, and sure enough the deranged man appeared making his usual loud remarks and gesticulating at us.

Immediately Sharpe strode across to where the man was passing, and fetched him a colossal and athletic high kick with the hobnailed boot he had put on. It felled the unfortunate man instantly. He tried to rise, spitting out teeth and blood; Sharpe, ignoring my cries, kicked him again, in his face. He still moved until Sharpe gave him the *coup de gras*: a horrific kick that left him motionless in the gutter. These proceedings had brought the strange chant to an end and we left the man.

For reasons you might guess I could do nothing; I couldn't attract attention to Sharpe. I felt extremely uneasy; Sharpe would surely know that having seen the outrage I might be tempted to report him to some authority, thereby blowing the whole gaff once and for all. What might he do, to circumvent this possible disaster for him and his colleagues? I needn't have worried. When we got home, I asked Sharpe why he had done it – perhaps in a slightly censorious voice, as we had a last whisky before turning in. He replied in amazement: 'What d'you mean why? *I* didn't know *you* wanted to. There's no need to be annoyed! I'd have let *you* do it if you'd said. I assumed you let *me* because I was your guest!'

Next day, to my relief, he was gone - his work done. I was well paid. I bought a new house, a new car - a Mercedes - and a whole cellar of fine wines. They didn't bring the satisfaction I had anticipated though. I fear there may be trouble ahead, bad trouble. I should notify someone – but I daren't. All I can do is throw this tale into my next story collection.

25 What would *you* have bloody-well done?

We were in Newcastle.

'We're going to have to *recover* the situation' Millman had said. He was putting it mildly. We knew the methods. With this man we tried almost every one. He had evidently been trained to resist anything. We took it in short shifts. I'm not squeamish; I used to watch a lot of gory films in my youth and when, because of my intelligence corps background, I was approached, I accepted, after I heard all the sophisticated ethical arguments which Millman put to me.

'Just theory; there's little chance we'll ever need to do it,' he had said. We had only been trained on water boarding. But so had our man and he always came up smiling. He knew we couldn't drown him. But we had further resources. We had been encouraged to do our own 'contingency research' on the subject. All the things man has done to man down the aeons. 'This is entirely down to you; you just have to grasp the enormity of the threat. There's no time. You're taking the decision not us. It will be left to the individual operative to weigh the pros and cons, decide on a course of action, and implement it. There will be no official involvement. This conversation never took place.' Millman went on.

When the time came, it was hard for us and harder on him. In my breaks I used to think of my mother, who was so proud when I got a degree at that fifth-rate university. I should have refused point blank, shouldn't I?

We had less than two and a half hours. But he did break, finally, after I'd done some terrible things to him and then run out of options, except one. I wondered who else hadn't had that conversation with Millman. But at the last a barbaric act was to be played out by me, on my own initiative. When his first-born was ushered in I saw an expression I hadn't seen before on his face. He usually wore a sly smile when he wasn't in distress from one of our interventions. Now it vanished. I prayed he would break at that moment, but he didn't. Perhaps he would have in time, but there *was* no time. The longer I hesitated, the more confidence returned to his stubborn features. There was now only the last futile hope that actual bloodshed might do the trick. My destiny had arrived. I did the unholy thing. Out of the blue he balked when the second one was led in.. Perhaps he hadn't believed anyone in our civilised democratic country would do it; or perhaps the second one was that special one that many parents have. Anyway I didn't have to pull the trigger again. As she was brought in, before she saw the mess, he screamed the word 'No!'

By then there was an hour and fifteen minutes, but his directions were clear and they found it right in the centre - a Russian one - old and crude, but of apocalyptic power, hidden in an old disused sewer under the Tate Modern. They had got it there part by part over four years. Their faith in God had kept them going they said. The public were shown endless clips of the bomb-disposal heroes who made it safe - brave army men working under extreme pressure: God was not mentioned. Not much was said about how they found it. If they hadn't there would have been no complaints from 'disgusted' of Tunbridge Wells in *The Times* – there wouldn't have been a Tunbridge Wells, or The Times either.

Go on then. Bite the bullet. What *would you* have bloody-well *done*?

26 Little Red Riding Hood

What did happen all those long years ago? People have come from far and wide to interview me – as they did those stupid girls who took pictures of fairies. Urgent questions, on and on. It served me right for not telling the truth when I went back to Mamma that day. She excitedly blabbed it all around the area and soon I was besieged with people who were desperate to find out the 'truth'. At first they thought it was a case of lycanthropy – it was widely accepted in those days. But even they were not naive enough to believe in a talking wolf – any more than you are, hopefully! Did it look like anyone I knew? Did it have pink eyes like Dermot, the idiot savant who lived with his father – the woodman? Etc. Then came some monks who thought some local saint often appeared in the form of a wolf to help lost travellers. They tended to downplay the fact that I had originally said that it had devoured my grandmother.

After them came the most persistent seekers after the 'truth' of all. Luckily, by that time I was a big girl and I knew all about the dirty deeds they had in mind, and I didn't need the rude little dolls they brought with them to understand their persuasive questioning. They were divided into two camps. Some were sure I knew the wolf's true identity, but was covering for him because he had threatened me with dire consequences if I let the cat out of the bag. I preferred that group; they seemed more open-minded. The second group were sure it was the huntsman. Well they soon got it out of me that I often spoke to him on the way to my grandmother's, and that he had once given me two ounces of dolly mixture which came out of his own ration book. And he had come to the house that day: to give grandmother two rabbits he had killed, and to show me how to skin them. Of course he was arrested, but after a long interval, when they never got me to say that he had done anything, they finally let him go. Looking back, I can see that he was about seventeen, and it must have been hard for him. I never saw him again. After that, things began to die down, although an animal rights group threw manure at me when I re-enacted my foolish tale at a pageant.

The last thing was a resurgence of the abuse business, but now my grandmother was in the frame. It seems in the great struggle for equality, we women are beginning to do our bit even in this sphere. Luckily for her she had died before the furore began, and I guess the seedy looking guy who was on that assignment thought that might mean I would badmouth her memory for the price he would give for the story. I didn't though.

Well you want to know what really happened, don't you? And you are afraid I will say 'Nothing at all – just a nice stroll through those idyllic fairytale woods.'

Well I did see a wolf that day: a dying one – shot by the huntsman with his crossbow. My frail old grandmother and he were standing looking at it. My grandmother beckoned me. 'There: he is dead now. The woods are safe for all the little girls and boys. There are no wolves now in the forest.' I saw that a tear had appeared on the huntsman's cheek. 'Don't be so sentimental,' my grandmother said. 'It was an old wolf – it would have died soon anyway.' I looked into its eyes, so calm and grave.

'What big eyes it has, Grandmamma.'

'Yes, and it has big teeth too. Big enough to have eaten you with them, if it could!'

Its sad eyes slowly closed, and its panting stopped.

'But why did we kill it if it would have died anyway?'

'In the end, child, it's them or us, and all the lions, tigers and bears will go the same way, until one day *we* go the same way. That's the way the world is, now and ever shall be, world without end. Now be quiet, and we will go and have those two nice rabbits for lunch.'

That's what happened that day. That night I told my tale; it was the only way I could deal with the horror of it all.

27 Tick Tock Man

My epiphany happened whilst I was lying on my bed, passing the time, having been sent to my room by my wife. Part of me was waiting to see if I would be called to dinner, but as I often do, I was also letting my mind range over a number of interesting issues, with only the ticking of the clock to break the slightly oppressive silence. It was during this incarceration that a thought struck me that gave me that sense of worth, that welling up of self-esteem that marks our arrival as a significant player in the human firmament.

How had I ended up in that unenviable situation? I don't mean that particular episode. My wife is a very intelligent and reasonable person, and only rarely uses this particular sanction. But I have not fulfilled my potential, generally. I think I got off on the wrong foot at the beginning. It was my name that did the damage, I'm almost certain of that. I was christened Herbert! Herbert Littlehampton. I think my father was instrumental in bringing this about. It was an unconscious Freudian blow struck by the castrating male, against his replacement, the carrier of the alien genes that had cast him with too great a likeness to his mother. He himself was well placed to understand the effect of his sly manoeuvre.

He was called Charles, and must have spent his life between the roles of the powerful, slightly pompous Charles – a hard one to sustain – and the hopeless comical nincompoop Charley. Probably he constantly resented the fact that he had not been born in the United States, where there was the third, infinitely preferable option, of Chuck. Chuck is a tough no-nonsense male, attractive to women, competent, able to choose any job: test pilot, lumberjack, or leader of a band of marines called Chucks Cheetahs. But compared to me, Dad had it easy. Even the *full* name Herbert is a name for an awkward, clumsy loser. 'Look at that Herbert' people exclaim when a runner, already well behind the pack trips over the water jump, in a steeple chase. Or 'we don't want that Herbert ruining everything' when one attempts to join an informal group of what one had thought of as like-minded people. Inevitably, in the forces I became a tick-tock man – the appellation one acquires from marching with the arms in the same movement as the legs instead of in a contra movement. And all because, feeling awkward about my name, I couldn't relax into the true marching gait. There you are, then, that's how I became a tick-tock man: it seems a co-incidence now that my world has changed so rapidly. But thus I remained as I minced stiffly along in the temporal flow of life.

'Well change your bloody name!' you say? You think I haven't done that? All you have to do when you turn up in a new community is say 'I'm Harold', and you'll become Harry, or better still Hal. But it doesn't make a scintillion of difference. They may not know I'm a Herbert, but I do – that's the problem. You are what you think you are. You're English if you think you are. Or you are Irish if you think you are. I had a school friend, Declan, whose great grandmother had been Irish. He spent his time boning up on Finn McCool, King James' rebellion and the Black-and Tans, and tried to learn to play hurley (in Penge, mark you) as well as talking about 'You English' in reference to the potato famine and the Troubles. And he was always fooling around with shamrock on the appropriate occasions.

Silly, you think? Not at all! He was Irish, because he thought he was. But no matter how many Herberts there are they will never form a group with any of the solidarity Declan felt with the Irish. In fact I only ever met one other Herbert, and the last thing I felt was any solidarity with *him*. And I only came across one Herbie and no Berties whatsoever. I didn't like the Herbert because I could see he was a bit like me, an archetypal Herbert: tall and gangly, self-conscious with a goofy expression. He thought I was called Hal, and I played up his name, pronouncing it with mocking emphasis. The Herbie's name wasn't Herbert, it was some Hebrew name, and therefore he had no shame in his name at all. Being Jewish didn't cause him any grief either – he was a jack-the-lad type, and he would pounce on any whiff of anti-Semitic talk with gusto, quickly intimidating the offender, hinting darkly that his compeers in the East End would be glad to pay a visit and robustly explain his mistake. There were of course no groups of menacing fellow Herberts to fall back on in my case. As for Berties, they went out of fashion a hundred years ago. But they would have been no use to me. Who is a Bertie? The weedy butterfly who grovels around the hero in a twenties musical, usually ending up marrying a loud American comedienne, that's who. No, until I made my great discovery there was no escape. But there was an escapement, oh yes!

As I listened for the sound of my wife's movements metamorphosing into the more harmonious symphony of forgiveness, I monitored the ticking of the clock. And like Aristotle leaping from his bath, I suddenly sprang up in a high voltage shock of enlightenment. The clock! It doesn't do what they say. The fools! The clock does *not go tick tock!* Careful listening had made me realise that each sound is slightly different, probably recycling as the escapement wheel completed one revolution! Of course I was overjoyed: the long years in the wilderness might be coming to an end! Later I examined the whole escapement system, and confirmed my suspicions, in engineering terms, in psychic terms, and most of all in social terms. But at this joyous moment I went straight downstairs without waiting to be called from my exile – such was the effect of my discovery on my confidence. My wife looked surprised – perhaps even a little intimidated by my sudden eruption, but she said nothing.

'I've just made the discovery of a lifetime' I gushed. 'I am the only man in the world who knows that clocks don't really go tick-tock.'

'Well what do they go then?' she asked with some asperity. 'Tock-tick I suppose'

'No, it's far more *complicated* than that. And I'm going to start by writing to the *New Scientist* about it.' I retorted.

'What a fool you are!' she said, as she often does. 'No editor in his right mind is going to publish a boring triviality like that! Anyway you'd better go back upstairs.'

Of course this was a setback, and as I went up to my room I did have just a momentary doubt about the discovery. I listened again to the clock, and found I could switch easily between its own real rhythm so complex and seductive and the maddening repetitive monotony of the sound which all other people on earth were constrained to hear by their upbringing and routine habits of thought. But not I: *I* and only *I*, was free of the coils of time, inexorably propelling us to our doom.

My wife turned out to have been wrong. I aimed my letter at *The Last Word* section of the NS, and they published it under the name Harold Lancing. And it has been cited! I am Harold now, and Harold isn't an easy man to cope with. Freed from the pedestrian flow of time, and from my former ridiculous name, I strut around like a rooster and refuse to go to my room when told to do so. I have bought an SUV and I drive it around in an intimidating manner, ignoring my wife's screams when I cut up the lorries as they thunder down to the docks; I screech to a halt at zebra crossings, and play chicken with any car approaching me when there is no room for two cars in a side street. All around, I see you helpless lemmings in the thrall of the great Tick-Tock man waiting in the sky with his scythe. You may have suppressed a snigger when you thought of me cowering in my room, but know now, that only *I*, Harold Lancing, float free of the tyranny of time. See how your world has changed, how you are all revealed for what you are, yes, you, not I, are the tick-tock people. So tick-tock on, go about your inconsequential tick-tock lives like the clockwork soldiers you are, tick-tock, tick tock, a never ending stream of tick-tock people feeding the tin-souled tick-tock society that you were bound to create. As for her...tick-tick-tick-tick-tick...

28 The Fifth Planet

John looked out over the world, as he could see it. His name wasn't literally John, but John will do. The sun was lowering in the sky, spreading long shadows across the rolling landscape, and beautifying it as it always did at that time. All was right with the world. His children were grown up - apart from Alex - and their careers were satisfactory. His wife was a loving partner, supporting him in his work. And the great telescope array was complete - the first light had already bounced off the multi-mirrored reflectors. The signal processing project of which he was the leader was about to be put to its greatest test. Only one tiny fly in the ointment remained. David, his great rival was about to test his theories of the fundamental nature of matter, using the equally prestigious and equally new collider. Somehow, somehow, he would upstage John - he always did. It was John's recurring nightmare.

John locked his office and walked across the balmy quadrangle, looking at the flowers as he always did. He felt that he was at one with the beauty of nature, in a way that David was not. David was a sort of hooligan he thought. Not in the rough way of a manual labourer, but in a kind of insensitivity to the world - to the needs of the planet. Driving through the falling dusk John saw, away to his left the huge structure on top of the mountain where the observatory was located. Standing up, like a surrealistic addition to a landscape painting, the housing the telescopes was hard to comprehend so out-of-scale it seemed compared to the surrounding terrain and its tiny buildings. He felt a deep satisfaction accompanied by a thrill of excitement. The secrets of the universe would soon unfold before this giant eye whose existence was entirely due to John's determined labours. Now no-one, not even David could stop it. There could be no problem - any of the mirror elements could be replaced at short notice. They could adopt any shape. The software might have bugs. It could be fixed. Only the signal processing philosophy was untried. But it had been tested, and had triumphantly succeeded on a small telescope - small by comparison - a mere three hundred inches. It had been orders of magnitude better than the existing system, which itself had mollified the effects of the worlds very thick atmosphere sufficiently to render the use of the 300inch mirror possible. But would it work with the new telescope which dwarfed the smaller instrument by orders of magnitude? He had little doubt. The lights in the houses were on as he parked beside his home. Inside things were as always - his return welcomed, his wife and son peacefully occupied.

Over dinner Alex questioned him about the Telescope Array. 'Its tomorrow that it is going to be tested, isn't it Dad?'

'Yes it is son: it will be the greatest day of my life!'

'What will be the first science it does?'

'Well, the theoreticians can't wait to have it peering to the end of the universe. They expect to finally discover its origins. But of course it has to be tested, and that's the job of the engineering team. And I can point it at anything I like. I've worked on this for seventeen years. I guess I've a right to know the worst.'

'What will you point it at, Dad? Planets – stars: galaxies?'

'Well I leave all the galaxies to the cosmologists! But I aim to take a first look at some planets. That's what I was attracted to from boyhood. I intend use the time to look at our neighbours; a quick look at the Big Planet and the Red Planet - then ... the Blue planet! There's water all over that – and it's almost certain it has vegetation. But I'll be able to see it! The first man to see life on another planet! And David will have to admit defeat for once. Ever since he won the Academy Physics prize ahead of me for his PhD he always manages to upstage me. But he can't this time. I know he's rushing his collider tests to try to get in first – but he can't. And there's absolutely nothing he can do once I see what I'm hoping to see on the Blue World. He will never be able to bear it. And what could he possibly do with that stupid collider that anyone in the world will understand apart from the few physicists who speak that nonsensical gobbledygook? They told us all that when they confirmed the existence of the God particle they would know what the universe was made of. They didn't, of course, so then they started talking about the Infinity particle - that's how David got the money for his Infinity collider. No, after tomorrow he will be forgotten. And so will all the geeks who want to use my telescope to waffle away about the Big Bang and try to tell us where the universe came from. But my discovery…my discovery!

'Dad; these *are* the questions that mankind must address! It's the secret of the universe. Yet you belittle them, and you are a scientist.'

'Yes, you are right son. I sometimes let that feud with David get the better of me. If only I knew he wasn't going to get his shot in first!'

'They're not going until day after tomorrow, Dad, according to Peter. So If your telescope works your announcement will come the day before' Peter was David's son, who was Alex's peer at school.

'What's that? The day after tomorrow! That swine...he just can't resist trying to steal my thunder. One day of fame, that's all he wants to give me. But he may be shooting himself in the foot this time. Who cares if he turns up yet another stupid new particle, it won't cut any ice with the public if I can do what I think I can!'

*

The next evening, as the stars came out, John was at the controls of his new telescope array - for the first and probably the last time. After the official opening it would be booked solidly by cutting edge researchers, with no slots for ageing professors, long since out of touch with the coal-face. Tonight however, it was his.

There was no skill needed - he had but to type the co-ordinates of any point in the sky - or better still a name - the interface was as user friendly as that.

He typed a name, and the Big Planet appeared on the consoles. No bigger than it might appear in the field of view of any of the big reflectors. But with almost trembling hand John started the zoom function and he felt himself to be traveling toward the great yellowish belted globe. It was at its aphelion, and yet the clouds of gas gradually resolved into towering columns and plumes of turbulent-looking vapor, hanging before him. Finally the zoom stopped at its maximum, and he stared at the silent majesty of the scene. And before his eyes he could see the slow but unmistakable movements of the billows of gas that he watched. He recorded still frames, and movie clips - the first sight of the Big Planets living atmosphere.

Would that be enough? He hoped so. But he turned now to the Red Planet. This was the nearest prospect. It had ice-caps, and changed seasonally. But even on the lowest magnification he could see that the planet was obscured by one of its intermittent atmospheric disturbances. It appeared a featureless disc, with only the polar caps discernible from the rest of the blandly pink surface. Was there really anyone there?

So at last he turned to the Blue World. It floated into the screen, its blue seas white clouds and greeny brown land masses surely a sign of an environment where life might have sprung up. He might see signs...unmistakable signs. Even individual creatures if they were big enough; very big. He zoomed on one of the greenish areas. Without bothering to look at any lesser magnification he set for its ultimate limit - nearly a million to one. The hundreds of mirror elements all turned and deformed in perfect harmony, and the signal processors applied their miraculous non-linear time varying filtering to cancel out the effects of the planets thick atmosphere. In an instant he was gazing in mesmerised wonderment at what he saw. His whole being vibrated with excitement as he made the most important discovery the world had ever known. He saw an unmistakable forest of trees lining a shore, all in exquisite miniature. A world of life! A thousands-of-years-old question answered in a few seconds. And he, John, was the only one in the world who knew. His fame was assured. His telescope had earned its huge cost in its first few seconds. And in the next few it made another discovery, which completely overshadowed the first. He noticed a long shape, and as he watched it moved like an insect. A long neck and a long tail, it was surely some huge beast moving slowly along the alien shore of the Blue World. Then he saw another, and another: a herd of monsters each maybe thirty meters long. There *were* living beings on the Blue World, across the emptiness of space. He gazed upon the scene, directing the gargantuan telescope to follow the progress of the creatures. 'I have done this thing' John said, out loud. 'We are not alone. One day we shall visit the Blue World, and the expedition will be named in my honour.'

The news broke the following day, and by the evening John was the most famous scientist who had ever lived on the fifth planet - or ever would live, as it turned out, although an even more momentous discovery was made that very day.

He sat before the cameras, ready to answer the questions that he would soon be asked. He had eclipsed David once and for all. David was preparing to fire up his exorbitantly funded hadron collider, surely aware that his silly gamble had come unstuck. Who would care what stupid particle he collided with what, or what happened when they did? Not when he had seen and filmed the giant lizard on the Blue World steering ponderously along that strange alien shore.

'Tell me John; tell me how it feels to have made the most important scientific discovery of all time?' John was ready to speak to the television journalist modestly but honestly about the momentous results of his work. He savoured the coming moment of his life – its high point. David would have died rather than live to see this broadcast, he was sure. But for once there was nothing, absolutely nothing David could do! He opened his mouth to speak, but he never got the chance.

On the Blue World, in the middle of the night, a giant saurian lifted its head, woken from its sleep, raising its long neck like a great serpent, disturbed by the premature arrival of the day. An uncomprehending fear came to it when it saw the strangely bluish sun that was already in the zenith. It was many days before it became dark enough for the creature to attempt sleep again. Davis had had the very last laugh.

Millions of years later an astronomer on the Blue Planet puzzled over the gap in the neat mathematical series that gave the positions of the planets. Finally he wrote 'Between Jupiter and Mars I put a planet.' The search was on. Soon a planet was found – a rather small one; then others. First dozens then hundreds then thousands: the shattered wreckage of the fifth planet – known as the asteroid belt.

29 Chiaroscuro

Once, in another time, another place, there were two large continents, separated by an ocean. Over the ages, two continents came to dominate them: Uscuro in one, and Chia in the other. Both were thickly populated lands, but Chia was larger, and had a larger population. Uscuro was a very well organised place, and had been the spearhead of the advance of technology and civilisation. But its factories had closed, and its farms were now mainly nature reserves where the Uscurons would reverently watch the workings of nature. Its cities were green and pleasant - almost like parks. There was peace and prosperity. Indeed the Uscurons lived what appeared to be almost ideal lives. They had all the gadgets one might need, to ease the chores and burdens of every-day existence. They had many ways of entertaining themselves, using electronic devices. Their means of communication were very advanced, and they used the most environmentally friendly means of transport to whisk them to the four corners of the earth to enjoy life, or conduct business. Each Uscuron had a very limited number of offspring and the population was stable at a number very suitable to the clean, green way that they felt appropriate.

Between Uscuro and Chia there was a good working relationship. The Chians were at a rather earlier phase of development than the Uscurons. Their attitude to threatened species of animal, for example, was rather suspect. The government, which liked to be on good terms with that of Uscuro, agreed that, for example, the lesser dwarf tortoise rat was in danger of becoming extinct and that all means possible should be taken for its conservation. In one part of Chia, though, the inhabitants had found that forty lesser dwarf tortoise rats, if put through a food mixer, could supply a nourishing glass of broth that would save a child from dying of an unpleasant disease. As this was the main region where these tortoise rats lived, it was a matter of great concern to the Uscurons. Children's reading courses were filled with tales of tortoise rats being saved from imminent death in Chia by the brave and enterprising actions of Uscuron schoolchildren.

The Chians were also a good deal less fussy about what came belching out of their factory chimneys than were the Uscurons - who had had to close most of their remaining factories for that reason. (The majority had already closed because the Chians worked for lower wages, and the Uscurons got all they needed from Chia.) Indeed the Chians had agreed to build factories with their polluting clouds well away from the borders with Uscuro on that account, which was part of the deal to transfer factories from Uscuro to Chia. The Chians made all manner of things - cars, radios, computers, toys, TVs, cameras, almost everything in fact. They weren't very good at designing things though, because they hadn't really got to that stage, so they built Uscuron designs under license.

The Uscurons had licensed so many things that were produced in huge numbers that they gained a lot of money from Chia manufacturing. They also picked up a lot of interest on the loans they had made to the industrious people of Chia, which had enabled them to set up all the factories in the first place. If one bought a TV for a hundred Uscuro dollars, at least eighty went for the

IP, the pollution taxation and the interest payments on the loans to the factories. Only about five dollars ended up at the factory - and the Chian who had assembled it got less than one dollar – he could hardly afford to buy the things he made. This meant that most of the TVs went to Uscuro. For some items the ratio was even greater - an A3, an older type rifle, for example cost the Chians fifty dollars altogether, of which only one dollar was production costs. This produced a huge bonanza in Uscuro, as the Chian government equipped their army with weapons, which replaced their home-grown muskets. They had quite a large army - The Right Hand of Darkness it was dubbed in Uscuro, where it was seen as an insurance against the social unrest that the government of Chia always seemed to fear. In Uscuro there was a small standing army, equipped with a lot of wonderful new weapons that were being invented on a daily basis by the ingenious engineers who found jobs in the arms industry in lieu of the now non-existent civilian manufacturing sector.

The situation remained like this for many years, with Uscuro existing on its knowledge, and Chia existing on its huge industrial and agricultural production.

One day a young man in the Uscuron defence department noticed that a Chian rifle that had been taken from an asylum-seeking Chian soldier incorporated some excellent modifications, giving it far greater accuracy, and a better range. These were exactly the developments planned for the A6, the next rifle to be adopted by the small, highly flexible, highly trained, highly mobile, superbly equipped Uscuron army. That they had been grafted on to the obsolete A3 was a tribute to the rapidly advancing skills of the Chian armaments engineers. But it was also discovered that this rifle had no license serial number on it. The Uscuron authorities found the latter development far more offensive than the former. Spies had discovered their new tricks: so what? They already had better ideas on the stocks. But manufacturing without a license - this was serious money! A commercial storm followed, but the Chians claimed that their modifications to the A3 meant that the A3 was a new rifle, the Z1, invented by them, and was thus not covered by the agreement. There were a number of other licenses that they did not wish to renew, since their modified variants seemed to them to be outside the scope of the former agreements. The Uscurons raised the matter at the highest levels: whatever the modifications there was 'background IP' to be considered. The big financiers of Uscuro started some belligerent talk. The Chians must be 'taught a lesson'. The Uscuron media began to say a lot of nasty things about Chia. Their simpler life-style was mocked. Their having imported all the manufacturing jobs from Uscuro - a sore point with the Uscuron hoi-polloi - was suddenly seen as an outrageous trick. The possibility of a trade war was floated. After all Chia depended on its huge exports to Uscuro for its rapidly improving economy. In government circles there was a considerable consternation. In the end, common sense prevailed, and a summit was arranged. Abe Seed, the President of Uscuro went personally to see Xy Zee the Chairman of Chia. President Seed was received with great honour, and the actual talks took place in a high, all glass, building, the conception of a brilliant young Uscuron architect.

Xy Zee could speak Uscuron, although President Seed could not speak any Chian languages. Xy Zee and Abe Seed dealt with a lot of the little problems that always occur between large neighbouring nations, and lots of positive joint statements were issued. But when the president raised the problem of the Z1 the chairman smiled sympathetically, but made a gesture of helplessness.

'We can't afford to pay the license fee for all those rifles, Mr. President' he said. 'There are just too many. Look!' He gestured behind the president. Abe Seed turned to look through the huge glass wall behind him. There, as the sun shone through the drizzle, was the Chian army or a large part of it - stretched out on a vast concrete plain; standing in serried ranks were soldiers, massed in their millions, farther than the eye could see, all holding a Z1. Their reflections in the wet concrete glittered in the lowering sunlight. The slight mist that arose from the ground was enough to prevent the president seeing the shores of this sea of riflemen, each standing as still as death, each with his rifle at port position. Above them flew squadrons of planes, all looking very like the latest Uscuron design; they had been assembling Uscuron aircraft for a few years now.

'The money due from the licensing of all those rifles - it's a lot of money, Mr Chairman.'

'It is a very great deal, Mr President. We understand why your newspapers are calling for a trade war…even some sort of …'

'Yes, Mr Chairman, I've seen the newspapers.'

'A trade war would be very expensive for us, of course, Mr President. We would hardly be able to pay the interest on our loans, even. We should not be able to pay for any new designs or new licenses. My son, for example, would have to wear plain roller-skates instead of Atomic Tortoise Speedsters, which would not please him. That is, of course, assuming immoral entrepreneurs did not supply copied transfers which were not of the official issue, in spite of the efforts that we would make to ensure

211

that this sort of thing did not happen. During a trade war this is always possible, I regret to say. Even your own great country would not find a trade war without some drawbacks, I think? The difficulty of becoming self-sufficient in manufacturing again would be very great. It might mean that your country would suffer some serious hardships in the almost complete vacuum that would appear, if we regrettably had to reduce, or even ban exports to your great country. '

'We don't want a trade war, Mr Chairman. Of course there are people calling for some sort of military demonstration, I regret to say.'

'I do not encourage that sort of talk in our media, Mr President. I point out that your country possesses more sophisticated military equipment than ours. They say we outnumber your army by twenty to one; that, even if your own superior equipment gave you a five to one advantage in hit rate, you would soon have nothing left. But I say that war is not good for anyone!'

'May we announce that there will be further discussions to clear up this point of licensing law?'

'We may indeed. And I am sure you agree that these discussions should include the arrangements for setting the license fees, and the interest rates. This is a subject of interest to both our great nations.'

Abe Seed wiped his brow with a handkerchief. He nodded pensively. The talks moved on to some less crucial issues, on which Chairman Xy was very accommodating. It was agreed, for example that forty-seven of the political prisoners in Chia would be released, and allowed to emigrate to Uscuro. Uscuron activists would be allowed to send representatives to the region where the tortoise rats were indigenous, and make representations on behalf of the tortoise rats. In future Chian exports would all carry labels to confirm that no cruelty to animals or children had been involved in their production. Uscuron inspectors could visit any factory or farm to verify the labelling, provided notice of intent were given in good time to allow manufacturing know-how and technical secrets to be suitably concealed. The period was to be determined by further, lower level, negotiations. In fact Abe got everything he had gone to get. There was to be no immediate change in the currently agreed licensing fees, interest rates, and pollution taxation levels. Even the Z1 would be licensed after all. The only things that he had given way on was changing one letter in the first and last paragraphs and one word in the second paragraph in the trade treaty which otherwise was allowed to stand exactly as before.

One sentence which formerly read 'License fees are to be determined by the licenser.' was changed by a single letter, only, the final 'r' becoming an 'e'. Lender was similarly changed to borrower in the paragraph relating to the interest on the loans. And finally the sentence that read 'The licensee is responsible for paying the pollution taxation raised in the country of the licenser' changed only the last letter of the second word to read 'licenser'. Xy Zee fully understood that President Seed would have difficulty passing the necessary bills through the Uscuron legislature, and agreed that no changes would be made for at least a year, and that the changes would only be valid if they were 'fair and reasonable'. If agreement could not be reached, the changes would be implemented on a purely temporary basis until a consensus *was* obtained. President Seed finally agreed and put his signature to the joint statement when he saw that Xy could go no further with his own ruling committee.

Even so, when Abe Seed got home there was a terrible outcry in the section of the press whose readers were deemed capable of understanding the significance of the changes. There was a lot of talk of boycotting Chian goods, but in the absence of any realistic alternatives, everyone from government downwards carried on buying toys, electronic gadgets, clothes, shoes, cars, tools, cranes, aeroplanes, ships and just about everything else from Chian manufacturers. This enabled them to continue in their near-utopian life-style. Behind closed doors the military looked at the logistics of the situation. President Seed suggested that it was now or never. But the generals, who had some statistics on the rapidly developing Chian military capability, soon convinced him that it should be never. Although most of the few remaining factories in Uscuro specialised in armaments their combined production was a drop in the ocean compared to that of Chia. Of course there was always the doomsday weapon. Banned in principle, it still lurked in silos up and down the country. But the Chians now had the doomsday weapon as well. And who wanted doomsday?

30 Basic Enfrazi

Preface

Many *enfrazi* enthusiasts from all over the country, and some from other parts of the world have written to me in recent years suggesting that I write a small pamphlet for the benefit of beginners, and to hopefully offer the benefit of my experience to those aspiring to a more advanced level. I hope my small effort will meet with their approval and be of interest to other readers.

Equipment

A lot has been written on the subject, and much of it nonsense. Some retail outlets offer to equip a newcomer to the activity with a surfeit of unnecessary clothing, apparatus and materials for astronomical sums, but I would not recommend wasting ones money in this way. All that is needed in my opinion is a stout pair of walking boots and a sharp pen-knife. Powder can be purchased from any good dental laboratory if it is desired, and a large shistle can be borrowed to scrape down any deposits formed during a jump. More affluent participants could use binoculars dusted with fungicide or even a lightweight oscilloscope provided it is washed down with Glauber's salt after each expellation (the word 'expulsion' should never be used in this context).

Materials

A number of commercially produced preparations can be purchased for a few pounds, but I always prefer to make up my own the night before a meeting. A kilogram of coconut fibre ground up with plenty of sharp sand and a fish-based paste can be added to a gallon of fairly concentrated potassium permanganate as a base. This should be boiled for three hours and the resulting roux placed in a couscouseire and steamed over a dilute solution of rabbit skin size for fifteen minutes. The resulting *blatten* can be pulled out into a brown pointed cylinder and forced through a manioc-colander (or a sieve will do at a pinch) into the characteristic blown-jets. After a half an hour they should be brittle enough to break - if not, there's nothing for it but to start again. The jets should now be ground into a fine powder and dissolved in sulphuric acid. The final solution should be stored in gutta-percha containers until required. A little egg custard can sometimes take the tartness of the flavour away, and facilitates the necessary adherence - I have used this tip, which I got from Wike Metz after my first national trial (many years ago!), and on every serious occasion since.

For revamping old runs I generally just use well-rotted horse manure from which the first fierce heat has gone, and spray it on through an Atkinson nozzle. This should be done well before the second outings, and in wet weather is probably better avoided altogether.

Finally for presentation quality single rubbers one should use either meringue or better still a pomade of tuberose, lavender or some such perfume. On no account should old cake decorations painted with Humbrol be used, as I have seen done on occasion.

Clothing

A word about clothing. Smart but workmanlike denims in grey or blue are my favourite, except for serious competition when livery can be worn, preferably student colours rather than the ceremonial which are unfortunately so popular today. Women should wear at least knee-length skirts stapled together along the hem to prevent embarrassment to onlookers during sudden polarity reversals, or air-funnel attempts. (My wife uses an old army ground sheet which I have had converted into a suitable garment.) Men should wear caps, not large broad-brimmed hats with plumage - these are likely to be damaged, and in any case can inconvenience ground-staff. Handkerchiefs should be kept in buttoned pockets so that they are not seen flying out of sleeves (or worse in the case of ladies) at the apogee of a hurl-jump.

Specimens should be retained in boxes for inspection by judges, not tossed away in delight, or thrust into pockets where they can suffer unnecessary discomfort.

All paraphernalia should be carefully collected at the end, and powder burned in a purpose-built incinerator which vents at least twelve metres above local roof height.

Operational Tips

Leaping on during the first pass should not be attempted by beginners, or those who suffer from blackouts or incontinence.

Double throws can best be attempted after one or more short whips, otherwise vomiting can follow.

A large specimen can be stunned with a lead-filled rubber truncheon, sprayed, and then thrown back against the boom, a procedure dear to the hearts of younger spectators.

Small specimens without markings need only be thrown once, but marked specimens are better thrown two or three times or if necessary, gassed.

Whilst opponents are planning, it is good manners to walk quietly away, only returning (on the catapult if desired) when the next essay is attempted. No points need be lost like this if prompt responses are made, and it is good etiquette.

Never let go during the acceleration phase of a triple pick up, or in the middle of a mixed salvo. I have seen trousers accidentally torn off in such cases, and there is seldom any success in the subsequent hosing.

PICTURES

Plate 1 shows Wike's body being retrieved from the moat - a sad occasion for us all. I may be seen second from the left sitting on a tricycle, in the skull cap and khaki drill shorts.

Plate 2, from 1947, shows a lady player in an inverted swallow. Costumes were less formal in those days!

Plate 3a shows a Chinese player, 'Looney' Lee, the first foreign winner of the championship in a full mud-ball strike. At the time he was not thought to have survived, and I was temporarily presented with the shield as shown in **Plate 3b**

Plate 4 The correct mounting stance. Note my left knee which comes on a level with my right ear, the sole of my right foot bent back level with my neck. The right hand encircles the lard slab and I am waiting to catch the third hook. The skull cap has protected my head from the manure-jet.

Plate 5 Players being violently expelled from the chimney during last year's final.

31 The Red Compulsion

Sentencing, the judge spoke more kindly than Laura had expected.

'The court has accepted your account of the assault as the truth. You have shown remorse, but have been unable to offer any motive for this senseless crime. You say that you had not the slightest intention of perpetrating the act as you entered the room. Yet according to the medical evidence the jar was hurled with a force on the limit of what a human being could impart. Your husband was unlucky in that he turned his head in trying to avoid the impact, which caused the missile to hit him in the temple. You have been rightly found guilty of manslaughter, but many questions remain unanswered.' Laura received a light custodial sentence. In jail she received several letters from Viola, and Glenda ostensibly expressing concern at the outcome of the affair, but with a subtle hint of approval.

Leonard looked up as Laura opened the door to the sitting room and looked in. 'I'm off - I might be a bit late, we're going for a drink afterwards. You needn't wait up' she said without a smile. He nodded. He had wanted to watch the late film but she mightn't be pleased to find him still watching TV when she got back. Oh well – he could watch *American Chopper* – that finished by ten and it was unlikely that she would appear before then.

The group were going to discuss Green Travel. That would take her mind off it – although ghostly greengages rose up in her minds eye for a few moments when she collected her thoughts. She had boned up on hybrid vehicles – none of the others would have a clue. Glenda would be stridently calling for an immediate moratorium on flying. Amongst the dire consequences of the global effect of reckless tripping-off on holiday in aeroplanes she had noted in a recent phone-call that: 'Studies show that in some tropical regions small lakes might boil in heat waves' What rubbish that sounded; but the mere word 'boiling' gave her an uneasy feeling. Laura felt that Glenda got pleasure from the idea that the better off members of the group would have to stop going off to places like Thailand for their expensive holidays And Viola would be asking everyone to sign a pledge not to have any more children. 'Western children consume more carbon per head than 40 children from Burkina Faso' she would probably say, as she usually did. What that had to do with Green Travel? She was looking forward to the debate next week though. 'This house believes that a rape suspect should be presumed guilty until proved innocent' Glenda would be hot on that.

What Glenda would say if she knew the struggle going on in her mind sent a shiver down Laura's spine. She would consider it high treason. She remembered one or two similar outré compulsions she had had at school, and how throwing her discus had always dissipated them. But she couldn't go back to that and become some monster on steroids.

Leonard settled in front of the TV 'What are you doing Pauly, wasting your -------- time out here? That --------- bike is gonna be ready by Thursday or you're out on your ------- ass.'

'I need time to visualise the...'

'You get f------ in there. Everyone else is working their ------- ass off and you're behaving like a ------- fairy.'

This was the business thought Leonard. That's what real men were about: cutting steel, welding, wiring up the electrics – swearing, farting and playing practical jokes on each other. And at the end – that beautiful chopper - this one was for Space-Race a private launcher company. All in a good cause too – to be auctioned for an anti-malaria charity. Still, he listened uneasily for any sound that could signal Laura's unexpected return. She hadn't specifically vetoed *American Chopper*, but there would be hell to pay if she caught him watching it. She would be having a cup of coffee now probably.

Sipping her coffee Laura felt very uneasy. The jam tarts were the last thing she wanted to see; just when she had put childhood delights to the back of her mind. She ate one so no-one would start asking questions, but found herself wondering whether the jam was home-made... no, no it was too awful. She felt as she imagined an alcoholic might feel as he hurriedly passed an off-licence. Things were better after the break. Her technical knowledge dazzled the others – she rolled *fuel cells*, *lithium hydride* and *Tesla* off her tongue and all were silenced except Viola who kept saying in a strident voice 'There's absolutely no technical solution to the environmental problem of cars; or the traffic jams. We've got to go back to horses.' 'Well I thought we'd just agreed that cows blow off more CO_2 than a Boeing 737' Glenda burst in. 'Surely horses fart just as much as cows?'

That would have left things on a good note but just before she left, she was handed a sheet of labels to print off the addresses in the database, for mailing the newsletter. As Laura looked at them a terrible shock went through her system. She seemed to see words like bramble-jelly and strawberry dancing on the blank labels. On the way back she though bitterly of Leonard. Of all the men she might have chosen he seemed to have been the worst possible. He was not the most exciting husband in the world, she had admitted to herself not long after they had married. That was putting it mildly. He was the most boring husband in the universe she now knew. He wouldn't talk – or if he did he only talked about the most uninteresting things. He wouldn't do anything – she had to *drag* him on holidays. And he would weakly agree with whatever deliberately provocative assertion she made. Luckily her career was making up for the deficiencies of her married life, with her professional life and her political activism

Leonard was already in bed by the time she got back. She saw his pathetic watercolour set-up in the utility room – careful conventional paintings of suburban buildings. Genteel Victorian ladies used to paint that sort of thing. Why couldn't he be a degenerate artist, like Kokoschka, who had painted himself with that frightening but thrilling rage in his eyes? She picked up the jar of water he had been using, opened the back-door and hurled it down the garden, enjoying the sudden exertion of her discus throwing arm. Her mother had done that once, with a rotten little ceramic marmalade pot her sister had made at evening class and sent to her as a cheap Christmas present. She shuddered again. She had been an obedient girl, and this episode had upset her. She had only known her mother as a kindly, loving person who had sacrificed everything for her family, and this flash of anger had been quite out of character, until the terrible day when her mother had left.

She got stuck for a while in a traffic jam and the stupid thoughts kept returning. She had a guilty yearning for those happy days in the sunny garden with washing fluttering in the summer breezes, her father poking around in the vegetable patch and her mother setting out an *al fresco* lunch for them all, after doing the ironing. And most of all helping her mother make ... in the afternoon. The happiest time of her life. She knew now from Glenda, Viola and the others that really it was a humiliating servitude for her mother. But still she recalled the smell of the fruit, the sealing of the jars, and her pleasure when her mother had praised her copper-plate writing on the labels.

When she got home. Leonard was thinking about ironing. He was pretending to be asleep. Laura had got Leonard to do her ironing when they had first met. He hadn't minded, there was something exciting about the little pile of variously coloured knickers on the top of the main body of items. But she had to show him what to do – he had never done it in his life. He recalled how she had taken a photograph of him, coming suddenly into the room with a camera. He hadn't had a clue why she did that. Now he knew. It was to show her friends she was starting him on the right foot.

Next day was Saturday and Laura's yearning for the long gone days when she had helped her mother home-making grew worse. Nothing Laura could do seemed to help. She started to print out the labels for the group, but as she was looking for a new ink cartridge a packet of rubber bands came to her hand. She stood up as if she had sat on a drawing pin. She glanced out the window for respite, and saw the red currant bushes in full mellow fruitfulness, glowing in the autumn sunshine. She hastily looked away, as Leonard came into the room.

'I can't find my jam jar – didn't leave it in here did I?' he said looking perplexed.

'Oh, for God's sake' Laura answered in a tone of controlled irritation.

'Well never mind he answered – I'll get one of the ones in the garage where we put the things we got from your mother's house once I get back from shopping. There were a lot of jam jars amongst that lot.'

Laura winced, said nothing, but sighed noisily. The very mention of jam jars was a trial to her now.

When he had gone she sat rigid at the desk. She was sweating, and her heart was beating rapidly. She would go and throw the lot away, once and for all. She went to the garage and opened the boxes; a whiff of the smell of her mothers house triggered more memories. And the first thing she saw was a packet of jar covers, with a red fruit pattern – red currants it seemed. Her resolve dissolved. One or two couldn't hurt she thought. She knew what she needed, starting with one pound of red currants. A feeling of blessed relief surged into her, and she hurried into the garden with a saucepan. She would have to be quick, and keep the extractor on to get rid of the smell. As she worked she brooded on the horrors of it all. She blamed Leonard; and her mother. She knew the group would despise her for reverting to the very archetype of the submissive woman. Well at least *he* wouldn't dare open *his* stupid mouth. All went well and the evidence was gone by the time he returned.

Next morning Leonard was sitting in an armchair reading the TV Times when Laura opened the door with something in her hand. She looked decidedly peculiar.

'Would you like to try some of this jam I made,' she asked, in a brittle voice, thrusting a pot of home made jam towards him. He felt confused – as if it was their anniversary and he had forgotten it. He put on an idiotic smile, but he felt distinctly uneasy. 'Making jam at last?' he said, a simpering patronising expression coming onto his face. She saw a blinding flash and her discus-throwing arm gave huge convulsive jerk.

She looked in horror at his still, white form – his face at peace for the first time since their early days of love and kindness.

32 No Guarantees

It was the final straw. I saw her talking to her tutor in the corridor outside the computer-science lecture theatre when I came out. Looking at him was bad enough. A typical arts type, sailing along on the hot gas which so captivated his young female students. Even the set of his legs in their casual corduroy, infuriated me. His easy over-flexible lips were weakly yet assertively generating a smelly stream of self-serving unfalsifiable bullshit, in a fruity and sonorous whine. But that was nothing compared to my feelings as I looked at her. Her cool, intelligent and sensitive features were completely focussed on what the noxious old fraud was spewing out. The tiniest touch of a pink flush glowed over her high, noble cheekbones. It went through my gizzard like a red hot poker. Not that she displayed any of that loopy, smitten puppy-dog expression that half the girls on the programming option directed at me. They couldn't help it, and I let them down as gently as I could, but what a contrast was Heather. I was sure the beginnings of some kind of crush on this married poseur were burgeoning in her heart. Yet her features remained strong, her eyes bright and sparkling with no faked up fluttering, her lips gently closed in a half quizzical smile, her raven hair being softly but maddeningly ruffled by the breeze in the corridor.

Something had to be done. And that Irish witch Morna was the answer. A scrawny swarthy creature, a trainee banshee from the Bog of Allen, she had told me she could put a hex on anyone. 'You English are too set in your simple beliefs' she told me over the bar in the pub where she worked. 'The world wasn't made for you to map out like your own back yard as you're finding out. 'I can call up spirits from the vastly deep!' she said her goblin face breaking into a grin as she quoted Owen Glendower from Henry IV. I surprised her by getting the next line – spoken by Harry Hotspur: 'Aye, and so can I, and so can any man, yet do they come when you do call for them?' This sally from a rigid steel souled engineering type gave her a shock, and for a moment her guard went down. She had contempt for all the men around the university, and I was no exception. But just for an instant she looked at me with interest, but only made herself look more like an undernourished harpy than ever. She knew I was head over heels about Heather. Her parting shot as I left the bar was a mocking reminder of my plight. I was in the pub because I knew Heather went there on a Friday night, and this one was no exception.

'Well you can come sniffing around here on a Friday night from now till the cows come home, but she still wouldn't touch you with a barge pole' she said as I hovered to hear her sneering words. 'Unless, of course, you want me to ensnare her for you, which could be done: for a fee!' I had given her a light-hearted victory sign, and gone back to the computer science table, passing unnecessarily close to the English. Lit. table as I went.

*

'It'll cost you £200' she said.

I nodded: 'Payment on results?'

'Half now, plus you settle this bill' she said, as the waiter put down a plate with our tab on it.

'And do I get a refund if I'm not happy with the result?'

'No. There are no guarantees that you'll be happy. But I never failed yet!'

'This'll be the easiest £200 quid you ever made'

'You poor Englishman of little faith; how about we have a drop of brandy to finish?'

'No' I said, firmly. I'd been lucky so far, no one had seen me with the grubby little scarecrow, and I was taking no chances. I handed over a hundred pounds and got up. She looked at me with an almost hypnotic stare. 'It'll be all right now', she said, then added in a sly undertone 'Much good it will do you, arrogant pig!' The words followed me out of the door.

*

I saw Heather sitting with a group of girls in the canteen. As usual heads jerked up as the besotted creatures sensed my presence. And wonder of wonders, up came Heather's face. And I knew - I don't know how I knew - that she'd fallen, hook line and sinker, just like the rest of 'em.

But what in the name of Beelzebub had I ever seen in this girl? It seemed every girl I ever looked at formed some kind of deep yearning, a repulsive, cloying almost tangible pseudopodia ready to engulf me as would giant amoeba.

Oh well – I had to pay Morna off, she'd somehow done the business! It would be a relief to speak to someone who looked at me as if I was a sewer rat. Not that she had anything to feel superior about. Although in some ways…yes, in some ways, she... had…a certain...er...hmm...

We were married the following month.

33 Unit 7

It was suspected that the problem was in Unit 7. Something was terribly, horribly wrong. Until a month ago all our dreams were being fulfilled. We could override the self serving machinations of the bankers, media, moguls of industry, the military, the movers and shakers in every field. The new government had set Barbelo up for the good of mankind, whether at home or abroad. The whole economy was now in the control of the most powerful software that had ever existed, with priorities far beyond growth and affluence. Inequality, the environment, health, diversity and internationalism were perfectly balanced with the need for production, freedom and enterprise.

Barbelo was no big brother. Safeguards built into the software were part of it, but the most significant thing was communication. Barbelo could understand English. And for me that was the triumph and reward of a lifetime's effort: linguistics had finally mastered natural language. And I and my group had done it. Instructions were given to Barbelo in English! No supercilious programming experts were needed to translate our imperatives. Things were at last moving at a steady pace in the right direction. No settling scores between political opposites, no sudden ideological capers, just a gradual but inexorable switch from the money-centred profiteering of the past to the human centred future. And my success had brought rewards. I was in Unit Zero now – a stone's throw from the Z committee itself.

We had seen inequality falling by the month – no peremptory orders, no demonising of those who strove to produce the wealth, but no migration of the wealth of the nation into the pockets of the few. Just continuing subtle adjustments sent into the system like the worker bees in their myriads sent by their queen to pollinate the fruit trees, and ensure the fruitfulness of the summer.

Now something was wrong and could no longer be denied. Our international operations, based on the same principles as those for our own society, were under suspicion. And the suspicion was that the trouble was in Unit 7.

Unit 7 was our covert international effort. Since we could not impose Barbelo's even-handed and altruistic changes on the world, we used – like every other government – clandestine operations to promote our interests. But our goals were just ones. Yes, it was hacking – and believe me, Barbelo knows how to hack! Gone were the days of anarchic hacking by nerdy wreckers, petty criminals, one issue fanatics and subliminal self-serving government organisations. Barbelo had only the best interests of people all over the world at heart. But something must have gone wrong. We had arranged that no analysis of the detailed activities of Barbelo's work was accessible to anyone, and that the inputs to Barbelo could not be reviewed. Its rule was proving to be the saviour of our society, and we wanted no meddling in her directives by those few disaffected people that any just regime will inspire. But now it was impossible not to suspect that its work overseas might be behind the horrific rise in conflict of all sorts, all around the world.

There were now seventeen wars across the globe. Four in the Middle east, four in Africa, one in the

Balkans, one in the Baltic, one in Indochina, one in South America and one in the Sub-Continent. And the upsurge had begun soon after Barbelo began work, and had been increasing ever since. Civil wars and insurgencies were springing up like weeds, and world peace seemed to be on the brink. By listening to hearsay around the Barbelo Committee, but without knowing any detail, I knew that wars should be dying out by now.

Now here I was, as chairman of the Armageddon enquiry, going into the office of the head of Unit 7 – and the most awesome member of the Z committee – some said the least known but most powerful woman in the world. She was waiting for me looking decidedly uneasy, and a little angry. We had known each other at Cambridge. In every sense. We used to alternate between furiously arguing and exploring the byways of our darker inclinations in the world of the senses. We hadn't seen each other for thirty-seven years. I felt the tension and broke the ice. She won all the arguments - she was ten times brighter than me. She did have one weakness though - a slight tendency to dyslexia. It affected her spelling - but she more or less conquered that.

'If we don't get to the bottom of this we might be really approaching Armageddon. The problem's got to be in this Unit, and you are it's head. This goes beyond inter Unit politics.'

'My, aren't we enjoying ourselves? Go on get it out of your system, for God's sake. Come on 'women will fail when they get hold of the reins, women are too touchy-feely. We mustn't hurt the bunny rabbits, we must give Johnny his lollipop because he's crying…never mind about the food supply and a bit of discipline!' Go on say it! But you've got it wrong as usual. Your sneers did me good in the end: my cooking, my friends, my arithmetic, my spelling, my singing even my hairstyle. Well it's all grey now, I hope you're happy. But at least it made me understand the male psyche – conquer and command. It was a turning point for me'

'I got over that years ago. I only used to say that because of all that sanctimonious crap about women that you used to spout. Now come on – the whole world's hanging on the brink, and all you can do is revive old personal quarrels. But I have to say your hair looks wonderful in that colour – it really does.' I was struck by how her face which had always been striking, was now so beautifully set off by the bluish grey hair she had.

'Well if you ask me it was your department's brilliant idea about using natural language to communicate with Barbelo that has put sand in the works' she said, in a much calmer voice. Who knows if natural language actually works? It's only a theory, we could have put the ideas into code and been sure of what Barbelo would do. You just couldn't stand the idea that you and your pompous pals wouldn't be able to understand what was going on.

All those clever ideas about how she deals with mistakes, how she can use and understand idiom. How because of that she can use the internet as one gigantic memory. "She will be as good as God, and a very just, compassionate God in our hands," you said in your stupid report. I didn't even know it was you who wrote that rubbish at the time, it's all been so Top Secret. I'll tell you something though. I know Barbelo. Better than anyone. She not a she, she's an it! It doesn't know anything. It doesn't know good from bad it only knows what it thinks we told it. And we can't find out what it thinks we told it.

'Well do you know what you did tell it? I've heard that you input the data personally because it was too confidential for anyone else to see. It was handed down to you by the Z Committee, I gather.'

'I didn't do it personally. I only read it out; there were twenty senior people there on each occasion, and each typed a single word in rotation. I always took my turn with the others. We did it every week, with different groups of witnesses. I was the only one who knew it all, but I only typed one word in twenty.'

'So what did you input?'

'I can't remember *exactly* - it was seven years ago and it wasn't printed. On the ZC we had made a voice recording in stages, and the recording was digital and self-destructed after each input session.'

She was silent for we a while, seemingly musing. Then she spoke: 'But we *could* find out. We'd need the highest level permissions'

'I've got the highest level permissions. But how much *can* you remember of the stuff - the drift?'

'Not many of the exact phrases – but the sort of things to be adjusted by Barbelo. It knew what was going on in all the top IT systems on the planet. It planted small viruses here and there, Trojan horses, and it could monitor the results, and modify its sub-goals according to the results of each round of hacking. Our input keyed it in to what needed to be done, and it set about doing it. It was to be a long process'

'But what were the sort of things?'

'Some were just concepts, the same as we have here. Reduce inequality, reduce reliance on financial activity, reduce the weapons trade, reduce greenhouse warming, and so on. Everything: you know the patter as well as I do.'

'What about tangible organisations?'

'What you'd call touchy-feely things. Barbelo is very touchy feely: World Wild-life Fund; Friends of the Earth; the Peace Corps, Oxfam, Amnesty International, etc. etc. And the big girls...United Nations, NATO, the churches.'

'No chance that you made a drop off in the input?' I asked. I didn't dare say what I was thinking. Her spelling had had its occasional lapses.

But she knew what I was recalling. 'Barbelo picks up spelling mistakes easily. You should know that.'

'Of course I know that. She understood idiom, and she was tested on picturesque phrases, colloquialisms – everything, even metaphors.'

'I wasn't writing metaphors,' she said, and the thought went through my head that she might written one unintentionally.

'Well who else knows what you input?

'Only the other members of the Z Committee. We evolved the imperatives over a period of months, meeting regularly. At the final meeting I read them out – there were no minutes taken for security reasons – and after one or two minor changes everyone approved. But none of them will remember the detail - I can't, and yet you know that I had a more or less photographic memory. '

'Are you ready to put the past aside and let me just put my mind at rest about one thing?'

'Well you are the lead investigator.' She said, icily.

'Will you just type out the concepts and organisations you just mentioned – and any others that come to mind.'

She looked daggers at me. But she shrugged and began typing. She went on a long time.

'There could be minor spelling mistakes I dare say, but nothing Barbelo couldn't have handled.'

A chill was running down my spine. Only she knew all the words that she herself had input. Finally her printer chattered away and she gave me a full two pages of spiel. I took it and began to read. I saw that her spelling had indeed improved. But it was not perfect, and I suddenly began to feel uneasy at the first ambiguous spelling. Just like of old she had used a similar but wrong word. Promote the Unified Nations. Barbelo wouldn't know what she meant, but it wouldn't correct it - it wouldn't see it as a spelling mistake. It would settle for unification of nations. It made sense. I reassured myself. And in any case unification wouldn't have such a bad name if it hadn't been for Hitler and the cold war. She had always used written words like that – similar meanings, similar spellings – *similar* but not the *same*. She wrote forced for false. A false smile was always a forced smile in her writings. And there was the famous occasion when she wrote to me when I was in the RAF saying her mother was to have forced teeth. These were not spelling mistakes. Barbelo could only correct if the context was a give-away – which it wasn't here. But the second mistake was not like that. I froze. 'Promote Peace Corpse'. Had Barbelo read it as a metaphor? *Bring about the death of peace.*

When all other explanations are ruled out, the only remaining hypothesis must be the truth, so said Sherlock Holmes. And I although knew nothing of how Barbelo went about its business, I knew exactly how she would react to those two imperatives. *Wherever there is a possibility of starting up a war of annexation, go ahead.* There was no first law of robotics for Barbelo. That had been corpsed from the start.

I showed her the mistakes: showed *her*, the Mistress of the Universe. We thought spelling didn't matter any more. We had spell-checkers and at our level, literate lackeys to make silken purses out of sow's ears of our prose. And we had speech recognition. But on the big occasion all those safeguards were inoperative – for security reasons. It all depended on the girl who couldn't spell but got a scholarship to Cambridge because she was one of the finest brains they'd ever seen. And I was responsible. Barbelo was a machine – an algorithm. And the spell-checker had failed because Barbelo knew the words, and they made sense. The wrong sense. The spelling was right but the words were wrong. One or two misspellings from Optimus Prima and the world was coming to an end. She looked at me, her blue eyes filled with cosmic horror: a signalman who has switched the up express on to the same line as the down freighter and has no way to stop the tragic collision. She looked as beautiful as the day she walked out of the flat – and as vulnerable as when she asked me to check her CV for spelling mistakes. And now here we were; two clever-clogs who had unleashed the whore of Babylon – me by hubris, she by dyslexia. By now I had slumped down into my seat, defeated, but like Theodora of old, putting some spine into Justinian during a riot, her nerve had not gone.

'Alright then, let's bloody well fix it!' she said, standing up, an ageing but striking Amazon ready for the battle.

It took us only an hour to get the security permissions. Then she told me what to type. First: 'Estimate time to next period without war on earth.' Barbelo came back instantly. *140 years to unified warless world: error margin twenty years*. We were in interrogation mode. Now we moved into the most sacred database in the world, and invoked Edit Data mode. She directed me to the offending Imperatives. Up came the first: *Promote the Peace Corpse.* I deleted the last 'e'. Then *Promote the Unified Nations.* Unified became United. I looked at her. 'Now type: 'Estimate time to next period without war on earth.' Barbelo came back. *Two years and five months – error margin four months"*

We looked at each other, two lonely people who had rescued the world from their own blunders.

'What will you report?' she asked anxiously.

'That we found the problem and sorted it'

'No details?'

'Top Secret – for our eyes only'

'Well done, Lord Babel'. That was the nickname I had in the media.

'And well done Optimus Prima.' No one knew that name – hardly anyone knew she existed. Unit 7 was hidden from the world for obvious reasons.'

'I need a drink' she said.

34 The Horror of it All

Was I driving to work - or driving back - I didn't really know which. The blood throbbed ominously in my neck. The beta-blockers had given up, obviously, at least for the moment. I could feel my heart beating fast and furiously. My wife had scowled and snapped at me, her irritation and contempt for me showing in her every gesture. I didn't know when. Was it before I left - had I just left? My sons had dealt sneeringly with me too - whenever it was. The older one had shouted in my face, talking to me as if I was one of his less valued peers... He hadn't struck me again; but he was rude and unfeeling. I had to take it – I didn't want to fall out with him - he could be called up next year. The other I had had to listen to as he outlined my deficiencies in calm and rational tones.

I still persevere - we all must. I had reports to write - six of them. My hands gripped the steering wheel, white-knuckled. I smiled though - 'keep smiling' - I had learned that from Grandfather long ago in my youth. The radio reported thousands more dead, and signs that it all might go on for years. More young men on both sides of the stupid endless war were being taken away in boxes and more women as well now. The smooth competent tones of the newsreader told of the total collapse of the government in a poor famine-ridden country, where the dead were now left unburied in the streets. His voice reeked with phoney concern, topped off by a sense of his own importance. Home news was little better. A new cabinet had been formed which seemed likely to be even more self-serving and rapacious than the last. They intended to borrow so much from the Chinese that even they admitted it would take fifty years to repay. In nasal whines they justified the sleaze and incompetence of their rule, pulling the wool over the eyes of the public with unintelligible new laws. The last remaining manufacturing outfit in the country was rapidly going bust, shorted into bankruptcy by noxious blue-suited leeches filling their pockets, nevertheless stridently calling for pride in the nation. The very same people were forming a consortium to buy up the corpse at a knock down price with a cheap government loan, fire its workforce and strip its assets. I switched stations, no longer able to stand the newsreaders smug tones.

The last conversation I had had, as opposed to confrontation, had been with Fredericks, at work. After I had told him my tale of woe, as we drank our coffee, he had shaken his head. 'Times change, and we can't go back' he had said. 'And maybe 1956 wasn't all that wonderful anyway. It might have already been too late by then!' He was looking at the mechanism of my mysterious watch which even he, it seemed, couldn't fully understand. 'This is amazing. Damn clever when you think how old it is. Maybe it was made by the Babylonians – they did mechanisms you know'.

'Maybe you are right: it was from my grandfather. It was given him by a dying German, on the Somme. 'Look after it Tommy' he said, according to Dad. 'It belonged to King Solomon. My ancestor got it from a Turkish prisoner at the siege of Vienna'

'Well then you'll understand that I can't make it tick: it could be a four-thousand year old watch, worth a bloody fortune. He was gazing at the interior. 'But I think you *can* move what I think might be a symbol for the year sideways. It's weird. And you just get the same year, only in a different colour. I can change it if you trust me with it overnight!'

'Why not; what colours?'

'Oh you could have red, blue or green – a bit in your face, I guess. Ah, but there's one other – like straw on a grey-blue background. More natural it is'

'Do that then.'

He had returned it yesterday, or today: things are so bad I can hardly recall. It was now sitting in the glove compartment of the car. I went over a bump, and immediately afterwards I heard a ticking sound.

*

I realise it has started to tick again after four thousand years, and a very strange feeling overcomes me. Nothing seems familiar. Yet everything looks as it should look; I feel decidedly odd. The rain beats on my windscreen and the green trees and hedgerows are shrouded in misty spray. The radio has been playing - 'Pack up yer troubles in yer old kit bag - smile, smile, smile.' But it changes abruptly to light music. I guess that the disc jockey, like me, is sick of hearing about the Great War. But it starts me thinking. I am better off than my grandfather had been - cowering in the mud-filled trenches as he had. But the palpitations and butterflies won't go away. I dare say he had felt them too; and for better reason, poor man. I'm trembling now, forcing myself to stay calm, appear calm. It's not right. I never thought life would be like this. No hiding place. I feel tears in my eyes, tears of self-pity, self-contempt. The rain is very heavy now, cascading down, I see nothing by my headlights on the dark glistening road ahead. It's too much - I should stop really. I am in a little oasis, comforted by the cosy glow of the instruments, the warm loving voice of someone on the radio - Dinah Shore maybe – hadn't heard her for many a year. It's not the sort of stuff the younger generation will listen to. I'm almost flying now, but I can see little. I seem to have taken the wrong exit; I don't recognise the terrain, what little I can see. But the rain is easing and I see the fields either side in a heavy gloaming. I am right off track; I can see one of those old control towers left over from the last war - an old RAF station ploughed in probably, with just the ghostly ruin of its former nerve centre. The last Lancaster has long since departed for Valhalla. Or maybe an American base - the Mighty Eighth, as they modestly called themselves. Didn't know there was any of these old sites so near my route. Or maybe it isn't so near. I have driven a long time in that impenetrable spray. But why are there lights around? I went over another bump and the ticking stopped.

*

No one would ever believe that I heard it. The lights had disappeared. Why would there have been lights around? Would coloured lights have been reflected in tarmac - perimeter tracks, runways - could that be? No: a fayre - that must be it; all kinds of rubbish mass manufactured by dying children in Indonesia to be sold as crafts. There was a mist around and I couldn't see much beyond the beams of my headlights. I saw a grassy verge and decided to stop to have a quick look at the artefact. I pulled over and parked, and picked up the object. I shook it, and felt sure there was some clicking inside, and I felt a faint vibration, like an electric fence. It began to tick again.

*

I feel excitement. It must be worth millions. I get out into the cool misty air, to try to get some bearings and am glad I did. I can see the vague shape of a red wrought iron gate closed right across the road; I would have gone full tilt into it if I had kept going. An iron fence stretches away each side of the strange gate. On the other side of the fence I can make out in the gloom a large aircraft sleek and delta winged, yet with props spinning, smoothly and near silently. It is a maroon colour and away to the rear is another of the same type, only in green. I will have to open the gate otherwise the car will have to be turned around I see that it is padlocked. To the side of the gate is a cow-gate, of wrought iron. I move through it, seeing no-one there to challenge me. I approach in the general direction of the strange aircraft. In the failing light its windows glow yellow, and the same warm inviting light comes from the open door at the top of the ladder where the front-end of a queue of people is entering the fuselage. The light reflects across the puddles, and the rain scatters it. Fortunately I am wearing a hat - a birthday gift of a trilby. I walk through the cow-gate.

The aircraft and its intending passengers hypnotise me. It has a sleek modern look, and yet at the same time it looks like an older technology, with a large array - eight perhaps, of what must be turboprop engines in pusher form. The lighting seems like tungsten and the shiny maroon colour covers the whole thing with only the most discrete logos and registration numbers. There is none of the huge lettering one normally saw. I walk toward it and see the faces of the passengers: men women and children, well dressed, yet with no sign of the flashy designer outfits air travel usually brings out. I feel that they are going to an event, something that relates to them all. Their faces look fresh, and there is a feeling of optimism which, now that I witness it, reminds me of the pervading sense of gloom and doom that I normally sense amongst people. I guess they are all off for some exciting holiday - a package tour by some new company, which had started operations with a fleet of new economical planes in a striking livery. I was close to the plane now; the steward beckons me, and I walk towards the steps that rise up to the door. No tickets seem to be checked at the top or bottom of the ladder. What if...? I pass the steward who pats me lightly on the shoulder. 'Good trip?' he says as I go inside.

On the plane my seat is toward the rear. There seems more room than usual, and the seats are very prettily decorated and comfortable. I feel warm and safe in the glow of tungsten lighting that comes from pearl bulbs in sockets in the roof. The plane soon begins to move, taxiing quietly round the perimeter and pausing at the end of the runway. There seems considerable excitement amongst the passengers as the plane begins its take-off. The engines seem to lack the power of the jets I am used to, and I even feel some unease, as the plane's take-off run seemed to last an eternity before it glided smoothly into the air to start its ascent.

There comes a buzz of conversation in the plane, people seeming friendly and talkative. I see no faces of aggression, no loud drink fuelled talk. Something hard edged is missing on this flight; probably just an odd fall of the dice. Sometimes we are unlucky enough to encounter drunks, air-rage or terrorism; I happen to have picked a plane full of kindly considerate folk who seem only too happy with their situation.

I read the evening paper provided by a pleasant air-hostess. Little seems to be going on: a big project in Africa had just finished. A country, which I had thought was just about to go under with AIDS, foreign debt and encroaching desert, has apparently just reached a significant economic target, achieving for a trade surplus the first time. Shows how pessimistic one has become. I can't really put my finger on where I heard the bad news that had formed my preconception, but evidently I had got confused. It is a long but restful flight, wherein I alternate reading the articles in the large broad-sheet, dozing and enjoying a drink from the trolley.

Finally the plane starts its descent and I look out over the lights of the great city. A sudden surge of joy overcomes me, as I see it, and in some obscure way I feel it, and recall it, and all that it had meant to me, does mean to me. Then we are taxiing, and the flight is over. I walk along the exit corridor, my spirits rising with every step, though I don't know why. There is no baggage hall, no customs, just a concourse filled with light, and someone I know waiting. She is standing beneath the great illuminated dial of the clock, her diminutive dark-haired figure caught in soft low-contrast illumination. I have forgotten that she will almost certainly be there, but now I know why I had felt so much pleasure at the approach, and in the corridor. She catches my eye and starts towards me, and I quicken my pace; how well she looks and how beautiful to my weary eyes. We embrace, and I hold her tighter than usual, although we part quickly enough not wanting to make an exhibition of our joy. 'Dorothy! I thought you might be here - I hoped against hope!' I say.

'I hoped the same, Tim' she says, and a shadow flickers across her face. I catch it, but smile.

'Let us take a few minutes before we get on the tube' she says. For some foolish reason I had expected her to bring the car, so we could carry my luggage. Now why do I want to take the luggage when it will be delivered this evening? I sip a coffee, and ask about the boys.

'They are fine. They are looking forward to your return. Lionel, Jim and Joss are working together, and Scott is out running with Matt.'

'And what of you, my beloved Dorothy?'

'Oh, just pottering around, as always. But there's some good news - excellent news as far as I am concerned!'

'What news?'

'It has been accepted: my first - after so many years!'

I jump to my feet, and punch the air. At last her persistence and courage has been rewarded. She has succeeded. Just as the boys are growing to maturity the door had opened to her.

'Have you told them at...?'

'Oh yes. If things go well I shan't need to carry on there...!'

'How have they all reacted?'

'Oh everyone is so pleased for me. They are so excited. '

'I wondered if there might just possibly be...just a tiny little bit of jealousy. Marc and Sylvia...'

'Oh Tim! Not at all! You are so strange tonight. Wasn't it a good trip?'

'No, not really, it wasn't. But I'll tell you later. Let's have a little celebration about your news. You, you of everyone I know, deserve this, and the world deserves to read what you have written.'

'Well don't be so dramatic Tim! You deserve half the credit, you've been so supportive!'

'Supportive? What have I done?'

'Well as I'm sure you have noticed I haven't made any jam, have I?'

We laughed.

'Perhaps that's Sylvia's mistake' she said, still laughing. 'She does make jam! Well she and Marc will be coming tonight. They are so excited. Marc wants me to do an article for the house journal.'

'The tube is busy this evening' Dorothy says. I am surprised at her remark for some reason. 'Why it's nearly half empty' I say, and she laughs. 'Well that's one way to look at it. But it does get busy around here at this time. Sylvia said she saw someone having to stand the other day.'

'I suppose the Metro is better!'

'Of course! Fewer people and more interesting!'

She says it with a pleasant rising lilt in her voice, so that I know she is teasing, but even so she quickly adds. 'I don't mean that; people are people, everywhere!'

At home Jim and Joss are just leaving. They smile at me. 'Did you have a good trip Dr Mann? Joss asks. I smile and nod. 'We're washing cars tomorrow' Jim said.

'I really ought to pay you chaps' I say, but Lionel laughs loudly. 'Dad, we aren't going to charge our parents, are we? You must be still feeling light-headed after the trip.'

'Well thank you boys, I really mean it.'

After his friends leave Lionel stands looking at me.

'Are you OK dad? You look as if you have had a hard trip. Can I get you something. You should take it easy. It's so good you are back!'

At that moment Tigridia appears meowing lustily for her meal. 'Shut up you stupid animal!' I say, but the words sound out of place. Dorothy and Lionel look at me a little shocked. Lionel goes quickly off to feed her but Dorothy looks at me with a smile but wide eyed. 'Tim Mann, where on earth have you been? Wherever it is you must get it out of your system quickly. I think Lionel is a little upset. I'll go and see him.'

I hear her speaking in the kitchen. 'Dad has had a very difficult trip, he just needs to rest and relax, he means no harm to Tiggy.' I can't believe that a boy Lionel's age can be so easily upset by a sharp word to a cat.

She returns with a glass of whisky and smiles. 'To be taken twice a day. If symptoms persist take a holiday.'

'Sorry I spoke like that. I just didn't think.'

'Oh he's OK, He has been a little touchy since those boys got a detention last month.'

Later Scott appears. He smiles at me but says nothing for a moment.

Then he speaks. 'Father, would you have a moment to deal with a calculus problem with me, any time tonight?'

'Yes, and now is as good as any'. I expect him to name some distant hour but he comes straight back. 'Great

- I'll get it.' He disappears then returns. 'Its *log*, you see, how do you differentiate a *log*?'

I show him the method, and his eyes light up.

'I see. So it's one over x – I never expected that. Maths is like poetry in some ways, isn't it?'

I get a sudden flashback of a sullen face and shrugged shoulders, and a sarcastic mumble 'oh yes very interesting' but it fades immediately.

'That's at the bottom of a lot of physics,'

'Is it? Well dad, thanks for your time. I want to take Clara to the pictures tonight, is that OK?'

'Yes, sure; you'd better get on then.'

'It's OK, Dad, she's already here,'

'Well, bring her in son, bring her in.'

'I was going to, but Mum just thought you might need to be on your own!'

'Oh no, I'm not going to be rude to Clara like I was to Tigridia. Just bring her in.'

She is a girl about Scott's own height, tall and graceful, but shy, as she would be.

'Clara, this is my father. Father this is my friend Clara'.

'How do you do Clara?'

'How do you do Mr Mann?' she says, giving a slight bow of the head.'

'I am very well, thank you Clara. Scott's mother and brother think my trip has turned me into a barbarian!

But it's a very great pleasure to meet you! Scott's glowing description of you is fully justified'

'Thank you Mr Mann!'

'How old are you Clara - if one may still enquire your age?'

'Sixteen Mr Mann'

'Well I hope you have a very good evening. What film are you going to see tonight?'

'Armageddon, Dad' Scott pipes up. 'It's a scenario where a Great War broke out in Europe in 1914. The idea is that Europe was a powder keg at that time, just waiting for a spark to make it blow up into Armageddon. Apparently there was an attempt to assassinate some Archduke or other in 1914 but it just failed. In the film it succeeds and that became the spark. There is a war afterwards that lasted on and off for about thirty years. The message is that for all the death and destruction, life would be better now. Technology would be more advanced, and we'd all have far more money. You'd have had rebellions all over the world, and everything would have been sorted out much quicker.'

'Trust you to want to see some gory thing. You young people are so desperate for adventure.'

'No Dad...'

'In fact *I* wanted to see it, but I don't agree with its view,' Clara says, her brown eyes very earnest. 'I am doing a project on it. I think everything would be much worse, because it would have made us all so hard, selfish and cruel. Everyone, not just the few'

'You'd better get off', I say, and when they've gone I lie back, my heart pounding again, the first time since take-off.

Later, after Sylvia and Marc have gone I tell Dorothy the whole terrible thing. It's not easy; it all has a misty yet nightmarish air. Only Dorothy in the whole world would understand. Only Dorothy would believe. 'And the thing is, I keep thinking that *this* is what's not real - *this* is the land over the rainbow.'

'No, this is real.' Dorothy says. 'Good always triumphs; that other would perish, if it ever existed'. Safe in her arms I know she is right. In the bright balmy days that follow, the memories mostly fade. But sometimes, as when the fine cool rain suddenly dampens us after the sparkling sunlight, as we stroll in the Great Gardens, I can't stop trembling. Then Dorothy looks at me, and her strong kind eyes calm me. 'Tim Mann, wherever you went, you're home now, where you belong.'

I sigh, and I say 'Yes, but the horror of that world, the horror of it!'

35 Lost and Found

A million bananas were coming to see me. I cleaned up as best I could – the place looked like it hadn't been refurbished since it was patched up after an air-raid seventy odd years before. Why they chose me I didn't know. I went out front and straightened the sign:

Marley Phillips, Private Detective

Up steps through door and first on left.

As I shaved I looked in the mirror at the gaunt, almost spectral figure that only needed a copy of Big Issue to complete the picture. I kicked the cat out of the swivel chair and sat at my desk. The client was the CEO of a company with headquarters in the financial heart of the city. I couldn't get from the minion who he was. 'Be in your office at ten o' clock, you'll find out then.' It was five to ten and I had a cup of espresso in my hand – my only luxury. 'You need to be discreet; got it?' The last words had been barked at me. 'You start running off at the mouth and we'll sue your ass off – for a beginning. After that you better watch out for your kids, OK?'

I had no ass. My wife had sued it off years ago. I couldn't watch out for my kids, I never saw them. Maybe they'd send me a pair of gloves made out of the cat. Suki was all I had, apart from a near bankrupt business, and the last bomb-site in London as a place to sleep and work. But I smelt the bananas, and I needed them.

I heard a car draw up. Outside I saw a Lexus with a chauffeur in a suit that would have paid my rent and my alimony for six months. I heard the footsteps on the outside stair. No suede hush-puppies. The clack-clack of some heavy female ordnance as it glided in the front entrance; a sensible knock, and immediate entry. A too-tight navy suit, shiny black hair with no hint of grey. Fifty if she was a day. I knew I must launch the smile-and-grovel software immediately. 'Come in, I'm Marley Phillips' I said. 'The lackey who telephoned was coy about your name?' The software wasn't delivering.

'Are you asking me who I am?' The voice was husky and commanding. The sort of voice you'd like to hear in a porno-film. 'Well I told you who *I* am ma'am' She looked put out – maybe I wasn't grovelling enough.

'I know who *you* are'

'Well you would wouldn't you – you're a smart lady who can read the yellow pages, otherwise you would never have made CEO'

Why I was adopting this bantering style I couldn't figure out. Somehow from the moment she cruised in, a sleek but heavy and menacing battleship I had been imagining kicking her fat bottom; or stroking it.

'You always were a smart-ass Marley. Like when you got us strip-searched at Bordeaux airport showing off your crap French.'

I stared at her. It was She. As large as life. Larger in fact. The love of my life who had gone off to make her fortune. And she'd done it, it seemed judging by the wheels and the pretty boy in the flat hat who was waiting with them and anything else she might want. I saw her face suddenly where before had only been a bunch of bananas.

'How touching – you've recognised me! Perhaps you can even dredge up my name if I give you the first letter!'

She was hopping mad – and a little sad.

'The light was behind you.'

'Well you better get the name – otherwise your dreams of the corporate millions will crumble into the dust.'

'Er…let me see…Betty Boop?'

'Funny man! You ought to be on the wireless – Tommy Handley could have used you: Billy Prick the Private Dick. Well, I'll be off now. Your powers of detection seem somewhat limited.'

She turned on her heel and headed for the door.

'Come back Julie Wells.'

She turned.

'It's Julia Oakes now.'

'Any kids?'

'Two'

'Aren't you the lucky girl – had your cake and ate it! Who's the lucky man?'

'I dumped the lucky man ten years ago. And the lucky man is blackmailing me. And that's where you come in.'

'Can't you just pay him off? You can't be short of a few bob'

'He wants to ruin me. He hates me! And he wants to have the kids to stay with him in the holidays. And that's not on.'

'What's he got on you?'

'Pictures of me – unsuitable for a family slide show.'

'I'd have to see them of course' I added with a smirk.

'No-one gets to see them. Whatever it takes, you've got to settle it.'

'Just how bad are these pictures?'

'Bloody bad.'

'I take it the lackey didn't know what all this was about.'

'Of course he didn't!'

'Right – well I'll see what can be managed. It'll cost me a bomb. And it'll cost you a nuke. But then it'll be over'

'Right'

We relaxed. We had got the worst over.

'So what happened about all the happy families then? You dumped me for that – how did it all work out?' Her voice had an edge.

'Bloody badly. Be careful what you wish for! It was a nightmare. Or you could say I never found what I was searching for.'

She looked at me, and I looked at her. The years had fallen from her. She was as beautiful as before now –

and there was more of her, which for me was good. Voluptuous is my thing.

'You always used to find what you were searching for in the back of the old Ford V8'

'Well that's now lost in the mists of time.'

'Do you think it doesn't exist then?'

'Even if it does one would need a sat-nav to find it now I imagine.'

A small plaster cast of a Shaolin monk flew past my ear and shattered on the wall behind.

'What use would a sat nav be to you without a barrel of Viagra you dried up louse?' she squawked.

'Well maybe we can find out' I croaked, 'May heaven guide me'

'And may it imbue you with more than the usual three minutes' she hissed...'

We didn't need any more words.

A desk is better than a kitchen table, I can now say with some authority.

36 The Place

Would you like to be alone in the Universe? Well here I am: alone in a universe. The sky is dark and uniform, a midnight blue in colour. There are no stars and at first it was pitch-black, but now there is enough light coming from somewhere to faintly perceive that I am sitting on a wide plain of what could be a sandy rock. My first thought was that it was hard and almost plasticy, but I could feel at least a slight texture. Now I notice that if I run my fingers around, a faint feel of very fine loose grains tends to rub off. I can't analyse it or anything, I brought nothing with me except the sterilised suit of clothes. A whole new universe mustn't be contaminated obviously. I have a small pack which contains highly nutritious biscuits and liquid concentrates, as well as a canteen of water, of which I have already drunk a significant quantity. I have been here three hours, by my watch. I am anxious that one horizon or other begins to lighten. Wherever I am, I hope there is such a thing as day. I still feel the sky is very gradually lightening, but I am not certain, and would dearly like to be sure. Just as I become certain that the lightening is real and not borne of my hopeful imagination, a very strange thing occurs. I suddenly see that there are stars in the sky, hard to discern, because of the increase in ambient light, but undeniable. This seems illogical, since they should have been easier to see before.

I am the right stuff: prepared even to die, in the advancement of human knowledge. Neil Armstrong's small step was a huge step for mankind – or so we thought. But it was a spark beside a supernova compared to what will be the effect of my getting back in one piece. A chance discovery in an obscure physics lab in a deadbeat university changed everything. The theory of the multiverse, that overheated outpouring of the high priests of theoretical cosmology could be tested, and relatively easily if you could suck up enough energy to drain all the wind farms in the North Sea, and find some young blood whose survival instinct was far outstripped by a thirst for action. One person could go through, and one only. And if the predictions were correct he would have a high chance of finding himself in an environment similar to the one he left behind. An international collaboration with money from China, know-how from the US and a gale of hot air from Europe got the project off the ground and from amongst the hundreds of testosterone-fuelled fools who volunteered I was chosen after a battery of tests. No experience was necessary. Now here I am, in another universe. And I seem to be all alone. And I don't think I can get back.

The air is breathable; there seems no temperature difference from that of the place from which I have come. The stars are unfamiliar, as I expected, yet their distribution looks to be of the same kind. A couple as bright as Sirius, a half dozen like Vega and Betelgeuse, and a host of lesser ones scattered around exactly as one would expect. Yet I had expected something unexpected; this was too perfect: exactly as they had expected – a similar environment. Gutmann, the philosopher, had had a sort of sly knowing look on his face when he had told me exactly what *he* expected. 'You must expect the unexpected, but only the unexpected you expect.' But there was something in his eyes: that smart-ass look that all these post-modern guys from Yale have on their faces. I was always puzzled as to why they had a philosopher on the project. Surely *they* didn't know anything useful? Yet he seemed right at the heart of the thing.

'But what if I do come out where there's nothing?' I had said; although they had told me endless times that it couldn't happen. 'I mean our universe is mostly empty space isn't it?'

'Don't worry: there'll be something there once you get there. It might not look like it when you arrive, but it'll soon appear.'

Well here I am; I don't expect things to be exactly as I expect, so I scan the brightening sky and immediately find something I hadn't expected, which I expected. A distinct binary of first magnitude stars: unexpected – there is no such beautiful phenomenon in Earth's sky. The sun seems about to arise on the now roseate horizon, and I can make out some shapes in the morning mist. Houses...houses like those I know, except more shiny and metallic. As I look I see more differences, differences in the architecture. I stand up, and realise I have been lying in a road, a dusty road, made of concrete – but concrete of a reddish colour – like red brick. It reminds me of when as a child I had daubed poster paint on cartridge paper to create a picture of an inhabited Mars whose roads I thought must be red – because I knew it was called the Red Planet. When I tried to paint the people in its streets I ran out of ideas, and could imagine nothing more than human beings with blue skins.

I begin to walk along the road toward the first house, and wonder what fate awaits me. By the time I reach it the sun is up and a hint of warmth is in the air. As I approach the house a woman comes out of the front door, and looks at me – somewhat surprised. My first thought is that she looks very much like a typical woman from the base, but then, as I get closer I see that she is in fact an unexpected blue in colour, and wears what looks like a silvery plastic jump-suit. She seems excited. She waves to me, a little uncertainly, but when I wave back she smiles and begins to speak. She is speaking English, but with a heavy accent. It is an accent I have never heard before, but I get the gist of it.

'It's amazing' she says. 'You talk English exactly as we expected.'

'Of course I can talk English. But how can you. Please don't tell me you have been listening to our radio broadcasts and learned the language.'

'That's exactly it – you get leakage between universes in the multiverse. I knew you would understand.'

'That's the most predictable thing I've ever heard anyone say. Did I have to change universes just to hear a bit of nineteen-thirties science fiction hokum, straight out of the old comics I found in my dad's attic when I was about ten? Please!' Yet somehow I had expected it.

'Where do you think you have come from?' she says.

'I *know* where I've come from; another universe like this one.'

'Oh it's amazing…and can you remember what it was like?'

'Of course I can. I was there only a few hours ago!'

'You weren't. I imagined you. My husband and I have been experimenting. He's a psychologist – I'm a philosopher. We are Pragmatic Post-Modernists and we have been trying for two years to prove that we create everything that we see and hear. You didn't *exist* a few hours ago. We've finally perfected the technique, using a hypnotic drug. It allowed me to create something by utter conviction. No-one believed it was possible. Now we have proved it! And you've already created a whole universe of your own; it's full of people like you, who kill each other in mass conflicts, isn't it?'

I shrug. 'It's been known,' I say.

'That's what we didn't expect! *We* never do that, we are very peaceful.' she replies. Oh it's amazing. It really is true, true…we create what we see…there's nothing out there…I've just created you! And you are just what I expected.'

All the conversations I had had with Gutmann come back to me. 'We create the stars by looking at them' he used to say, infuriating all the physicists and engineers. 'Everything is an illusion – consciousness itself' he had said. Suddenly it dawns on me, I know what has happened. I look at her, shaking my head.

'No' I say. 'I created *you*, and your whole universe.'

She looks at me as I look at her; gazing into the boundless ocean of consciousness, and suddenly we both know the secret of the universe. We know where it came from.

37 The Community Spirit

The rat escaped from the nest and ran free across the yard. It had existed for two weeks. It knew very little. There was a piece of pipe-work buried in the earth at one corner of the yard which stuck out about four inches. Why it was there did not concern the rat, but its original purpose was long forgotten. The rat looked down into the dark hole. It was a very inexperienced rat, and it did not occur to it that the rough corroded exterior of the pipe and the first six inches inside it were different from the smooth interior below the ground. It wanted to scramble down. Holes were part of its heritage. The diameter of the pipe was such that the rats extended limbs were insufficiently long to enable it to hold itself in position by pushing its legs against the sides. It heard something suddenly spring into life, and it briefly glanced to see a creature much bigger than itself silently bounding toward it, a sleek dark shape with luminous yellow eyes. Following its instinct, it darted down the pipe, feeling the tiniest of sensations as a great sharpened claw nearly ended its short period of freedom, and its life. It reached the smooth section, lost its tenacious grip and fell about eight feet to the pile of grain that filled the bottom two feet. It was unhurt, its small size preventing it from achieving any dangerous momentum, thus saving it from injury.

Ephraim was to go with his mother to his first day at school. He had been looking forward to it. He wanted companions, but he didn't know any other boys or girls. His father didn't encourage him to talk with other local children. 'It will only end in tears' he said, getting on with his hobby. Every evening Ephraim would watch him cut veneers of exciting shapes, and then fit them together on a surface, building up a scene. 'We don't want you wasting your time with the kids around here. The boys play with guns; the girls all watch TV and visit social networks. And they all have mobile phones'.

His parents had taught him up to the end of primary school age. His mind developed well, fed by his parents loving guidance. He was allowed to listen to certain programs on the radio, and was taken to see some films at a cinema in the town – which usually showed award-winning continental films. He read incessantly, except that on summer days when the scent of mown grass was in the air he would go to the yard just across the road to look at the various wild flowers and insects that could be found there and to watch the cats sneaking around. He saw one catch a bird one day, and went home in tears.

'Yes darling, people shouldn't keep cats, they are natural killers, and destroy the diverse wildlife all around here. They are almost as bad as dogs.'

'Are dogs bad?' Ephraim asked. He secretly wanted a dog.

'Dogs are dreadful, and their owners worse. Don't approach dogs, they can be quite aggressive, and may even bite you. They are very dirty, and you can catch a disease which makes you go blind just by going into to the park where they go with their owners.'

At last he was on the way to school. Now he would make friends; people to play with. His mother was going to explain that he was a vegetarian, and that he must always clean his teeth after lunch. She expected that he would be up the top of the class but she didn't say anything for fear of pressurising him.

The rat had to live in the pipe. A little light found its way to the bottom; the dew ran down the inside and it could lick it off; it didn't need much and this supply was adequate. It ate some of the grain every day, and knew instinctively not to eat its own droppings. It was lonely, and its nature drove it to try to scramble up several times a day, but it couldn't. It tried burrowing through the grain, with the idea of gnawing its way out of the bottom then burrowing upward. Rats are good at that, but it came to a steel bulkhead about three feet below and that was the end of that project.

Eventually the rat reached the size where it could wedge itself in the pipe and scrabble its way to the top. The surface, whilst smooth, had a matt texture and was not slippery. It started, and slowly moved up. It became fatigued. It looked up at the light at the top of the pipe and redoubled its efforts. It was not a fool, this rat. It knew that danger lurked above, and when it reached the top it stopped like an observer looking out of the turret of his tank. Its eyes took some time to acclimatise to the bright light of day. It looked around, and was horrified to see a black and white cat strolling not so very far from where it was stationed. It very sensibly froze, knowing instinctively that the only thing cats could see was movement. It was fortunate, though it didn't know it, that this cat was the dominant male of the neighbourhood; the other cats had made themselves scarce at its approach. The cat was merely passing through on a patrol around its extensive territory, and was soon gone, but the other cats always gave the situation a half-hour or so before returning to their usual activities in the yard. The rat therefore had the opportunity to explore in safety. It followed a fascinating and compelling scent which it felt was very important to it. In fact it was the scent of a member of a tightly knit community of rats that lived in a disused drain culvert nearby which they had extended and improved.

Ephraim saw the rat as they passed the yard, and noticed that it was of a pale colour with its eyes half-closed and that it had an almost jaunty eagerness about it, as if it, like him, was on its way to school for the first time, and looking forward to meeting its future playmates. He said nothing since his mother had a horror of rats and would scream and run away if she saw one.

His mother wanted to speak with his form teacher before leaving him and as he crossed the school playground with her, two year-nines looked at him, and one sniggered. They glanced, grinning, to each other and nodded. Ephraim was not used to boyish ways, and mistakenly thought that this was positive evidence of smiling goodwill. Nevertheless the sight of so many youngsters, none of whom he knew, made him feel just a tiny bit of uneasiness.

The rat soon discovered the way into the culvert, and there it saw fifteen or so other rats. Its first reaction was one of pleasure at finding the place where it belonged. But things were not quite as simple as that, and in unison the other rats went into stylised gestures of hostility which were their natural way of defending their community. The gestures were perfectly aligned with the rat's own psyche and it died instantly from shock, as a rat may do in such a situation. It had enjoyed two and a half minutes of freedom.

Ephraim's mother was about to go out to collect him after school. She had just come back from her sister's where she had spent the day. 'I do hope he has enjoyed it', she had said. 'The teachers seemed quite nice; his form tutor is environmentally conscious, and the head stressed that there's no elitism and that competition is not part of their culture – it's all about community life, and co-operation.' Her sister smiled. 'What about the other kids? He hasn't had much experience of his peers, has he?' Ephraim's mother shrugged. 'Well he hasn't been exposed to bad influences at least' she said.

She hoped things had been as good as he expected. She felt quite concerned about his day, she didn't know why. But she longed to see him run out of the school gates smiling, perhaps with some new friends of his own sort. All day she had felt quite excited – it was one of rare these moments in life upon which a whole future of good or ill depended. At last it was time; she put on her coat and opened the front door. A policeman was standing there with a woman, evidently about to ring the doorbell. He asked if they could come in, showing her his identity card and introducing his companion as a counsellor. He was very uneasy, and suggested they all sat down. He said what he had to say, and his hands shook. He had never heard of a case like it. The first day at school could be daunting but...

38 Winter Wonderland

The memories of the warm saloon bar had faded, and Johnson soon regretted his decision to walk the six miles back to the base. He hadn't wanted to go with Sershall and the others in the ancient Rover - the driving on the way had been bad enough, and after what Ellis had drunk he wasn't sure they'd make it back at all. Now the weather was turning nasty. What a way to spend Christmas Eve

'Anything can happen tonight', Sershall had said, with his irrepressible optimism. But it had been a typical stupid evening with that loudmouthed crew. The locals didn't like them, and there was no chance of meeting any girls or interesting better-off people. If only he had been an officer it would have been different. But the erks were for the most part from the lower echelons of society with limited visions of their future.

He had struck out along the old Roman road. There was already a layer of snow on the ground which must have settled whilst they were drinking. It was dark, and difficult to see where he was. Clouds were constantly obscuring the moon.

He had, as usual, failed to get in amongst his own kind, when he flunked it at the Hornchurch officer selection board. Ground crew in the Mob was a third rate option, and he detested service life anyway. The Yanks had more idea, spending their off-duty hours in Whitton's bar in Lincoln. That was more like it; there one could imagine oneself on Fifth Avenue, or in the Yale Club..

Johnson found himself shivering. It had begun to snow again and it was a long way back to the camp – six miles he guessed. For the first half hour the almost autumnal weather had held, as he strode along the ancient road, but now it had turned very cold, and the snowflakes were blowing at him almost horizontally. He kept going, but the settling snow made the road white, and barely discernable amongst the scrub and hedgerow. He hadn't even taken a coat, just his cream-coloured mackintosh of which he'd once been so proud, contrasting as it did with the schoolboyish navy of most his fellow sixth-formers, which he had put on over his uniform. The snow was beginning to drift making him uneasy: he had had no idea how quickly it might build up. His feet began to sink six inches, then ten inches. He was seriously cold. He begun to realise he had made a serious, maybe dangerous, mistake; just his usual luck.

He had failed his A-levels on account of swanking around town in this very Burberry. He had pubbed and danced, and never once looked at his notes. Now he was stuck in the cold war and getting colder by the minute. The dark was so intense he could scarcely see even the white wilderness that had built up around him. Ellis was probably driving calmly into camp now. There was probably time for mug of cocoa and a fried egg sandwich. He was still miles from camp. Worse, the going was getting slower. He was fighting his way through deep snow avoiding the drifts. He knew he mustn't stop - he could die of exposure, yes die!

What a stupid way to end his so far unsuccessful life. And he'd never had one decent chance. Other people like himself always had the right contacts. Contacts he might have made at Oxford, or in the Officers mess. None of his peers here knew that had had pretensions to obtaining a commission, his sham estuarine accent saw to that. But he knew he was a man of whom much had been expected. It was still owed him! He would get out of this.

But now he felt the snow on his face turning into ice, as the driving wind was getting up more, becoming chillier, an icy whip cutting into his face. He began to feel an ache in his chest as the struggle of proceeding became greater and greater. He had to slow, determined though he was to keep going. Only an hour or so before he had been by a log fire in a cheerful pub. Now he was one small trip from dying of exposure within three miles of camp. But he was damned if he would! He had a life to live, beyond the cold war, beyond the Mob, beyond his current social milieu.

Ahead to one side he suddenly got a glimpse of a light. About time he found a cottage or something - after all the place wasn't the North Pole. With a surge of energy he staggered toward it. He stumbled, nearly fell, felt the blizzard rising again in his face, lost sight of the light, but kept going. Then the source of light appeared out of the driving snowflakes, right in front of him; nothing more than a telephone kiosk, its feeble light reflecting dull tungsten yellow on the snow which piled up around it. Johnson cursed, having envisaged a warm cottage, some soup and a bed for the night. But the numbing pain of the excruciating cold drove him to pull at the door of the red box. His fingers almost tore off as he had to break a seal of ice which had made the door fast. He pulled it wide open and stumbled through. It closed behind him and he was in, the dreadful snow banished; he could still see it driving past and against the windows.

He immediately felt warmer. He would survive, protected as he now was from the snowstorm. Indeed it was quite obvious that the kiosk was heated, because he felt a balmy breeze gently caressing his freezing skin. He wondered if it was because of just such situations - a haven in the storm; or because the equipment could not be allowed to freeze. What did it matter? He pulled down the folding seat and sat down, eyes closed with a feeling of well being. Just this tiny structure had changed his life from a downhill progress to his doom, to a new chapter - a second chance. The sight of the evil white snow swirling around in the darkness whilst he sat in perfect comfort cheered him considerably.

He noticed a cabinet by the phone, and wondered what was in it. The directories, he guessed. He realised he could use the phone to get out of his current plight. He felt light-headed in the welcome warmth; the situation was too delicious to bring so quickly to an end. Anything could happen, Sershall had said. He pulled out a book from his pocket - a penguin edition of some Fitzgerald short stories. He would sit and read for a while. He read peacefully for a few pages, and was about to pick up the phone, but opened the directories cabinet first, to look up the number of the camp. The Snowdrops would have to come out in one of their land-rovers to rescue him. Torn away from their poker game into the frozen night on Christmas Eve – how pleased they would be!

Inside the little cupboard he saw four glasses and several bottles of spirits. He could hardly believe it. It must surely be liable to theft. Perhaps it was only stocked when weather like this was expected. Perhaps it was remotely unlocked, in response to life threatening conditions. He took down a glass and placed it on the little miniature bar which he now recognised for what it was. The kiosk was marginally larger than the normal sort and the area to the left of the phone he now saw was a bar, with one stool that his eyes could make out in the gloom of the orange bulb. He filled his glass with rum and one of the small cans of Coke that had been lined up with the glasses. Sipping the drink he read on, of the magnificent Yale men and their flapping ladies. Yes, this was the life. As if a tiny mote of Fifth Avenue had been smashed off by a meteorite and had floated down here in a storm with the other snowflakes.

He finished one story, refilled his rum and coke and was about to start another when he realised that in the fascinating orange gloom of the bar area there was another person. He could hardly believe that he could have entered the box without realising that someone was in it - he supposed it was because he hadn't initially realised that the area on the right went back a little. Someone else must be sheltering from the storm. He wondered why he hadn't spoken, but simultaneously with his mental query the man spoke.

'Hi there; my name's Tom, Tom Curtain. I guess you just got here! '

'I'm Harry, Harry Johnson. Yes I just came to shelter from the storm!'

'Blown up a bit has it? I don't recall you from Yale...are you a Harvard man?'

'No, I'm English.'

'Oh I see: Oxford and all that!'

Johnson mumbled something with a sheepish grin. He saw that Tom had a companion, a beautiful girl with dark hair and expensive looking clothes.

'Harry, meet Eve! Eve, this is Harry, an Oxford man!'

'Hi Harry! You look like you really got caught in a storm. You should take off your raincoat it needs t'dry. Burberry isn't it?'

Harry nodded unostentatiously, and removed his mac; he was glad the wetness improved its shabby appearance. Their clothes all looked expensive and brand new.

'I got caught alright. There's a fair blizzard blowing out there.'

'Yeah; wasn't too bad earlier, Tom and I were out in the garden!'

'There is a garden?' said Harry incredulously.

'Sure, we'll go and take a look in a moment.' said Tom. 'But look, I need to make a call to my stockbroker. I just heard that shares in General Wireless are going to double when the announcement comes out. You got any cash? I'll get some shares for you too, it's as easy a killing as you'll ever make. '

Harry's heart sank, until he remembered the money his father had put in a bank account for him on his twenty-first birthday. 'None on me of course; but there's a thousand quid I could easily get my hands on tomorrow.'

'OK – you're good; you won't need it anyway - we'll sell 'em again in two hours and you'll be a thousand quid in. What's that in dollars, huh?'

'About seventeen-hundred I guess.'

'OK'

Tom picked up the phone, and soon had his broker on the line.

'Yeah, thirteen thousand altogether; I'll call again at one.' he turned to Eve and Harry. 'Let's get some more liquor, then you can see the garden, and we'll be back in time to take our profits.'

They walked down the dimly lit room past other men and women talking and laughing, all with East Coast American accents. He was introduced to Anson, Dwight and Sally, Phillip, Gloria, Harold and others. He was accepted without question. For once he didn't have to fake a London accent - his natural voice was fully acceptable. At the end of the bar there were double doors which led into a garden, decorated with fairy lights, where the snow had stopped, and was being cleared by discreet serving men in white jackets. Couples sat around in the once more autumnal air, and enjoyed the scene. At one o' clock everyone watched the ticker tape as the General Wireless shares zoomed up, and there were cheers as they reached three times the original price. Tom called his broker again and sold.

'You did alright there, buddy, three thousand dollars clear profit!' Tom said.

'That's swell,' Harry answered concealing his shock of delight, with an Americanism that he felt appropriate.

'You can take half out, and I can put the rest into Searbuck - they are going to rise on a take-over rumour, what do you think, Harry?'

'Yeah, let's go for it Tom'

Tom made the call and then turned to Harry.

'How 'bout a highball Harry m'boy – we gotta celebrate our killing?'

'Sure Tom, let me do the honours!'

The night advanced and Tom and Harry had drink after drink, whilst Eve and Sally laughed in their angelic voices. Each deal Tom pulled netted thousands, and by the time people began to leave Harry had over forty thousand pounds in his bank account. He understood at last how life had passed him by. He had always met the wrong people. Never his own kind; never people who could put him on the road to success. Now for once he had made a successful contact, made the transition. After the hubbub died down he relaxed in the little seat by the phone.

Sershall found him at six o'clock - he had taken the SWO's bowser with its snowplough out onto the road at first light without permission. It was against regulations, but no pal of Sershall's was going to freeze to death on account of a few silly regulations. The big tanker, with its huge wheels, pushed its way along the obliterated but straight road until Sershall spotted the telephone booth. Ellis had suggested that Johnson might be there, and so he was. Sershall was just able to rouse him, and get him into the cab. On the return journey he recovered a little but Sershall took him to the MO straight away, and he spent three days in sick bay. The SWO found out about Sershall's hi-jacking his bowser, but he said nothing.

Harry Johnson was different after that, so Sershall thought. He seemed less of a mate, more aloof. After they were demobbed, and when he was in London a year later, Sershall telephoned to suggest a meeting. Harry seemed a bit put out.

'OK Sersh, but I'm partying with some friends tonight, and they're, well they're rather well heeled you see. I've moved on a bit lately, socially you know, but come along anyway Sersh, I'd like to see you.'

Sershall went along, and was stunned by the glittering assembly - he knew now what Harry had meant, and although Harry was friendly, he felt like a fish out of water and soon left. Somehow or other that winter night, Johnson had broken the mould of his former life, Sershall thought, as he sat in the Horse and Jockey in time for last orders with his mates from the factory. But it was nothing like those nights out in the Mob, where anything could happen.

39 The Summons

I decided to drive myself. I wanted no lackeys or yes-men around me if the answer was yes. I had told Father Shanahan the day before when I met him in the street. Nothing was said about my dereliction of his church, but somehow I found myself telling him of my fears. 'Have faith my son' he had said, predictably. I didn't. I hoped and prayed it was not so, but I was scared. With more than two-billion at my disposal I have never had reason to fear anything in the last twenty years. Not since I nailed that first million.

I had shorted Rover Air, a medium size cut price airline, who specialised in package tours; I had got a two-hundred thousand pound loan from a bank, through a guy who worked in their investments branch, who owed me a big favour. I had set up a company called British Air Transport Capital and through it I borrowed more than four million Rover Air shares. I had noticed that their share price had been shaky for a few weeks – fuel was at its peak price at the time. If they had struggled on for a year they would have come through as the bottom dropped out of the oil market. But I set about ruining them. I had a friend who worked in the financial press who also owed me some favours, and got him to write some articles advising people to avoid their shares. I kept selling the shares and watched the drop my transactions caused. Others began to sell and soon everyone saw that their shares were in free-fall and eventually achieved junk status, whereupon I bought them back at a few pence each and returned them to the broker I had got them from. I got a clear million and a half after repayment of my loan. I never looked back. The airline went bust obviously, and I bought up some of their assets at a knock down price. But today was another story. I was sure my money would save me if I could be saved, but if I couldn't...

Lots of people appeared as if by magic at my arrival. I looked in vain for Mr Sandolin, the head of the department in which my case was being dealt with. I was ushered up to the imposing office and asked to wait in a sumptuous antechamber with books, magazines and a TV. But I wasn't kept waiting for a moment. The head nurse, or whatever she was, knocked firmly and immediately opened Sandolin's door. 'Sir Patrick is here, sir' she said, beckoning me. I had been knighted only the year before – for being so rich, I guess - but for the first time being referred to by my title gave me little pleasure.

I stood up, feeling as I had done when I went out to face the infamous Arumugan in my first game for the school, after he had skittled our first four and broken the captain's ribs into the bargain. Sandolin reminded me of Arumugan. I tried to read his face as I crossed the lush carpet and accepted his lavish gesture to sit down. He seemed poker-faced which I thought was a bad sign.

He looked up, with a sober gaze, meeting my eyes.

'Well let's take the bull by the horns; I deeply regret to inform you that you do have the illness that we suspected, and that it is deeply entrenched and advanced and has spread to your vital organs,' he said.

A shock like a physical blow struck me and I was hardly able to answer him. But I was determined to keep my *sang froid*.

'Well I feared that' I said in the firmest voice I could muster. 'is there any hope at all?'

He slowly shook his head.

'I won't try to deceive you Sir Patrick; you are too astute a man for that. But we can keep you going for three months at least. And I shall personally see to it that you won't suffer.'

'Oh my god!' I said, unable to control my horror. I thought of my enemies, who were legion, and of the hypocritical things they would say whilst concealing their delight. And of the shares in my companies that would drop like stones if this got out. 'And there's nothing to be done?'

'Treatments at this stage can only be palliative – they cannot prolong your life I fear. But we are quite capable of preventing any news of this from leaking out. Your records are being treated as totally confidential; none but I and one of the consultants, who is completely trustworthy and sworn to secrecy know the true situation. If you agree to it, this can be the situation for many months whilst you deal with your affairs' He seemed very focussed on this point.

As I drove home I let the news sink in, driving out of my way until I felt I could face the world. All my money could not buy me what every person I saw on the street had. The purveyor of The Big Issue, the mother and child returning from school, the bus driver, the policeman, the well heeled business men…even the dogs and cats, could look forward to a future life stretching ahead, yet I, with the prodigious wealth I had accumulated could expect nothing but a few depressing months. I would have handed it all over to the first person I met if I could have restored my health. I could soon make more – I knew the ropes. No-one in the world could save me. A fool might try to barter his life for his soul, by going through some idiotic ceremony to summon up Satan. But to what purpose? If there *were* such a thing as a soul, the whole problem would disappear – one would live forever. So who on earth would exchange an eternal soul for a few more years on earth, and the eternal fires at the end of them? But if there wasn't, then there was no Satan, and no reprieve: Catch 22.

A few days passed, and I found myself brooding and snapping at people. I cancelled what had seemed like important engagements, and took no pleasure in the fabulous trappings of my wealth. Days turned to weeks and this black depression continued, although I did my best to resume some of the activities that had formerly absorbed my life. I tried to prepare my affairs to be affected as little as possible by my demise, but avoided any actions that might alert my family or staff prematurely. I still felt surprisingly well apart from some bouts of indigestion from which, in any case, I had always suffered, so I had as yet no reason to reveal the truth. Things would probably have gone on like this until I was consumed by my disease and the light faded from my world. But then something happened.

I received a letter from a life insurance company who had somehow got wind of my health problem. I had numerous policies ensuring that my wife and family would not suffer in the event that I met a premature death and that my various charitable foundations would be protected from the earthquake that would subsequently assail my financial empire. The policies were all looked after by my personal assistants. I had told none of these about my impending doom, so I could only conclude that Sandolin had broken his promise. Of course it was maybe that he was legally bound to do so, by some clause or other in the policies, which involved co-operation with this company. They had therefore not contacted any of my subordinates, perhaps in accordance with some formal agreement with Sandolin.

I read the letter with some increasing annoyance. It came from *Afar Life Underwriting* with all the usual headings and references to my life insurance companies and ran as follows:

Dear Sir Patrick Barroby

As you may know this company underwrites a number of the policies you hold with the above named companies. It has come to our attention that you have recently received a medical diagnosis which puts a limit on your life expectancy of six months at the outside. We are naturally very concerned on your behalf at this development.

However, in addition to our personal regrets we note that our professional relationship is seriously affected. You are bound by your contracts to pass information such as this to us at the earliest possible moment, yet you have not done so. Such an omission puts the validity of our contract in doubt; in order to preclude the possibility of terminating our relationship you are therefore summoned *to a meeting at our offices on Maundy Thursday. Until that date and on a promise of your attendance, the contract will be treated as continuing. We are in hopes that a satisfactory arrangement can be arrived at for the future.*

Your most obedient servant

Nicholas Luke Chort

On behalf of Afar Life Underwriters

There was a flamboyant signature which betrayed a certain relish that the writer felt in the power that his position gave him in the situation.

I was outraged, yet suspicious. I had not heard of this company . I had not kept an eye on my policies as the money they would have to stump up was a fleabite compared to my capital and the value of my assets. I felt it was probably a scam, but either way I was in no mood to put up with this arrogant missive. Whoever it was he was too big for his boots, and I would have some fun grinding him into the dust. I would go carefully though, as he was in a position to blow the gaff on my secrecy, and my affairs needed several more weeks to render my empire immune from the results of the coming bombshell. But the prospect of battle reinvigorated my fighting spirit and I had the clout to intimidate him if necessary.

I would therefore attend the meeting. I would have to swallow the arrogant word 'summoned' but they would pay for it. I would appear calm and confident. I would threaten them with legal action and exposure. I would crack them as a macaw cracks a Brazil nut, and I would enjoy doing so. My last mission on earth! I would go out in a blaze of glory. Fob them off with lies about my situation, but prolong the negotiations until my affairs were in order, then strike with all the forces at my disposal. My MP's would ask for them to be investigated, women from Chort's past would 'come forward' as the saying goes. Ah yes, life would be short but sweet for me, but not so sweet for Chort!

A few days later on the appointed Holy Day (I was brought up catholic) I found my way to the Shard – where ALU were situated. I had thought that I would be going to some pretentious offices overlooking the grand panorama of the great city which I and a few others ruled from our lairs. I was surprised to discover though, that the Shard went down as well as up, and ALU seemed to dwell at the bottom of it five floors below ground, where the air was warm and quite oppressive.. The atmosphere was almost reverent as a female lackey in a sharp black business suit with a bright orange blouse ushered me along several warm corridors to a door with ALU written on it. She took me through into an antechamber with several doors off it including a very impressive one with N L Chort written on it. She bade me be seated and entered this office with a knock – all rather reminiscent of my debacle at the hospital. She disappeared closing the door behind her, leaving me to pick up their house magazine. It was a special issue subtitled 'Evil – the Route to Money and Power?' I flicked through it, and it appeared to be a series of interviews with power-seeking people from the fanatical right and also the most notorious and least salubrious members of the super rich class. I was not featured I noticed: I felt a mixture of jealousy and relief. The female reappeared, beckoned me and smiled, raising her eyebrows: 'The Chort is ready to see you now Sir Patrick.'

I have heard that Hitler had an almost mesmeric charm when he chose to use it, but I was totally unprepared for the impact of this man's charisma. He had the most riveting gaze imaginable, dark cropped hair, a neat but upturned moustache and a sharply pointed jaw. His hazel eyes spoke of vast knowledge and experience, those of a man who knew everything one knew, and an ocean more besides. And there was a slight but moving resemblance to my father, whose death when I was nineteen had nearly destroyed me. He wore a perfectly fitting charcoal grey suit with a burnt umber tie from some organisation featuring striking orange and yellow stripes. His voice was deep and resonant. He sat behind a modest desk, in a smaller office than I had expected, with some superb engravings of Gustav Doré arranged sparsely around its walls.

He smiled, and his smile warmed me. 'I'm so glad you found the time to drop in Sir Patrick…you must be a very busy man' he said.

'You were rather insistent' I said a little coldly, difficult though it was in his overwhelming presence.

'I don't think you will regret this interlude' he said, leaning forward with that keen-faced and genuine warmth that is so hard to resist. He paused, then out of the blue asked me if I would like to smoke. I was shocked by this, so taboo is this activity in our time, but since I saw myself as doomed, I did not object. I nodded and waved my acquiescence.

'One must go to hell in ones own fashion, mustn't one?' he opened a wooden case on his desk and took two long thin cigars from it and looked at me.

'Here you are , Sir Patrick. They are the finest this world can provide – flown in from Cuba each week.' I took one and he followed suit. One couldn't hurt – the damage was already done.

I hadn't smoked for two years. Much good my painful abandonment of the exact brand that he offered had done me. I accepted one gratefully. Together we lit the forbidden fruit. We were empowered.

The young woman appeared with a tray of coffee, and placed it on his desk. He thanked her and turned to me. 'It's Yirgachefe, from Ethiopia, I have interests there.'

A few puffs of the cigar, and a few sips of the coffee and I was feeling myself again, better than I had for years. But I was too old a hand to be turned from my purpose by his exquisite hospitality.

I echoed Sandolin's opening gambit 'Well let's take the bull by the horns; you want to avoid paying up when I keel over, and you hope that my failure to tell you my medical development will enable you to do so.'

A twinkle came into his eyes, and he leaned back in his chair with a disarming smile. He lifted his hands and lowered and raised them in a calming gesture.

'Sir Patrick! I must confess to some little deceit – the only way I could lure you to this meeting. We have no interest in your insurance policy. It is perfectly safe. Indeed I have no power to influence it, nor any connection to it! I have *summoned* you here – I used the word ironically – because I had been disappointed in your reaction to the result of your hospital visit; precisely, in fact, because you failed to *summon* me!'

I was totally unprepared for this. The man was making a fool of me. I stood up, and took my briefcase. 'If you have anything worthwhile to say, Mr Chort, you had better cut to the chase; I am, as you say, a busy man.'

'Would you class saving your life as worthwhile, Sir Patrick?'

I stopped in my tracks. Could he be selling some new and efficacious treatment? After all, Sandolin had contacted him, and might know of something – untested, but potent. Was money the object, some gigantic sum to offer whilst the medical profession's hands were tied?

I sat down. 'So fire away –I'm interested. How much are you asking, and what are the research results?'

'I don't offer you some scientific quackery, Sir Patrick. I offer you immediate cure. A thing only I am able and willing to do.'

'Immediate?'

'Yes, immediately on satisfactory conclusion of our business; by the time you leave this building after concluding the deal. You can leave with your illness, or you can leave without it. If you leave without it, neither I nor anyone else can offer you a cure.'

'How can anyone do that?'

'In am not *anyone*, young man. It is within my power!'

I was struck by his patronising way of referring to me, out of keeping with his well mannered style.

'I would guess that you are hardly older than I' I said calmly.

'I am very much older than you Sir Patrick. Indeed I was old when your Christian forbears added the prefix 'old' to my first name.'

'To your Christian name?'

'Hardly'

'Old Nicholas' I said...and then realised what he meant.

He looked at me, his eyes boring into me, in a manner that held me in his gaze unable to avert my eyes. Then he stood up, and towered over me, in a way that I felt sure that no mortal man could achieve.. True, my psyche has always been very affected by size, but even his face looked different. No less friendly, but more authoritative – a powerful boss, inducing the feelings I had got when starting out when first I met the titans of the financial world. I looked away, cowed as I hadn't been since facing bullies at school – or the headmaster.

I looked up at him again; high up...he seemed even taller now, taller than mere psychic impact could make him. He raised his hands and spread his fingers and rays of flickering orange light splayed out from their tips. Burning hands. I knew then that he was what he said he was. With his height, his power radiated from him, like the light from a quasar...like the angel of light he had once been.

'You are Satan then?' I murmured.

He sat down, and without any sense of transformation he was Mr Chort again.

'Well now, no more party tricks, no need for any horns, hooves, or orange tights I hope.'

I shook my head. 'No, no need at all. I believe. But then you are going to ask for my soul, which will prove that have one, and if I do I won't trade it for anything. So it looks as if I may be stuck with my illness and imminent death.'

'Not so, Sir Patrick, I don't want your soul. I would probably acquire that in five months in any case, so if you refuse my offer you will lose both your mortal life and most likely suffer the eternal fires, within a very short time. And recall that it is He, not I who disposes of men's souls as he chooses.'

In partial shock, but with my brain still functioning I grabbed at the only chance I had. 'So what do you want?'

'What is usually required of men such as you. You will liquidise three quarters of your assets, and invest it in the projects of the ALU foundation, of which you may have obtained an idea from glancing at the magazine in my waiting room.'

So I was to support a lot of semi-Nazis – and keep a quarter of my empire. I didn't care about the politics. No amount of money would stop these political lunatics from being ground into the dust by the good old fat-cats and their establishment running-dogs. And I could get all my money back and more…a new challenge, and one I would enjoy more than any that had gone before. And whilst I was getting it I would become a great benefactor to the world, opposing all evil, and fighting hunger and poverty – what an intoxicating challenge. But…

'How do I know you won't rat on it, and give me the disease back once I've signed the money off?'

'You know how. Set up a trust that pumps out the money, starting six weeks from today, for such time as you remain alive: and all monies to be returned to your own legacy on your death.'

He was right – it could be done. But then another thought occurred to me.

'And how do you know I wont rat on you, and axe the trust once I have the all clear. I suppose you will magic the illness back?'

'We will have no need for that. You will set up the trust so that you have no power to stop the funding before your death, no matter who you try to bribe.

'So be it' I said and I looked at him and he at me; there was a strange trust between us. We shook hands.

'Thanks Nicholas. Are you sure that you are not Santa Claus?'

'Call me Luke, Patrick, it's the name I prefer – you know, Luke - Lucifer! 'It was a pleasure to do business with you, Patrick.

We arranged a second meeting for the afternoon to give me time to consult my legal beagles on the soundness of the documents prepared by ALU for the setting up of the trust. I knew that he couldn't cheat on me, since if he failed his part of the bargain I would be dead before ALU got anything from the trust.

He came with me and put his hand on my shoulder as I left. I felt a fellow feeling with him.

I arranged in secret to enter a private clinic who understood the need for secrecy, and submitted to an extensive series of tests. They needed a tense week to collate all their results, but when they had, I knew by the face of the specialist that all was well.

'You have nothing to worry about Sir Patrick. You have a mild form of irritable bowel syndrome and that's all. Liver, kidneys, lungs...all are very healthy for a man of your age.' I had said nothing of course about my previous diagnosis.

So Luke had kept his promise instantaneously as he had said. Wonder how he fixed it? I rejoiced with my wife that night and got on with my life. I passed the six months and was as fit as a fiddle. But I had begun to want to talk to someone who knew something about Lucifer. Something kept occurring to me again and again. Especially when it became impossible to deny that there were increasing signs that the far right were rising.

I lived in a pleasant area of North-West London and witnessed a menacing scene a few months after my miraculous recovery. A large body of young men were marching in an intimidating manner through the beautiful street on which I was. Harsh shouts and laughter, sneering expressions and a plethora of black, red and white marked their progress. I drove carefully past them and swept on, feeling very uneasy.

I went round to the old Church and found Fr. Shanahan. I told him I had a theological question for him. He smiled and took me into the clergy house where he offered me a cup of coffee. When we were settled I blurted out my question.

'Can Satan perform miracles?' I said.

He sat forward, and with is hands making almost an praying shape answered me.

'It has been a matter of debate in and out of the church for two thousand years. Most in the Catholic Church believe that he cannot. But he can perform the most spectacular conjuring tricks; imagine, having seen the amazing displays of human illusionists and conjurers, what such a being could do without violating the laws of nature...of physics. Your Protestant theologians like to say that he can, and brand Fatima, Walsingham, Lourdes and other appearances of the Virgin, as his miracles, given to deceive us and return us to idolatry.' We parted amicably, and to some extent my fears were allayed. He had not ruled it out entirely.

For the next year or so I gradually went back to my old life, energetically rebuilding my financial and commercial empire. Only the nagging fear that came when I saw increasingly emboldened politicians of the right using words and language which I had thought were outlawed, and banished from our speech. Prosecutions failed defeated by expensive defence councils and mobs in the street outside. I did my best to finance liberal causes, and sponsor media outlets which preached against the rising wave of divisive activity.

In my own life I had grown closer to my dear wife, Bathsheba who was increasingly uneasy about the new situation. We went abroad to places where we could forget our troubles. We were sitting in an Indian city on the terrace of a cafe, drinking pastis, when I heard loud upper-class English voices, both of which seemed very faintly familiar. Round the corner came two men and two women. The men, both dressed in Old Harrovian 'Henley' blazers, were striking to me, but in different ways. One, because I quickly recognised him as Mr Sandolin. His face froze as he saw me and he quickly turned away to cross the road. The other's face also betrayed horror. But that was not the striking thing about him. He was the tallest man I ever saw, and I knew him.

I watched them scuttle away toward the theatre opposite the cafe. They parted when the tall striking man walked confidently through the stage door into the building. I saw with a shock that it was putting on Dr Faustus.

.

40 A Problem with Human Cloning

The first thing you should know is that I myself am a clone: I am *well placed* to delineate the problem areas in the field of human cloning, especially in my own case. I can thus tell you that the crucial complication is that a human clone has all the original attributes of the being from whom she, or in my case he, was cloned, with *one exception*. It has no soul. Does that mean I don't have a soul? As it happens, it doesn't mean that. I do have a soul, as you will see – but one not cloned from my original's soul. That can't be done. You all know that science is one thing and the whole spiritual business another, and that science does bodies, not souls. Those who cloned me had been well prepared for this difficulty. But their lack of insight into the subtle complexities of the soul-body entanglement meant that their plans went badly wrong, and more than once. They first introduced iron as a crystal of ferrite into the clone cell, just as a man who wishes to culture a pearl adds the tiny impurity which initiates the growth of the precious jewel. They had completely misunderstood the relationship.

The oyster analogy was perfectly sound. But the body is not the oyster. The soul is the oyster. Only a few souls have bodies, just as in the oyster community, very few have pearls. The body is the soul's exquisite response to a minuscule contamination of its substance. But the *body* can't grow a *soul*. Rather the iron atom caused a rejection in the body. It grew a nightmare entity that lurked in the incarnate receptacle where the body usually houses its original incorporeal progenitor. It gloried in its chance existence, and both the cloned body and the false soul had the same urgent desire. The body yearned to rid itself of the iron abomination, whilst the unclean entity desired its freedom. Some time in its first few days of life my body ejected its noxious passenger and we went our separate ways. My creators witnessed the whole cycle, and felt a pity and guilt for the evil they had wrought. Their close and insightful observations of the normally hidden transactions between temporal and spiritual processes convinced them that they could supply me with a soul of my own. They had already known that it was in the metal iron that the links were forged. Its ferromagnetic influences induce the radiant forces which surge between the temporal and spiritual worlds. It was the metal that fertilised the world that men built. It was the metal of the mysterious magnetic lodestones that first pointed the way to the ocean of living radiation that pervaded the universe, and the knowledge that it could be manipulated. My soul had to be imbued with that half-spiritual metal, yet be combined with the foundation upon which all life rests – the coal black essence of us all. With iron, and this carbon, in the white heat of the furnace they cast my new soul in the mould that only they of all humankind understood.

Afterwards, afraid and ashamed of their work, and fleeing the consequences that they dimly foresaw, they disappeared from my life. They left me with she who reared me, changeling though I was. In the aftermath of the ungodly deeds, the forces of evil were stirred by my monstrous doppelganger who rejoiced in the death and destruction that came to us in the quiet suburb where we lived. His laughter could be heard in the chattering of the guns. His frenzied hatred exploded on our houses, and his sudden sulky silences sent cold steel through our hearts as his devilish avian missiles swooped to kill. Peace came when he finally subsided, his energy temporarily spent. But it came too late to save my cast iron soul, hard but brittle. It was shattered, as he had wanted. My surrogate mother saw that, but looked on me, and blessed me as a true mother can, and loved me for the good that she still saw within. The shattered world was re-grown with steel at its heart, and iron in its soul. It became a place of gleaming steel-framed towers, speeding vehicles and huge steel ships that plied the seas, trading glass beads for souls, and which do so yet.

In the blessed dawn of the world at peace, my mother left no stone unturned in her efforts to imbue me with the soul I lacked. Finally her hopes were raised and she took me to an ironmonger she had discovered, tucked away in the back streets of the bomb-busted region of the city in which we lived. It was run by a grey-haired and bearded man who eked out a living from its tatty-looking spades, baths and other household ironware. Encouraged by his kind wise face she had asked if he sold iron souls. He had shaken his head. 'We don't, I'm afraid,' he had said. 'But I do have a steel one.'

She had not waited to see it, but had rushed back to the house and taken me to the shop. In a shed at the back he rooted around, with sounds of heavy metal objects being disturbed and moved. Finally he emerged, followed by a corroded and run-down looking soul which shuffled along as if it had no self-esteem. Where the storekeeper had got it from he didn't say, and we didn't enquire. We were sure it was something to with the war. My mother looked askance at the price he wanted, but he reassured us. He told us that we would have no regrets. It needed attention, he admitted, but said that it was perfectly in tune with the new world that men had built. I would have a soul upon which to build a dream of a bright modern future. It wasn't stainless steel, he agreed. But such a thing was beyond the bounds of humankind to make. As it was, we took it home, cleaned the rust off it with Jenolite and polished it to a dull shine. At last I experienced once more the long-forgotten joy of having a soul. Though it was only an external stand-alone one, it bound itself to me so that we could never again be put asunder.

It strengthened and ennobled me, steering me through the pitfalls of growing up. Now many decades later, it watches out for that brooding horror that feels it has been supplanted, but which fears cold steel. Yet throughout my life my steel soul, though saving me from perdition, has rendered me unlovable; a being with whom long acquaintance produces a feeling in others of its cold offhandedness; a robotic figure; a heartless tin man who first charms, then chills, and finally, worst of all, bores.

41 The Whirlwind Romance

'You will forget me as soon as you get back.'

She would not. How could she forget the man who had in the space of a single week changed her from a thirty five-year old spinster who compiled indexes and helped at jumble sales into a woman? How could she forget the bright smiling eyes which had spotted her as she dutifully read the guide which explained that the ruin was the remains of a fortress built by the Romans two thousand years before? How could she forget running across the white hard sand chased by the bronze Adonis whose hands, when he caught her around the waist, were so strong and gentle; hands which lifted her as if she were made of polystyrene? How could she forget him, waiting for her in his white shirt where he said he would wait, by the harbour wall, his hair ruffled by the breeze, his face lighting up as she trotted down the steps to the little group of quayside restaurants and cafes, his noble eyes looking into hers, burning with devotion?

How could she forget that heavenly meal, the white wine she had sipped, the calamari, the merguez and the cous-cous they had eaten? Or his white teeth flashing in the light of the lanterns, as he poured out his words of love, whilst the dark sea slowly breathed its life-giving force onto the shore? Or forget the walk, arms round each other, weaving up the pavements passing through the crowds; Or forget how for once she too had a partner, and the best of them all? And in his room, she was a beautiful orchid, as he said. An orchid that was about to open at last, finally and without shame, could she ever forget that?

Totally fused in the waves of ecstasy that undulated through their bodies, she was transfigured forever.

'I will not forget you! It is you who will forget! Once I've gone back to England. Will we ever see each other again?'

'Of course we will my love. If you wish it; it is my hearts desire.'

'Oh if only I could be sure. I am not naïve! I can see that you are a man who must have the choice of women. What hope can I, a pathetic church mouse, have?'

'I will give you something when you leave: something that when you open it at home will reassure you. I am not a rich man, but I can give you my love, and what will prove it!'

She knew he had no work, and when he came out of the shop she felt guilty. He had a gift-wrapped parcel, and a few cheap items which he had chosen, to remind her of the week of love: a little statue of the great cathedral, a small tin of the calamari they had eaten that night, and a box of sweets made with local liqueur that she had sipped later in his room. She put them into her hand luggage but put the parcel which was quite bulky into her suitcase at the check-in. She could see that he felt shame at the cheapness of his gifts. 'These are nothing' he said 'but, this, this is from my home, you will see: something to prove to you that I am not a man quick to change his feelings. Open it in when you get home…and then you will see! I did not like any tourist girls, until I saw you. Now I have found the woman who I will love and cherish all her life. A woman just for me, with no others in the past; a woman like the women of old, as you say, a one-man woman! That is my dream.' She put it into her suitcase before she checked it in.

They parted only when she went through gate to the departure lounge, his strong arms at last relinquishing her. She sat in a haze of pleasure: she had at last inspired love, and inspired it in such a man! She would give him all the loyalty he desired. She would cook, wash and clean – iron his shirts, and make jam…never mind the jeering of her feminist friends.

A voice came over the loudspeaker system. Her name was called.

*

'Did you pack your bag yourself as you said at the check in?' the chief of the security officers asked.

'Yes I did!'

'How then did it get into your baggage? How is it that you didn't know what was in it?'

'It was a present from the person who saw me off! He told me not to open it until I got home.'

'You would never have got home if the plane had taken off with that in the hold. Are you stupid – not to check?'

'It was a present.' She broke down in tears.

42 The Harbour of Souls

This town never saw its docks ablaze and the sky a lurid flickering red as did the one in which I was born. That giant port survived the ordeal, but it didn't survive the attack of the metal boxes which drove its workforce from the dockside and squeezed the life-force from the nation. This town eclipsed that other, but unlike that other its soul is nothing but a steel skeleton which twitches away on the skyline, a strange symbiotic entity which sucks in the tangible and blows off the spiritual.

Gazing at the tugs scurrying up and down the great river charmed me as a child; now I watch the huge floating warehouses moving purposefully into the haven, their engines throbbing like the black hearts of those evil drones that oppressed us so long ago. There are neither wharf-side taverns nor any press gang waiting for drunken sailors outside them. There are no missions, nor any alien seamen staying in the town. One may see a few small groups of lost-looking Asians, clutching plastic bags filled with fresh fruit, and hear occasional aggressive Eastern European accents from groups of big, purposeful-looking men. None of the indigenous population of the town ploughs the sea as they would have of old. A few wield the mighty gantry-cranes, the rest drive the lumbering wandering lorries or stare at databases and spreadsheets on flickering computer screens. The passenger ferries - crewed by natives of the port - have long since gone. There is no romance of the sea, no gates made from whale jaws, no colonies of sea-folk from the corners of the globe to strengthen the land with hybrid vigour, no army of boys looking out at the horizon, their eyes wide with wild dreams, their spines tingling with the sound of the sirens of ships bound for blue water. Oh no. This town is not pervaded by the mysterious miasma of the oceans of the world, nor provided with a rat's nest of vaporous alleys, where red-lit buildings exude the languid music which lures the toilers of the sea; at whose windows pale painted faces appear whenever a ship's siren drowns the silky sounds of the sultry saxophones. Oh town of mine, so much you do, so little you show, how much less you know! Or so I thought.

Yet there are places one has never been, and stumbling upon one, that dread day, I learned the darkest secret of the land, the crawling chaos which is inexorably engulfing us all, yet which few hear and few see, and of which none speak.

I decide to stop painting – I have reached that stage where nothing works, and woodenness rules. It has just stopped raining. The sun threatens to break through, and once again glitter on the wet red-bricked buildings. I look moodily out of the window at the flamboyant Victorian seaside architecture, with its turrets, gables and wrought-iron balconies. But I have seen it all, and it fails to charm. I am depressed. I must go down to the harbour again, where there are no tall ships and no star is needed to steer them. No-one stirs in the house as I leave; my two sons are tapping away in their futile computer fantasy-worlds; their masculine spirits are trapped in a world of no-risk, no-pain hunt and destroy. I make for the dock, hoping to see some big ships moving - anything to establish some sense of a real world, where people do real things and make some permanent mark in the intangible psychic quicksand in which I feel myself sinking. The rain tries again but I ignore it. Occasional spitting drops land on my lips, and I seem to taste sweetness - honey, maybe.

My Irish ancestry reminds me that this is a sign that the banshee is abroad, and the wail of a siren brings a smile to my lips. He who hears the wail of the banshee...! I walk to the car park on the levee where retired couples sit in their cars and eat packed lunches, or frankfurters that can be purchased at a snack-van. All around, behind tall spiked fences, containers can be seen, piled up to amazing heights: China Shipping, Maersk, K-line, Yang Ming, Cosco, MSC, USA Lines, Triton, and countless others, all very paintable, and all painted already by better hands than mine.

But I see a path at the side that leads directly along the shore, into a place I thought was inaccessible, from which a furtive-looking figure is just emerging; I eagerly set out along it - thrilled by a new vista of possibility. I see why I didn't spot it before. There is a gate which must usually be closed, and which would blend into the high spiked fence when it is; but now it's open, chained back against the railings. I walk along, close to the floating tug platform. Then the route turns inland along the side of the container compound, and suddenly veers off to where I can see a ship inland. I walk uncertainly towards it, and suddenly emerge from the high stacks of containers to where there is a dock basin, a wide cut, on the other side of which is the ship, and beyond which is a little row of older-looking shops, with what seem to be sea-folk going about their business. I walk to the end of the basin. Then round I go, and I am on the wharf beside the ship, which is not a container ship, but a real cargo boat being unloaded by a dockside crane which lifts panniers of boxes onto a waiting lorry.

I had seen such ships coming up the estuary but assumed they went on up river to the inland port. Behind the ship I am amazed to see a café, a tavern, a newsagent and a general store, as well as some kind of engineering works. It all has a late-on-a-hot-Friday-afternoon air about it. What is this ship's cargo - cedar wood and sandalwood? Or pig iron and cheap tin trays? It looks more like a sturdy British coaster than a quinquereme of Nineveh. I decide to have a drink at the pub - *The Outward Bound.* I enter the place, and note that it is chiefly populated not by the bearded and piratical sea-salts of my childish imagination, but by people who look as if their home ports are in the China seas – the great archipelago of Conrad's writings, perhaps. I buy my beer, and take it outside. I watch the unloading. To do so I have to look over the top of the stack of identical coffin-shaped boxes that I guess are awaiting shipping. So we still export something then, I think, with a little relief. In fact the boxes look quite hi-tech, with bright lights twinkling and flickering on the side, indicating the existence of some electric life-force within. Almost all are blue, forming strange configurations which wax and wane, but which raise a feeling of sadness within me. There are a few rare pink lights which form seductive flower-like shapes. I am suddenly surprised when a man joins me at my table: how very unexpected. Is he a weirdo? Is he looking for a fight? Is he gay, looking for a pick-up? Is he going to ask for money? Is he going to complain about asylum seekers? I hardly dare look at him.

'Are you from the town?' he suddenly asks in a booming baritone. I look up and see that he is a powerful man, bearded, and wearing vaguely nautical clothes. He is not English, but I feel English is his native language. The accent is not American, nor Australian, nor South African; maybe some smaller spin-off of the great colonial diaspora of the nineteenth century. Yet he seems so confident, so sure of himself. I look stunned, I can hardly reply, I am so shaken by this attempt at contact. It's not what we do here. 'I came here so that I can keep an eye on the ship,' he said. 'I won't disturb you.'

'Ah, yes. Well I *am* from the town, yes: and you?'

'Oh no; I came in on that ship. And I'll be going out on her. She's my ship.'

'It's not a container boat, I see.'

'No. There's still a plenty of us left.'

'Can I ask what's being unloaded?'

'Oh yes. It's coloured glass beads mostly. Special ones...people like 'em. There's an endless demand, it seems.'

'Like the ones they do at Mardis Gras?'

'No. Not that: although people *will* do anything for these. I'll show you, come and have a look.'

We walk up to where the last palette has just been unloaded. The skipper grabs a brown cardboard box, from a pile. Without a word of explanation to the crane-driver he slits along the plastic tape and opens it for me to have a look at the beads. I look in, but they are not beads. This seems to be a consignment of game controllers - joysticks and consoles all in nice boxes. And there are DVD players, and i-pads.

A lorry is revving up - the skipper puts the box back and a fork lift approaches.

'They aren't beads.'

'Oh most of 'em are. And we only saw the boxes - there will be glass beads inside, you know. It's to do with marketing you see – that's the way the importers work.

We resumed our drinks as the crane began to pick up panniers of the long boxes.

'Is this a regular run?'

'Oh yes. It's a regular run; it's good business; fully laden both ways!'

'Where do you go?'

'We get the load in the Far East.'

'And where do the exports go: come to that, what are they?'

'They go everywhere – to the four winds you could say! You can have a look at them. I've to go back aboard. We turn this round pretty quick. There's a lot to do.'

I stroll over to the pile of boxes. They click and hum and smaller banks of lights flicker. The biggest blue light stays steadily on. I find a tiny label on the side - the word 'soul', followed by a long number and the date. There is a name at the other end. I look from one box to the other, frantically, like a man looking for his child after a tsunami, reading the names. I finally find one I know as well as my own and beside it the other. As I cry out, the huge grab lifts the pannier on which these two boxes rest amongst fifty others.

I shout to the skipper who is looking over the stern of his ship. He looks down at me and shakes his great bearded head. I sit mesmerised and powerless as the boxes are cleared off the dock, and I am woken only by the boom of the ship's siren as it moves slowly off the levee, and I watch it steam slowly away into the sunset until it is nothing but a tiny brushstroke on the far horizon. Then I leave the dock and set off home in a hurry. I am in a feverish state, afraid that some devilish new world has surfaced. Once home I run up the stairs and burst into my elder son's room. But there he is.

'Hello son,'

He doesn't look over his shoulder. He mumbles an inarticulate word, impatiently, between clicks of his keyboard; situation normal.

Over dinner, which my wife and I eat alone as our sons don't join us for meals, my wife asks me if there is anything wrong. I tell her the story although as I do so I realise that it is almost too ridiculous to recount. But she seems to understand, and nods her head with tears in her eyes. 'There weren't many pink ones you say? I told you it would have been better to have girls.'

43 Disappointment

Friday

How can people remain silent and go on with their petty affairs when, as usual, our government is going along with the slaughter of innocents by their so-called ally, like the lap dogs they are? What pigs so many members of the public are! Just the death of one innocent child in the pursuit of power and money under the pretext of fighting to preserve democracy, freedom, free speech or whatever is the current flavour of the month makes me feel the suffering right down into the depths of my soul. But I gather the bastards are planning something big next week, which is timed to coincide with the anniversary.

Piers heard about it from a source that has always been reliable – he won't tell me who it is or where they work, but I think it's in the ministry. He says it is aimed at a military strong-point where nevertheless there are a lot of civilians around so that there could be as many as a hundred 'collateral' casualties including women and children. The very thought sends me into the pit of despair. The pain will be with me for weeks.

My feelings goaded me into action: I've arranged a meeting for the following day and publicised it extensively, and it should attract a lot of press interest – I've got speakers from the opposition back-benches, university lecturers, and I'm hoping some TV people will come along. Everyone who's anyone seems to know what's in the wind. My meeting may thus be a watershed in public opinion. Surely this will at last get the message into their complacent little lives. And I've been asked to do an article for next weeks edition of the Weekly and although nothing was said, it's obvious they want it to come out just after the raid has been carried out, which shows they must know about it.

I can see on the news that their public and ours are being prepared for the outrage. The destruction of the strong-point is described as being a crucial necessity in the struggle, and there is much talk of the defenders using a human shield to protect it…and so on and so on. Endless reruns of atrocities supposedly committed by the insurgents and 'heart-rending' tales by families of victims, cameras eagerly zooming in if there seems to be the slightest hope of the interviewee breaking down into tears. Gallant survivors explaining how they tried to save colleagues etc., etc. So now the bastards can torch a hundred women and children with a clear conscience, and I can see that the public are swallowing it all, hook, line and sinker. Oh if only I could protect those poor innocents, stop the bombers in their tracks, bring the perpetrators to their senses, let humanity prevail! Anyway, I'd better take up my pen, despairing though I feel, and start on the article, and on my introductory speech. I'll leave this journal until it's all over.

Monday week

Can you believe it? They called the whole operation off at the last moment! Of course nothing was said apart from some mumblings about 'restraint' and 'not interfering with the peace process', so Piers said. And if you believe that you'll believe anything. They just didn't dare affront international opinion or even their own lot; but don't worry – they'll be up to some devilry over the next weeks. Evil is evil and it doesn't go away because of one political miscalculation. In my opinion, they could have gone ahead with no comeback – they had manipulated public opinion masterfully, and I gather the planes were all tooled up on the runways with their engines running. That'll be another ten million wasted, which could have gone in hospitals or overseas aid. But I've heard that the oil barons were against it for some financial reason; they probably thought it would send the price down again. So the ruling swine are not only callous and indifferent to human suffering, but they are stupid as well!

The meeting was obviously a complete flop; I had to improvise a speech which sounded pretty lame even to me and none of the distinguished speakers turned up apart from a broken down 'concerned' comedian who embarrassed everyone by his confused but assertive ramblings. I couldn't cancel it because I had no reason – I would have put Piers in a tricky position if I had let the cat out of the bag as to what we knew. I would have pleaded illness but my wife told me I should 'face the music' if I wanted to keep her respect. She doesn't always appreciate the full import of my work.

This morning Piers phoned to say I should hang on to the article for a future slot, as they didn't think it was worth publishing now. Typical – always thinking of the bottom line. The pain of this stupid and humiliating cock-up will be with me for weeks.

44 Kazbekistan

I sat at a table on the terrace of a restaurant in the square of a beautiful town in the middle of France. The evening sun shone, and I was at the beginning of a three week holiday. I found the item in which I was interested and began reading it. Although I knew more or less what it would have to say, a rising sense of terror gripped me and I felt a shiver go down my spine. But I sat back and contemplated the delightful environs of where I sat, and let the horror gradually recede, until I was at peace. It was one of those short moments of almost unalloyed pleasure. The ambience was exactly as I had imagined from the many books I had read, and it was my first night in the Promised Land after a difficult drive across Eastern Europe.

We had saved for three years to afford the trip, Natalya and I, and our two little boys, Kyril and Ivan were wide-eyed at the new sights and sounds. Kazbekistan is a good country, but it cannot compare with the West, for people like myself with ambition. I put down the newspaper; I spoke good English but I wished to give our order in French, whilst my wife and the boys visited *Les Toilettes.* As I ordered the drinks I knew they would like, I caught a look of surprise in the waiter's eye as he listened. After he went I sat on, awaiting the return of my wife and the two dear boys. They seemed to be an uncommonly long time in returning, and after a while I became a little restless. I found the toilet - a unisex type, and it was unoccupied. I was puzzled, and a little irritated. My wife occasionally made little unannounced deviations from plan, and no doubt this was one such. But it was a thoughtless one, leaving me sitting bored, at the mercy of a waiter. Probably she was buying the boys some comics or puzzle books, to keep them occupied after the meal.

I returned to the table and got out my English newspaper, and broke my French-only resolution. The front page of the paper was a typical summer affair, no more interesting than would have been the boring Kazbekistan equivalent. Some idle speculation as to which politician might be planning to supplant the leader of his party and a scandal involving a large company. No international news of moment and nothing to hold ones interest. I finally found an article inside about a new type of fuel which greatly interested me, and I read it in detail. I put the paper down, and suddenly felt extremely uneasy. Fifteen minutes had passed, and I could in no way explain the continued absence of Natalya. I felt a rising panic. I found the waiter, and asked him as best I could if he had seen my wife and children. He repeated something several times, until at last I caught his meaning. I had come alone to the restaurant. I realised then that he was confused, since we had parked our car - a Polish built Fiat, and walked into the restaurant together. On a sudden impulse I went out of the restaurant and hurried to the place where I had parked the car. There was another car parked exactly where I had parked mine. I looked frantically around as one does in this type of situation. I knew the car was gone but wanted some miracle to put it somewhere nearby.

Then the obvious truth dawned on me. Natalya had taken the car, and left. I tried to think of some sensible reason. Had she noted some inappropriateness in the parking place that I couldn't see? But I knew the truth. She was gone. I didn't know why on earth she might have gone, but gone she must be. Natalya was a wonderful wife, and we were very close. But she had one part of her mind -from her Kazbeki grandmother - that I could never fathom, and I knew she had left me, for some reason, good, or ill. I got up with heavy heart, and returned to the restaurant, where I explained to the waiter that my wife had taken a sick child back to the hotel. I ordered a beer and reviewed my position. My wife had in her possession my passport, our money and indeed everything we had for the holiday.

In this sorry situation I thought my troubles could hardly be worse, but they were actually far worse than I knew. I soon realised that I had to visit the *Gendarmerie*, since I had no idea how to proceed in such a position. I guessed that somewhere was a consulate which would be handling the affairs of Kazbekistan, probably the Russian one. But I needed to explain my position to some French authorities before the few Euros I had ran out. The details of my announcing myself, and explanation of my problems are not greatly interesting. The French police were most civil and polite, and after speaking to various officers, I was finally brought before a fairly senior officer. He spoke English better than my French, and sympathised with my case having been given the details. He asked me my name.

'Mikhail Rudelski' I replied

'She may return quite suddenly, my friend,' he said, reassuringly. 'One often sees such things in this business. It's not so rare. But in the meantime we shall contact the Kasbeki Consulate. My assistant is in the process of doing that. I think things will soon be cleared up. We have a call to all cars in the region to intercept your wife who will, I am sure, be able to help us.'

At this point my troubles began in earnest. His assistant reappeared,   with a query. He wished to clarify my nationality. He suspected Kazakhstan, but wondered if I might actually be from Uzbekistan. I smiled - the mistake was a common one, even in the East. 'No - it's actually Kazbekistan - I know the former Russian Republics can be confusing!' The assistant listened, looking very dubious. She went off with a shrug of the shoulders, and returned some time later. 'Perhaps Monsieur would care to speak to the Russian Consul himself in the absence of any representative of the country of which you speak?' I went to the phone, and had an increasingly irate conversation with a typically obstructive official of the old Soviet kind. I knew he was deliberately using some loophole to deny the existence of Kazbekistan. They had never forgiven us for our independence, and although I am basically pro-Russian, these types of tyrannical bureaucrat infuriate me. I slammed the phone down, and returned to the French Inspector.

I rapidly explained what the problem was, and he raised his eyebrows. He spoke quickly in French to the assistant who went away. He seemed less warm though very courteous still. We spoke little, and after ten minutes his assistant returned with a large up-to-date atlas. 'Perhaps Monsieur would like to point out Kazbekistan on this map!' she said, with an air of one who has herself perused the map for some time without success. I eagerly took the atlas, which was open at the most suitable page, where I knew Kazbekistan could be found. It showed all the new republics, so I took it very pointedly. But when I looked I saw that something was gravely wrong. I am not exceptionally good with maps, my wife believing that my excellent linguistic skills come from an over development of the left cerebral hemisphere at the expense of the right. But where I expected to find the little gull shaped country there was nothing I recognised. I shook my head. The atlas was probably misprinted - Kazbekistan is small on such a scale. But by now my hosts had become suspicious and impatient.

I was treated from then on, first as a possible illegal immigrant, then after days of interrogations, as an idiot. I was allowed to try any way to justify my faith in my reality. Encyclopaedias, telephone calls, more maps, but never once did I find a scintillion of hope that such a place as Kazbekistan existed or had ever existed. I existed only in that I was walking about, but in all other ways I might have been a ghost. Neither my wife, nor my car, nor my children could be traced. My hosts arranged for me to see doctors and psychotherapists. They finally concluded that I was suffering from psychotic delusions following sudden onset total amnesia. I was kindly adopted by the country where I found myself. I was found a job as a petrol pump attendant, acquired a French passport, and eked out a lonely and meagre existence. As for me, I believed that I was completely sane, the victim of a cosmic accident. I came from an alternate time stream, and was suddenly shot into this one by an eddy in the fabric of space time. But I knew I could never hope to convince anyone of the true case.

Over a few years, only one trivial incident lent any credence to my contention. Seated in a train that was being slowly passed by another, I caught sight of a face that I knew - a scientist colleague who had been a specialist in General Relativity. He saw me and *smiled*, waving. He knew! A wild thought came to me. Somehow his experiments had caused my current problems. I told no one, well aware of how such a story would be received.

Things began to resolve themselves when I met Marc Thiebaud, a psychologist who had read of my case and was fascinated by it. He seemed to at least listen to my alternative universe explanation for my strange plight, and I stuck to it through all difficulties. Such delusions are not uncommon these days, he told me, since the concept of parallel universes has become a familiar one. For a long time he seemed to make no progress in my case. He seemed impressed by my ability to give the most detailed explanations of my native land. He agreed that I spoke Russian, although with a noticeable accent, at least according to a Russian colleague of his. He didn't think this argued against my story, though, as he knew that numerous accents and dialects are spoken all over the former Union.

One day he admitted to me. 'Your case is quite baffling. We must go back to first principles. When, by your reckoning did you transfer into this alternative time-stream?'

I told him that it was clearly whilst I sat waiting for my wife and children at the restaurant. He questioned me very closely, and seemed interested in the fact that I had read the newspaper, and my unease as I did so. He asked if anything in the paper had struck me. I shook my head – indeed I could hardly recall anything about it beyond the fact that I read it. He wanted to read that newspaper and, after a little effort, he obtained a copy from London. When I next saw him his eyes glittered with excitement. He had read it and I could see that he had come to some earth-shattering but probably erroneous conclusion. I laughed inwardly - one knows, somehow, when one has swapped time streams. I don't know how, and I didn't expect to convince him. But I saw the futility of his new hopes.

He had seen this article about a company scandal. A scientist in academia had confessed that he had been paid by a large conglomerate to acquire by illegal means some internal reports from the research department of rival firm which he had reason to visit. This company were known to be developing a technique which would virtually put the conglomerate out of business. He had been caught in the act of leaving the site with the stolen papers, and had made it clear that higher-ups were involved, and justice was being obstructed. It seemed that company directors and leading political figures were involved. Marc, having read the paper in great detail felt that this article was somehow crucial to my problem. He followed the case up, obtaining the succeeding editions of the papers, and gradually came to his conclusion.

He came to me one day, and said, quite suddenly: 'Does the name Mike Ruddle mean anything to you?' It didn't, and I told him so. 'Nevertheless, that's who I think you really are.' He then told me that a man of this name was a director of the company involved in the information theft scandal and had personally initiated the crime. He had left England on the news of the arrest of the burglar. He had informed his wife that he was headed for Eastern Europe, where he thought he could remain until the affair was forgotten. He believed that I had had a breakdown on the journey, and woven the strange story unconsciously. Mike Ruddle had evidently been an Eastern European specialist, and would have easily been able to maintain the illusion in his mind, and also convince others. He had no doubt, planned to adopt a new persona in the East. He had needed little more than a memory disorder that might arise from stress to actually *become* the personality whom he had planned to assume. No doubt he had friends in the East who would have been generously persuaded to oil his path. The press had reported him being seen in Uzbekistan, Ukraine, Azerbaijan and other places, but of course he had never turned up. I could see that the facts more or less favoured him, since they fitted so well. But I knew it to be nonsense – a convenient construct.

But Marc was not finished. 'What is your wife's name?' he said out of the blue. 'Oh, Natalie' I said. 'You said Natalya, before' he replied his eyes lighting up. 'Oh, yes - it's the French version' I replied. He nodded mysteriously

The next time I saw him whilst we were going through our usual motions his phone rang. He picked it up and after a couple of words said 'Yes, he is'

'It's Natalie Ruddle for you'

I took the phone and said 'Hello darling!' but the phone went dead. I realised what I had said. Like a sudden recollection of a long forgotten dream, things flooded back. First fragments, then whole memories: my house in London, my children, finally my work. Thiebaud was triumphant. His psychic ruse had worked. All his Gallic bravura came out in his gesturing hands. It was the solution to an abstract problem for him. He made no attempt to advise me, betray me or lecture me. In fact his only momentary irritation was when I pointed out the strangeness of my choice of the non-existent Kazbekistan as homeland; he mildly corrected me. 'The subconscious is a funny dreamlike place - such a mistake is common; if it *was* a mistake! If you had chosen Kazakhstan, where would you be now my friend?' And a little thought showed me how right he was.

I went back to face a possible trial, but in the happy knowledge that the involvement of some government high ups had made it unlikely - due to my health - in fact they had hoped I wouldn't turn up at all. My reunion with Natalie was a very happy one. I had learned a serious lesson, and intended to bring to life, for real, that imaginary moment of tranquil happiness outside the restaurant where I had had my breakdown. I had been a solitary guilty fugitive, stopping on his drive to freedom, suddenly yearning for a better world. We sat in a delightful tavern en route for home as she breathlessly told me of the last three years developments. 'Evan has done well in his first year exams, and he's going to specialise in petro-geology. He still has an eye for money.'

I laughed. 'Remember all those bribes that got him through school on the straight and narrow?'

'Well Cy is more dedicated as a scientist - he wants to be a radio astronomer - and he got grade 1 in A-level maths!'

'Oh great! Nat, you have done better than anyone could have hoped! Whilst I - I've let the family down. But things will change.'

She squeezed my hand. 'I know!'

'A pity the boys take after me,' I said. 'I suppose - we could do with another sensitive artist in the family!'

'Well Kate's doing marvellously at art for GCSE!' Natalie said, her face lighting up.

I said nothing for a long moment. Then I spoke: 'Who's Kate?' I said.

45 The Martyr

In a way Gavin was hoist with his own petard, as they say, because that's how we met: through his conservation work. I was young, and it looked like a nice summer holiday doing dry stone walls. He was the leader – five years older than I. Several of the girls on the project were head over heels in love with him: his slightly unkempt hair, his way of looking into people's eyes as he talked passionately about the work he did; his lithe body as he leapt over obstacles leading his disciples, his earnest manner. And finally the inevitable attraction to power that some of us feel – whether we admit it or not - made him irresistible.

He had approached me as I carefully laid another piece on the dry stone wall, and told me how it was far more efficient than any modern structure. 'Walls with mortar are typical of our rigid controlling society.' he said 'Once the rain gets to them, and when they get frozen in winter, they crumble as nature humbles our arrogance' Only he and a few carefully chosen companions could save the world from 'Invasive controlling Western technology' and I wanted to be chosen. 'Of course these old walls are living organic entities – they can move. And the moss lives within...' I saw his eyes burning with desire for the planet, the dry stone walls, the moss, and perhaps...could it be? 'I think it wouldn't be a bad idea for you come along with me to the next *Green Drink* that we have' he asked in a slightly absent manner as he corrected the position of the last stone I had laid. The Green Drink turned out to be an evening in a local pub where Gavin held court surrounded by admiring young environmentalists.

I became the regular companion to Gavin. His proposal didn't go quite so far as saying 'It wouldn't be a bad idea', but rather suggested the inevitability of our union. 'We might as well get married' he said one day, and I was overwhelmed. From amongst his huge crop of obedient female followers *I* had been selected to support him as he locked horns with the Forces of Darkness; my next weeks were spent in a love-fired burst of joyous activism, as my archangel and I challenged and put to flight all the demons of hell. The greedy bankers, the multinational developers, the warmongering oil barons, the chemical-pesticide-wielding farmers, the polluting industrialists, the white supremacists, the cruel cosmetics manufacturers, the filthy smokers, the fascist police, the self-serving pharmaceutical industry, the stupid communists who had dried up the Aral Sea, the additive-addicted food processing industry, the controlling media, and the all powerful supermarkets.

I had long since picked up the tune and now began to learn the words. It was almost like marrying my father who had been fanatical catholic. He knew the lives of the saints almost by heart; he had prints of the great mediaeval religious paintings on the walls of his study, haloes littered around like helium balloons at a fiesta. My mother didn't permit them in the lounge – her friends from Golder's Green and Hampstead would have been shocked and horrified. He would murmur about the odour of sanctity that apparently accompanied the decay of saintly bodies. On Good Friday he would take a sneaking look at the palms of his hands from time to time in the hope that he would see the first signs of stigmata.

The marriage began successfully and it wasn't until after the two children were born that I found things changing – or, to be more exact, I found myself changing. Firstly some of Gavin's moral taboos became decidedly inconvenient. Buying Nescafe would draw down censorious looks as would a tin of processed food, or a frozen microwave meal. We didn't have many rows, but the pained but loving expression that would come over his face as he gently expressed his surprise when he found a non-recyclable plastic bag in my hands, after a quick trip to Tesco, was worse than a raised voice and stern scowl. Going on holiday by air would have been tantamount to harpooning a threatened species of whale.

He continued doing sponsored walks and expeditions up the four peaks or other mountains. I, who had to stay at home with the children, and who would have loved a holiday in some balmy southern clime, had to make do with pictures of all these young dedicated-looking acolytes smiling and seemingly fawning on Gavin who would be gazing up ahead with animated face, in an almost heroic pose, in some rugged and desolate mountain terrain that would have deterred all but the most besotted follower. I could hear the deep sighing inhalations of the 'good mountain air' and see the assembled devotees relaxing in the glowing evening, with a bottle of cider and a burgeoning joy at their own beatitude.

Not that I feared that he ever took advantage of any of them. However much such a man might be alerted to sexual opportunities by tightly stretched hiking shorts straining over striving behinds during the ascents, or eyes beckoning him from young but not absolutely innocent faces in the gloaming of sunset, I didn't think he would ever exchange his elevated charisma for the pleasant half hour of undignified panting and thrusting that his nature might be urging. No doubt some of the rather awkward looking young males who appeared on the periphery of the groups around Gavin took their chance with a willing and windswept partner when it came. Perhaps an enterprising pair even disturbed a rare threatened Mountain Ouzel on the point of nesting for the first time in sixty years, as they went body to body behind a convenient bluff or in a one-man bivouac – and why not I say? He would have ostentatiously said nothing, but withdrawn all smiles. In *his* mind he had taken them *all* with the point of his moral lance. And you don't get much bigger than that. My naïve confidence in the impregnability of his self-esteem made it all the more of a shock when it all happened.

Things had become even worse when he got heavily into asylum seekers, and the outrageous injustices they suffered. He was always going off to hostels, coming back with a briefcase full of asylum application forms and a sanctimonious cast of feature, talking of overweight middle-aged, middle-class bigots. One evening I had taken the children to my mother but decided to give my organic cookery class a miss. On my return I heard a loud rhythmic moaning upstairs. Shocked I went up and pushed the half-closed door of the bedroom from which the sound came. I saw nothing but a jerking female bottom and Gavin's precious briefcase and I instantly and silently withdrew without being seen. By my quick action I avoided seeing him and his no doubt proud face at the climax of her throbbing ecstasy. I thought she was dazzled by his status as the local campaigning guru.

I said nothing when I came back to the house at my usual time. But over the next days I was smouldering with anger, and brooding over all that I had had to put up with, all that the children had suffered by his absences and his lack of interest. He was a modern day saint. I used to appear by his side, looking demure, but perhaps a little smug and possessive. Now I had lost the whole purpose of my life in one incongruous moment. There would be no asylum for me. I would end up looking like one of those stupid politicians' wives who stand outside some pretentious mansion with the sly-looking culprit, not looking too pleased, and promising to 'stand by my husband' . On some level I had known. All the attention he got, all the gratitude, all the admiration for the uncannonised saint: all for his ego, his lust for power, the best power of all, power over peoples minds.

But the children's simple faith in him: it would never be lost. No-one yet knew: *no-one ever would.*

My confidence in my purpose grew in my mind in proportion to my certainty of Gavin's hypocrisy. I acquired my little friends from a great palm house where I had once asked the attending gardener what they were. It took five seconds to pick two when no-one was looking. I brought them home in a brown paper bag along with some mangoes, papayas, star fruit, passion fruit and bananas I had bought at the Indian shop; I prepared him well by telling him that it was looked down on by some of the mothers at the primary school where the children went. I told him they had turned up their noses at the exotic fruit, saying 'the things *they* eat!' He had immediately fired up in a post-imperialist lecture. 'What does she mean 'they'? The 'other', I suppose: typical middle class attitude. The English are notoriously unadventurous about food. They go off to France and start trying to find fish and chips – or a Macdonald's, which is even worse.' The English came out in bad light in Gavin's philosophy – they had initiated the rape of nature with their dark satanic mills, which had begun exuding the evil black smoke from their potent and dirty thrusting chimneys in the Industrial Revolution.

'Well, you can see that I don't go along with the xenophobic prejudices,' I said as I put down the bag of fruit. 'Makes a change from apples and oranges doesn't it?'

He eagerly tumbled the fruit into a bowl and examined them. I guess the only ones he didn't recognise were the Sea Mangoes. 'What are these?' he asked.

'Oh, well actually they may be a mistake. I'm all for celebrating diversity, but I'm afraid I tried one, and they taste so foul that no-one in his right mind could possibly eat one of them. They are a sort of very small mango – but they aren't sweet. *They* obviously eat them, how I don't know.' My emphasis of the word 'they' did the trick. He bit into one, and although I could see he didn't like it, he chewed it up and took the large seed out of it, nodding his head. 'You need to get out of your comfort zone' he said, smiling eagerly.

'Why don't you admit it was revolting?' I said, rather defiantly. 'The other one will end up in the dustbin, and you know it!'

One would probably do the job, two certainly would, the book had said. He quickly gobbled the other up. We had lunch and we enjoyed a papaya and a normal mango. The kids were in bed and we were watching television when he began to feel unwell. In the middle of a boring program about how food manufacturers evaded the labelling system using loopholes and lobbying, he suddenly groaned and said he had a tummy ache and felt as if he was getting a fever. He went to bed early, but I heard him getting up, going to the bathroom and staggering back. When I went to see him he had violent stomach pains and was sweating profusely. He couldn't move. He told me to phone a doctor. I went downstairs and turned on the television. I felt right had been done. His cloying love of righteousness was a sham. Every action he had taken in pursuing the goal of becoming a 21st century saint was nothing more than a power trip, his family neglected for media fame and the vulgar accolade of a mindless lemming-like crowd of acolytes.

It was the perfect crime: the poison in the fruit was known to be undetectable except to special techniques used in India, where its use was common in one region and when it was suspected. No chance of that in an autopsy in Golder's Green. I didn't go upstairs until about three o' clock in the morning. All was silent. The room was filled with a strangely fragrant odour. He was stone dead. And I didn't need to switch the light on, in the otherwise dark room, to see him sitting up in bed, his face at peace, as beautiful as he had had been the day he first looked into my eyes. The light around his head gradually faded.

The next day I got hold of his diary. He had never let me get even a peep at it. But the last entry read *'Sorting out a safe house for Amal. She had escaped from the hostel in nothing but a night-dress. Left her sobbing on the bed; I'll tell dear loyal Di about it later when the dust has settled. She's been a tower of strength to me over the last years, and never uttered a word of complaint.'*

I knew now what the light at the head of the bed and the fragrance were.

46 Shall not be Forgiven

They were very unlucky. Things had seemed good when they got the local drama society to put on their play *Godsmell!* It had had a religious theme, and had been a riot. They had themselves taken the leading roles; Jemima played the part of God, Alex played the part of Jesus and they took turns to play the Holy Ghost. The line which got the most laughs was when the man playing Nietzsche read out an obituary for God who, as Nietzsche predicted, had died. It was really very witty, Alex having had great fun writing it. It ended 'God leaves two descendants: one Son and one Holy Ghost.' The only person who didn't laugh was the vicar who had come along to enjoy what he had thought was a play on a Christian theme. He shook his head. He mumbled something: 'All sins shall be forgiven, but the sin against the Holy Ghost shall not be forgiven,' as he passed the authors in the foyer on his way out. Nobody cared about that.

But their fame was short lived, because on the way back they collided with a big Maersk container lorry which flattened their BMW and they were killed instantly.

God seemed a nice old boy, who most certainly wasn't dead. But he was obviously very uneasy with them.

'This is a terrible thing. We'll just wait for my Son before I explain the problem. It's really a piece of exceptionally bad luck you see. I had no problem with the play. I thought it jolly funny – one Son and one Holy Ghost! But that's really the difficulty, you see.'

At this point Jesus came into the office.

'Hello Father!'

'Hi Son! This is Jemima and Alex – the ones I told you about.'

Jesus smiled very warmly.

'Pleased to meet you; I have been on your case for ages, but I'm afraid I can't sort it out.' He looked up at them.

'Don't worry about me not doing all that 'yea, I say unto thee' business: that's all dropped out of use now. Anyway, the situation is not good.'

'Have you investigated the whole thing, Jesus?'

'Yes Father, and I've written a report, it's here on the laptop, so the paperwork is all done at least.'

'And there's no way out?'

'Nope!'

'Oh dear!'

God turned to Jemima and Alex.

'Well, the plain simple fact is you have to go to the other place. Jesus will explain it over a coffee if you would like that. I shall just have to read you the formal thing – it hasn't been updated I'm afraid: we're a bit behind the times up here.'

God picked up a tattered thermally sealed card and read out:

'Depart from me ye cursed, into the ever-lasting fires that were prepared for the devil and his angels.' He looked up almost sheepishly. 'Well that's it I'm afraid. Can you take them to the coffee lounge Jesus?'

'Yep!'

'You see things have changed radically here,' Jesus said. 'Very few people go down there nowadays. They are all redeemed and so on, and they've really got rehabilitation sorted out in purgatory. They have psychologists, excellent cognitive therapists and some of the top saints as well; and you can watch the Purgatory House on TV – I think you can get it in hell.'

'Well why can't *we* go to purgatory, Your Holiness?' Jemima burst out. 'We are very much of the liberal intelligentsia and we used to live in Highgate and everything. We lead very ethical lives.'

'Of course you do my dear – we are well aware of the fact – that's our job you see. But the fact is that you committed the sin against the Holy Ghost, and though all sins shall be forgiven, the sin against the Holy Ghost shall not be forgiven. Much though I admired the production, the acting and not least the script!'

'Did you think the script was good?' Alex asked eagerly.

'For God's sake, Alex, we're just about to be cast down into hell for all eternity and you're fishing for complements about your damned play.' Jemima said in a high pitched and angry voice.

'Yes, perhaps we might put that on the back-burner for the moment, Alex. Excellent though the play was, it nevertheless adopted a mocking tone when dealing with the Holy Trinity, and the Holy Ghost has clearly asserted his right to have the performance classified as a sin against the Holy Ghost and yourselves as the perpetrators.'

'So where do we go now?' Alex asked.

'Well, I hardly like to tell you, but you will have to go down. In the old days we had so many that there was a special corps of courier angels who spent their time taking the damned halfway down the stairway - it isn't paved with good intentions of course,' Jesus smiled.

'Various fallen angels used to share the duty of meeting them halfway. But there are so few now that the couriers have been redeployed as guardian angels – we need all that we can get, with the demographic situation on earth, as you can imagine.'

'What about *our* guardian angels?' said Jemima. '*They* didn't protect *us* did they?'

Jesus shook his head. 'No – things are getting very slack nowadays. They hardly know the difference between a venial and a mortal sin – as for the Holy Ghost most of 'em have had no contact with him for a thousand years. They've been admonished of course, but I doubt they were too worried about it. Anyway, I'll take you to the top of the stairs; you'll be able to find your own way down, I should imagine.'

He ushered them through plushly carpeted corridors turning various corners until they came to a pair of impressive double doors, which opened automatically on his approach, and he turned to them smiling forlornly. 'Yes, we have all the latest conveniences here, as you can see. But I have to say goodbye to you now. Asmodeus will be waiting for you at the bottom. And that's about it. Good luck, my friends.' Alex looked at Jemima and she looked back, her eyes full of fear. Alex took her hand, a gesture he hadn't made for a long time. Together they started the long downward journey. The further they got, the warmer it seemed to get, and bonfire and barbecue scents began to waft up. The early part of the staircase was nicely decorated, rendered in a shade of orchid pink, but everything began to get run down as they descended, and soon the walls were just bare red brick, some of it scorched black as if, alarmingly, the infernal fires sometimes reared up the stairwell.

'It isn't fair!' Jemima half-sobbed. 'Why are we the only ones? What about all the paedophiles, the property developers, the multinational corporations, climate-change deniers? What about Hitler, what about George W Bush?'

'Hitler would have come down here ages ago, if he did. And Bush is still alive, isn't he?' Alex answered. 'And he may not go to hell anyway.'

'Oh shut up!' Jemima didn't mean to be rude but the situation was just too much.

On they went, and gradually the sounds of a big roaring fire began to echo up the staircase. And it was becoming decidedly hot.

At last they came round a curving corner and out into a sort of atrium cut out of lava-like rock. Evidently waiting for them was a huge and powerful-looking horned figure wearing a tank top, and calf-length black cargo-trousers. His skin was a violet colour but its shiny surface reflected the orange flames that flickered up from a crevasse about fifty metres from where they stood, creating a myriad of strange highlights which were in constant motion as he moved. He had an ugly, brutish face, but wore a hard-bitten smile. He looked eagerly at them, and spoke in a gravelly voice, with a distinct estuarine accent. He started to nod his head appreciatively.

'Hello there!' he said in a friendly voice. 'My name is Asmodeus, and I would like to take this opportunity to welcome you to this place!'

Alex seemed dumbstruck, but Jemima was very encouraged by Asmodeus's pleasant manner.

'Are we the only ones, today?' she asked innocently. Alex tried to get her to be quiet. He thought Asmodeus was just playing them along, and would suddenly seize them and throw them over the precipice.

'Well you are, and indeed you are the first for months! We are very glad to see you.'

'Is there any chance we could have a job in the library or something, rather than being cast into the pit?' Jemima went on, ignoring Alex.

'Well you can work in the library if you want. The Marquis de Sade used to spend a lot of time in there but he hasn't been in recently, I hear. He may have got a pardon, I suppose,' he added, shaking his head. But we don't cast into the pit any more. For one thing, we have to be more humane. That sort of thing was all a bit mediaeval. For another, most of the pits have gone out. There've been a lot of cuts, you see. We are funded per resident soul, and of course there's nothing like the money about that there used to be. A lot of the fallen angels have had to go back upstairs and kow-tow to the establishment – the rebellion is more or less over. *We* still fly the flag, though!' he said with a wry smile, lifting his pitchfork up with an energetic thrust. 'Those were the days! I recall having that fat *manzer* Goering on the end of this, seventy odd years ago. I lifted him right up, so I could hurl him way out into the middle of Central Pit, and that took some doing even for me!' He looked well capable of it though, thought Alex.

'There's a big fire below that precipice, though, isn't there?' said Jemima.

'Oh yes, that's still funded for the moment. First impressions are important. But there aren't many flats left where there's a good view of the fire and brimstone.'

'Surely there must be lots of free accommodation now if the population has declined so much?' said Alex.

'Not as fast as the funds have dried up. But in fact talking of Goering reminds me that his old apartment is free, and it looks right out over Central Pit, in the middle of Pandemonium.'

'That sounds good,' said Alex. 'But where has Goering gone?'

'Oh he's in Purgatory now. He sits around with his cronies drinking in a *bierkeller*, talking about the good old days. In principle he's taking classes in inclusiveness and celebrating diversity, but I don't think he attends many.'

'What about Hitler?'

'Oh he's still here. He sits around mopping his brow and ranting, but no-one listens to him. But there's no reforming him. He really believes all that stuff, and he prefers it here to grovelling around in purgatory.'

'So when can we see the flat?'

'Well you can see it now, but I'll have to ask the boss if you can have it. I can probably get you in next week.'

He led them through the dark and smoky streets of hell, where there seemed to be few people. A dull red glow pervaded everything but there didn't seem to be a lot of fire and brimstone. He took them to a tall block of charred red brick, unlocking a door let them in. They had to climb a lot of stairs, but in Goering's old apartment there was indeed a splendid view of the grim city of Pandemonium, whose name was now singularly inappropriate. Alex could see magnificent flames belching up from Central Pit. On the wall there was a picture of a Nuremberg rally which Asmodeus took off the wall and hurled out of a window.

'Well, what do you think?' he said, a quiver of pride in his voice. 'You'd be hard put to match this in heaven, the demographics getting out of hand as they are.'

'It seems fine,' Alex said. 'What do you think, Jemima?'

Jemima burst into tears. 'It was all your fault, you smug pompous fraud, with all that smart-arse stuff about religion; anything for a bit of attention. Your mother told me when you were small you used to throw tantrums to get attention. I never liked that play at all really!'

Asmodeus and Alex looked at each other. Asmodeus beckoned Alex over to a window. 'This isn't going to work out too well for you, is it?'

'Doesn't look like it.'

'If you give me a moment I might be able to find something better. It will be a great sacrifice though.'

He picked a mobile phone from his waistband and punched in a number.

'Hey Nick. This is Azzy; any chance of a favour? I want to go for option zero with those two who did the *Godsmell* play – you heard about them, did you?'

There was a long pause when they could hear a drawling cultured voice on the other end but not what it said. Asmodeus answered, 'Well what do you think? You going to talk to the Big Guy, or maybe Jeez?' More words, then Asmodeus concluded: 'You're going to speak direct to the Holy G, then? Oh great. Well I'll make my way over, and just hope it's sorted by the time we get there.' He hung up.

'I think I've swung it. Nick gets on well with the Holy G; they are similar types really; not in ethical orientation of course. But you know, fire and brimstone – tongues of fire etc. Same sort of style.'

'Where are you taking us now?' Jemima said in a pitiful but rather shrewish voice.

'Somewhere I think you will like,' replied Asmodeus. He took them along narrower and narrower streets which became alleys, until they came out into what looked like an old bombsite. As they did his phone rang and he answered. They heard the same voice again, sounding quite upbeat. 'Oh that's great! Was he difficult about it?' The voice was heard again. 'Oh well, I'll be there to receive them then – good timing, a plane-load of global warming-deniers? We can hold on to them can we? For the moment, then…yes I'll give it to them.'

He hung up and turned beaming. 'It's all fixed. And here comes someone with the keys.' A small sexy-looking demoness approached and handed Asmodeus a big key, and an envelope. She hung around by Alex until Asmodeus shooed her away.

'Follow me,' he ordered.

'Who was that?' Jemima asked.

'She's just some succubus that's running his errands.' He led them to a door. He handed them the envelope. 'Follow these instructions carefully. The HG isn't the type to give a second chance!' He opened the door and without another word he kicked Alex through it with his clawed foot, and then thrust his fork gently into Jemima's chubby behind and pitched her after him, slamming the door behind them. Lying in a muddy hedge they looked up and the first thing they saw was the word 'Maersk' writ large in blue and black.

'You two were very lucky,' the policeman said. 'Your car is flat underneath that, but you were thrown clear. You smell a bit smoky though – has there been a fire?'

*

The play was not performed again, and Jemima and Alex's smart friends were horrified when Jemima took to arranging the flowers in the local church and helping with the jumble sales. As for Alex, he is jockeying for position to become a churchwarden, and the Vicar is often invited to a high tea at the house of his former enemies. He had been wrong in what he said after the play; but then he wasn't to know that even the Holy G had mellowed down the centuries.

47 The Number 3

When I was thirteen I used two buses to get to my school. The 56, and the 231. Occasionally, though, instead of the 56 a Number 3 would come. This route is very special. For one thing the buses that served it were more modern and powerful than the pre-war crop that served all the other routes. They were a brighter red, and the interiors were more luxurious. They smelt new inside. For another it had yellow eight-penny tickets which I never saw on other buses and it was a much longer route than the others around my way. And most of all because it played a key role in the sadness of my later life. On the way to school the buses were headed for Bellestead. I had never been there, but a cousin of mine who had been bombed out had recently moved there. I could tell that my mother somehow resented them being able to say that they lived in a flat in Bellestead. On the way home they were going to a place called Crampton Green. It sounded all right, but it was, according to my mother, an 'awful place'.

I was very interested in buses and trains at the time, and it was my absolute ambition to go and see what Bellestead and Crampton Green were like, via the Number 3 bus route. I nagged my mother constantly to let me go to Crampton Green, and eventually she gave in. I went on a Saturday, leaving at about two 'o clock. I got a front seat upstairs and drank in the smell, the comfort of the red and green upholstered seat, and the throaty roar of the engine. I didn't get an eight-penny ticket, since I was a half fare, but I got a fourpenny half. The journey was a long one – it had been agreed that I get off at Crampton Green, and take the next bus back. I drank in the rat's nest of streets, through which the bus found its way, seeing places I had never seen before at every turn. Their mere unfamiliarity was sufficient to lend them a magical air, when seen from the top deck of a Number 3. I saw too, buses of types I had never seen, bearing strange numbers, 118, 201, and a 234A – the 'A' intriguing me greatly. Finally, after nearly two hours we pulled into a stand of buses all parked on one side of a wide road, and the conductor called out 'Crampton Green – all out!' I stepped off into a late November afternoon's gloom only broken by the lights of the shops which lined the other side of the road. I had been given some money by my mother, together with coupons to buy some sweets. I had to cross a busy road to get to the shops, and did as I had been told. I stopped a passer-by and asked her to 'see me across the road' She stopped, and looked at me, in my red cap and blazer, evidently quite surprised. She had a dark, sallow face, black hair and large hoop earrings. She seemed not to understand me and suddenly jabbered words in a tongue I didn't understand. I pointed across the road, and naively offered my hand. She suddenly smiled, and took me across, weaving between the slow moving cars. I heard other people speaking foreign languages, and saw people dressed strangely, as well as people who seemed very poor. There were more of them, too than there would have been at our shopping centres. The other buses lined up at the terminal line were even older than those I was used to. One had an open staircase at the back. Over about two minutes I absorbed the fact that I was in a foreign land. A thrill of fear and excitement surged up in me. It was my first experience of a world beyond the one I knew.

I looked for a sweet shop, but I was confused by the fact that there were lots of goods actually stacked up on the pavement outside the shops, plus some stalls, and crowds milling around them. I stood looking around, until a voice nearby said, 'Are you lost?'

I looked around and saw a girl of about my own age standing behind a fruit stall, her pale face lit by the lights of the shop she was evidently attached to. Her face was very pretty, with large eyes, and a long mane of jet black hair. And it was a kind sympathetic face. She spoke in what my mother classified as a 'common' voice, but in a soft almost husky tone.

I shook my head. 'No, I was going to buy some sweets actually. You don't sell them do you?'

At that moment a customer came, and she gave me a nod. 'Wait', she said, and turned away. It was some time before she was free again, after dispensing some decrepit looking oranges and apples – that was about all she had.

'There's a sweet shop just up there – look, where it says Ben's Newsagents. '

I thanked her and went to buy a quarter of chocolate toffees. I knew I should get back, but I thought I might thank the girl, and returned to her stall. I offered her a toffee, and she seemed grateful out of all proportion to the gift. I stood nearby and we talked. I told her I had come on a Number 3, but the number was of no interest to her. The bus was enough. 'I've never been on a bus.' She told me. I was shocked.

'How do you get to school?' I asked

'I walk. Most of us do.'

'Do you live here?'

'Not all that far. Look, I'll show you where!'

I knew I ought to get home, but I followed her, and she took me along the street to a side turning, which went straight across a lot of railway lines. She ran across the bridge and I followed. She pointed to a large dirty brown building with children throwing stones at each other, outside. 'That's where we live.'

A boy a bit bigger than me came up.

'You're a posh kid, aren't you?' he said, in a rough menacing voice.

'You shut up Ronnie Stokes. Or I'll tell your mum it was you who broke all those windows in the garage.'

He scowled, gave me a push and went off.

'I must get back to work – Dad'll be angry if he sees the stall empty.'

He was there, a morose stout man, standing at the stall. He cursed her, and aimed a slap at her, catching the side of her face. I was horrified that anyone could want to harm this pleasant creature. He stumped off. She looked at me, a sort of shame on her face. I thought she might cry, but she didn't. I gave her five toffees, which for me was an unusually generous act. 'I have to go now.'

'Will you ever come back?'

'Yes. I'll get a double rover ticket and take you on a Number 3!'

We stood a moment, mute, looking at each other. Then I saw my bus arriving, having turned round and begun its return journey. I sat at the back, upstairs this time, and felt the tiredness of a long satisfying day. I had seen that the world was a much more exotic place than I had thought. And I had met a most charming person. Crampton Green had a lot to recommend it.

At home I lorded it over my young brother, who was not allowed out by himself yet. And I told my mother about the girl.

'How romantic!' she said. 'What was her name?'

'I don't know!'

She laughed and I knew she would tell Auntie Polly about the thing in a way that would make me seem foolish.

'She was like us, wasn't she?'

'No. The people there are different from here.'

'They are just common that's all!'

'She isn't common,' I said, with some vehemence.

'Well it doesn't matter, you probably won't see her again. We can't afford to have you going off on four-penny tickets every week.'

'I might one day, though' I said.

After that my mother began to talk about my cousin Jeremy and the girl Becky, who lived at his house, in Bellestead. Becky's parents were out of the country. I heard my father say they were stinking rich.

'You really ought to go and see them you know. You used to get on so well with them! Becky is a very pretty girl now, I bet! And Polly was telling me on the phone that Jeremy has a new Hornby train lay-out, he'd love you too see.'

This sounded a good idea, and my mother agreed to talk to Auntie Polly about it. They had stayed with us after they had been bombed out, and relations were only just recovering. Now Uncle Tom was back from Germany, and had – as I had heard my father say – fallen on his feet.

I persuaded my mother I could find my own way.

'I'd like to have a Rover ticket, it'll be almost as cheap, and I can try out a lot of bus-routes. I could go in the morning, and make a day of it. Please Mum!'

My mother hesitated, but since I used to work out the travel arrangements for the whole family, she had no fear that I would get lost.

With the money she gave me for the Rover ticket, and some of the half-crown my Uncle Kyril had given me, I bought a Double Rover, and set out on the day. I headed for the northbound Number 3 bus stop, and was soon on my way to Crampton Green. Things all worked out well. When she saw me her face lit up, and I guess mine did as well. I told her my plan.

'I've bought two weekend Rover tickets one for you, one for me... Today you can come with me to our park. Meet the gang. Then tomorrow we can go on to Bellestead. I've never been there!'

She looked very pleased, but seemed dubious about her chance of getting off her stall. She looked around, then suddenly hared off, toward a group of girls who were standing some distance away, playing cat's cradle. She spoke to one for a moment or so, then returned.

'Lucia's going to do it – Dad's away this week.'

'Who's looking after you?'

'No-one! I look after myself – and Dad!'

Lucia approached; she was similar to the girl herself, apart from her ash-blonde hair.

She looked curiously with her great grey eyes.

'What's his name?'

'I don't know! What is your name?'

'Edwin'

'Edwin!' Lucia laughed mockingly.

'I think it's a nice name,' said the girl.

She got on the No. 3 bus with an expression of wonderment, and seemed afraid to go upstairs. But once we had paid the conductor, and the bus was wending its long route to where I lived, she seemed at ease.

'My name is Jess,' she said, with an air of one who knew herself to be an object of my interest. I told her we would probably go to the cinema the next day, with my cousin. She said she had only ever seen one film, at school, about hygiene, and nutrition. She had never been to a cinema.

We went straight to the park, where the others were playing around the bomb-crater that we called 'our crater'. The others all looked at Jess, especially the girls, Marie, Diana and my sister Molly. We played tag, and took her round the park, showing her the overgrown ornamental lakes and statues. They showed her their pet rabbits, which she was allowed to stroke. We had tea in our house. My mother seemed very polite and inquiring of Jess, asking if her mother would allow her to eat with us. 'I can telephone her,' she said.

'My mother is dead', Jess replied. 'She was killed in an air raid'

'Oh, how terribly sad!' said my mother.

But she was obviously very nonplussed when she found out that Jess's father was away.

After tea we went back in the park, and sat round the bomb-crater with the others. They started to ask Jess questions to embarrass her – they always did it to strangers. Knickers and bottoms were mentioned, but Jess seemed able to rise above them, in a strangely dignified manner. I took her for a walk to where the brandy-bottle lilies were growing on a big fishing lake. We sat in the late afternoon sun smelling their intoxicating fumes. Then she asked me the time, and I was able to show off my watch – not many boys had one. 'Its quarter to five' I said showing the face of the watch.

She had to go. We waited together at the bus stop and when the No. 3 finally came – after many false alarms – and we agreed that she would come the next day in the morning.

I had felt a delicious pride in being the one to be in charge of the strange pretty person, and went straight back to the bomb-crater to see what the effect had been on my gang. They were as curious as I had hoped. The boys voted her a 'jolly good sport', because she had run as fast as any of them in the games, and hadn't cried when someone had tripped her up. Marie had liked her, but Molly and Diana were more reserved.

'She's not all that pretty,' Diana said.

'She's a damn sight prettier than you!' Arthur said, laughing.

Diana's mouth went into a sulky moue. She was trying not to cry.

'Don't be beastly to Diana. I'm going to tell your mother!' said Molly.

'Tell her!' Arthur said – but he shut up all the same.

'Is she going to be your girlfriend then?' Diana said, having got over her moment of pique.

'No, of course not! I don't want a girlfriend!' I shouted indignantly.

'It would be nice, she'd come here often then!' Marie said. She had taken a great liking to Jess.

'I'm telling you I don't have girlfriends, cant you get that into your fat heads?'

'Did you kiss her at the bus stop?' Diana was in full cry now, getting her revenge on me for what Arthur had said.

'Let's go into The Forsaken Land.' Marie said, and I was thankful. The Forsaken Land was a bomb site where a beautiful mansion had been destroyed and Diana didn't dare go there because she thought it was haunted.

My mother said in a casual voice, as I was cleaning my teeth.

'You don't want to get too friendly with that girl, Edwin. She lives so far away! And she'd only feel awkward with you and your friends.'

I said nothing. Somehow I didn't want her to know I was going to Bellestead with Jess.

The next morning I waited for the bus at the agreed time, and when it came, there was Jess smiling at me from the top window. She seemed very elated; her face was glowing with excitement. I too was excited – the journey was a long one, and it would be the first time I had been to Bellestead. I had often wondered what Bellestead was like. We didn't say all that much but enjoyed the increasingly airy suburbs that we went through, with their tree-lined streets and well-dressed inhabitants. Women wore beautiful dresses; men had an air of authority. She would ask me from time to time where we were, and I gave her names I had seen on the bus map, which may or may not have corresponded with the actual places – but she seemed happy that I could answer.

She asked me how old Molly was. I told her she and Marie were thirteen and Diana the same as me. When we got to Bellestead I was overwhelmed with the modern look it all had. So many of the buildings were white, big blocks of flats with flat roofs, residential areas with white houses with curvy windows, like those I had seen in my Puffin book which told of new types of town and city. There were streamlined cars, and I saw no bomb sites. The streets were lined with cherry blossoms, and the people looked so smart and rich. Many women wore fur coats and fur hats. Even the buses were of a more modern type, and the No. 3 now appeared old and disreputable compared to the gleaming streamlined types that operated here, with their strange numbers. And I saw green buses, exactly like the red ones, except that they were painted in green – they were country buses, coming in to the outskirts of the city. I could hear Jess talking, but hardly heard her, in my reverie. But she plucked at my sleeve, insistently, and when I finally looked at her I saw that we had parked, and that it was the terminus.

We got off, and walked along the street with its wide paving in a pinkish colour, past the line of other buses which also terminated at that place. Some were green, and I picked up a bright mauve ticket with the value of 1 shilling – beyond my wildest imaginings. I showed it to Jess – but she found it no more amazing than the tickets we already had, which she hoped to keep. But her mouth fell open, and her eyes widened as we passed the great department stores and tailor's shops. She stopped before a milliners with countless hats being modelled on dummy heads. One in particular, made from peacock feathers, she gazed at for some time. We found a café where one could buy ice-creams, and I bought us one each. There were only two flavours, and I chose strawberry, because I had only seen vanilla before. She chose vanilla – because she had seen others eating vanilla ice-creams and had never had one herself.

We sat in a little green square by a bed of flowers. I looked at my watch, and told her that we had to go to the clock tower where we were scheduled to meet Jeremy and Becky. We got there, and very soon after I saw Becky's laughing face. 'Edwin! Come on we're going back to the house for lunch, then we're going to go and see a Danny Kaye film!' Jeremy smiled at me. He was a soft looking boy, with blue eyes and waves of yellow hair – but he wasn't actually soft, in fact he had more nerve than I did. They hadn't realised that I was with Jess, and as we moved off she hung back. I called her and she followed looking doubtful – much more than she had in the park at home. Becky looked at her. She seemed very surprised to see her, and looked her up and down. Jeremy just called her to come on. 'She's Jess!' I said, in a rather explanatory way.

'Oh. Well come on then – lets see what Aunt Polly says.' Becky called her Aunt Polly, although she wasn't her aunt.

Becky was wearing a rose coloured beret, with a white fur coat, and she looked ravishingly pretty, even more so than I had remembered. She had twinkling eyes and was taller than Jeremy although she was younger. She took my arm as we walked along, and began testing my maths – she knew I was very good. 'You are amazing, you know, Ed, you must be the best in your year, by far! Don't you think so Jess? Can you add fractions like that?'

'No,' said Jess.

'Well Jerry can't, and neither can I – so we're all impressed, Ed.'

Calling me Ed was excellent. I wanted to play jazz, and it was more the sort of name a jazz trumpeter would have.

'What is your best subject, Becky?' I asked. The others seemed content to listen.

'Oh English! I like poetry, and reading'

'Do you know a poem?' Jess asked, but Becky either didn't hear or didn't care.

'I was first in English, and first in French!'

'You'd be first in Polish too, if they did it.' Jeremy said.

'Jess asked if you knew a poem' I said, feeling awkward at Becky's ignoring her.

'Oh yes! Patriotic, or fairies, what you want!'

'Fairies!' Jess said.

"Up the airy mountain, down the rushy glen,

We daren't go a-hunting...."

We all jeered. 'Not that one!'

"For fear of little men!"

She turned to me. '*If music be the food of love – play on…*'

She looked mock-lovingly into my eyes, holding my hand. I pulled away, reddening, I should imagine.

We were turning into her road now, walking past the flowering cherries, which lined the street of huge cream blocks of what were top-range flats. We entered one, with tulips and wallflowers bedded out in its spacious grounds. Then we were in the foyer and Becky summoned the lift. Jess' eyes were wide open, larger even than Becky's, in that slender sallow face. I tried not to look impressed by the lift, although I was, but Jess even gripped my arm when the lift suddenly jerked upwards – she hadn't even known what it was – she thought it was a little room, she said. Becky squealed with laughter.

Then we were at the door of their luxurious flat. Auntie Polly was very welcoming although she looked questioningly at Jess. Becky quickly explained.

'This beautiful *creature* has come with Ed. Her name's Jess. She was very impressed with the lift'

'Well Edwin, you should have told me you were bringing a friend. Your mother phoned just now, and she didn't mention anything.' She looked at Jess for a moment. 'I really am not prepared. What about you, Jess. Does your mother know where you are?'

'Her mother's dead' I said.

'Oh dear! Well where do you live?'

'At Crampton Green'

'Crampton Green? Crampton Green! Why that's miles away. Who looks after you?'

'I look after myself'

'Well come in anyway. I'll give Nan a ring.'

We sat in a huge lounge, with a splendid carpet, and highly polished wooden floor round the edge. Jeremy's Hornby was laid out, and I immediately went to play with it. It had two electric locos, a Royal Scot and a Mallard, as well as an electric suburban train, exactly like those we used to go into the centre. Jess knelt down to watch, but Becky called her.

'Don't play with those bores. I'll show you my pictures of Van Johnson. I've a signed one.'

Jess moved away, and I watched spellbound as Jeremy operated the complex layout. His old wind up tank engine was nowhere to be seen.

Auntie Polly returned, and called us together. 'We are all going to have a nice drink on the balcony, then I'm going to give Jess a box of chocolates to take home with her. Then she needs to start back, because, otherwise its going to be getting late for her. Is that alright Jess?'

'Yes'

'But Aunt Polly' I exclaimed. 'Jess has never been to the cinema, she was looking forward to it.'

'Well she'll go with you all another time. We only have three tickets you see.'

So after a pleasant drink of Tizer outside, Jess was taken to the bus stop by Auntie Polly and me. She kept the ticket, and Auntie Molly gave me money for another.

'She was a very nice polite little girl, Edwin, But she wasn't exactly our type you know. And in any case she was too far from her home. She probably wouldn't have been used to the sort of food we eat, it might have made her sick, do you see.'

I felt relieved. Aunt Polly was very sensible, I now saw.

Becky was at her best over lunch, laughing and joking, and praising me for qualities I hardly noticed, my general knowledge, my school football badge, and other things.

'Ed's a dark horse, isn't he Auntie Polly. Bringing these sultry beauties from exotic climes. She was certainly a scrumptious bit of stuff!'

'Becky! Your father would be very angry if he heard you talk like that!' said Auntie Polly.

'Sorry Aunt Polly! She was a bit threadbare, though. Did you see her coat – it was coming apart at the seams.'

'One mustn't make fun of people in less fortunate circumstances Becky.'

'I thought she was jolly nice' Jeremy said. 'Who cares about her coat You could give her one of yours – you've got enough.'

'My old coats are to be given to the WVS. They are for more deserving cases. But let's go. I want to see the film!'

Outside Becky took my arm. She was a precocious girl and she had a lot of appeal.

'I was just jealous of Jess really. But now she's gone we can have a whale of a time. Come on!' She broke away and began to run.

After that day I went back and forward to Bellestead, beginning a long active friendship with Jeremy and Becky. But eventually Becky went off to the USA, and I never saw her again.

The No. 3 stopped going to Crampton Green, it terminated about halfway there. When Becky went off I remembered Jess, and became quite obsessed with her. I began to treasure the memories of our short friendship. There was no easy way to get to Crampton Green, and I had to just dream about her. But one day my father gave me a bus map that he had got on his way to work. After studying it I found a two change method of going to Crampton Green. When I got there I found that the stalls had all gone, and there was a big building project sprawling all over her sacred ground. I mooched around, but no friendly voice sounded in my ear, and in the end I went back, and listened to some sentimental music. Molly thought I was mourning Becky, she had got so interested in that, that she had forgotten Jess.

Years later I did see Jess. She was getting into a new Jaguar – a man in an expensive-looking black coat was in the drivers seat, but he looked deferentially at her. She was wearing a white fur coat and had on a beret – not pink, but peacock blue - sporting a little feather and just as stylish as Becky's had been. Me? I was coming home from work, on a No. 3 bus.

48 The Christmas Present

It was Christmas Eve. I lay there, sweating, trembling, pulse and blood pressure sky-high. Suddenly a deep manly voice boomed in the air. I looked up and saw him, holly crown and all. 'I am the Ghost of the Christmas Present,' he boomed.

'Holy Shit' I answered.

'As one of the few just men in the land you shall receive any gift you ask'

I told him the only thing I wanted for Christmas. He faded, glaring.

I dozed off for a few moments and woke feeling refreshed. Then, looking at the date on my mobile, I blessed him: January 2.

26586120R00193

Printed in Great Britain
by Amazon